PRAISE FOR *THE LAST DETECTIVE*

"Unexpectedly moving . . . [a] pleasingly peculiar
tale of English eccentricity
pushed to the limit."
—*The Washington Post Book World*

"This whodunit, with top-rate writing and plotting,
is a treasure."
—*Chicago Sun-Times*

"Witty . . . a perfectly realized murder mystery."
—*The Wall Street Journal*

"Cunningly deceptive . . . a brilliant performance
. . . We shall be lucky if we get
a more baffling or entertaining crime puzzle
to read this year."
—*Times Literary Supplement*, London

MORE PRAISE FOR *THE LAST DETECTIVE*

"Everything meshes perfectly in this air-tight tale:
Lovesey's books should be force-fed
to fledgling crime writers who believe
plotting is unimportant."
—*Booklist*

"[*The Last Detective*] is not only a good story
but a compelling one."
—*The Boston Globe*

"Peter Lovesey, one of Britain's best, is in top form
here. His ingenious story, cleverly told,
is full of surprises and his abrasive but oddly
endearing hero is a true Diamond in the rough."
—*The San Diego Union*

"*The Last Detective* is a mystery of unusual depth for
the discriminating reader."
—*Murder by the Book*

Also by Peter Lovesey

PETER LOVESEY

The Last Detective

BANTAM BOOKS
NEW YORK TORONTO LONDON SYDNEY AUCKLAND

THE LAST DETECTIVE

A Bantam Crime Line Book

PUBLISHING HISTORY
Doubleday edition published October 1991
Bantam edition/July 1992

*CRIME LINE and the portrayal of a boxed "cl" are trademarks of
Bantam Books,
a division of Bantam Doubleday Dell Publishing Group, Inc.*

ISBN 0-553-29619-1

Published simultaneously in the United States and Canada

*Bantam Books are published by Bantam Books, a division of Bantam Doubleday
Dell Publishing Group, Inc. Its trademark, consisting of the words "Bantam Books"
and the portrayal of a rooster, is Registered in U.S. Patent and Trademark Office
and in other countries. Marca Registrada. Bantam Books, 666 Fifth Avenue, New
York, New York 10103.*

PRINTED IN THE UNITED STATES OF AMERICA

OPM 0 9 8 7 6 5 4 3 2 1

The Last Detective

PART ONE

The Lady
in the Lake

1

A MAN stood thigh-deep in water, motionless, absorbed, unaware of what was drifting toward him. He was fishing on the north shore of Chew Valley Lake, a 1,200-acre reservoir at the foot of the Mendip Hills south of Bristol. He had already taken three brown trout of respectable weight.

He watched keenly for a telltale swirl in the calm lane where he had cast. The conditions were promising. It was an evening late in September, the sky was overcast, and the flies in their millions had just whirled above him in their spectacular sunset flight, soaring and swooping over the lake in a mass darker and more dense than the clouds, their droning as resonant as a train in the underground. The day's hatch, irresistible to hungry fish.

A light southwesterly fretted the surface around him, yet ahead there was this bar of water known to fishermen as the scum that showed a different pattern in the fading light. There, he knew by experience, the fish preferred to rise.

So preoccupied was the man that he failed altogether to notice a pale object at closer proximity. It drifted languidly in the current created by the wind, more than half-submerged, with a slight rocking motion that fitfully produced a semblance of life.

Finally it touched him. A white hand slid against his thigh. A complete arm angled outward as the body lodged against him, trapped at the armpit. It was a dead woman, faceup and naked.

The fisherman glanced down. From high in his throat came a childishly shrill, indrawn cry.

For a moment he stood as if petrified. Then he made an effort to gather himself mentally so as to disentangle himself from the undesired embrace. Unwilling to touch the corpse with his hands, he used the handle of the rod as a lever, lodging the end in the armpit and pushing the body away from him, turning it at the same time, then stepping aside to let it move on its way with the current. That accomplished, he grabbed his net from its anchorage in the mud and, without even stopping to reel in his line, splashed his way to the bank. There, he looked about him. No one was in sight.

This angler was not public-spirited. His response to the discovery was to bundle his tackle together and move off to his car as fast as possible.

He did have one judicious thought. Before leaving, he opened the bag containing his catch and threw the three trout back into the water.

2

A LITTLE after 10:30 the same Saturday evening, Police Constable Harry Sedgemoor and his wife Shirley were watching a horror video in their terraced cottage in Bishop Sutton, on the eastern side of the lake. PC Sedgemoor had come off duty at six. His long body was stretched along the length of the sofa, his bare feet projecting over one end. On this hot night he had changed into a black singlet and shorts. A can of Malthouse Bitter was in his left hand, while his right was stroking Shirley's head, idly teasing out the black curls and feeling them spring back into shape. Shirley, after her shower dressed only in her white cotton nightie, reclined on the floor, propped against the sofa. She had her eyes closed. She had lost interest in the film, but she didn't object to Harry watching if it resulted afterward in his snuggling up close to her in bed, as he usually did after watching a horror film. Secretly, she suspected he was more scared by them than she, but you didn't suggest that sort of thing to your husband, particularly if he happened to be a policeman. So she waited patiently for it to end. The tape hadn't much longer to run. Harry had several times pressed the fast-forward button to get through boring bits of conversation.

The violins on the video soundtrack were working

up to a piercing crescendo when the Sedgemoors both
heard the click of their own front gate. Shirley said bitterly, "I don't believe it! What time is it?"

Her husband sighed, swung his legs off the sofa, got
up, and looked out of the window. "Some woman." He
couldn't see much in the porch light.

He recognized the caller when he opened the door:
Miss Trenchard-Smith, who lived alone in one of the
older houses at the far end of the village. An upright
seventy-year-old never seen without her Tyrolean hat,
which over the years had faded in color from a severe
brown to a shade that was starting to fit in with the deep
pink of the local stone.

"I hesitate to disturb you so late, Officer," she said
as her eyes traveled over his shorts and singlet. "However, I think you will agree that what I have found is
sufficiently serious to justify this intrusion." Her grat-
ingly genteel accent articulated the words with self-importance. She may have lived in the village since the
war, but she would never pass as local and probably
didn't care to.

PC Sedgemoor said with indulgence, "What might
that be, Miss Trenchard-Smith?"

"A dead body."

"A body?" He fingered the tip of his chin and tried
to appear unperturbed, but his pulses throbbed. After
six months in the force he had yet to be called to a
corpse.

Miss Trenchard-Smith continued with her explanation. "I was walking my cats by the lake. People don't
believe that cats like to be taken for walks, but mine do.
Every evening about this time. They insist on it. They
won't let me sleep if I haven't taken them out."

"A human body, you mean?"

"Well, of course. A woman. Not a stitch of clothing
on her, poor creature."

"You'd better show me. Is it . . . is she nearby?"

"In the lake, if she hasn't floated away already."

Sedgemoor refrained from pointing out that the
body would remain in the lake even if it had floated

away. He needed Miss Trenchard-Smith's cooperation. He invited her into the cottage for a moment while he ran upstairs to collect a sweater and his personal radio.

Shirley meanwhile had stood up and wished a good evening to Miss Trenchard-Smith, whose tone in replying made it plain that in her view no respectable woman ought to be seen in her nightwear outside the bedroom.

"What a horrid experience for you!" Shirley remarked, meaning what had happened beside the lake. "Would you care for a nip of something to calm you down?"

Miss Trenchard-Smith curtly thanked her and declined. "But you can look after my cats while I'm gone," she said as if bestowing a favor on Shirley. "You don't mind cats, do you?" Without pausing to get an answer, she went to the door and called, "Come on, come on, come on," and two Siamese raced from the shadows straight into the cottage and leaped onto the warm spot Harry had vacated on the sofa as if it were prearranged.

When Harry came down again, Shirley glanced at what he was wearing and said, "I thought you were going upstairs to put some trousers on."

He said, "I might have to wade in and fetch something out, mightn't I?"

She shuddered.

He picked his torch off the shelf by the door. Managing to sound quite well in control, he said, " 'Bye, love." He kissed Shirley lightly and tried to provide more reassurance by whispering, "I expect she imagined it."

Not that tough old bird, Shirley thought. If she says she found a corpse, it's there.

Harry Sedgemoor was less certain. While driving Miss Trenchard-Smith the half mile or so down to the lakeside, he seriously speculated that she might be doing this out of a desire to enliven her placid routine with gratuitous excitement. Old women living alone had been known before to waste police time with tall stories. If this were the case, he would be incensed. He was damned sure Shirley wouldn't want to make love after this. Whatever there might or might not be in the lake, the mention of a corpse would color her imagination so vividly that nothing he did or said would relax her.

With an effort to be the policeman, he asked Miss Trenchard-Smith to tell him where to stop the car.

"Anywhere you like," she said with an ominously nonchalant air. "I haven't the faintest idea where we are."

He halted where the road came to an end. They got out and started across a patch of turf, his torch probing the space ahead. The reservoir was enclosed by a low boundary fence, beyond which clumps of reeds stirred in the breeze, appearing to flicker in the torchlight. At intervals were flat stretches of shoreline.

"How exactly did you get down to the water?" he asked.

"Through one of the gates."

"Those are for fishermen only."

"I don't disturb them." She gave a laugh. "I won't tell anyone you broke the law."

He pushed open a gate and they picked their way down to the water's edge.

"Was this the place?"

She said, "It all looks amazingly different now."

Containing his annoyance, he drew the torch beam slowly across a wide angle. "You must have some idea. How did you notice the body?"

"There was still some daylight then."

Fifty yards along the bank was a place where the reeds grew extra tall. "Anywhere like that?"

"I suppose there's no harm in looking," she said.

"That's why we're here, miss."

He stepped in and felt his foot sink into soft mud. "You'd better stay where you are," he told Miss Trenchard-Smith. He worked his way through to the far side. Nothing was there except a family of ducks that put up a noisy protest.

He returned.

She said, "Just look at the state of your gym-shoes!"

"We're looking for a body, miss," PC Sedgemoor reminded her. "We've got to do the job properly."

"If you're going to wade through every clump of reeds, we'll be out all night," she said blithely.

Twenty minutes' searching resulted only in Miss Trenchard-Smith becoming more flippant and PC Sedgemoor less patient. They moved steadily along the shoreline. He shone the torch on his watch, thinking bitterly of Shirley alone in the cottage with those unlikable cats while he danced attendance on this scatty old maid. Almost 11:30. What a Saturday night! In an impatient gesture he swung the beam rapidly across the whole width of the water as if to demonstrate the futility of the task. And perversely that was the moment when Miss Trenchard-Smith said, "There!"

"Where?"

"Give me the torch," she said.

He handed it to her and watched as she held it at arm's length. The beam picked out something white in the water.

PC Sedgemoor took a short, quick breath. "What do you know?" he said in a whisper. "You were right."

The body had lodged among the reeds not more than ten feet from where they stood, in a place where waterweed, bright viridian in the torchlight, grew densely. Unquestionably a woman, face upward, her long hair splayed in the water, a strand of it across her throat. The pale flesh was flecked with seedpods. No wounds were apparent. Sedgemoor was reminded of a painting he had once seen on a school trip to London: a woman lying dead among reeds, evidently drowned. It had impressed him because the teacher had said that the model had been forced to lie for hours in a bath in the artist's studio and one day the artist had forgotten to fill the lamps that were provided to keep the water warm. As a result the girl had contracted an illness that didn't immediately kill her, but certainly shortened her life.

The story had been given to the class as an example of obsessive fidelity to the subject. Sedgemoor had stood in front of the painting until the teacher had called his name sharply from the next room, for it had been the only painting of a dead person he had seen, and death is fascinating to children. Now, faced with an actual drowned corpse, he was made acutely aware how idealized the Pre-Raphaelite image had been. It wasn't merely that the girl in the painting had been clothed. Her hands and face had lain elegantly on the surface of the water. The face of the real drowned woman was submerged, drawn under by the weight of the head. The belly was uppermost, and it was swollen. The skin on the breasts had a puckered appearance. The hands hung too low to be visible at all.

"There's a wind blowing up," said Miss Trenchard-Smith.

"Yes," he responded in a preoccupied way.

"If you don't do something about it, she'll drift away again."

The duty inspector at F Division in Yeovil picked out the significant word from PC Sedgemoor's call. "Naked" meant a full alert. You can generally rule out accident or suicide if you discover a naked corpse in a lake. "And you say you handled it? Was that necessary? All right, lad. Stay where you are. I mean that literally. Stand on the spot. Don't trample the ground. Don't touch the corpse again. Don't smoke, comb your hair, scratch your balls, anything."

Sedgemoor was compelled to ignore the instruction. He hadn't cared to admit that he was calling in from the car, where he had stupidly left his personal radio. He set off at a trot, back to the lakeside.

Miss Trenchard-Smith stood by the body in the darkness, sublimely unconcerned. "I switched off the torch to save your battery."

He told her that assistance was on the way and he would see that she was taken home shortly.

"I hope not," she said. "I'd like to help."

"Decent of you to offer, miss," said Sedgemoor. "With respect, the CID won't need any help."

"*You* were glad of it, young man."

"Yes."

She was unstoppable. Women of her mettle had climbed the Matterhorn in long skirts and chained themselves to railings. "They'll want to identify her," she said with relish. "I'm no Sherlock Holmes, but I can tell them several things already. She was married, proud of her looks, and her shoes pinched. And it appears to me as if she had red hair. It looked dark brown when you first brought her out, but I would say on closer examination that it was a rather fetching shade of chestnut red, wouldn't you?" She switched on the torch and bent over the face admiringly as if it had none of the disfigurement caused by prolonged submersion. "No wonder she let it grow."

"Don't touch!" Sedgemoor cautioned her.

But she already had a lock of hair between finger and thumb. "Just feel how fine it is. Don't be squeamish."

"It isn't that—it's procedure. You don't handle anything."

She looked up, smiling. "Come now, you just dragged her out of the water. Touching her hair won't make a jot of difference."

"I've had orders," he said stiffly. "And I must request you to cooperate."

"As you wish." She straightened up and used the torch to justify her deductions. "The mark of a wedding ring on the left hand. Traces of nail polish on the toes as well as the fingernails. Cramped toes and redness on the backs of the heels. Neither a farm girl nor a feminist my dear Watson. Where are they? They ought to be here by now."

It was with distinct relief that Sedgemoor spotted across the landscape the flashing light of a police vehicle. He swung the torch in a wide arc above his head.

In a few bewildering minutes their sense of isolation was supplanted by activity on a scale the young constable had only ever seen on a training film. A panda car, two large vans, and a minibus drove over the turf and halted. At least a dozen men got out. The area was cordoned off with white tapes and illuminated with arc lamps. Two senior detectives approached the body and spent some time beside it. Then the scenes-of-crime officers moved in. The forensic team arrived. A photographer took pictures and a screen was erected. Miss Trenchard-Smith was led to the minibus and questioned about the finding of the body. The detectives took more interest in her green Wellingtons than in her deductions about the victim. The boots were borrowed, photographed, and used to make casts. Then she was driven back to PC Sedgemoor's house.

Sedgemoor was not detained much longer. He made his statement, surrendered his muddy gym-shoes to the forensic examiners, waited for them to be returned, and then left the scene and drove home. Miss Trenchard-Smith and her cats were still there when he arrived a few minutes after midnight. She was still there at 1:30 A.M., drinking cocoa and reminiscing about her days in the ambulance service during the war. As she graphically expressed it, sudden death was meat and drink to her. This was not the case with Harry Sedgemoor. He refused Shirley's offer of cocoa and went upstairs to look for indigestion tablets. He had to be on duty at eight next morning.

3

IN THE BRISTOL CITY MORTUARY a body lay on a steel trolley. In profile the swell of the stomach suggested nothing less than a mountainous landscape. Or to an imaginative eye it might have been evocative of a dinosaur lurking in a primeval swamp, except that a brown trilby hat of the sort seen in 1940s films rested on the hump. The body was clothed in a double-breasted suit much creased at the points of stress, gray in color, with a broad check design—well known in the Avon & Somerset Police as the working attire of Detective Superintendent Peter Diamond. His silver-fringed bald head was propped on a rubber sheet he had found folded on a shelf. He was breathing evenly.

Peter Diamond was entitled to put his feet up. Ever since the phone beside his bed at home in Bear Flat, near Bath, had buzzed shortly after 1:00 A.M., he had been continuously on duty. By the time he had gotten to the scene at Chew Valley Lake and viewed the body, the local CID lads had set the wheels in motion, but there had remained decisions only Diamond could make, strings that only the man in charge could pull. He'd pulled more strings than Segovia.

Clearly a naked body in a lake was a suspicious death, warranting the attendance of a Home Office pathologist. Resolved to get the top man rather than one of the local police surgeons who was simply empowered to certify that death had occurred, Diamond had personally called Dr. Jack Merlin at his home seventy miles away in Reading and spelled out the facts. Fewer than thirty forensic pathologists were on the Home Office list for England and Wales, and several lived closer than Merlin to Chew Valley Lake. Diamond had set his sights on Jack Merlin. Experience had taught him to shop around for the best. In practice two or three pathologists bore the brunt of the work for the whole of southern England, sometimes motoring vast distances to attend the scenes of crimes. Dr. Merlin was grossly overworked, even without the emergency calls, obliged by the system to perform many routine autopsies a year to provide funds for his forensic science unit. Reasonably enough, if he was called out to a corpse, he liked to be assured by the detective in charge that his attendance was indispensable.

Without altogether succumbing to Diamond's early-morning charm, Merlin had responded at once. He had gotten to the scene by 3:30 A.M. Now, ten hours later, he was performing the autopsy in the room next door.

The sight of that unoccupied stretcher had been irresistible to Peter Diamond. Ostensibly he was there to witness the autopsy. The emphasis on scientific and technical know-how in the modern police made it increasingly the custom for senior detectives investigating suspicious deaths to watch the pathologist at work. Diamond didn't embrace the opportunity so readily as some of his colleagues; he was content to rely on the pathologist's report. Not for the first time on the way to an autopsy he had taken the slow route and meticulously observed the speed limits. On arrival he'd spent some time cruising along Backfields looking for a parking space. Upon finally checking in at the mortuary to learn that the pathologist had started without him and Inspector Wigfull, his reliable assistant, had already gone in, he'd grinned and said, "Botheration. Bully for John Wigfull. Time out for me."

For the now-dormant detective superintendent, those first hours had been as stressful as they always were when you had to impose order on a situation so disorderly as sudden death. But the CID machine was humming now, the procedures set in motion with the coroner, the scenes-of-crime officers, the missing persons register, the forensic science laboratory, and the press office. Diamond could justifiably take his nap while waiting for the news from Jack Merlin.

The door of the dissecting room opened suddenly and woke him. There was a whiff of something unpleasant in the air: cheap floral perfume sprayed from an aerosol by a zealous technician. Diamond blinked, stretched, reached for his felt hat, and raised it in a token greeting.

"You should have come in," he heard Dr. Merlin tell him.

"Too close to lunch." Diamond hoisted himself ponderously on to an elbow. It was true that he wasn't used to missing lunch. He had stopped buying suits off the peg when he took up rugby and started thickening. The rugby had stopped eight years ago, when he was thirty-three. The thickening had not. It didn't trouble him. "What's your snap verdict, then—subject to all the usual provisos?"

Merlin smiled tolerantly. Soft of speech, with a West Country accent redolent of blue skies and clotted cream, this slight, silver-haired man projected such optimism that it was a pity the people he attended were in no state to appreciate it. "If I were you, Superintendent, I'd be rather excited."

Diamond made a gesture toward excitement by heaving himself into a sitting position, squirming around, and dangling his legs over the side of the trolley.

Merlin went on to explain, "It's the opportunity one of your sort dreams of—a real test of his sleuthing ability. An unidentified corpse. No clothes to identify her from a million other women. No marks of any significance. No murder weapon."

"What do you mean—*'one of your sort'?"*

"You know very well what I mean, Peter. You're the end of an era. The last detective. A genuine gumshoe, not some lad out of police school with a degree in computer studies."

Diamond was unamused. "No murder weapon, you said. You're willing to confirm murder?"

"I didn't say that. I wouldn't, would I? I'm in the business of making incisions, not deductions."

"I just want any help you can give me," said Diamond, too weary to argue professional demarcations. "Did she drown?"

Merlin vibrated his lips as if to buy time. "Good question."

"Well?"

"I'll say this. The body has the appearance you would expect after prolonged immersion."

"Come on, Jack," Diamond urged him. "You must know if she drowned. Even I know the signs. Foam in the mouth and nostrils. Bulging of the lungs. Mud and silt in the internal organs."

"Thanks," said Merlin with irony.

"You tell me, then."

"No foam. No over-distension. No silt. Is that what you needed to know, Superintendent?"

Diamond was accustomed to asking the questions, so he tended to ignore any addressed to him. He stared and said nothing.

Someone stepped out of the autopsy room carrying a white plastic bag. He spoke something in greeting and Diamond recognized him as one of the scenes-of-crime officers. The bag now on its way to the Home Office Forensic Science Laboratory at Chepstow was known in the trade as the guts kit.

"Drowning is one of the most difficult diagnoses in forensic pathology," Merlin resumed. "In this case, decomposition makes it even more of a lottery. I can't exclude drowning simply because none of the classical signs are present. The foam and the ballooning of the lungs and so on *may* be present when a body is retrieved from water soon after a drowning occurs. They may not. And if they are not, we can't exclude drowning. The majority of cases of drowning I've seen over the years have lacked any of these so-called classical signs. And after a period of immersion . . ." He shrugged. "Disappointed?"

"What else could have killed her, then?"

"Impossible to say at this stage. They'll test for drugs and alcohol."

"You found no other signs?"

"Other signs, as you put it, were conspicuously absent. Chepstow may give us a pointer. This is rather a challenge for me, too." Merlin didn't go so far as to rub his hands, but his blue eyes certainly gleamed in anticipation. "A real puzzle. It might be more productive to determine what didn't kill her. She was definitely not shot, stabbed, battered, or strangled."

"Thanks for nothing. And she wasn't mauled by a tiger. Come on, Jack, what have I got to go on?"

Merlin turned to a cupboard marked POISON, unlocked it, and took out a bottle of malt whiskey. He poured generous measures into two paper cups and handed one to the superintendent. "What have you got to go on? You've got a white female in her early thirties, natural reddish-brown hair of shoulder length, five foot seven inches in height and about a hundred and ten pounds in weight, green eyes, pierced ears, a particularly fine set of teeth with a couple of expensive white enamel fillings, varnished fingernails and toenails, a vaccination mark just below the knee and no operation scars, the mark of a wedding ring on the appropriate finger, and yes, she was sexually experienced. Aren't you going to make notes or something? This is the distillation of twenty years wearing a rubber apron, I'll have you know."

"Not pregnant, then?"

"No. The swelling of the abdomen was due entirely to the putrefactive gases."

"Can you say whether she has borne a child?"

"Unlikely is as much as I'm prepared to say."

"How long had she been in the lake?"

"What sort of weather have we been having? I've been too busy to notice."

"Pretty warm the last fortnight."

"At least a week, then." Merlin put up his hands defensively. "And don't even ask which day she died."

"Within the last two weeks?"

"Probably. I suppose you've checked your missing persons?"

Diamond gave a nod. "Nobody fits."

Merlin beamed. "You wouldn't have wanted it so easy, would you? This is when your technology is put to the test. All those incredibly expensive computers I keep reading about in *Police Review.*"

Diamond allowed him to make his dig and get away with it. He felt he couldn't do otherwise, knowing, as he did, the conditions that Merlin and his colleagues were sometimes obliged to work in, public mortuaries with inadequate space, lighting, ventilation, plumbing, and drainage. Mortuary building would never be high on the list of social priorities. Mind, there were points Diamond wouldn't mind making himself about pay and conditions of work in the police, but not to Jack Merlin. So he simply repeated in a tone of disparagement, "Computers?"

Merlin grinned. "You know what I mean. Major Inquiry Systems."

"Major Inquiry Systems, my arse," Diamond commented. "Common sense and knocking on doors. That's how we get results."

"Apart from the odd tip-off," said Merlin, and added quickly, "So what will you do about this woman? Issue an artist's impression? A photo wouldn't bear much resemblance to the way she was before she got into the water."

"Probably. First I want to collect any evidence that's around."

"What sort?"

"Obviously we're searching for the clothes."

"At the scene?"

Diamond shook his head. "In this case the scene is unimportant. The body floated there. I gather from what you said that it must originally have sunk to the bottom, and later risen, as they do, unless they're weighted."

"Correct."

"So it came to the surface and floated with the breeze across the lake. We have to search the perimeter."

"How many miles is that?"

"Ten, near enough."

"That represents a lot of canceled leave, I should think."

"It's a pain. But we may get lucky. The lake is popular with anglers and picnickers. I'll be putting out an appeal to the public on TV and radio. If we can pinpoint the place where the body was put into the water, that will give us a start."

Merlin cleared his throat in a way that signaled dissent. "There's a hefty assumption there."

"A deduction," said Diamond with a glare. "Come on, what else am I to assume—that this young woman decided to go for a solitary swim when nobody was about, first removing her wedding ring and all her clothes, and then drowned? You'd have to be bloody naive to put this one down to natural causes." He crushed the cup in his hand and dumped it into a bin.

4

THE MURDER SQUAD worked from a mobile incident room from Sunday morning onward. It was a large caravan parked on a stretch of turf as close as possible to the reeds where the body had been found. Each time Peter Diamond crossed the floor it sounded like beer kegs being unloaded. The sound was heard until well into the evening as he directed the first crucial stages of the inquiry. Five telephones were steadily in use and a team of filing clerks transferred every message and every piece of information first on to action sheets and then onto cards. The standard four-tier carousel for up to twenty thousand cards stood ominously in the center of the room. Diamond felt comfortable with index cards, even if some of his younger staff muttered things about the superiority of computers. If there was not a quick resolution to the inquiry, he'd be forced to install the despised VDUs, and God help the moaners when the things broke down.

The search for the dead woman's clothes was first concentrated on the sections of shoreline with easiest access from the three roads that enclosed the lake. A bizarre collection of mislaid and discarded garments began to be assembled, tokens of the variety of human activities around the lake. The items were painstakingly labeled, sealed in plastic bags, noted on the map, and entered on the action sheets without much confidence that any were linked with the case.

Divers were brought in to search the stretch of water where the body had been found floating. It was not impossible that the clothes or other evidence had been dumped there. This was an exercise that had to be gone through, although most people, including Diamond, reckoned that the body had drifted there from farther along the shore, or even across the lake.

At the same time, house-to-house inquiries were made in the villages and at each dwelling with a view of the lake, seeking witnesses to any unusual activity beside the water after dark in the previous month. A sheaf of statements soon confirmed what the squad already knew, that the area was popular around the hour of sunset with anglers, bird-watchers, dog owners, and courting couples. Nothing remotely resembling a naked body being dragged or carried into the water had been seen.

For Peter Diamond this dragnet process was a necessary, if largely unrewarding preamble to what he thought of as real detective work: the identifying and questioning of suspects. For all the care that was being taken to refer to what had happened as an "incident," this was a murder inquiry. He was as certain of that as one day follows another. Since his appointment to the Avon and Somerset murder squad three years previously, he had led five investigations, three domestic, two large-scale, all but one resulting in convictions. The odd one out was an extradition job, still to be resolved. It could drag on for another year. However, he was satisfied that he had nailed his man. An impressive record. And it might have been more impressive if his service in Avon had not been regularly interrupted by all the ballyhoo over the Missendale affair.

Four years before, a young black man called Hedley Missendale had been convicted of murder in the course of a theft at a building society in Hammersmith, West London. A customer, an ex–sergeant major, had tried to tackle the thief and had been shot in the head, dying almost immediately. The investigation had been headed by Detective Superintendent Jacob Blaize, of F Division of the Metropolitan Police. Diamond, then with the rank of detective chief inspector, had been Blaize's second-in-command. Missendale, a known thief, had been pulled in quickly and had confessed under interrogation from Diamond. Then more than two years later, after Diamond had won his promotion to superintendent with the Avon and Somerset force, a second man had confessed to the crime after undergoing a religious conversion. He had produced the gun used in the killing. A second investigation by a fresh team of officers had been ordered, and late in 1987, after serving twenty-seven months of a life sentence, Hedley Missendale had been pardoned on the recommendation of the Home Secretary.

The press, of course, had roasted the police. Blaize and Diamond had been openly accused in the tabloids of beating a confession out of an innocent black youth. An official inquiry had been inevitable. Jacob Blaize— broken by the strain—had accepted full responsibility for the errors and had taken early retirement. The press then switched the full force of their attack to Diamond. They had wanted his head on a platter, but he had stood up well to tough questioning at the inquiry. What had yet to be seen was whether his strong rebuttal of the criticism had influenced the board of inquiry. People said he'd damaged his own case, because the principal charge was that his forceful personality had secured the bogus confession, and he had defended himself ruggedly at the hearings.

Eight months after the hearings, the inquiry team had yet to publish its findings. Meanwhile, Peter Diamond was unrepentant, and willing to argue the rights of his conduct in the case with anyone rash enough to take him on. No one did; the mudslinging went on from a safe distance. His response was to prove his worth as a detective, and this he was doing—between appearances in London—with fair success. The string of cases he had investigated in Avon had been properly handled without a suggestion of intimidation.

Diamond was proving a hard man to stop, a burly, abrasive character who spoke his mind. Computer technology was "gadgetry," accepted with reluctance as an aid to the real detective work. Some of the career-minded people around him thought it a miracle or a travesty that a man so outspoken and with the Missendale inquiry hanging over his head could have progressed to the rank of superintendent. They failed to appreciate that his bluntness was a precious asset among so many backbiters.

Whether he would ever earn respect in Somerset and Avon it was too soon to predict. His detractors said that his successes so far owed too much to help from paid informants. They couldn't fault him for using grasses; but they waited gloatingly to see him handle an inquiry when no help could be bought.

The Chew Valley case might be the one.

Sunday was disappointing. Nothing of significance was found.

On Monday Diamond recorded interviews for BBC Television and HTV West for their regional news broadcasts after the early evening news. An artist's sketch of the dead woman was shown, followed by Diamond beside the lake appealing for help in identifying her. He asked for information from anyone who might have witnessed suspicious behavior over the last three weeks. An invitation, he commented afterward to the TV crew, to all the voyeurs in the valley to wipe the steam off their glasses and share their secondhand thrills, but he had to admit that it was worthwhile. A thirty-second spot on TV brought in more information than a hundred coppers on house-to-house duty all the week.

Late that night, while the calls were being processed, he called Jack Merlin and asked for the results of the laboratory tests.

"What exactly were you hoping for?" the pathologist asked in that benign, but irritating way he had of sounding as if he were from another, more intelligent form of life.

"The cause of death will do for now."

"That, I'm afraid, is still an open question until all the results are in, and even then—"

"Jack, are you telling me those flaming tests are still going on? The autopsy was yesterday morning, thirty-six hours ago."

For this petulant outburst, Diamond was given a lecture on the time scale necessary for the processing of histological tissues, which required at least a week, and on the pressures the Home Office Forensic Laboratory was under. "Currently they're so pressed that it could be weeks before they deliver."

"*Weeks?* Have you told them it's a suspicious death? Don't they understand the urgency?" Diamond had picked up a pencil and put it between his teeth. He bit into the wood. "You're still not willing to say if she drowned?"

"All I will say is that as yet the cause of death is not apparent." Merlin was retreating behind the form of words he used in giving evidence.

"Jack, my old friend," Diamond coaxed him. "Can't you speak off the record to me? Can you help me with an estimate of the date of death?"

"Sorry."

"Terrific!" The pencil snapped into two pieces.

There was a longish silence. Then: "I am doing the best I can in the circumstances, Superintendent. I won't be steamrollered. You must appreciate that the service is undermanned."

"Jack, spare me the charity appeal, will you? Just call me the minute you reach an opinion."

"I always intended to."

Diamond dropped the phone and left it dangling below the desktop. The telephonist retrieved it without complaining and removed the pieces of pencil. Diamond ambled across the floor again to see what had come in as a result of his television appeal, knocking the carousel out of alignment as he went.

John Wigfull, his second-in-command, summed up. "We've heard from seven callers convinced that the victim is Candice Milner."

"Who the hell is Candice Milner?"

After a pause to decide whether the question should be taken seriously, Wigfull said, *"The Milners—* that soap on the BBC. Candice was written out of the story a couple of years ago, at least."

"Give me strength! What else?"

"Two deserted husbands called in. In one case the wife left a note saying she was going away for a week to unwind. The home is in Chilcompton. That was six months ago."

"Six months. She ought to be in missing persons."

"She is. The photo doesn't bear much resemblance. We passed it over."

"I'll take another look at it. You'd better send someone to talk to the bloke tomorrow. What else?"

"Slightly more promising, this. A farmer by the name of Troop from Chewton Mendip had a row with his wife three weeks ago and she hitched a lift with the lorry driver who collects the milk churns. Husband hasn't seen her since."

"Didn't he report it?"

"He was giving her time to come to her senses. There's a history of fights and walkouts."

"And he reckons the sketch looks like his wife?"

"He's not saying, sir. His sister-in-law thinks so. She was the one who phoned us."

Diamond's eyes widened a fraction. "Anything on file? Complaints of violence?"

Wigfull nodded. "Just the one, on twenty-seven December, 1988. Farmer Troop seems to have kicked his wife out of the house, literally, and refused to let her in again. The sister reported it. A PC from Bath was sent out and saw the bruises. The woman refused to proceed. She said it was Christmas."

"Goodwill to all men." Diamond took a deep, disapproving breath and let it out slowly. "What can you do? You and I had better follow this one up ourselves, John. Chewton Mendip can't be more than five miles from the lake. I'll see the sister-in-law in the morning—and you'd better find out the name of the gallant knight of the churns."

Wigfull grinned appreciatively. Any sign of good humor in the superintendent had to be encouraged. They weren't exactly bosom pals. Wigfull had been appointed as Diamond's assistant in the worst of circumstances, when the Missendale scandal had first made banner headlines. In the few months before, Diamond had made an impressive debut with Avon and Somerset and cleared up two murders, assisted by an inspector he had got along well with, called Billy Murray. But within hours of Diamond's involvement in the Missendale case becoming known, instructions had come from county headquarters that Murray was transferred to Taunton, where a vacancy had arisen. John Wigfull, from CID (administration), was his replacement. Rightly or not, Diamond was convinced that Wigfull was a plant, the headquarters man under instructions to report any excesses. Unlike Billy Murray, Wigfull did everything by the book. He'd gone to a lot of trouble to ingratiate himself with the squad. He hadn't succeeded yet with his superior.

"Anything else?" asked Diamond.

"A fair number of sightings."

"But of what?"

"Horizontal jogging, mostly."

"No reports of violence?"

"Nothing yet."

"Not much, is it? I may go on the box again toward the end of the week. Let's see if Chewton Mendip amounts to anything. Is that where the sister lives as well?"

She was Mrs. Muriel Pietri, and her husband Joe owned a motor repair business beside the A39 that had a sign that promised LOW COST HIGH-CLASS REPAIRS. WE GET YOU BACK ON THE ROAD. The police often visited the place to follow up hit-and-run accidents. Diamond himself called there early next morning. Someone lower in rank could have handled the interview, but the prospect of question and answer was so much more appealing than another morning in the caravan.

The sickly-sweet vapor of paint hung in the air as he maneuvered his bulk unskillfully through a narrow passage between damaged vehicles, collecting rust on his gray check suit. He had brought a sergeant with him to take the statement.

Mrs. Pietri stood at the open door in a floral print frock that she probably wore for visitors. She was made up for the occasion—the works: foundation, lipstick, mascara, and some sort of cheap scent that made the paint quite fragrant in retrospect. She was a slim, dark-haired, slow-speaking woman, burning with the enormity of what she believed had happened. "I do fear the worst this time," she said in the broad accent of Somerset as she led them into her scrupulously tidy front room. "Carl's behavior is a proper disgrace. He do clout my sister summat wicked. Terrible. I can show you photographs my husband took with one of they Instamatics last time poor Elly came here. Black and blue she were. I hope you'll be giving the bugger a dose of his own medicine when you visit him. He do deserve no blimmin' mercy, none at all. Won't 'ee sit down?"

"You saw the artist's sketch of the woman we found?" said Diamond.

"On *Points West* last night. That be Elly, without a blimmin' doubt."

"Sergeant Boon has a copy of the picture. Take another look at it, would you? It's only an artist's sketch, you understand."

She handed it back almost at once. "I swear to it."

"What color is your sister's hair, Mrs. Pietri?"

"Red—a gorgeous, flaming red. It were her best feature, and it were natural, too. Women spend fortunes being tinted at the hairdressers for hair that color and it never looks half so good as Elly's did."

Her use of the past tense reinforced her conviction that the dead woman was her sister. Diamond made it just as clear that he was keeping an open mind. "Flaming red, you say. Is that what you mean—pure red?"

"Natural, I did say, didn't I? Nobody's hair is pure red, except for they punks and pop stars."

"I need to know."

She pointed to a rosewood ornamental box that stood on the sideboard. "That color, near enough."

"Her eyes—what color are they?"

"Some folk called they hazel. They always looked green to I."

"What height is she?"

"The same as I—five-seven."

"Age?"

"Wait a mo—Elly were born two years after I. Saint George's Day. She must have been thirty-four."

"You said that your husband took photographs of her."

"Not of her face, my dear. The backs of her legs, where she were marked. It were in case she wanted evidence for a divorce. I don't believe I got a picture of her face, not since her and I were kids at school, anyways. We were never a family for taking pictures."

"But you said your husband has a camera."

"For his business. He do photograph the damage in case the insurance people get funny."

"I see."

"It were his idea to take they pictures of Elly's legs."

"Photographing the damage."

"I can find they if you want."

"Not now. Tell me how you heard that your sister is missing."

"Well, being that she lived so near, she used to call in here regular for a bit o' gossip Tuesday morning. She didn't come last Tuesday, or the Tuesday afore that, so I got on the blower and asked that bugger of a brother-in-law what happened to my sister."

"And?"

"The blighter tells I this bit o' hogwash about Elly taking off with Mr. Middleton who collects the milk. Your sister is a shameless woman, he did tell I, no better than the whores of Babylon. He called her other things, too, that you wouldn't find in the Scriptures. Riled I proper, I can tell 'ee."

"When is this supposed to have happened?"

"Last Monday fortnight, he did say. I didn't believe a word of it, and I were right. She must have been dead already, lying naked in Chew Valley Lake, poor lamb. Do you want I to come with 'ee and identify her proper?"

"That may not be necessary."

"Will you be going over to arrest the bugger?"

"I want you to sign a statement, Mrs. Pietri. The sergeant will assist you." Diamond got up and walked out.

Over the radio he made contact with Inspector Wigfull. "Any news?"

"Yes," Wigfull answered. "I just called at the milkman's cottage."

"Middleton?"

"Yes."

"And?"

"Elly Troop opened the door."

5

IN THE MODERN POLICE, as any detective will tell you, a murder mystery is rarely, if ever, solved by scintillating deductions from clues that baffle inferior minds. Unless the killer's identity is so obvious that the case is cleared up in the first hours, the investigative process is likely to be laborious, involving hundreds of man-hours by police officers, forensic scientists, and clerical staff. If any credit attaches ultimately to a conviction, it is diffused among numerous individuals, and has to be qualified by administrative delays, false assumptions, and sometimes fatal errors. These days criminal investigation is not a sport for glory hunters.

After the unproductive interview with Mrs. Pietri, Diamond returned to the mobile incident room and pounded the floor again. He demanded another look at the missing persons files for Avon and Somerset and the adjacent counties and vented his anger on a filing clerk when he found that the list hadn't been updated since he had last seen it. The atmosphere in the caravan was sulfurous as he reduced the girl to tears, blaming her for other shortcomings in the list that were apparently not her responsibility.

Inspector Wigfull's return should have defused the tension. Wigfull, the sunbeam of the squad, as Diamond

unkindly dubbed him, always had a word of encouragement for everyone, including the civilian clerks, each of
whom he knew by their first names. His was the shoulder to cry on. He smiled a lot, and when he wasn't smiling he still appeared to be, because of the tendency of
his exuberant mustache to curl upward at the ends. This
time the mere sight of him coming up the steps—playing a catching game with his car keys—triggered Diamond into another tirade.

"You took your bloody time."

"Sorry, sir. Mrs. Troop was in a bit of a state. She
needed advice."

"John, if you want to join the bloody marriage
guidance people and hold hands with weeping wives,
why don't you go ahead? I happen to be working on a
murder inquiry, and if that isn't your particular bent, I
suggest you tell me right now so that I can ask for someone I can rely on."

"She'd been assaulted by her husband, sir. I was
telling her to lodge a complaint this time."

"Social work," said Diamond as if he were speaking
of some disease brought on by lack of hygiene. "You're
supposed to be a detective. Meanwhile I'm stuck here
like a lupin waiting for a bee."

"Has there been a development?"

Diamond flung out his hand and knocked over a
box of paper clips. "Of course there bloody hasn't. How
can there be when you're listening to sob stories over
coffee in Chewton Mendip? Three days, and all I've got
for it is a sunburned scalp. We're literally up the creek
until we can put a name to this corpse."

"Should we have another look at missing persons?"
the hapless inspector suggested.

There was a tensing of shoulders right around the
room, unnecessarily as it turned out. Diamond, deciding
that he had raised his blood pressure to dangerous
levels, said in the mild register that he knew was more
effective than a bellow, "That is what I have been trying
to do."

"But in this area alone?"

"And Wiltshire." He snatched up a sheaf of flimsy papers and flapped it. "A bloody long list, growing by seventy-plus every week."

Wigfull cleared his throat and said, "Surely the PNC can help us."

Diamond had to think a moment. His mind didn't work in abbreviations, and people who knew him better were more tactful than to press the cause of the Police National Computer. "Yes," he said with contempt, "by giving us twenty thousand names."

"You limit it by keying in the data you have," Wigfull tried to explain. "In this case, females under thirty with red hair."

In reality, Diamond had a reasonable grasp of the PNC's functions; otherwise he couldn't have survived in the CID. What he deplored was the general belief that it was the cure-all. "For the present, we'll work with the county lists," he said. "I want updates on each of the names I've marked. Call the local stations. Get descriptions, real descriptions, not sodding data, as you insist on calling it. I want to know what they're like as people. By three-thirty this afternoon. I'm calling a conference."

"Very good, Mr. Diamond."

"That remains to be seen. You may have sensed that I'm feeling somewhat frayed at the edges, Mr. Wigfull. Somewhere out there is a murderer. We're making precious little progress toward arresting him. Jesus Christ, we don't even know how it was done."

"Looks as if we'll need the PNC," said Wigfull.

Diamond turned away, muttering, to check more responses to the local appeal for information. Copies of the artist's sketch had appeared in Monday's *Bath Evening Chronicle* and the *Bristol Evening Post*. "Two more for Candice Milner," he presently called across to Wigfull. "It says a lot about contemporary values when people can't discriminate between real life and a flaming television serial." It would take a breakthrough of cosmic proportions to shake him out of this embittered mood.

Wigfull's work on the phone had yielded results of

a sort: he had fuller details of three missing women whose descriptions broadly tallied with the woman found in the lake. "Janet Hepple is divorced, thirty-three, a part-time artists' model in Coventry. Red hair, five foot seven. She left her flat seven weeks ago, leaving rent unpaid, and hasn't been seen since. Evidently this was out of character. Everyone spoke of her as honest and reliable."

Diamond was unimpressed. "And the second?"

"Sally Shepton-Howe, from Manchester, missing since May twenty-first, when she had a row with her husband and ran off. She sells cosmetics in a department store in the city. Hair described as auburn, green eyes, thirty-two, good-looking. A woman of her description was seen that night at Knutsford Services on the M6 trying to hitch a lift south."

"Asking for it. Who else?"

"This is an odd one. An author, from west London, Hounslow. Writes romance. What are those books women buy everywhere?"

"Bodice rippers?" someone suggested.

"No, the name of the publisher."

"Don't ask me. I only read science fiction."

"Anyway, she writes them. She's called Meg Zoomer."

"Zoomer. Is that a pen name?"

"It's real, apparently, the name of her third husband."

"*Third?*" said Diamond. "What age is this woman?"

"Thirty-four. She appears to carry on as if she's one of the characters in her books. Hungry for romance. She wears a dark green cloak and grows her hair long. It's chestnut red. Anyway, she drives about in an MG sports car looking for experiences to use in her books."

"Someone's having you on, John," said Keith Halliwell, the inspector supervising the house-to-house inquiries.

"They'd better not be," Diamond said grimly. "This

is a murder hunt, not a night out at the pub. Let's have the rest. When was Mrs. Zoomer last seen?"

"May nineteenth, at a party in Richmond. She left soon after midnight with a man who seems to have been a gate-crasher. Everyone assumed he came with somebody else. Tall, dark-haired, aged about thirty, powerfully built, a trace of a French accent."

"Straight out of one of the books," commented Halliwell. "What did he drive—a Porsche, or a four-in-hand?"

"Wrap up, will you?" Diamond snapped. He regarded Halliwell as a pain, which was why he was on house-to-house. "Who was the informant?"

"The woman who lives next door, sir. She took in the milk each day until there was no room left in her fridge."

"Has anyone shown her the picture yet?"

"That's being done. And Scotland Yard are trying to locate Mrs. Zoomer's dental records."

"A model, a shopgirl, and a writer." Diamond sniffed. "That's all?"

"Those are the missing redheads more or less fitting our description, sir."

"I thought you would come up with more than that."

Wigfull countered this by saying, "With respect, sir, the PNC would have given us more."

After an uneasy silence, Diamond said tamely, "All right. See to it."

Wigfull tilted an eyebrow in Halliwell's direction and it was his undoing.

"As we're going to cast the net more widely," continued Diamond in a reasonable tone, "maybe we should broaden our data base."

The jargon from the lips of the Last Detective ambushed everyone. "In what way, exactly, Mr. Diamond?" Wigfull innocently asked.

"Brunettes. People have different ideas about red hair. Our woman isn't what you'd call ginger. The hair is reddish brown."

"More red than brown, sir."

"Some people might call it brown. Check the bru-nettes on the PNC as well."

That silenced Wigfull rather pleasingly. The confer-ence continued for another twenty minutes, dispiritingly chronicling the failure of the door-to-door inquiries, the searches, and the appeals in the media to throw up any-thing of real significance. At the end of it, when they had climbed out of the minibus and were flexing their limbs, Inspector Croxley, a quietly ambitious man—an ascending angel, by his own lights—who was coordinat-ing the search around the lake, approached Diamond and said, "I didn't raise this inside, sir, but it crossed my mind. We're all assuming murder because she was found nude, but there isn't any evidence of violence."

"Up to now. The pathologist's report isn't in."

"If it does turn out to be the writer, I wonder what you think of suicide as a possibility, sir?"

"What?"

"Suicide. I saw a thing on television once about a famous writer. I mean a documentary, not a play. She was out of her mind, I admit, but she killed herself by walking into a river. Back in the 1940s, this was, in the war. She drowned. We know this Zoomer woman has fantasies about herself, the way she dresses and what have you. Suppose she got depressed and decided to do away with herself. Isn't this the way she might do it—a dramatic gesture?"

"Starkers? Did this woman on TV strip off before she drowned herself?"

"Well, no, sir."

"That's gilding the lily, is it?"

"I beg your pardon."

"The dramatic gesture. An extra touch?"

"Something like that. It's only an idea."

"I'll say one thing for your theory, Inspector. I've heard of cases when people have left a heap of clothes on a shoreline. It's not uncommon. That Labour MP—"

"Stonehouse."

"Right. The difference is that he faked his suicide.

People were meant to find the clothes and assume he'd drowned. What we have here, Inspector, isn't a pile of clothes and no corpse. It's a corpse and no clothes. You find me a pile of women's garments including a long, green cloak, and I might buy your theory." With a swagger, Diamond ambled off to the incident room.

Wanting to get away from the constant bleep of the phones, he chose to hold his case conference in the minibus parked beside the incident room. So at 3:30, the four senior officers in the squad sat with him in the rear of the vehicle in uncomfortable proximity and in turn reported their findings.

Occasionally during the long summer, when his caseload had been less, he had bought sandwiches for lunch and found a seat among the tourists on one of the wooden benches in the Abbey Churchyard, the paved open area facing the west front of the Abbey. There he'd regularly whiled away a pleasant twenty minutes reading *Fabian of the Yard,* which he'd acquired in the Oxfam shop for 10p.

Fabian of the Yard. Lovely title. No wonder so many big-name detectives from Fred Cherrill to Jack Slipper had used that *"of the Yard"* tag for their memoirs. *Diamond of Avon and Somerset* didn't have the same ring to it. Good thing he wasn't planning to go into print.

At intervals in those summer lunch breaks he had looked up from his reading. The towers on each side of the great west window were decorated with sixteenth-century carvings representing angels on two ladders, to Diamond's eye more curious than decorative. These weather-beaten figures were perched at mathematically precise intervals on the rungs of the two ladders reaching up to heaven. Many people assumed that it was a representation of Jacob's ladder. The official version, however, was that it was Oliver King's ladder, for the bishop of that name who rebuilt the church, starting in 1499, had stoutly insisted that the dream of a ladder to heaven was his own, and who can doubt the integrity of a bishop? Fixed in perpetuity in their positions, unaltered except by the eroding effects of wind, rain, and contamination, those luckless angels seemed emblematic of hope deferred, rather than of celestial promise. Peter Diamond knew the feeling. Staring up at the west front one lunchtime, he had been charmed by a revelation of his own, picturing the senior CID of Avon and Somerset clinging to the rungs. The image often came back to him when he saw them together.

Midway through Wednesday morning came a call from Dr. Merlin, the pathologist. For no obvious reason Diamond had started the day in a benign mood. He strolled across the room, cheerfully thanked the girl who handed him the phone, put it to his ear, and said, "Glorious morning here, Jack. What's it doing in Reading?"

"Look here, I've been badgering the lab on your account," Merlin announced, sounding quite piqued at the bonhomie. "Off the record they've given me some early results."

"And?"

"Nothing has been found to indicate conclusively how she died."

"You call that a result?"

"It supports my preliminary opinion."

"I never doubted you."

The absence of doubt in Diamond's mind appeared not to settle the question for the pathologist. "It's still quite conceivable that she drowned."

Diamond sighed. "We've been over this before. Aren't we any closer to a definite cause of death? Let's put it this way, Jack," he added quickly, not wanting the phone slammed down. "Is there anything I can rule out? Toxic substances?"

"Too early to say. Nothing very obvious, but you have to remember that if someone has drowned, especially in fresh water, there's a tremendous increase in blood volume—up to a hundred per cent within a couple of minutes—due to the osmotic absorption of fresh water through the lung membranes. This has the effect of diluting any concentration of drugs or alcohol in the blood by up to a hundred per cent. So any analysis result on a postmortem sample may give only half the true value which was present just before death."

"Jack, suppose she didn't drown. Suppose the body was dumped in the lake after death. Is there anything pointing to a cause of death?"

"Essentially she appears to have been a healthy young woman. We can rule out coronary artery disease or myocarditis, or diabetic coma, or epilepsy."

"I sense that you do know something," said Diamond. "You're keeping me in suspense, you bugger."

"I'm telling you these things, Superintendent, because without them my conclusion is tentative, at best. At the autopsy I found a number of pinhead hemorrhages in the eye membranes and there were some in the scalp and to a lesser extent in the brain and the lungs. The presence of petechial hemorrhages is open to different interpretations depending on other findings."

"All right, mate, I get the point. You can't be a hundred percent certain. But what would you put your money on?"

Merlin's tone revealed that he didn't much like his opinion equated with gambling. "In the absence of external injuries, one is drawn along the road—"

"Oh, come on, man!"

"—of asphyxia as the cause of death."

"Asphyxia?"

"So you appreciate the difficulty. Drowning is a form of asphyxia."

Diamond groaned. "But I just ruled out drowning."

"I didn't." After a pause, Merlin said, "There's a phenomenon known as dry drowning."

Diamond wondered briefly whether he was being sent up. "Did you say *dry* drowning?"

"It happens in about one case in every five. The victim's larynx goes into spasm with the first intake of water and very little of it enters the lungs. They drown without actually gulping or inhaling water. Dry drowning, you see."

"What about those hemorrhages you found?"

"Would be observed, as in any case of asphyxia."

"Meaning she may have drowned after all? That doesn't help me much. It doesn't help me at all." Diamond was heating up again. "This wasn't a swimming accident, Jack. People aren't allowed to swim in reservoirs. Anyway, she was nude. Her wedding ring was missing."

"Are you listening to me?" said Merlin.

"Go on."

"To answer your question, if you exclude drowning as a possibility, and if we can eliminate drugs and alcohol, the most likely explanation is that before she got into the water she was smothered with some soft object, say a cushion or a pillow."

"We've got there," said Diamond to his audience in the caravan.

"I didn't say that. I'm trying to balance the probabilities. Death by smothering is hard to detect at the best of times," said the pathologist tartly.

"You said the same about drowning. I sometimes wonder, Jack, if you'd say the same about a dagger through the heart." Diamond banged down the phone and looked around. "Where the hell is Wigfull?"

"Outside, sir," said a sergeant. "The press has arrived."

Diamond swore and left the room.

One of the filing clerks said to nobody in particular, "I wish we were back in headquarters."

"Why?" the sergeant asked her.

"He intimidates me, that's why. I don't like to be so near him. You can't get away from him in this poky caravan. There's more room in a proper incident room. And he breaks things. Have you watched him? He breaks things, paper cups, pencils, anything he gets his hands on. It gets on my nerves."

The sergeant grinned. "That's how he got where he is today, by breaking things."

Outside, at a signal from Diamond, John Wigfull terminated the press interview and the two men took a walk along the edge of the lake, past fishermen spaced at intervals. Wigfull waited until Diamond had given him the gist of the news from Merlin and then said with his habitual optimism, "That's a big step forward."

"It may be, when we eventually find out who she is," Diamond said, and was moved to confide to his assistant, "I can't even feel sorry for the woman without knowing anything about her—her name, her background. I need to care about what happened to the victim, but I don't. She's just a stiff. That isn't enough."

"We know a certain amount," Wigfull pointed out. "She was married. She cared about her appearance. She wasn't a down-and-out."

"Someone ought to have noticed that this woman is missing by now. It's over two weeks. She must have had people she knew, friends, family, or workmates. Where are they?"

"I'm following up on those missing women we talked about yesterday and I've got a long list of brunettes who could be worth checking out."

Diamond aimed a vicious kick at a fir cone.

They retraced their steps in silence. Before they reached the encampment of blue and black vehicles inside the taped cordon, a police motorcyclist rode along the track and stopped by the incident room. He went inside, was evidently told where to deliver his message, came out and walked across to Diamond, and handed him a brown envelope, sent from police headquarters at Bristol.

"My promotion, no doubt," Diamond quipped sourly as he opened it. Inside was a faxed diagram. "No," he said. "It's from the Yard. Mrs. Zoomer's dental record. I regret to inform you, Mr. Wigfull, that by the look of this, your eccentric author has two superfluous wisdom teeth. Two more than our lady of the lake."

Later that afternoon, the decision was taken to decamp. The house-to-house inquiries and the search of the lake perimeter had been completed. The scenes-of-crime officers had long since left. It made sense to transfer to Bristol.

The midges in their millions were casting their evening haze over the water when the last police car left the site and headed through Bishop Sutton toward the A37. In the backseat, Diamond remarked, "You know what depressed me most about that spot?"

John Wigfull shook his head.

"Those goddamn fishermen. They were showing us up."

Just short of Whitchurch, a message came through on the car radio. It was the desk sergeant at Manvers Street Police Station in Bath.

"Don't know if this is relevant to your inquiry, sir. A man has come in and reported that his wife is missing. Her name is Geraldine Snoo, sir."

"Snoozer?"

"Snoo. Geraldine Snoo."

Beside him, Wigfull opened his mouth to speak, but Diamond put up a restraining hand.

The sergeant added, "She's thirty-three and he describes her hair as auburn."

"When did he see her last?"

"Almost three weeks ago."

Diamond cast his eyes upward in an expression of gratitude that was almost worshipful. "Is he still with you?"

"Yes, sir."

"Keep him there. For God's sake don't let him leave. What's his name?"

"Professor Jackman."

"Professor? Hold on. You say his name is Jackman, and he's the husband, but you just gave me the woman's name as Snoo."

"That's the name she's known by, sir. She's an actress. Well, that's an understatement. She's a star. Do you ever watch *The Milners* on TV? Geraldine Snoo played the part of Candice."

Diamond had taken too strong a grip on the window handle. It jerked out of its socket.

6

IF A SOAP-STAR had to live anywhere, it might as well be Bath, that squeaky-clean city in the south-west. Ribbons of Georgian terraced houses undulate elegantly between seven green hills, diverting the eye from anything more unsightly. Stone-cleaning is second only to tourism as a local industry; the Yellow Pages list fifty-four firms. High-pressure water-jets have transformed old blackened buildings into gleaming backdrops for television plays of the sort the British are supposed to do best. With two thousand years of history, Bath chooses to ignore all but the Roman and the Georgian periods. Some people say that it's just a theme park, that if you want to see a real city you might as well drive the thirteen miles farther west to Bristol. If you tried, as Peter Diamond did most mornings, you'd suffer the curse of a real city—its traffic. With the soap star and the stone-cleaners, he was content to make his home in Bath.

His house on Wellsway was only twenty minutes' walk from here—south of the railway. Not the smartest end of town, but the best a senior detective could afford.

He almost waltzed across the car park and up the steps of Manvers Street Police Station. Already he had brushed aside the trifling embarrassment of his remarks

about the people who had phoned in to say that the
dead woman was a TV star. He didn't believe in fretting
over past mistakes. Infinitely more was at stake than his
own self-esteem. What mattered in a major inquiry was
the ability of the man in charge to seize his opportunity
when it came. Diamond was sure that the moment had
arrived. His luck had changed now that he had turned
his back on that pesky lake.

He was met by the desk sergeant, whom he knew
well.

"Is he still here?"

The sergeant nodded and made a dumb show of
pointing toward a door.

Diamond scarcely lowered his voice. "What line is
he taking?"

"He's very concerned about his wife, sir."

"He ought to be after three weeks."

"He's been away from home a good deal, he says.
He thought she was with friends."

"And left it until now to go looking for her? What
do you make of him?"

The sergeant pursed his lips. "He's not my idea of a
professor, sir."

"They don't all look like Einstein. Is he telling the
truth about his wife is what I want to know."

"I think he must be, else why would he come in
here?"

Diamond answered with a look that said he could
think of a dozen reasons. "Does he know about the
body in Chew Valley Lake?"

The sergeant nodded. "Friends told him."

"And what's a murdered wife between friends? Has
he seen the picture we distributed?"

"He hasn't mentioned it."

"Right. Don't stand there like a Christmas tree.
There's plenty to do. I propose to set up the incident
room here. We were on our way to Bristol, but this has
changed everything. Get it organized, will you? And I
need someone to take a statement."

With the confident air of a man about to do the

thing he enjoys best, he thrust open the door of the office where the professor who had lost his wife was waiting. "My name is Diamond," he announced, "Detective Superintendent Diamond."

It was immediately clear what the sergeant had meant. The man standing beside the window had the look not of a professor, but of a sportsman. He might have just showered and changed after a five-setter at Wimbledon. Some padding in the shoulders of his black linen jacket clearly contributed to the effect, but he still didn't pass muster as an academic. He could not have been much over thirty. He wasn't wearing a tie, just a sky-blue cotton shirt sufficiently open to show a double gold chain across the chest. His thick, black hair was expensively cut and he had a luxuriant mustache. "Gregory Jackman," he introduced himself in a voice that was pure Yorkshire. "Do you have any news of my wife?"

Diamond in his customary fashion declined to answer. "You're a professor, I understand. Bath University?"

Jackman gave a nod.

"What's your subject?"

"English. Look, I'm here about my wife."

A woman PC came in with a shorthand pad.

"You don't object if she takes notes?" Diamond inquired.

"No. Why should I?"

"Have a seat, then. Just for the record, I should tell you that you don't have to say anything unless you wish to do so, but what you say may be given in evidence. Now tell me about your wife."

Jackman said without moving toward a chair, "I told them at the desk half an hour ago. They took the details."

"Bear with me, professor," Diamond said with painstaking courtesy. "I'm in charge and I'd rather hear it from you than read it in the occurrence book. Her name, first."

With a resigned air, Jackman planted himself on a

chair and said, "Geraldine Jackman, known to most people as Gerry Snoo. That's her stage name. She'll be thirty-four in a week or two if . . . God, I find this whole thing too appalling to contemplate."

"Would you describe her, sir?"

"Do I have to? You must have seen her on television. *The Milners.* Right? If not, you must have seen the lager ad with the bulldog and the girl. That was Gerry. She did a few commercials after she left the BBC."

There was a moment's hiatus. Diamond was studying his man's expression so keenly that he had to catch what he said by mentally playing it over again. "Oh, I don't see much television. Let's assume I've never seen her. What color hair does she have?"

"Reddish brown. Chestnut red, if you like."

"You said auburn to the sergeant."

"Auburn, then." On a rising note that showed the strain he was under, Jackman said, "What are you trying to do—catch me out? I wasn't dragged in here for questioning, you know. I'm here because my wife is missing. I'm told she may be dead."

"Who told you that?"

"Some people who know Gerry extremely well saw that picture you showed on television. They said it was exactly like her. They told me they got in touch with you."

"Not me personally. We had a massive response to our appeal for information," Diamond smoothly explained. "It takes time to check. But now that you have come forward—"

"Look, I want to know, one way or the other," Jackman cut in. Concern was etched vividly in his features, but so it would be at this stage of the game, whether he was innocent or not. "You found a woman. Where is she now?"

"At Bristol City Mortuary. Let's not leap to conclusions. It may not be necessary for you to go there if it turns out that your wife's appearance is unlike the woman we found." Patiently Diamond elicited a description, feature by feature, of Mrs. Jackman. It corresponded closely with the details of the corpse. Encouragingly closely.

He went on to ask, "When did you last see your wife?"

"On a Monday, three weeks ago."

"That would have been September eleventh?"

"Er, yes. I left early for London. She was still in bed. I told her when I expected to be back, and then left to catch the eight-nineteen from Bath."

"You had business in London?"

"I'm responsible for an exhibition about Jane Austen in Bath that opened that weekend. I had to see someone about a manuscript."

Diamond had never read a book by Jane Austen. He found it difficult to identify with the detectives in TV whodunits who quoted Shakespeare and wrote poetry in their spare time. Biography was his choice, preferably biography that included the words "of the Yard" in the title.

"And this exhibition kept you away for three weeks?"

"No, no. I was back on the Wednesday."

Diamond straightened in the chair and shut out all thoughts of Jane Austen. "Home again?"

"Yes."

"Then you knew your wife was missing as early as Wednesday, September thirteenth?"

"Missing, no." The professor reinforced the denial with a sideways sweep of the hand. "She wasn't home, but that wasn't any cause for alarm. She often stays over with friends."

"And doesn't tell you?"

"I'm not Gerry's keeper."

The answer jarred.

"But you are her husband. Presumably you like to know where she is."

"I don't insist upon it." There was a period of silence before Professor Jackman thought it appropriate to explain, "We live fairly independent lives. We are two people who need space to be ourselves. We married on that understanding. So when Gerry isn't around for a day or two, I don't immediately call the police."

"We're not talking about a day or two, sir."

"I thought we were."

"You've had three weeks to notify us," Diamond pointed out. He wasn't impressed by the slick explanations. The man was clever with words, as you would expect of a professor of English, but he couldn't gloss over the fact that he was suspiciously late in reporting his wife's disappearance.

"I wasn't at home all that time," said Jackman. "I've been buzzing about getting things organized for the new session. London, Oxford, Reading. I'm on too many committees. I was in Paris for a couple of days. I've given most of the summer to setting up this exhibition, so I'm way behind on my work in the English Department."

"What did you think your wife was doing meanwhile?"

"Visiting friends. Gerry knows plenty of people in London and Bristol."

"She doesn't work, then?"

"Resting, as they say."

"Do they?"

"Unemployed actors."

"Ah." Diamond knew the expression well enough. If he had appeared vague, it was the way his mind worked. He had been thinking of the words so often seen on tombstones. *Only resting.*

Jackman may have sensed something, because he went on to say precisely what he had meant. "Gerry has been off the box for eighteen months. She did a couple of commercials after she left the BBC, but otherwise the television work dried up."

"Why is that? Because everyone still thinks of her as Candice Milner?"

Jackman nodded. "That's part of it, certainly. There's also the fact that she's untrained as an actress. She was still in school when they offered her the role." Given the chance to take refuge in a narrative of less immediacy, he grasped it. "The way she was discovered was every schoolgirl's dream. The director picked her out of the crowd at Wimbledon. He went to watch tennis and found himself watching Gerry instead. In appearance she was exactly the young girl character he had visualized for *The Milners*. Extremely beautiful. You know the corny scene in all those Hollywood musicals when the Fred Astaire character says, 'Lady, I don't care who you are, I *must* have you for my show.' It really happened to Gerry, at eighteen. They tailored the part to her personality, so she played herself and became a household name. The other side of the coin was that she found it difficult to take on any other role."

"Did that depress her?"

"Not at first. Being in a twice-weekly soap is very demanding, you know—a treadmill of learning lines, rehearsing, and recording. Plus opening church fetes on Saturdays and dodging the gossip writers. She wasn't altogether sorry when she was written out of the script."

"And that was how long ago?"

"Getting on for two years now."

"So how long had she been playing the part?"

"She started when she was eighteen and she must have been thirty-one when it came to an end. Poor Gerry. It came out of the blue. The first she heard of it was when they sent her a script in which the character of Candice stepped into a plane that was to crash over the Alps with no survivors. I can remember vividly how angry she was. She fought like a tigress to save her part, but ultimately the director got through to her that they couldn't any longer keep up the fiction that she was an ingenue. So she turned her back on London."

Jackman related it with sympathy, yet there was a note of detachment in the account, as if he looked back with more regret than he presently felt. This didn't escape Peter Diamond, who had a sharp ear for evasion. The case might not be so complex as he had first supposed. He expected to crack it soon.

Rather than pussyfooting through more of the family history, Diamond took the drawing of the dead woman from his pocket, unfolded it, and handed it across. "This is the picture that went out on TV. What do you think?"

Jackman gave it a glance, took a deep breath as if to subdue his emotions, and said, "Looks awfully like Gerry to me."

Within minutes they were sharing the backseat of a police car on the way to the City Mortuary.

"I ought to mention," Diamond said, "that the body we're going to look at has been underwater for a couple of weeks. The artist's drawing was prettied up to go out on television."

"Thanks for the warning."

"If there's some means of identifying her by a mark or a scar . . ."

"I don't know of any," Jackman said quickly, then added, as if in an afterthought, "What happens if it turns out to be someone else?"

Diamond made a good show of remaining impassive. "Now that you've reported your wife's disappearance, it's an inquiry anyway, and we'd take it from there. Someone else would handle it."

"It's just possible that I was mistaken."

Diamond didn't trust himself to comment.

They arrived soon after 9:00 P.M. and it took some time to make the necessary arrangements. Mortuary staff had a different set of priorities from the police. At length the attendant arrived on a pushbike and unlocked the door.

Diamond didn't say a word. He was too interested in watching Jackman.

The body was brought out and the face uncovered.

"It goes without saying that I can rely on your cooperation."

Diamond's utterance was the first he had made since leaving the mortuary. Deliberately he put it as a statement rather than a question.

Professor Jackman was sitting forward in the backseat of the police car, one hand covering his eyes. Vaguely, he said, "What?"

Diamond repeated what he had said, word for word, like a schoolmaster being scrupulously fair.

Without looking up, Jackman answered, "I'll do whatever I can to help."

"Splendid." Diamond waited while the car stopped at a traffic light and said nothing else until it moved off again. "Tonight, I'll arrange for you to stay at the Beaufort, unless you prefer another hotel."

This time the professor swung around to face him. "A hotel isn't necessary. I don't mind going home. I'd prefer it, really I would."

Diamond shook his head. "Your house is off limits tonight, sir."

"Why?"

"I want it examined first thing tomorrow—with your permission. Until then, it's sealed. I'm putting a man on guard tonight."

"What do you mean—'examined'?"

"The forensic team. Scenes-of-crime officers. Fingerprints and all that jazz. You know?"

"*Scenes of crime?* You're not suggesting that Gerry was murdered under my own roof?"

"Professor, I'm not in the business of suggesting things," said Diamond. "I deal in facts. Fact number one: Your wife is dead. Fact two: The last place she was seen alive was in your house. Where else am I going to start?"

"I don't see what difference it makes if I spend one more night in the place, considering that I've been there on and off ever since Gerry went missing."

Diamond let it stand as a protest that didn't merit a response. Instead, he asked, "When you came to report your wife's disappearance this evening, how did you travel?"

"I took the car."

"So where is it now?"

"Still in the National Car Park beside the police station, I hope."

"Have you got the keys?"

"Yes." Jackman was frowning now.

"May I borrow them?"

"What on earth for? You're not impounding my car?"

A reassuring smile spread across Diamond's face. "Impounding, no. It's just the boring old business of checking facts. We make a print of the tires, that sort of thing. Then if we can find another set of tire prints—say in front of your house—we can eliminate your own vehicle from our inquiries." He was pleased with that answer. It sounded eminently reasonable, and he hadn't given an inkling of his real purpose, to examine the trunk of the car for traces of the corpse. When he had been handed the keys he asked casually, "Are you planning to be at the university tomorrow?"

"If my house is being searched, I'm going to be there to see what goes on," Jackman stated firmly.

7

THE SEARCH of Professor Jackman's house was not, after all, begun "first thing" the next day. The first thing, the first in Peter Diamond's day, was the bleep of the phone beside his bed at 6:30 A.M. A message from the Assistant Chief Constable, no less, relayed by the duty inspector at Police Headquarters. Diamond was instructed to report to Headquarters at 8:30.

He was willing to bet it wasn't for a Chief Constable's commendation. This, he sensed, was trouble.

He flopped back on the pillow and groaned. Whatever the reason for this sudden summons, it couldn't have come on a more inconvenient morning. The complications! He had somehow to unscramble his arrangements of the previous evening. Van loads of detectives, uniformed men, and forensic scientists were due to converge on Jackman's house at 8:30—precisely the time of the appointment in Bristol.

Sitting up again, he removed the phone from the bedside table and planted it on the quilt between his legs. His wife, Stephanie, resigned to their bedroom taking on the function of a police station, wordlessly dragged on a dressing gown and went downstairs to put on the kettle. Diamond picked up the receiver and made the first of several calls rescheduling the search for 11:00 A.M. He was unwilling to let anyone go into the house without him. In theory the responsibility could have been delegated to John Wigfull—a theory Diamond preferred to ignore. But he did ask Wigfull to visit Professor Jackman at the hotel and explain the change in arrangements.

On the drive to Bristol, he tried to fathom the thinking at police headquarters. He concluded sourly that Jackman must have gotten busy on the phone in his hotel room the previous evening. When trouble loomed, people of Jackman's elevated status didn't go underground like petty crooks. They rose above it by rallying support from the old-boy network.

This morning Mr. Tott, the Assistant Chief Constable, was sitting behind his desk in white shirt and pink braces, a spectacle so unlikely as to cause any officer of lesser rank to hesitate in the doorway. But Tott greeted Diamond warmly, using his Christian name, waving him toward the black leather settee under the window. As if utterly to remove all apprehension that a reprimand was in prospect, the assistant chief constable got up, went to the door, and asked for coffee and biscuits to be sent in. Then he perched himself on the arm at the far end of the settee with arms folded, looking—with his parted hair, flat to the scalp, and guards' officer mustache—as if he were posing for an Edwardian photograph.

All this forced informality had a dispiriting effect on Diamond. The last time anyone had treated him with such a show of consideration was on a tragic occasion when a doctor had given him the news that his wife had miscarried.

"Sorry to have messed up your arrangements," Mr. Tott said, managing to sound completely sincere, "but it was necessary to see you at the earliest opportunity. How's the murder inquiry going, by the way?"

That "by the way" was another jolt, for it implied that a matter quite different from the Jackman case was up for discussion. Diamond mouthed the next few responses while making a rapid mental adjustment. "We identified the woman last night, sir. Perhaps you heard."

"A television actress—is that right?"

"Yes, sir. She was married to the professor of English up at Claverton."

Mr. Tott grinned amiably. "So I heard. Better brush up on your Shakespeare, Peter." He paused, unfolded his arms, and said, "And I'd better come to the point. Over there on the desk is an advance copy of the report on the Missendale inquiry."

Diamond had read the signal right.

"I see." The bland response was the best he could manage after striving to suppress his troubled feelings for so long. More than eight months had passed since he had appeared before the board of inquiry—and more than two years since Hedley Missendale had been released on the orders of the home secretary and recommended for a pardon. A false confession, a wrongful imprisonment. Sections of the press had drummed the story up into a hate campaign against "rogue policemen," with accusations of racism and brutality. A campaign targeted on Chief Superintendent Blaize and Diamond. Jacob Blaize had been hounded into ill health and early retirement, which the press had maliciously and without justification written up as confirmation of their smears.

"I thought you should cast an eye over it as soon as possible," Mr. Tott said. "You'll be relieved to know that none of the wilder accusations was shown to have any foundation."

Diamond looked toward the desk. "May I?"

"Go ahead. That's why you're here."

Numbly, he got up, crossed the room, and picked up the report.

"The main findings are toward the end, of course," said Mr. Tott. "You'll find the paragraphs from page eighty-seven onward are of personal interest. Take your time."

Diamond flicked through and found the summary of the findings. His name sprang out of the text. He scanned the page swiftly, getting the gist of the comments. *We found no evidence of racial bias on the part of*

Detective Chief Inspector Diamond. . . . This officer acquitted himself impressively under intensive questioning. . . . As to Missendale's statement, there was nothing in it that conflicted with the evidence. . . . It was reasonable for Chief Inspector Diamond to deduce, as the court did, that Missendale's statement was supported by the facts.

He turned the page, feeling curiously unmoved rather than vindicated after the months of abuse from the media. Then his eyes fixed on a sentence.

"Christ Almighty!"

Mr. Tott had returned to his chair. "What's wrong?"

" 'We are bound to state that Chief Inspector Diamond's physical presence and forceful demeanor must have appeared intimidating to Missendale,' " Diamond read aloud. "That's out of order. I'm built that way. I can't help the way I'm made."

"Yes, it's unfair," Mr. Tott agreed in a tone that attached no importance to the matter.

But Diamond wasn't willing to let it pass. "Sir, there was no intimidation used to obtain the confession. The judge established at the trial that there was no oppression."

"Of course, but the inquiry team was charged to reexamine everything."

Diamond's eyes were already moving on. "I just don't believe this! 'We view with concern the fact that hair samples from the woolen hat snatched from the assailant in the struggle were not compared with hairs from Mr. Missendale.' "

"What's the problem?" Mr. Tott asked.

"We sent the hat to the lab."

"But you didn't follow it up, if I understand this correctly. You didn't take hair samples from Missendale."

"Sir, the man *confessed.*"

"It would still have been sensible to do so."

Diamond stared at him in amazement. "To what end, exactly?"

"As a comparison."

"This was 1985, sir. Before genetic fingerprinting came in. Even if we had followed up, forensic couldn't have told us whether the hairs in the hat were Missendale's, or Sammy Davis, Jr.'s. This report implies that if the samples had been compared, Missendale's innocence would have been established, but it simply isn't true."

"The report doesn't go so far as to say that."

" 'We view with concern'? It's suggesting somebody was at fault."

Mr. Tott said firmly, "The point is that it should have been done routinely. Nobody is accusing you of witholding evidence."

"They're accusing Jacob Blaize and me of framing him."

"Oh, don't be so melodramatic, man! If that were the case, you'd be out of a job. Your integrity isn't in question."

Diamond knew that he should have shut up at this point. He still felt aggrieved. "I told them at the inquiry what must have happened and they seem to have disregarded it. Missendale *was* framed, but not by me. He was a petty thief with a record, not much good at it. He had a low IQ. There were bigger operators in the background, too smart to be caught. It's obvious with hindsight that Missendale was their fall guy. They wanted the other crook, the guy who actually gunned down the sergeant major, to keep pulling the jobs, so they made it clear to Missendale that if he didn't fake a confession, they'd wipe him out. He was safer in prison. He had no future on the outside."

Mr. Tott nodded. "I'll take your word for it. Organized crime is behind so much of our casework these days. But this sort of theorizing falls outside the scope of the inquiry. They were looking at the particular circumstances in which the miscarriage of justice was perpetrated."

Diamond heard himself saying, "I'm far from satisfied."

"In a report that runs to over a hundred pages, it

would be surprising if anyone was satisfied with all that it contains. I think you'll find that this lays the whole wretched business to rest. The media won't be interested in the points that seem to be exercising you."

"But I don't believe it wipes the slate clean."

"I think I hear the chink of cups," said Mr. Tott.

Diamond waited while the coffee was poured in genteel fashion from a chrome and glass container. When they were alone again, he said, "I'd like to ask what effect this will have on my career with Avon and Somerset, sir."

"None at all," said Mr. Tott, and his voice was metallic in its positiveness. "What happened four years ago in London is history."

"Plenty of mud has been slung my way since then."

"Yes, and none of it has stuck."

"But you won't deny that you clipped my wings?"

Mr. Tott stirred his coffee and said nothing. It was transparently obvious that this was a reference to the replacement of Billy Murray by John Wigfull, so clearly a headquarters man.

"I'm not beefing about that. From your point of view it was a reasonable precaution after the Missendale thing blew up," Diamond conceded. "But I had a right to expect that this report would vindicate me, and I don't believe it has, not completely."

"If it makes you just a little more punctilious about procedures, it won't be entirely wasted, Peter. You must admit that you can be rather resistant to technology. The scientific developments of the past few years are mind-boggling, I grant you, but it behooves us all to make an effort to work with them."

"Up to a point, sir. There's still a lot that native intelligence can achieve. There's a danger in surrendering to technology."

"Come now. I'm not suggesting any such thing. It's a question of balance, of proportion."

Diamond closed the report and planted it on Mr. Tott's desk. "So what will happen next time some petty crook objects to the way I question him?"

"I would treat any complaint on its merits," said Mr. Tott, showing in his tone that indulgence can only go so far. "And I would take exception to any suggestion that I might show prejudice. I see no mud sticking to you, and I hope I don't see a chip on your shoulder, either. Is there anything else you wanted to say to me?"

"In which regard, sir?"

"About your present investigation."

"No, sir. Nothing else." In the stress of the moment he had already said more than was politic.

"I appreciate that," said Mr. Tott. "Wigfull's transfer to your squad was at my insistence. He is not—I stress this—he is not there as some kind of informer. I keep tabs on all my officers without assistance from the likes of John Wigfull. Is that understood?"

"Understood, sir."

"And accepted?"

"Yes, sir."

"Then I'll tell you about Wigfull." Looking down at his cup, Mr. Tott traced a finger slowly around its rim. "Knowing as I did that this report was imminent, but not knowing its findings, I had to face the possibility—the worst conceivable scenario—that you might have to be removed at short notice from the murder squad. I wanted a man capable of taking over, and without going into personalities, there was no one in your team I could confidently turn to. Wigfull was my choice. He hasn't, of course, been told the reason, but as a good detective, he may have worked it out for himself. I appreciate that his temperament and yours are not in tune. You, too, are a good detective. You are also a big man, as the report unjustly emphasizes. Be big in the best sense, big enough to get the best out of Wigfull."

Shortly after 11:00, the convoy of cars and police vans streamed into the drive of Jackman's house some distance up one of the secluded roads off Bathwick Hill. The leading car was Diamond's BMW. Beside him sat Jackman. John Wigfull followed in his Toyota with two detective sergeants and a constable. The other vehicles brought a scenes-of-crime officer from headquarters, two forensic scientists, and a team of uniformed officers.

Jackman's blue Volvo was at this moment undergoing forensic examination at Manvers Street. Diamond had commented when handing over the keys to the forensic lads, "Don't disappoint me, will you? They always believe they've removed every trace."

Brydon House looked suitable for a professor to inhabit, not quite within walking distance of the university, but convenient to it, as the estate agents had no doubt claimed when the Jackmans first took an interest in the property. It was an ivy-clad, four-square structure with a pillared porch and a first-floor balcony. Probably not much over a century old, it was set in spacious grounds behind a low drystone wall. Plots tended to be generous in size on the outskirts of the city and the houses were distinctive in design. The area was too far out from the center of Bath for the planners to have insisted on uniformity, and quite modern buildings in garish reconstituted stone stood alongside mellowed Georgian and Victorian villas.

Diamond invited Jackman to open the door. Then he gripped the professor's arm, preventing him from entering. "No, sir, you and I won't step inside just yet."

Disbelief and bewilderment were combined in Jackman's look as two men in white overalls stepped forward, sat on the porch, removed their shoes, and replaced them with socks made of polythene.

"If you don't mind," Diamond said, "we'll leave the spacemen to their work. How would you like to show me your garden?"

"This is a huge waste of everyone's time," muttered the beleaguered professor.

"I've got a brother-in-law in Doncaster," Diamond said, "and each time we visit him, I hardly set foot in the house before he draws me away from the ladies and says, 'Come and see the back garden.' Now, I'm no gardener. I wouldn't pretend to know when to prune the roses, but I do know enough to see that Reggie's garden is a bloody wilderness. Some of the nettles are chest-high. We poke about searching for the path while Reggie points to pathetic plants weighted down with blackfly and bindweed and tells me their names. After an hour of this, there's a shout from my sister that tea is ready, so we beat a route back to the house for a reviving cup. No sooner have I had a bite of cake than Reggie turns to me and says, 'You haven't seen the front garden. Come out and see the front.' I'm supposed to be a detective and I don't know why he does it. Is he afraid to go out there unaccompanied? Or is the house stuffed with stolen goods he doesn't want me to notice? I'm still trying to work it out."

Jackman seemed unwilling to supply a theory, but he had, at least, consented to walk beside the superintendent. They made an incongruous pair, the broad-shouldered academic moving with a sinewy step beside the fat policeman forced by sheer girth to throw out his feet in a ponderous strut. The setting for this spectacle consisted of stretches of lawn separated by clumps of shrubs and a number of well-established trees. There were enough apple trees at the far end to give it the status of an orchard.

Abruptly, Diamond moved from domestic matters to the business of the day. "Your wife. I need to know everything about her. Background, family, friends past and present—and enemies, if any—daily routines, personal finances, state of health, drinking habits, hobbies, places she visited, shops she used."

"We've only been married two years." Jackman's tone protested at the length and comprehensiveness of the list.

"Long enough to know all those things, surely?" Diamond pressed. "We'll take it from the beginning. How did you meet?"

This approach yielded a dividend. Jackman made a sound that was halfway to being a laugh, shook his head wistfully as some memory surfaced, and said, "It was because of a pigeon, or so Gerry always claimed. The pigeon may or may not have existed, but it became part of our private mythology. She was motoring along Great Russell Street in her Renault 5—"

"This was when?" Diamond cut in.

"Just over two years ago. As I was saying, she was driving along when this slow-witted or stubborn London pigeon allegedly stepped across the road and refused to take flight. Unable to bear the prospect of killing a living thing, Gerry swung the wheel and crumpled the fender against a parked van. You must be hearing stories like this all the time."

"I'm not in the traffic division."

"Well, this was in the month of May, I think, and I was in my final term at Birkbeck College prior to taking up the professorship here. I'd been working in the British Library that particular morning and I came out for a lunchtime stroll. I didn't see the pigeon, but I heard the bump. I was the first to reach the car, open the door, and inquire if she was hurt. I can see her now staring at me, pale with shock, and beautiful, surpassingly beautiful. She was suffering nothing worse than the shakes, so I helped her to move the car into a space, found her a seat in the nearest sandwich bar, and ordered strong, sweet tea. Then, not missing a chance to play Galahad, I went to look for the van driver. He turned out to be a Buddhist monk."

"A monk—in London?"

"Doing research, just as I was. I'd seen him once or twice in the reading room. When I told him about the collision, he was serenely unconcerned at one extra dent on his van. In fact, he went out of his way to praise Gerry's action in averting an accident to the pigeon. She was moving toward enlightenment, in his estimation. So I nipped back to the sandwich bar and set her mind at rest."

"Advising her, no doubt, to go to the nearest police station and report the accident," Diamond said sardonically.

Jackman stayed with his story. "I found her perched on the high stool, dabbing the edges of her eyes with that amazing red hair. The bump was the first she'd ever had, she told me, and she felt stupid at having caused damage just to avoid a scruffy pigeon. I remember springing to the defense of the pigeon and upholding its rights to cross the street without being flattened. Made her smile again. She had a stunning smile. Then she announced that she was due at the Television Center in twenty minutes, so I offered to drive her to White City. Embarrassing. It was transparently clear that I didn't know she was famous. I hardly ever watch the box."

They stopped at the edge of the apple orchard, where the grass was too overgrown for comfortable walking. Diamond pulled off a long stalk and chewed it, pleased with himself for having the patience to listen to this boy-meets-girl stuff. There was time enough to get to the violence. "You arranged to meet again, I take it?"

"Well, yes. We got on well. The attraction was mutual—though I suppose there was overglamorizing on both sides. She had a few O levels to her name, and that was all, so she was flattered to have a professor-designate in tow. And apart from finding her extremely attractive, as every red-blooded male in the country did, I rather basked in the envy of people who watched *The Milners* and couldn't fathom how some egghead professor had managed to hook television's top girl."

"What about her conversation?"

"What do you mean?"

"Was she on your wavelength?"

"Oh, she was as bright as a button. If her schooling hadn't been interrupted, she'd certainly have got to university."

Diamond noticed something in the way Jackman made this remark. It was spoken with a measure of detachment rather than the pride you would have expected from a devoted husband. Yet everything else he had said—all the memories from two years ago—had been related with warmth. The story of their first meeting rang true. Undoubtedly the man had been charmed by her and it wasn't difficult to see why she had been attracted to him. He was handsome. He wasn't stuffy. He wasn't at all the stereotype of the lofty intellectual.

Jackman went on to say, "We first made love under the stars in Richmond Park. Didn't realize the gates closed at sundown. Had to climb over the wall to get out, and our energies were somewhat depleted by then." Jackman smiled faintly. "We came to a more comfortable arrangement after that. She moved into my flat in Teddington. We married in September, a registry-office do followed by a trip up the Thames in a pleasure steamer for two hundred and fifty."

Diamond took mental stock of the number, troubled by it. Tracing the victim's friends, if it came to that, was going to require a large task force.

"Surprising, really," Jackman remarked. "The worlds of academe and showbiz got on famously. They strutted their stuff to a jazz quartet until well into the next day."

"This was September 1987, you said? So when did you move to Bath?" Diamond asked.

"Directly. My term was about to start. Gerry was still with the BBC. We had no idea that her days with *The Milners* were numbered. She rented a flat in Ealing to use when she was filming. As I mentioned to you, we were each committed to our careers, so we tied the knot less strongly than is traditional. We kept separate bank accounts. The house here is in my name; I'd already found it and set the legal wheels in motion before I met Gerry."

"Did she approve your choice?"

The professor put a hand to his face and passed it across his mouth and down to the point of his chin as he considered the question. "I think she liked it, yes. It's a little far from the center, but she had the car."

"The Renault?"

"A Metro. She bought a new one. It's in the garage. Want to see it?"

"Later." Now it was Diamond's turn to take stock. "If her car is still in the garage, didn't that worry you when she went missing?"

"Not really. She often used taxis for getting about, particularly if she was likely to have a few drinks."

"Was she a heavy drinker?"

"She could put it away, but I wouldn't say she drank to excess."

Inside the house, John Wigfull, in the approved polythene oversocks, had been called upstairs by the scenes-of-crime officer to look at the master bedroom. They watched one of the forensic team on his knees collecting fiber samples on strips of adhesive tape.

Wigfull folded his arms and took in the essentials of the room. "Twin beds, then."

"Some people prefer them."

"Would you—married to Gerry Snoo?"

A smile from the scenes-of-crime officer. "I'm a simple scientist, John. No imagination at all."

Both beds had been stripped to the mattress for forensic examination, enough to dispossess any bedroom of its character. It was a large, gracefully proportioned room decorated in a mushroom color and pale green. There was a television set and video recorder on a stand facing the beds. Two abstract paintings in the style of Mondrian enlivened the walls, yet to Wigfull's eye reinforced the feeling of hotel-like neutrality.

He got a strikingly different impression when he crossed the room and looked into one of the adjacent dressing rooms. It was a shrine to Gerry Snoo's television career. The walls were thick with silver-framed stills from *The Milners,* interspersed with press pictures of the actress with celebrities at parties. Her dressing table had the mirror fringed with light bulbs that was supposed to be in every star dressing room, and the wall behind it was festooned with silver horseshoes, telegrams, greeting cards, and sprigs of heather. Across the room was a folding screen entirely pasted over with press clippings. A system of shelving between the built-in wardrobe and the window was stacked with videocassettes and paperbacks of *The Milners.*

"Missing the big time, would you say?" the scenes-of-crime officer called out.

"Looks remarkably like it." Wigfull returned to the bedroom. "Have you found much?"

"A few microscopic spots on the quilt that could be blood. May be significant, may be not. We'll see what the tests show. Plenty of prints on the surface of the dressing table, presumably her own. Hardly any else-where. I reckon the chest of drawers and the wardrobe have been wiped clean. Did he do it?"

"The husband, you mean?"

"Who else? Murder's generally in the family, isn't it?"

Wigfull gave a shrug.

The scenes-of-crime officer snapped shut the metal case containing his instruments. "If he *is* guilty, I back your boss to nail him. I've seen the way Diamond works. It's cat-and-mouse with him. Playful for a bit. Then he pounces. If he doesn't bite their heads off, he breaks their backbones."

Wigfull said, "Before it comes to that, I'd like to know the motive."

"Obvious. They weren't sleeping in the same bed. She must have been getting it from someone else. Husband found out. Curtains for Candice."

In the garden, Diamond was patiently unraveling the story of the marriage. "You were telling me in the car about the blow it was when your wife was written out of the television serial. You seemed to imply that after the initial shock, she was quite positive in the way she faced up to it."

"That's perfectly true," Jackman answered. He was calmer now that the questions were more structured, more predictable. "Of course she made her feelings plain to the director, but once she saw that it was a lost cause, she responded sensibly, I thought. She told me she meant to make up for the years she had missed."

"What did she mean by that?"

"She had never been allowed the freedom girls in their teens are entitled to expect. At last she could break out—go on holidays, dance the night away, change her hairstyle, put on weight if she wanted, and never answer another fan letter. I suppose it was the teenage rebellion ten years delayed."

"Not the ideal start to a marriage," ventured Diamond.

The answer came on a sharper note, as if Jackman knew what was behind the comment. "We didn't view it that way. As I told you, we had agreed to leave enough space to be ourselves and pursue our interests independently. We didn't want the kind of arrangement where one partner tags along forever making sacrifices."

"But the basis of your contract—your understanding, or whatever you called it—had altered," Diamond pointed out. "She no longer had a career."

"So what? Just because Gerry was unemployed I didn't expect her to stay at home and darn my socks. She put her energies into building a social life for herself. She gave up the flat in Ealing, of course."

"Difficult for a woman used to London, coming down here and not knowing anyone," Diamond remarked, resolute in his belief that the marriage must have been fatally flawed.

"Not for Gerry. Word soon got round that she'd moved down here. The invitations came in thick and fast."

"Did you get invited, too?"

"Quite often. I couldn't usually join her. I had a brand-new department to set up, and that took up most of my time. I gradually got to know the crowd she spent her time with. We had the occasional party here."

"People from Bath?"

"Bristol. All around, I gather."

"You gather? You didn't get to know them *that* well, then? Weren't they your sort?"

Jackman gave him a cold stare. "People don't have to be my sort, as you put it. Anyway, I didn't make a point of asking them where they lived. If you want their names and addresses, I daresay I can find her address book."

"You mean you don't even know the names of your wife's friends?"

"I didn't say that. There were some people called Maltby. They were from Clevedon, I believe. Paula and John Hare. Liza somebody. A tall fellow by the name of Mike—I'm not sure where he lived."

"Don't bother," said Diamond. "I'll go through the address book, as you suggest. Did your wife ever mention falling out with any of the friends she made?"

"Not that I recall."

"Shall we move on again?" Diamond started back in the direction of the house by way of stepping-stones across a lawn still damp with dew that would probably remain all day. "I sense from what you've been telling me about your marriage that she might not have discussed her friends with you," he commented as he picked his way gingerly across the path.

"Probably not," the professor answered from behind him. Nothing appeared to wrong-foot him.

Ahead, virtually in the center of the garden, was a solidly paved area, darker at the center. Diamond mistook this at first for a flower bed, but as he got closer he saw that the blackness was the burned-out foundation of a building, roughly octagonal in shape. "Looks as if you had a fire sometime," he said conversationally.

"It was quite a feature of the garden," Jackman responded with the urbanity of the practiced host. "A summerhouse. It burned down on the night Gerry tried to kill me."

Diamond stopped with such suddenness that he practically lost balance. When he managed to find his voice again, it sounded quite different, shocked into a flat, breathless delivery. "I don't know if I heard right, professor, but I think we've jumped ahead a bit in the story."

PART TWO

Gregory

1

_____

LAST AUGUST 5, my wife Geraldine attempted to murder me.

The killing of a husband calls for a degree of disaffection, not to say loathing. Gerry was known to everyone as a warm, exuberant personality, a charmer. She was extremely good-looking, too. She had reached the stage of her life when "beautiful" was beginning to give way to words that were no less appreciative, merely more dignified: words such as "elegant" and "soignée." Her famous flame-colored hair was gathered and fastened high on the nape of her long white neck. The fact that she favored black skirts and blouses was in no way sinister; that was good dressing.

I'm bound to say that in the privacy of home it was a different story. In the last six months she had become increasingly difficult to live with. Her moods were unpredictable. She was subject to fits of temper, irrational outbursts when she would blame me for little things that thwarted her. I recall that she accused me of tampering with her car when it failed to start, of hiding her newspaper, and of emptying the hot-water tank when she had clearly left a tap running herself—silly, domestic things that she inflated into major incidents, claiming blatant evidence of malice on my part. Yet at other times she swung to moods of gaiety and amusement that could be almost as difficult to take, followed often by black, silent depression. All this worried me, naturally, but it stopped a long way short of personal violence, or so I believed.

Looking back now, I can see that the first intimation that Gerry was planning something came indirectly, from the doctor. Toward the end of July I went for my annual checkup, a routine that my employers at the university of Bath insisted upon. After the nurse had weighed me, checked my blood pressure, water, reflexes, and every function on her list, I was ushered into the consulting room for the verdict. My regular GP was not available, so for the first time I met the senior man in the practice. Dr. Bookbinder is one of the old school, pitted and grizzled, with a bow tie and cuff links. Although he had an antismoking poster on his wall and kept the window open, his room reeked of cigars.

"How do you feel?"

"Fit as a butcher's dog," I answered, and although I say it myself, I looked it, clear-eyed, sturdy, and cheerful.

"What are you—thirty-six, thirty-seven—indecently young for a professor. What's your subject? Nothing in the medical line, I hope?"

"English."

"Fine." Dr. Bookbinder's brown eyes glittered as he looked at me over his glasses. "You won't be telling me my job. I didn't know they bothered with the mother tongue up at Claverton."

"I'm in process of building up a department. The chair was created a couple of years ago."

"Chair of English, eh? Sounds all right, but don't be tempted to sit in it too long. The sedentary life can lead to constipation and piles."

"It's not all sitting. I stand up and stretch at intervals."

"Splendid. Is it stressful?"

"The standing up?"

"The running," said Dr. Bookbinder. "Of the department."

"Not really. I don't have many students yet."

The doctor glanced through the form containing the nurse's findings and stuffed it ham-fistedly into the buff folder that represented all of my life in medical terms. "Haven't read anything so boring since that book about the hobbits—or was it the rabbits? In insurance terms, professor, I would describe you as a ruddy good risk so long as you don't burn yourself out. You're married to that enchanting young woman who used to play Candice Milner on the television, aren't you? She's a patient of mine."

I nodded.

"She was in here on Monday," he went on. "It's one of the perks of this job that I tend to see the ladies more often than the husbands. No insult intended."

"None taken. I make a point of avoiding doctors unless it's inescapable," I riposted, uncrossing my legs prior to making my exit. "And since I'm not here to wangle a week off work, I shan't take up any more of your time."

Dr. Bookbinder made a downward movement of his hand to signal to me to remain seated. "When Mrs. Jackman makes an appointment, they go bananas in reception."

"The power of television."

"Want to know why she came to see me?"

Indiscretion was in the air. I didn't care for it. I remember saying guardedly, "My wife and I respect each other's privacy."

"Do you sleep together?"

My eyes widened. I pulled myself up in the chair in a formal attitude. "Does that have some relevance?"

"I wouldn't ask it otherwise, would I?" said Dr. Bookbinder.

After a moment's consideration, I said, "If you mean in the same room, the answer is yes."

"In that case I'm not being unprofessional. You must have noticed it."

"Noticed what, doctor?"

"Your wife's insomnia."

"My . . . wife's . . . insomnia?"

"That's why I asked you about the stress. It crossed my mind that you could, quite unwittingly, be passing on your concerns about the job to her, but you tell me that isn't the case."

Now, I don't care for half-baked psychiatry. I don't care much for psychiatry at all. So I told him, "I don't often discuss my work with Geraldine."

"Then we must look elsewhere for a possible cause of anxiety. Could it be traced to some dissatisfaction with her present mode of life? She has to put up with rather less of the limelight now."

"True. She does the occasional commercial, but otherwise the television work has dried up."

"Why is that? Because everyone still thinks of her as Candice?"

"That's part of it, certainly."

"You didn't notice she was losing sleep?"

"Frankly, no. We have twin beds, and when my head touches the pillow, I'm off."

"You don't inquire in the morning whether she slept well?"

"Not usually. My impression is that she's always sleeping soundly when I get up." I paused. "But I must say I feel very uneasy about this conversation, doctor. If Geraldine is worried about losing sleep, she could have mentioned it to me. The fact is that she didn't. She came to you in confidence."

"I made the not unreasonable assumption that you knew about the problem," the doctor told me. He followed this up with an insinuation that I didn't like in the least: "You *are* concerned, I take it?"

With difficulty I controlled myself. "Naturally I'm concerned, now that you've told me. I'll do whatever I can to help, if it's only making her cups of hot chocolate in the night."

The doctor sniffed. "You don't have to stay awake

and keep her company. That's no way to tackle insomnia."

"What do you suggest?"

Offhandedly he said, "Don't trouble—she'll get her sleep now. I've put her on phenobarbitone."

"Is it as bad as that?"

"We've run through the milder hypnotics. She tells me they had little or no effect."

"It's been going on for some time, then? I didn't know."

"This is severe, intractable insomnia, professor. We must break the cycle somehow, and in cases like this a good old-fashioned barbiturate will do the trick when some of the newer tranquilizers will not. When we have reestablished the habit of sleep, the natural pattern should reassert itself in a few weeks."

"You mean there's nothing I can do?"

"There's still the underlying problem. It *may* be physical, but of all the causes of sleep loss, anxiety is the most common. I can see that you're sympathetic, and that's helpful in itself, so if you can find out what is troubling your wife and do something constructive about it, you'll do more good than phenobarbitone in the long run. Please be discreet, however."

"That's rich!" I said.

"Professor, as an intelligent man, I'm sure you won't need telling that a patient's confidence in her doctor is vitally important."

"Point taken," I told him, and this time I didn't hold back. "And as an intelligent man, I ought to advise my wife to change her doctor. Good morning."

I got up and walked out.

Before starting the car, I sat for some time trying to understand why Geraldine should have been losing sleep and how it was that I had failed to notice. The possibility didn't cross my mind that the phenobarbitone was intended for me.

2

_____

LATER the same morning at the University of Bath, I found myself watching Miss Hunter—the personal assistant to the dean of letters—arrange six chocolate digestives on a plate. In the next room the University Steering Committee was in session and I had been summoned for item six on the agenda. I was scheduled to go in with the coffee. After twenty minutes I was getting restless. I still hadn't gotten over that uncomfortable session with Dr. Bookbinder. I remember helping myself to a biscuit and saying facetiously, straining to put myself in a better frame of mind, "Peculiar name to give it—the steering committee. What do they do in there—ride around on tricycles?"

Hilary Hunter likes a giggle. She seemed to enjoy the mental picture of five professors solemnly pedaling around the dean's office for the entire morning, but as a loyal PA she couldn't laugh at the dean's expense, so she turned and flicked the switch on the kettle. It had come to the boil twice already.

Another minute passed.

The buzzer on her desk sounded. She poured the coffee and picked up the tray.

I opened the door for her and murmured, "Watch out for the race leader in the yellow jersey."

It was like a nudge in the ribs for Miss Hunter. She made a snorting sound as she stepped through the door.

The Dean said, "Do you require a tissue, Miss Hunter?"

She shook her head.

"Leave the tray, then. We'll help ourselves. Jackman, do come and join us." The Dean gestured toward a vast chintz-covered settee. The comforts of life are important to him. He goes in for check-patterned woolen shirts and hand-woven ties. His flat cap and golf bag were hanging on the door. This year it was his turn to preside over the steering committee. The others were drawn from different faculties. I knew three of them slightly and sometimes propped up a bar with the fourth, Professor Oliver, the art man.

"How is the fledgling School of English faring?" the Dean asked in his ponderous way.

"Chirpy enough," I answered.

"Ha—yes. Ready to take wing?"

"What's on offer, then—a trip to the States?"

The Dean chuckled. "You're an optimist." He turned to his left. "Isn't he an optimist? Professor Oliver, would you be so good as to explain?"

"Me?" Tom Oliver asked in a spray of biscuit crumbs. He needed something to chew. Smoke-free committee meetings are an ordeal for a man who habitually keeps a pipe alight. He took a gulp of coffee and swallowed hard. "You probably know, Greg, that we're trying to buff up the university's image in the town."

"The city," said the Dean.

"Correction. The city. There was some criticism a year or two back that we'd built the proverbial ivory tower up here at Claverton and were ignoring the burghers."

"Now that's uncalled for," said the Dean.

"Burghers," Oliver repeated. "The good citizens. The suggestion was untrue, of course. With our strength in science and technology we've always been involved with local industry through sandwich courses. We provide a marvelous range of extramural courses. We have the Concert Society arranging musical events. At Christmastime we let hundreds of shoppers use the car park for the park-and-ride scheme. And of course the students have their rag week and so on."

"The sedan-chair race," contributed the professor of comparative religions, a featherweight who annually agrees to be transported around the course.

"That too. What I'm leading up to is that three years ago, before you joined us, Greg, we held an exhibition in the Victoria Gallery."

"The one over the public library," chipped in the Dean. "Fine exhibition, it was, for a pioneering effort."

A guarded look dropped like a visor over my features.

"It fell to me to organize it," Oliver continued. "My mandate was to put on a show called 'Art in Bath,' featuring painters who actually lived here at some point in their lives. A motley crew, I have to admit. Gainsborough, Sir Thomas Lawrence, Whistler, Lord Leighton, and a few lesser lights."

"Professor Oliver had one of his own on show," said the Dean. "An abstract, mainly in pink, as I recall."

Oliver said self-consciously, "I needed to fill a space. I would have preferred to put on a complete show of modern work, but the Society of Bath Artists had its annual show in the gallery a month before, and I was told firmly that this must be different in character, a more traditional exhibition."

Sensing, perhaps, that the positive aspects of the "Art in Bath" exhibition needed to be stressed more, the Dean said, "There was a first-class response to our request for the loan of pictures—from private collections as well as the more obvious sources. That's partly the point of an exhibition such as this. It's a way of involving the local people, reminding them that we exist. It got into the papers and on local television and radio. Professor Oliver got to be quite a media man in the end."

Tom Oliver's eyes rolled upward at the memory.

By now I'd heard enough of this. I sat back and

folded my arms. "Let's have it, gentlemen. What am I lumbered with?"

The Dean frowned. "No one has *lumbered* you with anything, Jackman. I would have thought a professor of English might have employed a more felicitous word than that."

"Clobbered?"

"We seem to be at cross-purposes," said the Dean. "I know you don't mince words, Jackman, but there's no cause to be obstructive before we have even outlined the proposition. I see this as a shining opportunity for the English Department to make a name for itself. You know, as the newest department in the university you have a lot of ground to make up on those of us who were here at the beginning. And with only two years' intake of students to administer I wouldn't have said you were overburdened. You won't be awarding degrees for another year."

"Fair enough," I said. "You want me to bang the drum this year. Do I have a free hand?"

"Within limits."

I shrugged. "I don't have a free hand."

"We have a proposal—rather an engaging one—originating from the city council itself. It has this committee's strong support, naturally."

"What is it?"

" 'Jane Austen in Bath.' "

There was a silence.

"Jane Austen, the writer," added the Dean, whose sarcasm wasn't complicated by subtlety. "In case you weren't aware of it, she lived in the city for several years."

"You learn something every day," I said. "Is that the deal—just Jane?"

"And Bath. The theme, the rationale, of the exhibition is a celebration of Jane Austen's years in Bath."

"A celebration?"

"Exactly."

I drew a deep breath and let it out slowly. "Pity she isn't still around to enjoy the irony of this."

The Dean bristled. "You had better explain that remark."

"Jane Austen's years in Bath were no cause for celebration. She was pretty pissed off with the place."

"Professor Jackman!"

"All right—it was the least happy phase of her life."

"That's rather sweeping, isn't it?"

The professor of comparative religions reached for the last chocolate biscuit and said, "What is happiness? What did happiness amount to for Jane Austen? We are dealing in abstractions here."

"As I recall it," I said, "when the Reverend George Austen informed his family that they were to move here from Steventon, where Jane was born and brought up, she passed out. Fainted. They had five years in Bath. It failed lamentably to come up to Steventon in her estimation. She had a series of unhappy experiences about that time—a broken engagement, the deaths of friends. Her father died here. They had to move into more humble lodgings, and after they finally left, she described it as a happy escape. Happiness amounted to escaping from Bath."

After another uncomfortable pause the Dean said doggedly, "The fact remains that she was a resident. And one of the world's great novelists."

"Not one of the great novels was written in Bath."

The Dean glared over his glasses. "Correct me if I'm mistaken, professor. Bath does, as I recall, feature prominently in the novels."

I looked around the room at the other members of the committee. "There's no ducking this, is there?"

"It isn't something to be *ducked*. It's an opportunity, Jackman. Everyone who has heard of it so far is extremely excited about the prospect. The city librarian and his staff have promised every assistance."

My heart sank. "People have been told already?"

"One or two crucial individuals."

"I wish you'd brought me in earlier."

Oliver said, "Greg, we only heard about it ourselves this morning."

I sighed heavily, got up, and walked to the window. "And I'm supposed to find enough exhibits to fill the Victoria Gallery?"

"The Assembly Rooms," said the Dean with an air of triumph. "We have been offered the Assembly Rooms."

"God—that's even bigger."

"It couldn't be a more appropriate venue. Do you appreciate the significance? Jane Austen must have danced there many times."

Tom Oliver said, "Actually, Dean, it was gutted by bombs in the last war."

"And perfectly restored."

"Right," I said, turning to face them. "It's a bloody great ballroom. How am I supposed to fill it? So far as I can remember there's one postcard-size portrait of Jane by her sister, and that's in the National Portrait Gallery because no other picture of her exists. If I get a loan of that, which is unlikely, it's not going to fill a hundred-foot ballroom."

The Dean shuffled his papers. "I'm confident that if you embrace the opportunity as Professor Oliver did three years ago, we shall have an admirable show."

I turned to the professor of comparative religions. " 'Embrace the opportunity'—how's that for an abstraction?"

Tom Oliver, wanting to be helpful, said, "You might make use of the novels in some way."

"Open at certain pages and displayed in glass cabinets?" I said. "Not exactly riveting, is it? It isn't going to pull in the crowds when they can pick up the same books in any shop in the town."

"City," murmured Oliver.

"You could photograph the houses she lived in," said the Dean.

"And blow them up to actual size?" At this stage, I was in no mood to take any suggestion seriously. "True, if I back them with hardboard and stand them upright like theater scenery, that might help to fill the bloody Assembly Rooms. I could dress my students in period costume and have them disport themselves around the scenery, commenting, 'Upon my word, the gentlemen of the steering committee are deserving of our plaudits, for a happier conjunction of town and gown than this was never conceived.' "

"Come off it, Greg," said Oliver before the Dean could erupt. "When you've had time to think it over, you'll have some bright ideas."

"It's window dressing, isn't it? Jane Austen is a name to pull in the tourists. Nobody stopped to consider what Jane herself really thought of the place. I suppose it's too late to point out this slight ethical objection to the genius who suggested it."

"But that is the very reverse of all we're trying to achieve," the Dean pointed out to me. "We want to make a gesture of support to the city, not humiliate them by scoring academic points. And, yes, it is too late. Far too late."

I asked fatalistically, "How long have I got?"

Oliver said, "It's essentially a summer exhibition."

"Opening on September ninth for three weeks," said the Dean as if he were passing sentence.

"That takes care of *my* vacation," I said.

"I'd like a progress report this time next week, if that isn't too much to ask."

I happen to be blessed or cursed with acute hearing. As I was leaving the outer office, I overheard the Dean saying, "What an obstreperous fellow. I don't recall this side of him emerging when he was interviewed for the chair."

Oliver said, "You weren't here, Dean. It was during your sabbatical."

"Ah."

"He's very well regarded by his students."

"I can believe it."

"He won't let us down."

"He had better not."

3

PLENTY OF PEOPLE cross Pulteney Bridge without even realizing that they're passing over the Avon. The reason, of course, is that it's lined on either side with buildings, like the Ponte Vecchio in Florence. You can't see the river without going into one of the shops and looking out of a window. I heard that when Robert Adam designed the thing in 1769, he had the Ponte Vecchio in mind, but if there's any resemblance, it's superficial only. Adam's bridge is charming and original, a Palladian structure built over the three arches, with a central Venetian window and domed tollhouses at either end.

The tollhouse on the west side, opposite the library, functions as a coffee shop called David's. Here I had come after my meeting with the steering committee. My presence had nothing to do with the new assignment; I had come to David's to unwind. After the sessions with Dr. Bookbinder and the steering committee, I thought I was entitled to a break. I couldn't stomach the Senior Common Room. My nature rebels against the attitudes and assumptions of most provincial academics. As the professor of a newly formed department I feel obliged most days to sit and listen to regurgitated points of view from the *Guardian* and *Independent*, or the failings of the cricket selectors, or the union, or the photocopier. Not that day.

David's is a haven for me. On the day nearly three years ago that I arrived in Bath to be interviewed for the chair of English, it seemed a happy omen when I chanced upon this bijou establishment no wider than a railway carriage, with its aroma of cappuccino, its narrow back-to-back seats and linen tablecloths, and the quiet clientele lingering over newspapers provided by the owner. At one end is a framed picture of Michelangelo's *David*. At the other the modern David dispenses tea and coffee from a serving area designed to utilize the limited space to the maximum. David is slim and supple, an essential requirement; one needs almost to be a limbo dancer to get behind the counter.

The most favored seats have a view of the river. The broad sweep of water below the bridge is dominated by the weir, a white, U-shaped structure in three tiers. However, its elegant lines mask a deathtrap. Thousands of gallons swiftly converge and drop on a confined area that form a whirlpool where year after year foolhardy swimmers and canoeists come to grief.

I took a seat by the window, easing my weight downward in a practiced way to avoid rocking the person at the next table. I ordered a coffee and thought about the interview in the doctor's office. The hell with Bookbinder. Later I would tell Geraldine exactly what had been said. Honesty in our marriage was more important than medical ethics that had been muddied by the doctor already.

I glanced at the front page of the *Times* and pushed it aside, and took from my pocket a paperback of *Northanger Abbey* that I had picked off my bookshelf in the office before walking down Bathwick Hill. I searched for and found a remark Jane Austen had put into the mouth of Isabella Thorpe: *"I get so immoderately sick of Bath; your brother and I were agreeing this morning that though it is vastly well to be here for a few weeks, we would not live here for millions."* It was like a balm. I felt restored by the words, which were much as I had remembered them. Of course it's erroneous to impute the views of fictitious characters to their author, and in justice the book does also contain some complimentary remarks about the city, but in my mood at that stage it pleased me to picture the councillors touring their exhibition and finding gracious pictures of Georgian Bath captioned with caustic quotes from Jane.

I sipped the coffee, telling myself to put subversive thoughts out of my mind. The exhibition had been dumped in my lap. It was my baby now, so I had better start to love it. A celebration of Jane Austen in Bath. In principle, I was more than willing to celebrate the six completed novels. If not, I was in the wrong job. The celebrating of their creator was more of a problem for me. I have never had any desire to join the legion of devotees who call themselves Janeites. Not that I find much to object to in Jane's character. In fact, the occasional waspish comments in her letters make her seem more worldly, more approachable, than the "gentle Jane" of the novels. My difficulty is more fundamental. I am out of sympathy with those who venerate writers and study their lives minutely. Any piece of literature has a life of its own, complete and independent of its author. So I balk at the trend of modern criticism to bury creative work in biographical data.

My thoughts were diverted momentarily by something I saw from the window. Below, three young boys had ventured out to the end of the weir and found a footing where driftwood collected. The current was not so strong there as in the center, where it raced over the edge, the result of several days of steady rain. The lads were picking up bits of wood and hurling them into the middle for the sheer joy of disturbing the shimmering uniformity of the flow.

The scene illustrated my difficulty rather aptly. There must be visual stimulation in this exhibition. Pages of text, however elegant, were not suited to public display unless they were supported by strong images. Yet the novels provided few striking pictorial possibilities. I always find illustrated editions of the Austen novels depressing to look at. They are little more than fashion plates. The dynamism is all in the text. Thinking it over, I could photograph the locations Jane Austen had used in *Northanger Abbey* and *Persuasion,* the two novels set in Bath, but to what effect? Who wanted to look at photos of Milsom Street and the Pump Room when they could see the places for themselves? No, I was going to be compelled to set aside my objections and use the biographical approach, providing pictures of Jane's family, the houses she had lived in, and the people she had met. The illustrations would be static, but at least they would not seem insipid.

Then how about moving pictures? It might be worth setting up a video and screening extracts from a television dramatization that had actually been filmed in Bath. I recalled a production of *Persuasion* not long ago. Presumably the BBC had obtained permission from the Bath City Council to film on location, so it wouldn't be unreasonable to ask for their cooperation in return.

I visualized several rows of chairs in front of a large screen at one end of the ballroom, and felt more optimistic. My gaze returned to the weir.

One of the boys was stepping along the edge toward the center. A stick, presumably one he had thrown, had lodged almost at the cusp of the curve. The other two watched as he moved quite confidently toward it. He looked about twelve or thirteen, and sturdy in physique. It was still a foolhardy thing to try. Notices on each bank of the river warned of the danger of swimming and canoeing here.

I remember telling myself with one voice that the boy was a little idiot and with the other that kids of that age needed physical challenges. If they weren't walking along the weir, they would probably be skateboarding down the ramps in one of the city car parks. The boy reached the center and drew the stick out of the water. He held it aloft like Excalibur.

Feeling, perhaps, that this was excessive, one of the others picked up a chunk of wood and slung it toward the show-off. It didn't hit him. He saw it coming and swayed aside. But he must have underestimated the strength of the current, because he was forced to take a step sideways to keep his footing. It took him closer to the edge. He seemed to sense the danger and teetered there for a moment with arms swaying. Then he was forced to step down to the next level.

The move was sensible. The concrete tiers were quite wide at that point and the difference in levels was no more than a few inches in depth. The force of the water seemed not to be a problem for him. He might easily have stepped up to safety.

He was unlucky, however. His foot slipped, he lost his balance, and fell on his back. The water carried him down to the next level.

I got up fast, concerned that the boy would be swept into the maelstrom of converging water. I believe I called out to David, "Someone in trouble," and ran out of the shop and across the bridge. Others may have seen the incident from Grand Parade, which overlooked the weir, but I was closer to the side with access to it. At the far end, I turned right, grabbed the iron handrail, and hurried down the enclosed flight of steps to the stone pier that supported the bridge. I ran to the railing. I had a clear view. The boy was not in sight. The other two stood as if petrified, staring at the place where the water poured off the weir and formed a bubbling vortex.

On this side of the river a sluice forms part of the weir construction, a huge floodgate on a pivot surmounted by a platform. To reach the weir on foot I would need to dash about a hundred yards to the steps on the far side and cross the platform. The lifebelt was almost as far away, attached to the railing beside the sluice. There wasn't time.

I wrenched off my jacket and shoes, climbed over the railing, and jumped. The drop to the river was about fifteen feet. I went under, surfaced, coughed out some filthy-tasting water, and started swimming. My actions up to this moment had been automatic. Now, as I struck out for the weir, the doubts came. Had there really been three boys down there, or only two? What a pointless and embarrassing exhibition this was if the kid in trouble had picked himself up already.

My right hand touched a solid structure under the water. I grasped the stone surround of the weir and with difficulty hauled myself upward, getting my leg up first and scrambling up sideways. I managed to stand upright, close to the point where the boy had gone for the piece of wood. The current dragged at my legs.

The boys at the end of the weir were waving and shouting.

I shouted back to them, "Can you see him?"

"He keeps going under," one called out in an accent redolent of Latin primers and striped schoolcaps.

"Where? Where did you see him?"

The boy pointed.

"There, sir! Over there!"

I glanced left and saw an arm exposed in the foam, a hand with fingers extended. Almost at once it sank from view.

I yelled, "Get the life belt! Get some help!"

I didn't give much for my chances in the torrent but you can't watch a child drown. I stepped down two tiers and felt my foot slip, so I dropped to my knees and crawled around the ledge to the point nearest to where the arm had appeared. I could see graphically how the inundation of water produced a churning effect that would prevent the boy from climbing back or being carried downstream. He would be submerged repeatedly until he drowned.

Desperately, I scanned the seething surface for another glimpse of the boy and suddenly saw him thrust upward again a mere two or three yards ahead. This time it was the torso that appeared, turning in the water like a log, lifeless apparently.

I launched myself after it, arms outstretched to make a grab. The cold water struck me like a charging rhino and forced me down. I went under, swallowing copiously. My ears roared. I was turned over, buffeted and disoriented. My head glanced against something solid. But I succeeded in getting a hold on the boy. I had him by the thigh.

I drew the limb to me and clung to it with both hands. The conflicting currents tossed us about as if we were cork. We were dragged down, hauled along the bottom, thrust upward, spun around, and slapped in the face. But I continued to hold the boy. And by degrees I was conscious of a lessening in the force of the buffeting. Now, when we came to the surface, there was time to inhale. I glimpsed foliage overhead, which meant that we were being carried to the outer extremity of the weir, where the current was less strong.

My shoulder scraped against the stone embankment. I found a foothold. I took a gulp of air and adjusted my hold on the boy, drawing a hand under his back, lifting the face clear of the water. It was lily white and lifeless. The head lolled back.

With this limp burden in my arms, I battled against the flow until I stumbled onto the lowest level of the weir at the outermost edge, just below the point where the boys had stood. I might as well say it, even if it sounds like something out of the *Boy's Own Paper:* The urge to do whatever I could to save this young life was giving me more strength than I knew I possessed. First I was kneeling. Then I managed to draw my right leg into a position where I could force myself fully upright. I staggered across the structure and climbed up to a place where the end of the weir had been built up to form the wall of the sluice.

Crouching, I rested the small body on the ground, and the daunting realization came to me that if the boy was to have any chance of survival, some life-saving technique was wanted. I had only the vaguest notion of what was necessary. As if prompted by my thoughts, a child's voice beside me said, "Kiss of life. Try the kiss of life, sir."

It was one of the boys from the weir.

I struggled to remember what one has to do. Resting a hand on the forehead of the unconscious boy, I tilted back his head. A trickle of water seeped from the edge of the mouth, so I turned the head, but no more was emitted. The mouth and nostrils appeared to be clear of weed or other obstructions.

The kid at my side said, "You have to pinch his nose and blow into his mouth."

I tried it. His lips felt clammy and gave no promise of life. I expelled several breaths, and saw the chest rise as the air penetrated the lungs. Nothing else happened. I seemed to be making no progress, so I tried pressure on the chest, pressing repeatedly on the lower half of the breastbone.

Without taking my eyes off the pale face, I asked the boy, "Did you go for help?"

"Nelson went. The boy that threw the wood."

The significance of the identity of the wood thrower was wasted on me. I was fast losing confidence in my ability to restore consciousness. I stopped kneading the chest and put my fingers to the pulse beside the boy's Adam's apple. If there was any life there, it was too faint to detect. I lifted the left eyelid. No movement. I pinched the nostrils closed again and clamped my mouth over the boy's.

It was difficult to tell at such close proximity, but it seemed to me that as I blew the second breath into the boy's lungs, the eye that I had examined gave a twitch. It remained shut, but the muscles around it appeared to flex. I could not be certain that it had happened. And I was not sure whether I had caused the effect myself with the pressure of my hand against the nose.

I stopped the blowing and drew back to get a better look. As I was putting my hand toward the eye, it opened and the iris moved. Both eyes opened fully.

The moment was profoundly moving. It was a deliverance. An acquittal. A life had been given back.

I murmured, "Thank God!" I am not religious, but no other words could encapsulate my feelings.

The boy coughed and spluttered.

"I'm going to turn you on your side," I told him, and the joy of communicating was never so exquisite.

The boy took several short breaths and then vomited some water. I massaged his back.

"He's all right! You saved his life!" The other boy knelt close to his friend. "Are you all right, Mat?"

"Is that his name—Mat?" I asked.

"Matthew. And I'm Piers."

"All right, Piers, let's have the shirt. We'll put it around his shoulders." And as the boy on the ground started to turn his head, I told him, "We'll get you home soon, Matthew."

Piers announced, "Here comes Nelson with a policeman."

I turned to look. Not merely Nelson with a policeman, but up to twenty people were strung out along the riverbank, running toward the weir. First they would have to climb a flight of steps and cross over the sluice gate. I took the opportunity to put in a word on Nelson's behalf. "Piers, if I were you, I wouldn't say any more about the piece of wood that was thrown. Matthew walked along the weir and fell in. That's all you need to tell anyone."

"I suppose it is."

"I'm certain of it."

"Right you are, sir."

Matthew himself managed to speak in a croaking voice. "It wasn't deliberate."

I glanced down at the pale face, the red-lidded eyes, and the dark hair flat to the forehead. He looked a bright kid. "That's right, son," I told him. "Sometime in our lives we've all done daft things we'd like to be overlooked." The "son" came naturally to my lips, although I had neither son nor daughter. At the marvelous moment when Matthew had opened his eyes, I had experienced something not unlike the joy and relief a father must feel at the miracle of childbirth.

Piers said, "The gentleman saved your life, Mat."

I said, "I think Mat needs to rest."

It wasn't a policeman Nelson had found, but a traffic warden. He led the rescue party up the steps and over the platform. They had to climb over a railing and let themselves down.

Someone had thoughtfully picked up my jacket and shoes. While I was putting them on, the boys gave their version of what had happened. The siren of an approaching ambulance cut the explanation short. A blanket was handed down. Matthew protested that he would rather go home, but he was wrapped in it and hoisted up.

It was my opportunity to slip away. The role of gallant rescuer didn't appeal to me. I'd rather be known as the obstreperous fellow who winds up the Dean.

4

LATE THE SAME AFTERNOON, I was drinking coffee in the kitchen of my house on Bathwick Hill, when the drumroll sound of the rollers on the garage doors signaled Geraldine's return from her pub lunch. In quick succession came the thump of the Metro door, the clatter of heels across the concrete floor, and the rasp of the door handle. She flung open the door. All those years in television and she still couldn't resist making an entrance.

This one was perfectly set up for her. "Christ," she said when she saw the white bathrobe I was wearing. "What's going on—infidelity?"

I smiled. If she was being humorous—and I couldn't be sure these days—it was worth encouraging. "Want a coffee?"

She nodded. She was pink from the Pimm's she'd been putting away. Her skin was drawn tight from cheek to jaw. For almost a decade the BBC makeup department preserved the peachy softness of her youth. Now it was gone. She had been written out of the series for two years, yet the image of Candice was impossible to forget when you looked at her. She was still a strikingly attractive woman, but the changes were striking, too—a poignant illustration of why the framed wedding photo in

most homes gets consigned to a drawer after a few
years.

She told me, "For a moment just now I thought you
were dead."

"Dead?"

"I saw the suit hanging up in the garage. At a first
glance I thought you were in it. What on earth is it
doing there?"

"It got wet, or at least the trousers did. I had a
ducking today. My things smell of river water, so I hung
them out there."

"*River* water? Are you serious?"

I spooned instant coffee into a cup, poured on the
boiling water, and told her about the boy in the weir.
When I had finished, she said, "You could have
drowned doing that. You could *really* have been dead."

There wasn't the depth of concern in her voice that
the statement warranted. On the contrary, there seemed
to be a note of wistfulness.

I let it pass. As a literary man I know the mind's
limitless facility for imagination. "Unlikely," I said
cheerfully. "I have a charmed life, like the pigeon in
Great Russell Street."

"*That.*"

"You haven't entirely forgotten, then?"

"I'm not likely to."

The Great Russell Street pigeon seemed these days
to have become a bird of ill omen. Our marriage might
have broken up already, were it not for the way we had
chosen to conduct it. Although Geraldine no longer had
professional commitments, we had kept to our pact to
conserve a strong measure of independence. I would go
abroad on courses without expecting Geraldine to tag
along; and she took her own skiing holidays. We each
had our own cars, beds, newspapers, books, and records.
She went to church; I didn't. We sometimes went separately to dinner parties. The theory was that when we
did spend time together, the experience was more precious because it was by choice, not circumstance. And

for the first few months it had worked, sexually and emotionally.

Given the free-ranging style of our marriage, Gerry's altered life after she lost her part in *The Milners* didn't threaten to spoil things too much. She had a pile of money from television and she spent it liberally. She soon linked up with a lively crowd from Bristol who were only too happy to hoist her on to the social merry-go-round she had missed before.

Now, two years on, our independence was about all we could agree on. Her erratic moods, the rages and the accusations, had turned the space we had created into a gulf. The sex had become perfunctory, and we both needed to be half-plastered to perform it. Our conversations were strained even when Geraldine switched to her exultant, highly animated states, because our worlds hardly overlapped. She had friends I had never met. "They would bore you," she'd say, "and, God, would you bore them!" There was an assumption in the way we treated each other that it would have to end in a separation.

However, I hadn't yet grasped that Geraldine's notion of separation was more absolute than mine.

And I still felt some responsibility toward her. I said casually as we sat drinking the coffee, "I went for my medical this morning. I saw Bookbinder, your doctor."

Geraldine gave me a sharp look. "I didn't tell you Bookbinder was my doctor."

"You didn't tell me you were being treated for insomnia, either."

"Bloody hell!" The jar of coffee tipped over as she swept her arm outward. "That's private and confidential. You had no right to ask."

"Hold on, Gerry," I told her. "Before you hit the ceiling, Bookbinder volunteered the information. He expected me to know all about it. I told him I didn't. It's news to me. I must say, I haven't noticed you lying awake."

She didn't answer. She glared at me with her green

eyes, threatening any minute to prove the truth of the axiom about redheads and their temper.

I said in conciliation, "Gerry, I don't want to make an issue out of this. If you haven't been getting your sleep, I'm sorry. On the few occasions I've had a wakeful night myself lately, I've heard you breathing evenly and assumed you were out to the world. But I suppose the tablets have solved the problem."

Her eyes widened and narrowed almost as quickly. "You heard about those, too? What else did you bloody find out? Did you read my medical files at the same time?"

After my attempt to take the heat out of the exchange, I found her response abusive. I rapped back, "You'd better complain to your doctor, not me."

She vented her fury in a piercing attack. "Snake in the grass! You've been trying to find out things, haven't you? Prying into my treatment. What are you plotting? Going to my own doctor behind my back—it's disgusting!"

The usual tack. I said, "Will you listen to me? I'm getting heartily sick of this persecution mania of yours. I was sent in to Bookbinder because my doctor—Marshall—is away. I went in to get the result of my medical."

"You fixed a date when you knew Marshall was away." She stabbed the space between us with her finger. "You trumped up this medical just to get in to my doctor and find out what my medication is."

"Give it a rest, will you?"

"It sticks out a mile! What are you up to, that's what troubles me. Are you trying to set something up with him behind my back? That's it, isn't it? You're in league with my doctor now, you bastard."

"If this was behind your back, why do you think I told you about it?" I pointed out.

"Because you're bloody devious, that's why," she shouted. "You're covering your tracks, pretending it's all out in the open when it isn't. Why did you mention it at all if you knew it would upset me? You're up to something, there's no question of that."

"Have you finished? You want to know why I mentioned this. I'll tell you. It's the reverse of what you're suggesting. The reason I spoke out is that I've always believed in being straight with you. And there's another reason: I'm damned sure you shouldn't be drinking or using the car if you're on phenobarbitone. A taxi might be sensible next time."

"Go to hell." She snatched up her bag and walked to the door.

I said, "I mean it. You're going to kill someone if you carry on like this."

She started to laugh.

I gave up trying to reason with her.

5

THURSDAY AFTERNOON of that week found me standing in front of a television camera beside one of the seven marble fireplaces in the main Assembly Room in Bath, the location so recklessly nominated for the forthcoming Jane Austen exhibition. As it happened, this wasn't directly concerned with the exhibition. I had been invited there in another connection, to contribute to a BBC *Points West* item about the history of the building. Even so, my thoughts kept darting ahead to September. The place was even more vast than I remembered. My gaze traveled up a Corinthian column and across the ornate ceiling to the orchestra gallery.

"Professor, would you mind coming in closer to Sadie?"

"If Sadie can stand the excitement," I answered.

"Enough. Hold it there." The highly strung New Zealander who was directing this interview asked the lighting man if he was happier and got a thumbs-up. "Fine. Are we okay for sound?"

While they continued to set up the shot, I spoke confidentially to Sadie, who was to interview me. "Before we start, I'd like to get one thing straight. Just now you mentioned the 'Jane Austen in Bath' exhibition. At this stage dear Jane is just a twinkle in my eye, and a faint one at that. I only heard about it myself a couple of days ago. You'd better not ask me what my plans are."

"No problem," she said. "Didn't Dougie make this clear? I won't ask you anything about it. After we screen the interview we'll mention that you're planning to hold the exhibition in September. That's all—a little advance publicity. We can drop it if you like."

"No, it ought to go in."

"Today's item is just about the uses the Assembly Rooms have been put to over the centuries. All we want from you, professor, is something about what went on here in Jane's time."

"You mean behind the pillars?"

A look of disquiet crept over Sadie's features. She said, "We were rather expecting that you would stress the more formal aspects, the dress balls and so on. I'm recording two more interviews to bring out the slightly more disreputable uses it was put to in more recent times. Apparently it was used as a cinema between the wars."

"A cinema?" Still with a straight face, I said, "I can't imagine *anything* more disreputable than that."

Every television interviewer dreads a wisecracker. Sadie eyed me without amusement and said firmly, "Everything will be edited, by the way. It doesn't have to go out until Friday. Dougie wants at least two takes in case of a problem, so if you cough or anything, you needn't worry. It won't be transmitted."

"My dear, I never worry."

Sadie wet her lips, turned away, and said on a lower note that I think was directed at the crew, "You worry me, ducky." She nodded to Dougie, the director.

"Quiet please," he said. "We're going for a take. Take one—and action."

We didn't get past Sadie's first question before Dougie said, "Cut." Something was amiss with the sound. While they checked it, I awarded myself a short break. I left the fireplace, strolled across to a row of Chippendale chairs that the crew used between takes, and picked up a newspaper someone had left there, the *Bath Evening Chronicle*. The headline ran: SHY HERO IN WEIR RESCUE.

I sat down and read on:

An unknown man plunged to the rescue of a drowning schoolboy at Pulteney Weir yesterday afternoon and hauled him to safety. The boy, Matthew Didrikson, 12, of Lyncombe Rise, a day pupil at the Abbey Choir School, was unconscious when brought to the bank, but his rescuer revived him with the "kiss of life" method of resuscitation. He was taken to the Royal United Hospital suffering from shock and water inhalation, but was not detained. Matthew's rescuer, a well-dressed man of about 35, left the scene without identifying himself.

Mr. David Broadbent, a retired optician, saw the entire incident from Grand Parade. He said, "The boy was playing with two others beside the weir and he started to walk out to the center. The current was strong after all the rain we've had lately. The lad appeared to wobble and slip, and the next thing he was in the water below the weir. The man must have seen it from Pulteney Bridge or thereabouts because he came running down the steps by the bridge and jumped straight in. He didn't hesitate. He swam to the weir and went in after the lad. It was heroic because people have drowned there in the past. Somehow he got a grip on the boy and they were washed to one side and he climbed out and dragged the boy onto the bank and gave him the kiss of life. I think the Royal Humane Society should be informed, because that man deserves a medal."

Dr. Rajinder Murtah, who attended Matthew at the hospital, said, "The boy undoubtedly owes his life to the prompt and sensible action of this unknown man." Matthew's mother, Mrs. Dana Didrikson, who is employed by Realbrew Ales Ltd. as a driver, said, "I would dearly like an opportunity to thank the brave man who saved the life of my son." Matthew, apparently none the worse for his adventure except for superficial grazing, will return to school tomorrow.

A police spokesman said, "At least three people have drowned at Pulteney Weir in the last ten years and there have been any number of incidents involving swimmers or canoeists. People don't realize that it's so deep below the weir that you could sink a double-decker bus there. For anyone caught in the undertow, it's a deathtrap."

A voice at my shoulder said suddenly, "There's no escape. I've tracked you down."

"What?" I slapped the paper facedown.

Sadie said, "We're going for another take."

On the evening the interview was screened I was caught up in a Board of Studies meeting, so I missed it. Gerry saw it and thoughtfully switched on the video recorder, which she failed to notice was tuned to Channel 4, so when I got in, I sat through ten minutes of a gardening program before I realized what had happened. But it was meant as an olive branch after the squabble we'd had about my visit to Dr. Bookbinder, and I thanked her for making the attempt.

"It's funny," she remarked. "You always look different when I see you on the box—almost dishy, in fact."

"*Dishy?*" I said, pretending to take umbrage. "We were discussing the social mores of Bath in Jane Austen's era. That was my donnish look."

"I wasn't taken in by that," she said. "It's just an act, isn't it? Greg Jackman putting it across that he's the professor just like some actor hamming it up as Julius Caesar."

There was more than a germ of truth in her comment, but I didn't much care for the analogy.

Sometime after ten that evening, when I was sipping a cognac prior to checking that the doors and windows were locked, the phone rang. Gerry was taking a shower, so I picked it up, expecting to find myself talking to one of her many friends who called at all hours with titbits of gossip.

"Is it possible to speak to Professor Jackman?" a woman's voice asked.

"Speaking."

"I thought I recognized your voice. I'm sorry to be calling so late. Is it terribly inconvenient?"

"Well, you found me at home," I said cautiously, trying to work out whether this was one of my students wanting to contest a grading. "Do I know you, then?"

"No. My name is Abershaw—Molly Abershaw." She paused as if I might have heard of her, then resumed, "From the *Bath Evening Telegraph.*"

I said with more tact than I usually employ, "Now that you mention it, I believe I have seen your name in the paper."

"And I saw you on television earlier this evening."

That was why she had recognized my voice. I felt more comfortable with the call now that I had some idea of its provenance. "You picked up the reference to the Jane Austen exhibition, I suppose?"

"Yes, indeed. That's in September, I gather?"

"Correct," I told her, refraining from adding that it scarcely merited a ten o'clock call this evening.

"You'll be wanting to publicize it, I'm sure," she went on. "We'd like to run a feature nearer the time."

"Fine," I said, not wanting to prolong the conversation now that the necessary goodwill had been exchanged. "It's early days yet, but I'll be happy to cooperate. And as you obviously have my home number as well as the university's, there should be no difficulty getting in touch."

"I'd like to ask you something else," she put in quickly. "I don't know if you know my paper. It probably gets pushed through your door twice a week. It's free, but we have a very good name for our news reporting. Earlier this evening I was speaking to the young schoolboy who was almost drowned at Pulteney Weir on Monday. He saw you on *Points West* tonight and thinks he recognized you. He believes you were the man who saved his life. Are you able to confirm it, professor?"

I hedged. "Why exactly are you asking me this, Miss Abershaw?"

"I thought that was obvious. It's a matter of public

interest. It was a very brave act and it deserves to be written up."

"But it *was* written up, on the day after it happened."

"Yes, in the *Evening Chronicle*. They weren't able to reveal the name—"

"—of the shy hero."

"Exactly."

"And you're hoping to get an exclusive?"

"*Was* it you, professor?"

Stupidly I admitted that it was, and from the elation that came down the line she might have turned a cartwheel. "Listen, I don't want any fuss," I added, too late, of course. "Anyone would have done what I did, seeing the boy in difficulties."

She laughed. "That's a load of balls."

"What did you say?"

"Give me a break. This story has been written a million times before without a single line being altered. Man saves child, or old lady, or kitten—and then walks away without identifying himself. And when he is finally traced, he says, 'Anyone would have done the same thing.' Would they—hell! These days nine out of ten would look the other way."

I took refuge in the same well-worn formula she was attacking. "I don't know what you want from me, Miss Abershaw, but the incident is over, as far as I'm concerned."

She said, "My paper will print your name. I thought you might like to be credited with a few intelligent remarks. Would you mind if we sent a photographer round in the morning to get a picture of you?"

"Yes."

"That's very good of you. Would about nine be convenient?"

"I said yes, I *would* mind. I'm not posing for pictures."

With steel in the voice, she said, "We are a major local newspaper, professor. We work closely with the university, publicizing events."

"Agreed, but this isn't an event requiring publicity."

"With respect, I believe it is."

"We'll have to differ, then."

Then she played her trump. "Don't you want to know how young Matthew is getting on?"

There was a threat of adverse publicity here. I said without much show of concern, "Right. Tell me. How is he?"

"He's fine, but he'd like to meet you and thank you personally."

"Oh, no," I said. "I'm glad he's all right and that's the end of it, as far as I'm concerned. Thank you for calling, Miss Abershaw." I put down the phone.

Out of curiosity mingled with apprehension, I picked up a copy of Molly Abershaw's paper next day. It was even more embarrassing than I expected. The main story, in banner headlines, was:

PROFESSOR'S RESCUE PLUNGE

The mystery man who leaped to the rescue of a schoolboy at Pulteney Weir last Monday and used the kiss of life to revive him was today revealed as a Bath University professor. He is Professor Gregory Jackman, 37, of Bathwick, who was appointed to the newly created chair of English in 1987. The *Evening Telegraph* this week appealed for help in tracing the hero of the rescue, who walked away from the scene without identifying himself. A number of our readers phoned with detailed descriptions of the man, but appropriately he was spotted by the boy he rescued, 12-year-old Matthew Didrikson, from the Abbey Choir School. Matthew recognized the professor when he appeared on the *Points West* program on television last night, in a filmed report about the Assembly Rooms.

Said Matthew when the *Telegraph* phoned him last night, "I'm positive that the professor is the man who saved my life. I switched to the program by chance and there he was. It was really amazing."

The *Telegraph* contacted

Professor Jackman late last night and he confirmed that he carried out the rescue. After making sure that Matthew was fully conscious and the ambulance was coming, he had walked away because, in his own words, "the incident was over as far as I was concerned." He said he was pleased to be told that Matthew has now made a complete recovery.

It made me squirm, of course, but I suppose it could have been more of an embarrassment. I had to be thankful that I'd given my last lecture that term, for the article would have been a perfect excuse for some kind of stunt from my students.

As it was, I planned a low-profile weekend. The only social occasion was a party that Waterstone's bookshop was throwing at lunchtime on Sunday to publicize a new book of poems by Ted Hughes, the Poet Laureate, who was coming to sign copies. I had never met Hughes, but I liked his work and the issues that he espoused, and I wanted to be there. If I could get away reasonably early, I hoped to drive down to Hampshire later the same afternoon to look at the house where Jane Austen had once lived in the village of Chawton. It was set up as a museum, so I was duty-bound to make a visit there soon, on the cadge for exhibits.

The weekend was one of those precious, if uncanny intervals in an English summer when the weathermen were prepared to hold out the prospect of sweltering heat. Across the nation last year's shorts were tried for size and straw hats were dusted off. Tables and chairs appeared outside pubs and cafés. Sales of suntan lotions, insect creams, lager, and lettuce increased phenomenally. And, unbeknownst to me, my wife prepared to murder me.

On Sunday morning, I needed to catch up on some office work, so I put in a few hours at the university before the sun made further work impossible. Then I drove down to Bath for the signing party, which was marred for me by an unexpected incident. When I arrived soon after twelve, the crush around the table on the first floor where Ted Hughes was already signing was a fine testimony to the literary taste of Bathonians, even if some had lowered the tone by climbing onto stools to get their sight of the great man. I looked for someone I knew and spotted a group of kindred spirits from the university. We were soon deep in discussion about trends in modern poetry.

The large woman who practically elbowed one of my companions aside and addressed me by name was unknown to me, although the voice was familiar. She introduced herself as Molly Abershaw, the reporter who had phoned me late on Thursday. I was peeved, to put it mildly. I reminded her that I had nothing else to say to the press.

Miss Abershaw had obviously had time to work out her battle plan, whereas I was reacting predictably. On reflection, I may have overreacted. She said with a smile that she wasn't there to get a statement, she simply wanted to introduce someone to me. Then she reached behind her and thrust a schoolboy in front of me—Matthew, the child I had pulled out of the weir. The poor kid looked thoroughly uncomfortable. Miss Abershaw tried to prompt him into some kind of statement of gratitude, but before he opened his mouth I said it was unnecessary.

You can imagine the mystification of the people I was with. They knew nothing of my adventure in the weir. But Molly Abershaw hadn't finished yet. She said that the boy's mother had come to meet me. By this time, I was in no frame of mind to be civil with anybody, and when a camera flashed and I realized that I had been well and truly set up, I acted fast. I grabbed the photographer, who was obviously from the newspaper, and insisted that he expose the film and hand it over. The wretched man was rigid with fear, and that's not a response I'm used to getting from people I meet. I demanded that roll of film and got it.

Not the sort of incident one expects at a literary party.

6

AS SOON AS POSSIBLE after the incident at Waterstone's I left the party. The drive to Chawton compelled me to think of other things. The cottage where Jane Austen spent the last eight years of her life is located this side of Alton, just off the A31, and is furnished as a museum by the Jane Austen Society. I took note of a number of items—manuscripts, family portraits, and other memorabilia—that I decided were worth making inquiries about for a possible loan. My list didn't include the lock of Jane's hair recently dyed bright auburn, or the microphotographs of pieces of her skin still attached to the roots. I had ditched most of my donnish scruples, but there were limits, even with a hundred-foot Assembly Room to fill. Before leaving, I explained my interest to the curator and sounded him out about the possibility of borrowing items. It seemed I would have to approach the society. There were the usual complications over insurance.

The worst of the day's heat had passed when I started for home, yet it was still an uncomfortable drive with the sun steadily penetrating the windscreen at a low angle. I stopped for a pint and a salad in Marlborough and got back to Bath shortly before nine—to an extra infliction. The mindless beat of disco music carried to me from my own garden even before I saw the lineup of large cars in the drive. I recognized a red Porsche and a gray vintage Bentley: Geraldine's Bristol crowd. The whiff of charcoal fumes and kebabs was in the air. A far cry from Jane Austen.

The front door stood open and a bearded man I had not met sat across the doorstep tapping the disco rhythm with his fingertips on a 1935 Silver Jubilee biscuit tin belonging to me that was quite a collector's piece, and usually displayed on the Welsh dresser. "Hi," the man greeted me without looking up. "What have you brought?"

"Nothing. I live here."

Now the man raised his face to squint at me. "With Gerry, you mean? Nice work, man. Want to come in?"

I stepped over his legs and walked through the house and found Geraldine dancing on the patio opposite an estate agent called Roger in striped shirt and red braces who never missed these shindigs. Gerry gave me a wave. The music was deafening, so I turned down the volume.

Continuing to wriggle her hips, she called out, "You're too early for the food. It needs another half hour to get up some heat. You've got time to get into something more relaxing." She was relaxing in an emerald-green jumpsuit. Her feet were bare.

To say that I wasn't in the party mood would be an understatement. I said, "For Christ's sake, Gerry—you might have told me you were planning this."

"Didn't get the chance, dear heart. You were up and away too early this morning. Never mind, I've fixed you up with a date."

"What?"

"A date. Skirt, or whatever charming expression you fellows use these days." The cassette ran out and she stopped dancing and came over to me and tried to loosen my tie. Her manner was elated in a way that it rarely was when I was alone with her. I guessed she was on vodka, because I couldn't smell drink on her breath.

"So get yourself into something sexy," she told me.
"She'll be here any minute."

I said, "Jump in the pool, Gerry."

"I'm not shooting a line," she persisted. "This woman with a name like a man's called on the phone an hour ago and asked for you. Wait, it's coming to me. Some 1940s' film star with dreamy eyes and a trilby. Dana Andrews. That was it. Her name is Dana."

"I don't know anyone called Dana."

"You will shortly. She was so desperate to speak to you that I invited her to my barbecue. She's the mother of that schoolkid you rescued from the river."

"Mrs. Didrikson." It had been that sort of day.
"You birdbrain. Those people are a menace. They turned up at the Ted Hughes signing."

"What's come over you, shyboots?" said Geraldine.
"I thought publicity was meat and drink to you."

"Not this local-hero stuff. I've had a bellyful. Look, I'm not having the press invading my house—least of all while this is going on."

"She's coming alone, she told me," said Geraldine.

"Yes, and pigs might fly."

I went up to the bedroom, picked some fresh clothes off the hangers, looked into the end suite, discovered a woman already using the shower, and had to wash in the bathroom instead. And would you believe it, someone had removed the mirror from the wall.

My first idea had been to tell Geraldine to give the Didrikson woman her marching orders the moment she arrived. But Gerry couldn't be relied on, even when sober. I would do it myself. I dressed, returned downstairs, stepped over the man in the doorway, and looked in the drive to see if another car had arrived yet. I walked out to the road. It was completely dark by now and blessedly cool.

In my days as a smoker this would have been a fine time to light up. I had no desire to join Geraldine's barbecue. I had nothing in common with her friends, although I was resigned to joining them ultimately. Trying to sleep would be futile.

I heard the approach of a car from the direction of Bath. Before it came into view, the headlights on full beam glowed high above the walls and hedges. Its progress was slow, as if the driver was looking for a particular house. Then the car itself appeared and the lights dipped. A Mercedes. It halted just across the road from where I was standing, but no one got out.

The driver was a dark-haired woman. She wound down the window and said, "Would I be better off parking in the road?"

"Are you here for the barbecue?"

"Not exactly," she said, hesitating. "You *are* Professor Jackman?"

"That's right, but my wife is giving the party. You can park there if you like. Not much comes along at this time of night."

She said, "I think we're at cross-purposes. I just wanted a few minutes with you, professor."

"You're Mrs. Didrikson?" I hadn't expected the woman to arrive in a Mercedes.

"That's right. Didn't you get the message that I was coming?"

"If you want to talk, this isn't the place," I said, seized with a pleasing thought. I could outflank Molly Abershaw, who had no doubt set up this meeting, and escape the party for a while by getting a lift to the nearest pub. "It would be easier in my local—the Viaduct. Do you have any objections?"

She hesitated. "Well, no . . . if that's what you'd like," she said.

I got in, chatted about the weather and the tourists for a mile, and admired the way she took the Mercedes around the tight bends on Brassknocker Hill. She handled it as if she enjoyed her driving. I was curious why she hadn't chosen to drive something more like a sports car, for she was really too short for the Mercedes. She was propped up on two thick cushions.

The pub was busy. As she wanted something nonalcoholic, I suggested a Saint Clement's and ordered a large cognac for myself.

"I was so upset by what happened in Waterstone's today that I had to get in touch with you," she plunged in as soon as we had our drinks. "Believe me, it came as a total shock to Matthew and me when that photographer appeared. We were there in the belief that it was a chance to meet you informally and thank you for what you did. It seemed a good idea when Molly Abershaw suggested it. Now I'm kicking myself for being so dumb. Can you forgive me?"

I had given her no more than a glance in Waterstone's. The incident had been so unexpected that I had barely registered who the boy was before the camera flashed and triggered my angry reaction. Dana Didrikson's deep-set brown eyes now studied me with apprehension as she awaited my response. She didn't look as if she was out for more publicity. The shape of her face, the high forehead and neat mouth and chin, suggested intelligence without guile. Her small hands were clasped tightly.

I said, "Forget it, Mrs. Didrikson. I blew my top, and I'm not too proud about that. Your son has fully recovered from the ducking, I hope."

"Completely. I can't dismiss it just like that. Not without thanking you for saving his life—and words seem totally inadequate."

"All right," I said, smiling. "In a moment you can buy me a drink and we'll both feel easier."

"And the cleaning bill for your clothes?"

"They were due for cleaning anyway."

"I should think the suit must have been ruined."

I shook my head. "You don't know my dry cleaner. He's a genius, an artist. He should be restoring Leonardo's frescoes. Instead he has my trousers to clean."

She was one of those women whose beauty is in their smile. "And now I've taken you away from your party."

"My wife's party," I told her. "Isn't it truer to say that I've taken *you* away from it? Gerry invited you, didn't she?"

"Oh, I didn't intend to stay." She blushed. "Sorry—

that sounds rude. I'm rather tired. It's been a heavy week."

"What's your job?"

"I'm a company driver, for a brewery."

"You sound like someone worth getting to know."

Another quick, self-conscious smile. "I don't get samples. And the car belongs to the firm."

"Is it hard work?" I asked.

"I have to earn a living."

"Are you, er . . . ?"

"Divorced." She said it evenly, without emotion. "Mat's father went back to Norway. We married too young."

"Is it difficult to raise a son? I don't have children."

She looked down at her drink, considering the answer. I particularly noticed that—the fact that she didn't trot out some superficial statement. "It's a matter of being alert to the way he develops. Mat's twelve now, just finished Common Entrance. He's coming to terms with manhood. He's neither small boy nor man. I keep reminding myself not to be too surprised by his behavior. My worry is that he'll lose his respect for me. How am I going to be a support to him if he disregards me? I see signs of it and I'm torn between reprimanding him and clutching him to my bosom."

"Difficult. Does he have any contact with his father?"

"No. We don't hear from Sverre. Mat is fiercely proud of his dad's reputation—he's a chess international—and he has a collection of press cuttings and some photos I gave him, but it's like worshiping a wooden idol. There's no response." She drew back from the table and flicked her dark hair behind her shoulders. "How did I start on this? Are you ready for that second drink?"

I watched her carry the glasses to the bar, exchanging some banter with a couple of men she recognized at another table. She was small, yet she conducted herself with confidence. Work must have toughened her. I felt privileged that she had been willing to tell me about her conflict in being mother and father to Matthew. When she returned with the drinks, though, she made clear her wish to turn to other matters.

"Did I catch it right on television the other night— are you putting on an exhibition about Jane Austen?"

"Under protest, yes. I drew the short straw. In my spare moments I drive around southern England looking for exhibits. There's a worrying shortage. If you hear of a fire screen she embroidered or a bonnet she wore going cheap, I'm the man to contact."

"*Anything* to do with her?"

"Absolutely. Strictly speaking, it's the 'Jane Austen in Bath' exhibition, but I won't turn any offer down— lace handkerchiefs, teapots, old shoes, tennis rackets."

"Tennis—in Jane Austen's time?"

"Joke—I've got to fill the Assembly Rooms with something."

"She lived in Gay Street, didn't she?"

"She did, indeed. Forgive me being tactless, but how did you know that?"

"It's part of a project Matthew is doing at school."

"Obviously I should enlist Matthew's help. Yes, apart from Gay Street there were three other houses in the city where the Austen family resided: in Sydney Place, Green Park Buildings, and Trim Street. She also stayed at Queen Square before the family moved here, and at one, The Paragon, where her scandalous old aunt lived."

"Jane Austen had a scandalous aunt?"

Now that I had vilified Aunt Jane and made Mrs. Didrikson curious, I felt in duty bound to tell the story. "It's been rather glossed over in the biographies. The aunt may have had The Paragon for her address, but she wasn't such a paragon herself. She was put on trial for shoplifting, which was a capital offense. She was supposed to have stolen some lace from a milliner's. Do you know the dress shop on the corner of Bath Street and Stall Street, just opposite the entrance to the baths?"

"You mean Principles."

I smiled at the name. "There's irony. Yes, that would be on the site of the shop. Well, one August afternoon in 1799, Aunt Jane bought a card of black lace there and walked out with a card of white that she hadn't paid for. Shortly after, the manageress stopped her in the street and challenged her. Aunt Jane claimed that they must have made a mistake in the shop, but they pressed charges and she spent seven months in custody waiting for her case to come up."

"That must have been an ordeal in those days."

"It could have been worse. Because she moved in elevated circles, she was allowed to lodge in the warden's house instead of a prison cell, and her husband moved in with her. Jane Austen almost went, too. Her mother offered the services of Jane and her sister Cassandra as additional company, but the accommodation wouldn't stretch to it."

"Good material for a writer."

"Whether Jane would have thought so is another question. The warden's wife had a habit of licking her knife clean after cooking fried onions and then using it to butter the bread."

Mrs. Didrikson grimaced. "But I suppose it was preferable to bread and water. What happened at the trial?"

"Aunt Jane was acquitted eventually, and it used to be accepted that the poor old biddy was the victim of a trumped-up charge and perjured evidence, but modern writers who have analyzed the quality of the evidence are more skeptical. She seems to have got off mainly on the strength of her reputation as an upright citizen. Witnesses galore were called to defend her character—members of Parliament, a peer of the realm, clergymen, and shopkeepers. All this was stressed by the judge in his address to the jury, coupled with the suggestion that a rich, respectable woman had no need to go shoplifting."

"Which is not necessarily the case," she remarked. "Rich women do steal. There can be motives other than personal hardship."

I nodded. "Lucky for Aunt Jane that post-Freudian psychology hadn't been heard of in 1800."

"Still, it *is* fascinating. I hope you can use the story in your exhibition."

"I daresay I will. You see, it's not so peripheral as it first appears if you think what might have happened if the jury had convicted Aunt Jane."

"Hanging?"

"Realistically, transportation. She would have ended up in Botany Bay. And then the Austen family almost certainly wouldn't have come to live in Bath the year after the acquittal. They lodged with her while they looked for a house of their own. *Northanger Abbey* and *Persuasion* might never have been written."

"Ah, but who knows what else might have come from Jane's pen? Was she a blood relative?"

"No, Aunt Jane was a Cholmeley. She married Uncle James and became Mrs. Leigh Perrot."

"Mrs. what?"

"Two words: Leigh and Perrot. She lived to a great age—over ninety."

"Innocence rewarded?"

I shook my head. " 'The good die early, and the bad die late.' "

The softening of her features each time she smiled challenged me to amuse her more. Before I tried again, however, she hoisted her bag on her shoulder and said, "I don't want to seem rude, but would you like me to drive you back?"

"Already?"

"I shouldn't keep you from your guests."

"I'm not too anxious to get back to the barbecue. Ah, but you said you were tired," I recalled. "I shouldn't have started on my Aunt Jane story." I drank up. "Let's go."

7

_____

AS THE MERCEDES cruised up the winding incline of Brass-knocker Hill, I said, "I've been thinking about your son. This may sound stupid after what happened, but does he like swimming?"

"I think so," Mrs. Didrikson answered. "He can manage a length or so. It isn't his strongest sport, by any means. They don't do enough at the school. Too much of their time is spent on singing, in my opinion. I shouldn't complain, should I, as I was daft enough in the first place to send him to a choir school?"

"What I'm leading up to is that we have a pool at the university. Oddly enough, it isn't much used at this time of year when most other pools are crowded. Nearly all the students have left. Do you think he would enjoy a swim?"

"Professor, you've done more than enough for Mat already."

"I'd like to meet him again. After all, he and I did meet first in the water."

She smiled faintly. "He wouldn't remember much about that."

"He'll remember the rebuff he got from me in the bookshop this morning. An incident like that can be wounding to a kid his age. I'd like to show him that it was nothing personal. How about one evening after school?"

The road ahead leveled out. After thinking about it for a moment, she answered, "I'm sure he would enjoy it."

"Tuesday?"

"All right. I'll bring him in the car."

"Say about seven? Why don't you join us?"

She answered tersely, as if she had seen the invitation coming, "No, thank you."

I had meant only to be civil and I underlined this by saying neutrally, "Just as you wish. Do you know where the pool is at Claverton?"

She laughed. "You're talking to a former taxi driver."

A Rolling Stones number boomed across Bathwick Hill when we stopped in the road opposite the house. Near-hysterical shrieks issued from the back garden.

"Good thing your neighbors don't live too close," Mrs. Didrikson commented. "When we have a barbecue, we have to watch the decibels."

"And I'm willing to bet that the moment you strike the first match there's always someone who pointedly marches out to take her washing off the line."

"Always."

"Will you come in for a drink? A bite to eat? A quick kebab?"

"Thank you, but I'd like to get back and tell Mat how this turned out. He was rather anxious."

I understood. I knew from the way that she spoke that it wasn't just an excuse. I got out, wished her good night, and watched her reverse the Mercedes in a neat arc and drive back in the direction of Bath. A capable woman. Beneath that armor suit of independence was a person of wit and integrity, qualities I rate highly.

The night was clammy, without much breeze. The temperature had not dropped much since sundown. The smell of fried bacon mingled not unpleasantly with the heavy scent of honeysuckle. I strolled around the side of the house in the direction of all the noise.

The floodlights around the swimming pool had been switched on and most of the party were standing around it being entertained by three women and two men who had stripped off all their clothes and were chasing each other around the perimeter with the object of pushing someone else into the water before they themselves took a ducking. Geraldine's friends liked to think of themselves as feisty—the feistiest people around—and the strain showed at times. I automatically assumed that Gerry was one of the three until I spotted her still in her jumpsuit, merely in the role of observer, her hand hooked over the shoulder of Roger the estate agent. The chase around the pool reminded me of a series of cartoons by James Thurber called *The Race of Life,* the naked figures pale, paunchy, and intense, more quaint than erotic. How long this had been going on was impossible to say, but the screams and laughter were forced at this stage, as if bestowed out of charity. At last one man was caught from two directions and he leaped off the side, tugging two women in with him. A mighty splash, hoots of laughter, and then the others plunged in as well. It would not be long before they were singing, "Come and join us," and grasping for the ankles of anyone rash enough to stand close to the edge.

I remember looking at my watch and recalling Mr. Woodhouse's dictum in *Emma* that the sooner every party breaks up, the better. Mr. Woodhouse, a standard-bearer for the modern obsession with health, would undoubtedly have had something pertinent to say on the perils of skinny-dipping.

Turning my back on the pool, I wandered across to the patio, where the barbecue wanted some attention if I was to cook myself a steak. With a hand shovel I drew some ash off the charcoal to reveal glowing embers and fanned them into more activity. The meat was set out on a tray covered with wire mesh. Plenty was left. I lifted the cover, picked up a steak and some bacon, tomato pieces, and mushrooms and spread them on the grid above the fire.

Presently I was conscious of somebody at my side.

Geraldine looped her arm around mine and said, "Where have you been hiding all evening?"

"I went out for a bit. Enjoying your party?"

"Immensely. Didn't your lady friend turn up after all?"

"She came. She couldn't stay."

"Pity." She looked at the steak. "I saved enough for both of you. You must be famished by now. Want me to take over?"

"There's no need. You go back to your friends."

"They don't need me. They'll only drag me in the pool and ruin my clothes. Listen to them." She picked up a fork and turned over a slice of the bacon. "Besides, I can't neglect my nearest and dearest."

"Your snake in the grass, you mean."

"What?"

"You called me a snake in the grass the other day. I'm supposed to be plotting God knows what with your doctor."

She squeezed my arm. "Darling, you know me by now. I'm a Leo. I can't help my personality. I roared a bit, as Leos do, that's all. Could you blow on the charcoal, or the steak will never get done? I saved some of my homemade sauce for you. They were on it like vultures. It's in the house."

"Where?" I asked. "I'll get it."

"It's all right. You keep an eye on this. I know where I tucked it out of sight."

I moved the tomatoes to the side of the grill to stop them from burning, my mind on other things. Almost enough material was now promised for the exhibition. The next challenge was how to present it interestingly. My earlier reluctance to get involved had been supplanted by a strong desire to make a success of the show. I still refused to make it a paean to life in Bath. I was resolved that Jane's feelings about the city should be scrupulously represented.

Then Gerry was back with a jug of sauce. "You're going to enjoy this. Got a plate?"

I picked one up from where they were stacked. "Hey, don't drown it."

Too late; she had liberally coated everything. She said, "Why don't you come down to the pool with it? You know most of them."

"Thanks. I'll eat it here, while it's hot."

"You don't really hit it off with my wacky friends, do you, prof?"

"I'm not complaining."

"I'll make some coffee in a mo and move the whole thing indoors. They'll be glad of a warm drink after their dip." She cleared some plates from a table and handed me a knife and fork and a paper napkin. "Listen, I knew you'd be wanting some sleep after being out all day, so I made up the camp bed in the summerhouse. You can slip away whenever you wish. They won't disturb you there. I left half a bottle of Courvoisier and a pack of cigars beside the bed."

Such wifely consideration was so rare from Gerry that I at once suspected an ulterior motive. I found it difficult to believe—even of Gerry—that she had the gall to invite her admiring estate agent up to the bedroom while her own husband spent a night in the garden, but what other construction was there to put on it?

I said, "I'm not tired."

"That's all right, then," said Gerry with such implacable charm that I was reassured. "Just remember it's there if you want to escape before the party finally breaks up."

She went off toward the house, leaving me alone on the patio eating my supper. The food was good, the sauce a trifle too peppery for my taste. I scraped some off the steak. Presently I was aware of someone standing nearby, holding a beer glass. It was Roger, the estate agent, his moon face glowing greenly in the artificial light.

"Hello there, brother Gregory. What's this—second helpings?"

I gave him a look without much fraternity in it. "I only just got here. I've been out."

"Business or pleasure? The latter, I hope. Six days shalt thou labor."

". . . and have a barbecue on the seventh?"

Roger laughed. "Speaking of labor, I have to be at my charming best in the office tomorrow morning."

"Gerry's making coffee," I informed him.

"I think we'll have to skip it. Have you seen anything of Val?"

"Val?"

"My wife."

"Er, no." I refrained from adding that I'd always assumed Roger was a bachelor from the way he carried on with Gerry.

"She was one of the first in the pool," said Roger.

"Perhaps she's gone indoors to get dry."

"No, there she is!" said Roger, and called out, "Val, darling, we're about to leave. Come and say good-bye to your host."

Val came over. By this time, she had gotten back into her clothes. When dressed, and with her damp hair flat to her head, she looked even more like one of James Thurber's creations. Her stare was withering. "So you're the husband."

I felt like the owner of an unruly dog.

Roger smiled feebly and said, "She means thank you for having us. Come on, my water nymph. Party's over for you and me. Nighty-night, Greg."

They moved off around the side of the house. Presently I heard their car start up and move away. I wondered if Gerry knew they had left.

When I had finished eating I strolled across to the house for a coffee. There, I couldn't avoid getting into conversation with some people who were vaguely connected with the Bristol Old Vic and wanted to impress me with their theatrical gossip. The vagueness was more of my making than theirs because unusually my concentration had started slipping. Black coffee didn't help. I was getting more weary by the minute.

Unable to listen any longer, I muttered some excuse and wandered out through the patio door. All that

I could think about was that camp bed in the summer-house. I moved as if wearing one of those early diving suits with weighted boots. It wasn't the drink that had done this; I'd had nothing since the cognacs in the pub and they never make me sleepy. Then I was conscious of pointed heels clattering on the patio behind me, and Gerry was at my side.

"Greg, are you all right?"

"Just tired," I answered, and I heard myself slurring the words. "Going to bed now."

"Can you make it that far?"

"Yes."

My thigh came painfully into contact with a table. I turned my head, but Gerry had already gone back to her party. The impact sharpened my wits momentarily. I thought, I've been given something. I'm drugged. I groped across the table and found the mustard dish, pulled it toward me, scooped up a generous amount on my finger and pushed it to the back of my throat. Instantly I retched, staggered to a tub of geraniums, and heaved up as much as I could of the barbecue supper. My head spun when I raised it. I still felt profoundly tired. I thrust my hand down my throat a second time, with a result almost as copious. The sweat on my forehead turned icy. Down the patio steps I tottered, then perilously around the edge of the pool, across the lawn, and as far as the summerhouse, an octagonal wooden structure open to the elements on two sides.

True to her promise, Gerry had made up the camp bed there. I dropped onto it like a felled tree, too exhausted to remove even my shoes.

It felt as if I were levitating. Not a pleasant sensation.

Homemade sauce, I thought as I pushed my finger down my throat again.

The next thing I knew was when I stirred, opened my eyes, and tried to remember where I was. It was still dark and quiet, yet something had disturbed me. My limbs felt heavy and my thinking was slow. I closed my eyes again.

Another sound, a movement close to me.

I remembered that I was in the summerhouse and that it was open on two sides. Possibly a breeze had gotten up and disturbed something. But the sound had been heavy, as if some living thing were in there with me. A fox? They sometimes crossed the garden.

Without otherwise moving, I opened my eyes. A faint light from the moon enabled me to make out a human figure—Geraldine, wearing a dark track suit. I wondered vaguely why she had come, but I was too weary to supply an explanation. I was too weary even to ask her.

I closed my eyes again.

A faint bubbling sound broke through my muzzy perceptions, as if liquid were being poured from a narrow-necked bottle. I looked, and that was exactly what was happening. Gerry was emptying the Courvoisier bottle, holding it upside down so that the contents tipped onto the floor. I registered that she must be drunk to do such a crazy thing. Too dazed to intervene, I observed her passively, as if watching a surrealist film too bizarre to interpret.

When the bottle was empty, Gerry turned, bent down, and picked up another that she must have brought in. She unscrewed it and began liberally dowsing everything, including the bed. I murmured a protest that came out as a Neanderthal-sounding series of grunts.

Geraldine ignored me. Next, she picked a cigar from the box she had left by the bed, put a match to it, and started smoking! Extraordinary—she never touched cigars. I watched her put it to her mouth and draw on it so that the tip smoldered and glowed. Then she crouched down and it was difficult to see her.

My eyelids drooped. It had been an effort to keep them open so long.

Sightless I may have been, but my sense of smell continued to function. I sniffed and caught the acrid whiff of smoke. It crept into my nostrils and made me open my mouth and cough. I heard a hissing sound. I opened my eyes and saw that the bed was on fire. Not merely the bed, but the entire floor was alight with trails of fizzing blue flame.

If I continue to lie here, I thought, I'm going to be incinerated with the summerhouse.

PART THREE

The Men in White Coats

1

THE INCIDENT ROOM in Manvers Street Police Station was not so crowded as the caravan had been. Paper clips no longer danced in their boxes each time Peter Diamond walked across the floor. Nor could the filing clerks feel his breath on the backs of their necks. Loose papers and file cards were not so likely to be brushed off the edges of desks. The carousel of filing cards, instead of dominating the room, had been relegated to a corner. Four Trojan horses—as Diamond dubbed them—in the form of computer terminals, stood on a table near the door. The Police Committee had decreed that no major inquiry should be without its computer backup, irrespective of the prejudices of one cantankerous detective. "We'll soon have them up and running, sir," Inspector Dalton, who came with the computers and four civilian operators, had rashly promised. To this, Diamond had responded, "Up where? Up yours, as far as I'm concerned."

Apart from that, the air of desperation beside the lake had been supplanted by confidence. They were working to a purpose now. In the hackneyed, but comforting phrase, a man was assisting the police with their inquiries. He had been in the interview room for an hour and a half.

Diamond and John Wigfull came out for a sandwich. Neither was wearing a jacket. The Last Detective was in his element. He had loosened his tie and unfastened the top button of his shirt. He didn't so much as glance at the computer screens. He expected all fresh developments in the case to come from the interviewing of Professor Jackman. With his weight securely deposited on a desk, he snapped open a can of beer and remarked to Wigfull, "You know what this amounts to—this story about the fire?"

Wigfull waited. He was no reader of minds.

"He's laying the foundations for his defense," Diamond said. "Mentally he's already in court, pleading mitigation. She tried to kill him on this previous occasion, so when it happened a second time, he defended himself. Didn't know his own strength. Panicked. Tried to get rid of the body by dumping it in the lake. See if I'm not right, John."

Wigfull's eyebrows were raised. "That isn't the way he told it yesterday."

Diamond was unmoved. "They always start by giving you the clean-as-driven-snow gambit. Left her sleeping peacefully and never saw her again. He's had plenty of time to concoct his story. That's only his first line of defense. He doesn't really expect to hold it long and he won't."

"You think he's ready to admit he killed her?"

"Not yet. Jackman's got a good head on his shoulders, remember. First, he wants to win us over and show himself in the best possible light. But this stuff about the summerhouse, this shows how his mind is working."

"You don't believe it, sir?"

Diamond said nothing, letting his silence make the point.

"The summerhouse *was* burned down," Wigfull pointed out.

"Agreed. Did he report it at the time? No. He can give it any slant he wants."

"Should we ask forensic to take a look at the site, see if the evidence bears out his story?"

"It's already in hand." Diamond couldn't help sounding smug. He enjoyed keeping mentally ahead of Wigfull, who was no idiot. With the air of an achiever, he tugged at the packet containing the egg and cress sandwich he had ordered. "Mind you, the lab will take weeks to come up with anything helpful. You and I can crack this today." Unable to find a way into the packet, he squeezed it. The result was a pulverized sandwich. Furious, he flung the whole thing at the nearest waste bin and missed.

"Want one of mine, sir—lettuce and tomato?" offered Wigfull.

"Rabbit food. Let's have another go at him. I need an early supper tonight."

"Are you going to caution him?"

A guarded look closed over Diamond's blunt features. "Is that advice, or what?"

Wigfull reddened. "I thought if we have reasonable grounds, we ought to issue the caution."

Diamond jabbed a finger against his assistant's shirtfront. "Don't ever tell me my job, Inspector. What I told you just now—about his guilt—was a gut feeling. If you and I are going to work as a team, you'd better get one thing straight: If I speak my thoughts aloud, that's my privilege. If I want yours, I'll bloody ask for them. Understood?"

"Understood, sir."

"I cautioned him last night, before he said a bloody word to me. Remind him when we go in."

Professor Jackman glanced down at his watch as they returned. He seemed so well in control that he might have been about to put the questions to them. On the desk in front of him was an empty mug and one biscuit, the last of a packet of three. Diamond reached for it and scooped it into his mouth in one rapid movement.

The constable taking shorthand slipped in unobtrusively behind them and took her place to the rear of Jackman, just as Wigfull was reinforcing the caution.

Diamond didn't waste time over small talk. "Getting back to the fire in the summerhouse, Professor, I take it that you got out without serious injury."

Jackman's response was even more to the point. "Yes."

"You managed to rouse yourself when you sensed the danger?"

"Not without difficulty. It took an exceptional effort."

"You're certain that you were drugged?"

"I'm convinced of it. She must have used the phenobarbitone she had from the doctor. God knows how many tablets she'd crushed and mixed in the sauce she gave me. If I hadn't made myself sick, as I told you, I wouldn't have recovered consciousness at all."

"You were lucky."

"You can say that again. In a matter of seconds I would have been incinerated. My shoes and trousers were smoldering when I got out."

"I suppose it's too much to hope that you kept them?"

"The shoes and trousers? I threw them away. They were no use anymore." His eyes narrowed. "You *do* believe what I'm telling you?"

Diamond answered equivocally, "I saw the burnt-out summerhouse." He leaned back in his chair and clasped his hands behind his neck. "What interests me, Professor, is what happened next. Your wife had tried to kill you. What did you do about it?"

"I was in no state to do anything. I flopped down on the lawn at a safe distance from the flames and watched the fire burn itself out. I still had some of the drug in my system and I must have fallen asleep, because the next thing I knew it was daylight and I was aching in every bone. Everything seemed like a dream except that I had in front of me the heap of ashes that had been the summerhouse. I went into the house to look for my wife. She'd behaved like a madwoman but she was no fool. She'd quit the place."

"How did you know?"

"Her car wasn't in the garage."

"So what did you do?"

"Slept a few hours more. I was still too muzzy to go looking for her. And when I came to, I started slowly clearing up after the party. I needed to occupy myself in a practical way."

Rebuking him mildly, as if remarking on a social gaffe, Diamond said, "You didn't notify us."

"You?"

"The police."

"I wanted Gerry's explanation."

"But you didn't know where she was. She could have killed herself. People frequently do after murdering a spouse."

Jackman said dryly, "People clever enough to dress up a murder as an accident don't spoil it by committing suicide. I knew she would come back."

Diamond exchanged a glance with John Wigfull. "You're telling us you just started clearing the dishes?"

Jackman rested his elbows on the table and leaned forward to make a point. "Look, I'm here of my own free will. I'm telling you what happened. I don't expect to have my behavior called into question."

With the air of a man whose behavior had been questioned too many times to matter anymore, Diamond commented, "We're simply trying to understand why things turned out as they did. Let's move on, shall we? When *did* you see your wife again?"

"The same day, early that evening."

"She came back to the house?"

"Yes." Jackman related the events with a directness that was vivid and convincing. "She didn't come into the house immediately. I watched her leave the car on the drive and walk around the side to the garden. She was wearing the black track suit that I remembered seeing her in. She stood for a moment staring at the gutted summerhouse. She didn't go too close to it, just stood about thirty yards away, fingering her hair. Then she turned and approached the house. She came in by the patio windows, which were still open." He smiled slightly. "Of course, she was shocked out of her skin when she saw me sitting in front of the TV with my feet up. She damn near passed out. I had to pour her a drink. I didn't accuse her right out. I wanted to see what she would make of it, so I asked where she'd been all day. She said she'd gone out early and spent the day on a deckchair in Parade Gardens catching up on her sleep. She said she couldn't face being in the house. Quite possibly she was telling the truth."

"And what happened when you *did* broach the little matter of the fire?"

"She denied it, naturally. Said I must have dreamed the bit about her coming into the summerhouse. She insisted that I must have dropped a lighted cigar and set light to the place myself—which you can bet is the story she would have put about if she'd succeeded in killing me. There's no chance that it was true," Jackman said quickly, as if sensing that he'd given them an opening. "In the first place, she definitely drugged me."

"Let's say that someone drugged you," said Diamond.

Jackman was quick to scotch that amendment. "Listen, Geraldine had the drug in her possession. She had the sauce put aside for me. She insisted on collecting it herself. She poured it all over the food. Within a short time of eating it, I was three parts slewed. She'd put the cigars and the spirits ready beside the camp bed in the summerhouse. It was all set up. And I'm certain it wasn't a dream when I saw her there because I noticed what she was wearing. She was still wearing that black track suit when she came back the next day."

"You mentioned that already. You've been over this many times in your mind, haven't you?"

Jackman nodded. "And the conclusion is irresistible."

"All right, professor," said Diamond cheerfully, as if he accepted every word of the story. "Why do you think it happened?"

"Why did she try to kill me?"

"Yes."

Jackman lodged his face ruminatively against his

hand. "I put it down to her mental state. As I explained, sometime before that evening she was showing symptoms of paranoia. She imagined I was plotting her downfall, or something. It was illusory, a fantasy, but plainly very real to her. I didn't appreciate how serious her mental state had become—until that night."

"Did she have any history of disturbance?"

"Only what I've described. I'm no psychiatrist."

"Paranoia," Diamond repeated, and with a gleam of mischief looked across at the constable taking notes. "Do you want the professor to spell that?"

The PC shook her head.

Diamond swung back to Jackman. "And how about you? Did you feel persecuted?"

Jackman tensed and drew back from the desk. "What?"

"Persecuted or threatened, at least. I should think you were entitled to feel like that after what happened."

"I wouldn't describe it in those terms."

"Would you care to describe it in your own terms, then?"

The professor hesitated, and when he spoke it was with reluctance, as if he were being drawn into alien territory. "Naturally there was a loss of trust on my part. I had to be on my guard in future."

"You thought you could look after yourself?"

"She wasn't going to rush at me with an ax, or something. At least, that's the way I saw it. A lot of planning had gone into the summerhouse incident, mainly to ensure that the killing would be passed off as an accident. She didn't want to be caught. If she plotted another attempt on my life, I thought I was capable of picking up the signals before it got really dangerous."

"Brave man," commented Diamond, without actually meaning it.

Jackman leaned forward to solicit more understanding. "When you've lived with a person, married them, shared their joys and disappointments, you've got to believe you have some influence, some hope of making sense to them. Okay, the magic had gone from our marriage, but we didn't have to destroy each other."

There was a silence. Neither Diamond nor Wigfull would say one word to deflect him from what sounded like the beginning of a confession.

Jackman appeared to see the expectation in their eyes, because he said, "I'll put that another way. I was willing to take my share of responsibility for what had happened. We'd made mistakes in our marriage. I'd alienated Gerry by failing to reach out to her mentally. The best thing I could do was try and remove the suspicions she harbored."

"Give her the benefit of the doubt?"

"There *was* no doubt," said Jackman flatly. "She tried to kill me and failed. The fact that I knew for certain was my safeguard."

Someone tapped on the door and opened it. Diamond wheeled around in his chair, ready to raise hell. He couldn't abide interruptions when he was interviewing a witness. But the intruder was the police doctor, accompanied by a constable carrying a kidney-shaped steel bowl containing a syringe and other items. "Ah," said Diamond, reconciled. He turned back to address Jackman, whose face was a study in disbelief and alarm. "I asked the doctor to step in. We'd like to take a sample of your blood for the forensic lab. It's a routine procedure. I take it we can rely on your cooperation?"

"Just a blood sample?"

Diamond grinned unkindly. "What did you expect —a truth drug?"

2

WHILE THE TWO DETECTIVES stood outside, Wigfull took
the opportunity to ask, "What's next?" His superior
wasn't much of a communicator.

"This." Diamond picked up a book and held it at
the level of his shoulder as if he were about to swear an
oath in court, except that the book had a laminated
cover of pink elephants. "Geraldine's address book."

"You want to go through the names?"

Diamond confirmed it with a grin. "With the help
of our friend in there, of course. Let's give him some
rope, John."

"And see if he hangs himself?"

"You're out of date, chum."

Wigfull nodded. Diamond's views on the death
penalty were well-known. He firmly believed Britain's
decline as a world power could be traced back to 1964,
the year of abolition. This wasn't the moment to get him
on that old hobbyhorse. "How will he give himself
away?"

"By pointing the finger at someone else."

"To sidetrack us, do you mean?"

"*Assist* us," Diamond said, affecting a pained look.
"We don't want to make any premature assumptions

about our professor, do we? He is cooperating to the best of his ability. You're a devious bastard."

"You're a sarcastic one," said Wigfull.

Diamond beamed.

When they returned to the interview room, they found Jackman buttoning his cuff, looking less self-assured than he had previously appeared. "Why did you want my blood?" he asked at once.

"You make me sound like a vampire," said Diamond. "I told you. It's standard procedure these days. Have you heard of genetic fingerprinting?"

"Yes, but what does it have to do with me?"

"There were traces of blood on the quilt of your wife's bed."

"I didn't notice any."

"They weren't very obvious."

After a pause that was open to several interpretations, Jackman asked, "Was she attacked in bed, then?"

"That's impossible to say yet. We don't even know if the blood was her own. There may be a perfectly innocent explanation if she scratched herself accidentally, as we all do from time to time. Or it may be significant. Either way, we won't know this side of next week. The forensic science lab isn't noted for quick results. And if your sample happens to match the bloodstains, I'm sure there's an innocent explanation. We can talk about it now if you want."

Jackman shook his head. "We'd be wasting our time."

"As you wish." Diamond dropped the address book on the table and they began the process of going through names. Whether anyone's address book is an indication of character is debatable, but Geraldine Jackman's was chaotic. For the few full names and addresses that appeared under each letter, many more were entered under forenames alone, often with no address listed, only a phone number. Some were circled or heavily underlined and many were scored through. Additional jottings had been added on most pages, times of trains, appointments, bank balances, and densely patterned doodles strung across the entries like an illustrated guide to cobwebs. A detective of the school of Sherlock Holmes would surely have deduced enough from those elaborate pages to convict the murderer and state exactly how the crime had been committed and when. Diamond's more workaday method was to observe Jackman's demeanor and listen to his comments as together the three men attempted to compile a list of Geraldine's friends.

Painstakingly, in the course of the next hour and a half, the task was completed—or as nearly completed as it was ever likely to be. By concentrating on local addresses and phone numbers, Jackman identified more than thirty of his wife's friends of the past two years. A scattering of names remained as mysteries, but his willingness to assist was not in doubt. He went meticulously through the book, interpreting the jottings. He could be faulted only in one respect. Inconveniently, he omitted to suggest that any of the names was a potential suspect.

Far from satisfied with the exercise, Diamond started probing. "When you were telling us about the barbecue, you mentioned an estate agent by the name of Roger, the character who was dancing with your wife."

"Yes. He's in here somewhere. Roger Plato." Jackman leafed through the pages. "Under 'R.' Two phone numbers, work and home."

Diamond reached for the book and peered at the entry as if he hadn't noticed it previously. "His wife isn't mentioned."

"As far as I know, she didn't go about with the Bristol crowd."

"She came to the barbecue, you said."

"Yes. I didn't know of her existence until that evening."

"But your wife knew, presumably."

Jackman gave a shrug.

Diamond snapped the book shut and said on a sudden aggressive note, "Was Plato sleeping with your wife?"

The attempt at a shock effect was too obviously stage-managed. Jackman showed that he was unimpressed and unruffled. "Isn't that a matter you should discuss with Roger rather than me?"

Diamond reverted smoothly to his more civil approach. "Let me phrase it differently, then. Did you suspect that he was sleeping with her?"

Paradoxically, this caused a flicker of annoyance. "No, I didn't. She wouldn't have been so obvious about it. She flaunted Roger like a new hat."

"Was there some other man?"

"I can't say. I simply do not know."

"Did you care?"

Jackman hesitated. "Yes."

"So the openness you talked about in your relationship didn't extend to taking lovers?"

At this stage in the interview the professor made a bid to seize the initiative by demanding, "Why are these questions necessary, Superintendent?"

Diamond answered candidly, "Because jealousy may be the motive I'm looking for."

"Jealousy on whose part?"

Unaccustomed to finding himself on the end of a sharp question, Diamond cast his eyes up to the ceiling and answered, "A wife who is being cheated, possibly."

"Or a husband?" said Jackman angrily. "You've made it plain enough that I'm your principal suspect, so why don't you say it?"

"Principal witness," Diamond insisted. "You're my principal witness up to now. I need your help. I'm not going to throw accusations at you when you're helping us." He reached for the address book again. "There are several names here that we passed over quickly. Andy. No surname. Bristol phone number. Did you meet a friend of your wife's called Andy?"

"No."

"Was anyone of that name at the barbecue?"

"I've no idea. I doubt whether I saw everyone who came."

"You mentioned stepping over someone in the

doorway who was using your Coronation biscuit tin as a drum."

"Silver Jubilee biscuit tin. I didn't discover his name."

Diamond tried another. "Chrissie—does that mean anything?"

"No."

"Fiona?"

"Look, if I'd recognized the names, I would have told you when we were going through the book. I thought I had made it abundantly clear already that we didn't live in each other's pockets. Gerry had a life of her own and I shared a part of it, just a part."

Diamond gave a tolerant nod and eased back in the chair. "Let's concentrate on *your* life, then. Take us through the weeks leading up to your wife's disappearance. How long was it after the barbecue that she went missing?"

"The barbecue was on August fifth. The last time I saw Gerry was Monday, September eleventh."

Diamond glanced at Wigfull, who made a mental calculation and said, "Just over five weeks."

"So how did you fill the time?"

Jackman gave an exasperated sigh. "For Christ's sake! I was working my butt off organizing a bloody exhibition."

The Jane Austen exhibition didn't interest Diamond. "What about your personal life? What was going on at home?"

"Nothing much. We were pretty suspicious of each other after what had happened. I think Gerry deliberately kept out of my way as much as possible—to let me get over it, I suppose. And I was getting in late."

"Did you continue to sleep together?"

"If you mean in the same bedroom, yes."

Wigfull put in, almost out of curiosity, "How could you relax, knowing she'd tried to kill you?"

"I felt safer knowing she was in the same room than if she were somewhere else in the house, where

God alone knows what she might have got up to." He made it sound reasonable.

Diamond, too, was making strenuous efforts to sound reasonable. "So this was the pattern of your life for the five weeks up to her disappearance: long days preparing the exhibition?"

"Correct."

"It can't have been very relaxing."

"Sometimes at the end of the day I went for a swim."

Diamond raised his finger. "Ah—I was going to ask about the swimming. You spoke earlier about the boy you rescued. What was his name?"

"Matthew."

"Yes. You invited him to the university pool."

"I mentioned it in passing," Jackman said. "I don't see why it should interest the police."

Diamond leaned forward on his elbows, covering his face in an attitude of fatigue or discouragement and ran both hands over his forehead and the bald curve of his head. "Professor," he finally said, "everything interests the police in an inquiry as serious as this. Everything."

With a slight shrug Jackman said, "Fair enough. Matthew came for his swim. He came a number of times. I would generally meet him outside the sports center about seven."

"With his mother?"

"She drove him up to Claverton, but she didn't join us. He and I had the pool to ourselves most evenings. I helped him lose some faults in his overarm style. He'll develop into a useful swimmer if he keeps it up."

Notwithstanding his declaration of a moment before, Diamond didn't want to know any more about Matthew's progress as a swimmer. What really intrigued him was the pretext that the swimming lessons must have given Jackman for regular contact with Matthew's divorced mother. He had noted how approvingly Jackman had spoken earlier of Mrs. Didrikson, even commenting on the beauty in her smile. "And when the swim was over . . . ?" he ventured.

"Mat went home."

"In his mother's car?"

"Most times."

"The exception being . . . ?"

"When I drove him home on a couple of occasions."

"Did you go into the house—for a coffee, or something?" Diamond added as if it scarcely mattered what the answer might be.

His casual air failed to woo Jackman, whose equanimity snapped. "For pity's sake! What are you driving at now? Do you want me to say the swimming was just a front for secret meetings with Mrs. Didrikson? Give me strength! This isn't 1900. If I really wanted to spend time with the woman, I wouldn't have to find some fatuous excuse."

"Perhaps you'll answer my question, professor."

"Perhaps you'll tell me what it can possibly have to do with my wife's death."

"That remains to be seen. Are you tired? Would you care for a break?"

Jackman sighed impatiently and said, "On two or three occasions I was invited in for a coffee. Is that what you wanted to know? And since you seem bent on pursuing this line of questioning, I took Mat to a cricket match at Trowbridge one afternoon and to a balloon festival at Bristol. I like the boy. I have no son of my own and it pleased me to spend some time with him. His mother was working on both occasions. Are you willing to believe that people sometimes act on innocent motives?"

"My beliefs don't come into it," said Diamond. "What about your wife? Did she mind you taking the boy to cricket and so on?"

"Why should she?"

"Perhaps with her suspicious mind she took it that you were making inroads with the boy's mother."

"Her suspicious mind, or yours?" demanded Jackman. "Look, Gerry was capable of twisting anything into a conspiracy, but don't forget that she invited Mrs. Didrikson to her barbecue in the first place, so she could hardly object if I exchanged a few civil words with the woman next time I happened to meet her. That's all it was. I haven't been to bed with her."

"How *was* your wife in those last five weeks of her life?"

"Her behavior, you mean? I didn't see a great deal of her. She spent the mornings lying in bed talking on the phone to her friends."

"Anyone in particular?"

"The entire galaxy, so far as I could tell. When we did meet she was pretty insufferable, either too moody to speak or spoiling for a fight—which I didn't give her."

"Was she like that with everybody?"

"No, she turned on the charm when the phone rang and it was one of her friends. She could be in a towering rage with me and then pick up the phone and say a sexy 'Hello, Gerry speaking,' before she knew who was on the end of it. That's the mark of a good actress, I suppose."

"What sort of things were you fighting over?"

Jackman clenched his fists and thumped them on the table. "How do I get this across to you fellows? *I* didn't fight. The aggression was all on her side. The issues were trivial. Example. The hand mirror from her dressing table went missing and she accused me of taking it. What would I want with an ebony-handled mirror from a woman's vanity set? I told her one of the women at the barbecue must have taken a fancy to it, but Gerry wouldn't accept that any of her friends was light-fingered. That's the sort of piddling thing she was getting agitated about. In the end to shut her up I offered her a shaving mirror I'd once used. She didn't need it. She had three adjustable mirrors fixed to her dressing table, another in the bathroom, and any number of wall mirrors around the house. But she told me she'd already been to the bathroom cabinet and helped herself to the shaving mirror. I didn't inquire what made a hand mirror so indispensable. In the mood she was in she wasn't amenable to logic."

"You're suggesting this was another symptom of the paranoia you mentioned?"

"I'm not suggesting anything. I'm stating what happened. I have neither the expertise nor the energy to go into her mental problems. How much longer do you propose to keep me here?"

Sidestepping the question, Diamond said, "I want to go over the last couple of days of your wife's life in detail. This is a useful time to take a break while you think about it. I daresay you could do with something to eat by now. I'll send someone out for sandwiches if you tell them what you'd like. Would you care for a warm drink or a beer?"

"I thought you served bread and water to people like me."

3

PETER DIAMOND removed his jacket and draped it over a filing cabinet, slipped his hands under his braces, and fingered the sweat on his shirtfront. The questioning had not developed as promisingly it should have done. This professor was turning out to be a stronger adversary than he had first appeared. There was progress of a kind—some of the replies were less guarded now—but Jackman was still mentally well defended. By declining to incriminate anyone else, he had resisted the lure that most guilty men would have accepted gratefully. Anyone in his position should have seized the opportunity to unload suspicion onto one of those names in the address book.

Far from discouraged, Diamond relished the challenge. At this stage, a tactical shift was indicated, a shift that might test the mettle of somebody else, as well as the professor. Without looking up from a copy of the evening paper that was on his desk, he told John Wigfull, "I think we should make this more of a two-hander from now on. You take him through the events and I'll catch him off balance when I see a good opening."

How satisfying was the jolt it gave to Wigfull, who had been quite resigned to a passive role. Diamond had always run his own show up to now, regardless of the fact that Wigfull had led at least two murder inquiries of his own before being assigned to this dubious role as understudy. It wasn't because he had a low opinion of the inspector's ability, rather the reverse. According to Wigfull's personnel record, he had joined the police at twenty-four, transferred to the CID in his second year, and worked his way swiftly through the ranks. He was the bright lad everyone had tipped for high office, the possessor of a degree from the Open University. He had breezed through the promotion exams and made the rank of inspector at a disgustingly early age. Then had the temerity to clear up a couple of domestic murders in Bristol. Bad luck for him that the Missendale report had exonerated Diamond, or he would certainly have been heading this inquiry by now.

"How are you holding up?" Diamond decently asked the professor when they returned to the interview room—and then spoiled it by showing that he had no interest in the answer. "The hours leading up to your wife's death: are you ready? Inspector Wigfull will be putting the questions." He rested an elbow on the table and sat chin in hand, like Nero in the Colosseum, prepared to be entertained by the contest.

Wigfull had taken the chair opposite Jackman. His curly mustache and widely set brown eyes made him appear less formidable than Diamond. He started in a tone that was mild to the point of diffidence, nodding briefly before saying, "If I have it right, sir, you said that you last saw your wife alive on Monday, September eleventh."

"Yes."

"Have you been able to recall anything at all of that weekend?"

"I'm unlikely to forget it," Jackman answered, but without irritation. "The 'Jane Austen in Bath' exhibition was officially opened by the mayor on that Saturday. I was racing around like the proverbial blue-arsed fly."

"Last-minute panics?"

"One, anyway. I'll come to that. In fact, everything

was in place by Thursday evening. I don't suppose either of you managed to see it, but I think it was a reasonable show. I won't say we filled the Assembly Rooms, but by some artful use of display stands and video equipment we managed to do interesting things with the space. There was some gratifying comment in the national press, and we made the local TV-news programs. But you don't want to hear about the exhibition."

"If it had any conceivable bearing on what happened . . ." said Wigfull.

There was a harsh intake of breath from Diamond and some ostentatious squirming on his chair. He could see the interview being sidetracked.

"I can't imagine how it could have played a part," Jackman admitted, keeping his eyes on Wigfull, "but Gerry's death is inexplicable to me, anyway. Shall I go through the weekend, as you asked? On that Friday, I spent most of the day at Heathrow meeting a weekend guest."

Wigfull's eyes widened. "You had a houseguest that weekend?"

Jackman answered casually. "He was Dr. Louis Junker, an American academic from the University of Pittsburgh. He's a specialist on Jane Austen, which is more than I can say about myself. Junker has published a number of papers on the novels and he's doing the research for a major biographical study. He got to hear about the exhibition and arranged his vacation around it. We corresponded through the summer and I invited him to spend the weekend of the opening with us. Unfortunately his plane was delayed six hours. Instead of arriving about ten A.M. on Friday, it came in at four. Good thing the exhibition was all set up the night before."

"Had you met Dr. Junker before this?"

"No, we'd merely corresponded. It's not uncommon for academics to offer to put colleagues up. I've enjoyed hospitality myself on my visits to America."

"Was he with you for the entire weekend?"

"Until Sunday. He attended the opening and

stayed all afternoon. Said a lot of generous things. I was run off my feet that day doing interviews and showing VIPs around, so I had to leave him to his own devices. Well, not quite. Gerry escorted him. She volunteered, much to my surprise, because she doesn't usually show much interest in what goes on at the university. She seemed to hit it off with Junker. I don't know what they found to talk about—she never opened a serious novel in her life."

"Was she acting normally?"

"Depends what you mean by normally. She could turn on the charm with other people. Her crazy out-bursts, when they came, were mostly directed at me." A sigh escaped from Jackman's lips, as if to chide himself for the bitterness he had just revealed. "Anyway, by Saturday evening, we were all exhausted. The exhibition closed at six and the three of us had a pub meal and came home. Sunday morning we spent quietly with the papers and then went to the local for a pint and a sand-wich."

"You and Dr. Junker?"

"Yes. Gerry lingered in bed as usual. She was up in time to see our guest leave. I drove him to the station about three-forty-five."

"You said something just now about a panic."

He nodded. "That happened later the same eve-ning."

"On the Sunday?"

"Right. I can't say whether this has any connection with Gerry's death. As a result of all the publicity before the exhibition, I'd been offered a number of items with Austen connections—a model of a ship once captained by Jane's brother Frank, some silhouette pictures of characters from the novels, early editions with special bindings, and so on. Most of it was unsuitable for my purposes, but on the eve of the exhibition I was made a present of two letters dating from the year 1800 that, if genuine, would cause a sensation in literary circles. They were apparently written by Jane Austen to her aunt Jane, who lived for some years in Bath."

"Some present!" Wigfull commented.

As if concerned that he might have overstated the importance of the letters, Jackman said, "They were quite short and they said nothing very startling, but their interest to scholars would be considerable. Obviously I couldn't put them on display without authentication. However, I was mightily excited about them, as you may imagine, and keen to add them to the exhibits if they proved to be genuine. Naturally I showed them to Dr. Junker. He knows Jane's handwriting better than I, and his opinion was that she had written them."

"Really? And how did you say you came by them?"

"They were handed to me by somebody who had seen me plugging the exhibition on TV. The donor didn't want any publicity, and I promised to respect that wish. I believe they were part of a batch of old letters sold by a philatelist for the postmarks. This was before postage stamps came in. Before envelopes were used. Letters would be written on one side of a sheet of paper, addressed on the other, then folded and sealed. The post office would frank them. People collect them for the postmarks, but they're not so sought after as are letters bearing Penny Blacks and other early Victorian stamps, and you can sometimes pick them up for peanuts."

"Unless they happen to have been written by a world-famous novelist."

Jackman permitted himself a fleeting smile. "You mean unless the seller is smart enough to know what he is selling. These were signed 'Your affectionate niece, Jane.' Janes were pretty thick on the ground in 1800. You'd need to know that Mrs. Leigh Perrot was Jane Austen's maternal aunt."

"What sort of price would a Jane Austen letter fetch?"

"Hard to say. There are about a hundred and fifty letters extant, and they rarely come up for sale. I think one could be sure of a five-figure bid in a London auction."

"I wonder if the donor had any idea of the value," Wigfull mused.

Jackman shook his head. "Highly unlikely. I intended to offer them back if they proved to be genuine."

His use of the past tense prompted Wigfull to say, "Something went wrong?"

Jackman looked sheepish as he admitted, "They went missing from my desk drawer. I should have had them under lock and key. Foolishly, I didn't. That Sunday evening, when I happened to go to the drawer, they weren't there. Of course I took everything out and went through all my papers. I pulled out the drawer to see if they had fallen behind it. I asked Gerry if she'd taken them out for any reason. She said she hadn't."

"She knew of the letters' existence?"

"Oh, yes. She was present when Junker examined them. Gentlemen, I felt sick to the stomach. I was damned sure somebody had been to that drawer and taken them. Of course I went through the house searching—I was at it until well after midnight—but there was no reason why those letters should have been anywhere but in the desk. Finally, I had a blazing row with Gerry and accused her of stealing them. It was bloody ironic— I must have sounded just as paranoid as she had when she'd accused me of tampering with her car and things like that. Quite a head case."

Diamond had contained himself admirably. Now he couldn't resist coming in with, "A blazing row? What do you mean by that? Did you knock her around?"

"No. I don't go in for violence." Jackman glared at him, affronted at the suggestion.

"When was this—Sunday night or Monday morning?"

"Monday, I suppose."

"You *suppose*?"

"I mean it must have been in the small hours. I told you I spent the whole evening looking for the letters."

"Where did this row take place—in the bedroom?"

Jackman's expression began to take on a hunted look. "Yes, as a matter of fact. She was already in bed."

"Asleep? You woke her up and accused her of stealing them?"

"Hold on," said Jackman. "She was still awake."

"You didn't take hold of her and shake her?"

"Absolutely not."

"A blazing row, you said."

"There was shouting. I said she must have taken them to spite me. I demanded to know where they were."

"Tell me precisely where you were standing when this exchange took place," demanded Diamond.

Jackman hesitated, frowning. "I don't know. I moved. I wasn't in the same position."

"Moved toward the bed?"

"Possibly. I didn't touch her, if that's what you're trying to get me to say. I didn't lay a finger on her."

"Not at that point?"

"Nor later."

"The next morning?"

"No."

"Sometimes, professor, people have blazing rows and don't remember very much of what they said and did." Diamond had switched to a more measured tempo. Interrogation ceases to be productive after a few minutes at the rhythm he had struck.

"That isn't the case," Jackman insisted. "I remember precisely what happened. We shouted some abuse at each other and she laughed at me, which only made me more angry. She said I deserved to lose the letters for not having locked them away. She was right, of course, but I didn't enjoy the way she rubbed it in when I suspected her all the time of having hidden them somewhere out of mischief or malice. After a while we just stopped talking to each other."

"Would you describe yourself as a man with a short fuse?" Diamond asked, reluctant to step down as the interrogator.

"What do you mean—a quick temper? No, I don't often lose control."

"But you did on this occasion."

"Only in the sense that I spoke my angry thoughts spontaneously. If I'd attacked her physically—which is what you seem to want me to say—do you think I'd be telling you this?"

Diamond gave a benign smile and commented, "Sometimes it's a relief to talk about it."

The response to that suggestion was that Jackman's mouth clamped shut, whereupon Diamond withdrew from the skirmish and gestured to his assistant with a lordly extended hand.

There was a pause. Then: "Did you consider the possibility," John Wigfull ventured, "that Dr. Junker had taken the letters?" It was as neat a way as any of restoring communication.

After sustaining his silence a moment longer, the professor consented to answer. "Of course it occurred to me later. Gerry was the obvious suspect, but I couldn't discount Junker. It's an unpleasant fact that academics aren't above stealing. They become so engrossed in a field of study that they consider it their right to acquire original documents and first editions, dishonestly if necessary. Every university librarian has horror stories of light-fingered researchers. To answer your question, yes, I began to believe that Junker couldn't be ruled out."

"But he'd left your house by then?"

"Hours before. As I told you, I'd driven him to the station in time to catch the four-twelve to Paddington. He was planning to visit Professor Dalrymple at University College on Monday, and then he was going on to Paris to begin his vacation. The more I thought about it, the more I convinced myself that I should go after him. So after not much sleep Sunday night, I got up early on Monday and caught a train to London."

"The eight-nineteen, you told us when you first reported her disappearance."

This small feat of memory by the inspector clearly impressed Jackman, if not Diamond.

"Yes."

"And that was the last time you saw your wife. Was she awake?"

Jackman tilted his head. "I told you that, too."

"What exactly was said?"

"I told her I was going after Junker, to ask about the letters."

Across the table, Diamond shifted in his chair and said, "That wasn't the way you put it to us. You said you had to see various people about the loan of manuscripts." A comment calculated to show that he, too, retained a memory of what had been said before.

Without turning to look at Diamond, Jackman said, "When I first spoke to you, I didn't think it would be necessary to bring up the business of the missing letters."

"You wanted to keep it to yourself?"

"If possible, yes."

Diamond commented to Wigfull, "Worth picking up these discrepancies. Carry on."

"What happened?" Wigfull asked the professor. "Did you catch up with Dr. Junker?"

"He didn't, after all, visit University College. He missed his appointment with Dalrymple, which made me suspicious. He'd phoned Dalrymple from Heathrow with some excuse about a late change in his flight arrangements to Paris, so I beetled off down to Heathrow with all speed and took the first flight I could to Paris."

"Did you know where he was staying?"

"No, and I knew he hadn't made a reservation, because he wasn't expecting to leave London before Tuesday, so when I arrived at Charles de Gaulle, I went straight to the Tourist Information Office at the airport and asked for their help. I said I needed urgently to find a colleague. He *had* called there and they'd sent him to a small hotel near the Sorbonne."

"Was he there?"

"Not when I arrived, but he had taken a room. I

booked in at the same place and settled down to wait for as long as necessary. Finally, about eleven, he came in. He was surprised to see me, but not obviously alarmed. I explained my reason for being there, putting it as delicately as I could that maybe the Jane Austen letters had got among his papers in error—an invitation, in effect, to return them to me, and no recriminations. I'd thought it through. I didn't want to bring charges. I just wanted those letters back."

"Did he have them?"

Jackman shook his head. "I'm satisfied that he didn't. If he *was* deceiving me, he did it brilliantly. He was troubled for me and yet sufficiently shocked that I could have suspected him of taking them. He invited me up to his room and we went through his luggage together. He turned out his pockets, his wallet, everything. I had to admit in the end that Geraldine must have taken them. I flew back the next day, meaning to get the truth from her—and of course she wasn't there."

"You didn't regard it as a police matter?"

"The theft of the letters? Who else could have taken them but Gerry? I believed I could get the truth from her without making it public. And I didn't want the donor of the letters to know that they were missing."

"You haven't given us the name of this generous benefactor."

"I told you. It's confidential."

Diamond said, "Come off it, professor. This is murder we're investigating, not kiss and run."

Adamantly, Jackman said, "I gave my word. That's it."

"There's such a thing as obstructing the police in the course of their inquiries, you know."

"I am not being obstructive. It has no direct relevance to Gerry's death."

"That's for us to decide."

"No," insisted Jackman. "The decision is mine."

4

"ANY QUESTIONS?"

Diamond eyed the CID officers assembled in the briefing room at Milsom Street. He expected no questions. His instructions had been plain enough. He wanted the interviews with the murdered woman's friends to establish when they had last seen her alive; when they had last spoken to her on the telephone; what had been said; and, finally—an invitation to the purveyors of gossip always encountered in such an exercise—whether they knew of any reason why she might have been murdered.

"Go to it, then."

Alone in the briefing room, Diamond turned to Wigfull. "You too, John. The boyfriend, Roger Plato. And his wife. What was her name?"

"Val."

He hadn't expected so immediate and confident a response. In a burst of bonhomie, he remarked, "Instant retrieval, eh? Why do we clutter the place with computers when we've got you? Take an hour off from the custody suite, John, and see what you can get out of the Platos. They're too important to leave to boys straight out of training school."

As a good detective, Wigfull was bound to respect

the reasoning behind the command, but he was plainly unhappy at being shunted to other duties. "What about the professor? We haven't finished with him, have we?"

"He can stew for a bit," Diamond said airily.

The prospect of the professor stewing for any appreciable time failed to satisfy Wigfull. "He was getting wrought up in there. He's free to leave unless we formally arrest him."

"He's torn, isn't he?" said Diamond. "He doesn't want to be uncooperative. That could go against him later."

"We've had twenty-four hours of his cooperation."

"And barely scratched the surface. There's more to come, depend upon it."

"Will you arrest him, then?"

"Would *you?*"

In the minds of both men were the time limitations set out in the Police and Criminal Evidence Act. An officer of Diamond's rank was entitled to detain a suspect for up to thirty-six hours without charging him, after which a magistrate's warrant would have to be obtained.

"I'd want to see the lab report first," said Wigfull.

"We won't get that tonight."

Wigfull said flatly, "He won't spend another night with us."

"And if we let him walk out of here," said Diamond, "he could do a runner."

After a moment's further thought, Wigfull said, "We can check whether he was on that flight to Paris on September eleventh."

"That's already in hand."

"And the University College professor—Dalrymple?"

"Boon is dealing with it."

"So what's the plan, sir?"

Diamond avoided a direct answer. "The case is stacking up nicely. Opportunity: Plainly—he was in the house with her. Motive: The marriage was on the rocks and she was bloody dangerous by his own account."

"It doesn't justify killing her."

"I'm not postulating a cold-blooded killing." Diamond's irritation sounded in his voice. "It's most likely to have happened during a violent argument. Those letters went missing, and—rightly or wrongly—he accused her of stealing them. A woman with fire in her belly isn't going to take that sort of abuse. She lashes out. If it *was* a violent row that Sunday night and he stuffed a pillow over her face and killed her, he'd know that it was curtains for his career—unless he disposed of the body. He put it in the car and drove to the lake and dumped it there after removing the clothes and the wedding ring. Next day, to establish some kind of alibi he behaved as if his wife was still alive and he suspected the American of stealing the letters."

The explanation, compelling as it was, appeared not to have swept up Wigfull in its wake. "If the letters were the cause of the argument that resulted in her death, why did he mention them to us?"

"Because he's a clever bugger, John. The way he tells it, they're his alibi. I've no doubt he was telling the truth when he said he flew to Paris and saw Dr. Junker. I'll bet you a double whiskey if we can trace Junker he'll testify that the conversations took place exactly as Jackman described them. And has it occurred to you," Diamond said, smoothly disguising the fact that it had only just dawned on him, "that the missing letters could be one enormous red herring? He could have killed her for some totally different reason."

"That is a possibility," Wigfull generously admitted.

Diamond nodded, drew closer, and thrust a fat finger in front of the inspector's face. "I've given you opportunity." A second finger sprang up. "I've given you motive. And now" a third finger—"his conduct. He behaved like a guilty man, waiting over two weeks—until after the corpse was discovered—before reporting that she was missing. Why? Because he hoped she would sink to the bottom of the lake and stay there. Once she was found and we put her picture on the telly, he had no

option but to come forward. People were certain to recognize the actress who played Candice Milner."

"Even the murder squad, eventually," murmured
Wigfull.

The irony didn't deflect Peter Diamond. "He'd had
plenty of time to concoct a story. It's not bad, but it's far
from perfect. He's scared out of his shoes by the prospect of what the lab will come up with. Did you see his
face when the doctor came in to take the blood sample?
That could nail him well and truly."

"The men in white coats have their uses," Wigfull
remarked.

Diamond gave a half smile. "As a last resort, yes.
They may even prove that his car was used to transport
the body. So, being an intelligent man, Jackman lays the
foundations for a fallback position—impresses upon us
what a nutter Geraldine was, and how dangerous she
had become. If the forensic evidence proves beyond
doubt that he smothered her and dumped her in the
lake, he's all ready to plead that he was provoked past
endurance. He'll get a nominal sentence." The way Diamond spoke the last words left no doubt of his views on
lenient sentencing.

It was an intriguing test of Wigfull's true role in the
investigation. Was he really only there in reserve, as the
Assistant Chief Constable had asserted, or was he supposed to prevent an outbreak of intimidation? If so,
Diamond had set him a problem. In the time it would
take Wigfull to get to Bristol and obtain a statement
from the Plato couple, Diamond was capable of tyran-
nizing the professor into a confession. More by accident
than design, the language he had just been using was
spiked with aggression: so many of the terms he had
used to analyze Jackman's situation were physical. *He's
torn . . . scared out of his shoes . . . Did you see his
face?*

"If you're planning another session with him, I'd
like to be present," Wigfull stated resolutely.

"No problem," Diamond airily said. "I'll wait for
you."

"But will *he?* I could interview the Platos later."

A grunt of dissent from Diamond. "The whole point of the exercise is that everyone is interviewed at the same time. We don't want one set of friends phoning another to warn them that the rozzers are on their way and tell them the questions they have to answer. Roger Plato is a big cheese, John. He's yours, right?" He pushed a piece of paper at Wigfull. Upon it the addresses of all of Geraldine Jackman's friends had been listed.

With undisguised reluctance, Wigfull took the paper and looked for the address of the Platos.

Diamond yawned, stretched, and said, "I might go out for a breath of fresh air."

He walked with Wigfull through the reception area. Immediately a group of people who had been sitting in a huddle got up and surrounded them. The press.

"Any developments, Mr. Diamond?"

"None at all. Why don't you get off home? I intend to, quite soon."

"You're interviewing a man? Are you holding him?"

"Will you be charging him?"

"We're interviewing anyone able to help."

The detectives made their way out to the forecourt where the cars were parked. Wigfull got into his Toyota, started up, and drove out.

Diamond watched him go. Then he turned and marched briskly back up the station steps.

5

DIAMOND MARCHED through the incident room without a word to anyone. Information was flowing in at a rate that kept six civilian clerks and the computer operators fully occupied. A heap of action sheets and computer printouts awaited inspection, but there was a higher priority for the man in charge. He was confident that he could extract a confession before John Wigfull returned from Bristol.

He pushed open the door of the interview room.

Jackman, on his feet in a stance that was assertive, if not actually combative, his face taut, obviously primed for the third degree, said, "Look, I'd like to have something clear from you. Am I under arrest, or what?"

"*Arrest?*" Diamond repeated, as if the word were unknown in the modern police.

"I came here of my own free will, to help you. I could walk out."

Diamond conceded the truth of this with a nod. "But I'd rather you didn't. We haven't cleared everything up yet, have we?" He felt profoundly encouraged that his man had become so tense. The laid-back academic had been a difficult adversary.

Jackman's expression had darkened. "What else is there? I've told you everything I know."

Diamond smiled benignly. "You've been extremely helpful, sir." A deferential touch that heralded a significant change of tactics. "Did I say earlier that my name is Peter, by the way? I wouldn't mind making this more informal now that we're alone."

The offer drew a hollow laugh from Jackman. "Informal?" His eyes traveled scornfully over the acoustic wall linings.

"We haven't been taping the conversations," Diamond was able to say truthfully. "Wouldn't do it without telling you. That's why the girl was taking notes." He paused briefly to make certain that the shorthand writer's absence was fully appreciated. "If you want to move somewhere else, it can be arranged. I would have suggested an evening stroll outside, but we'd have the press for company. You know how they are, Gregory."

Jackman, already unsettled by this outbreak of bonhomie, winced at the mention of his name. "Greg, if you must."

"Sorry . . . Greg."

Diamond might have been talking to his oldest friend. Contrary to the rumors that had circulated after his transfer to Avon and Somerset, he didn't actually bully suspects into submission. He was more subtle. He liked to win their confidence. When he judged that the moment was right, his normally abrasive manner gave way to a charm that was difficult to resist after hours of interrogation. By that stage, a smile from Peter Diamond was more productive than a clenched fist. He had believed at the time that this was how Hedley Missendale had been coaxed into confessing; the lad had appeared so bemused that he'd poured out the story as if he were proud to join the company of Bonnie and Clyde and holdup murderers in general. In Diamond's book, that isolated mistake hadn't destroyed the effectiveness of the technique.

"You'll have to forgive me for some of the things I said earlier," he went on in the same companionable vein. "In my job you get so obsessed with the facts of a case that human considerations get pushed aside. I mean, it's easy for me to overlook the fact that you came here as a volunteer, to render assistance."

"Which I have rendered to the point of exhaustion," said Jackman acidly. He seemed to find the charm resistible.

Diamond nodded. "Too true. You could probably do with another coffee, Greg."

"Is this where you soften me up before your sidekick comes back and puts the boot in?"

This brought a smile of genuine amusement from Diamond as he savored the notion of John Wigfull, Mr. Clean from headquarters, laying into a suspect. "He's gone to Bristol to talk to a witness."

"It was meant as a joke," said Jackman unconvincingly.

Diamond grinned again. "I'm beginning to understand your sense of humor."

"I think I would like that coffee."

"Fine. Let's go down to the canteen. I don't know about you, but I'm famished." He looked at his watch and picked up the phone. "Do you mind?" he asked Jackman. "I ought to have phoned before this. She's used to this, but she likes to be told." He pressed out a number. "Me," he said presently into the mouthpiece. "How's it going? . . . I'm not quite sure, my love, but soon as I can. What are you up to yourself? . . . I'd forgotten it was on. . . . Well, yes, of course, but don't wait for me." He replaced the phone and said to Jackman, "She's watching football. When I'm at home and want to look at it, she complains. I'll never understand women."

He deliberately pursued this theme at some length downstairs over toasted sandwiches and coffee, to a background of old Beatles' songs and a noisy card game in one corner led by a former sergeant, now employed as a civilian computer operator. Once or twice Diamond's reminiscences of quirky women he had met succeeded in relaxing the muscles at the side of Jackman's face, the next thing to raising a smile. Encouraged, he went on to talk disarmingly of his difficulties courting

Stephanie, his wife, who when they had met had been Brown Owl to the local troop of Brownies. He had visited them in Hammersmith as a community involvement officer, to instruct them in road safety, and had been enchanted by their winsome leader. A fuse had been lit that evening, and almost every spark and splutter in the consequent relationship had been witnessed by little girls in brown uniforms.

"I must have been bloody dedicated to put up with it," he recalled. "Steph had to take me seriously when I turned up to the summer camp with a couple of donkeys. The desk sergeant at Hammersmith had opened a sanctuary for old donkeys after he retired. He was a good mate. I think those donkeys swung it for me. Steph and I got engaged soon after. I was slimmer in those days." He grinned. "Relatively. Well, I could sit astride a donkey without someone complaining to the RSPCA."

He paused, crammed the last of the sandwich into his mouth, and asked, "Do you believe in love, Greg?"

"In *love?*"

Diamond nodded. "Is there such a thing, or are we all deluding ourselves? Is it just a con trick by songwriters and authors? Desire I can understand. Admiration and respect. But love is something else. I mean, did you love Geraldine when you married her?"

Jackman gave him a long look. "Is this what you've been leading up to? You want to know more about my relationship with my wife? Why didn't you come straight out with it?"

"Skip it, if you feel like that," Diamond responded, piqued. "I'm only trying to find some common ground."

"Peter, my old chum," Jackman said sarcastically, "if it's going to get you off my back, I'll tell you anything." He cleared his throat and said, "I'd better rephrase that. If there are things you want to ask, let's get them over with. I want to get home tonight. Yes, I believe I loved her. Later we ran into problems, but I retained some tender feelings toward her. Does that cover it?"

"Apart from her good looks, what was her appeal?"

"I thought we'd been over this. I was flattered that she seemed to prefer me to the glamorous TV people she worked with."

"That isn't love."

"Look, what are you trying to prove now—that I'm devcid of human feelings . . . some sort of psychopath? Do you have some theory about murder that you want to slot me into? I loved Gerry because she was like no one else I'd ever met. She was witty, observant, brave, and optimistic. In a unique and mysterious way, her mind was in touch with mine. The same things amused and delighted us. Will that do?"

The tribute was brief, but convincing.

"And then it went wrong," Jackman continued. "Catastrophically wrong. That precious contact between our minds was lost. I don't know why. Up to a point I can understand—her career falling apart—but why she turned on me as if I was the enemy, I'll never know. With her friends she was still the same Gerry, bubbling over with vitality. Not anymore with me."

"She made your life intolerable," Diamond prompted. "You made that clear."

"No," Jackman was quick to correct him. "Not intolerable. I didn't use that word. The point is that I *did* tolerate her."

"That'll teach me to feed words to a professor of English," said Diamond wryly, not wanting to stem the flow. "Let's just say that she was being difficult. Why didn't you divorce her, Greg? Wasn't that the obvious way to deal with the problem?"

"You're still implying that I solved the problem by killing her."

"I didn't say that."

"You didn't have to." He pushed away the plate with his half-eaten sandwich. "If you want to know, I wasn't opposed to divorce, nor was Gerry. I think we both knew that we were traveling rapidly down that path, but we hadn't discussed it."

"Why not?"

"First you've got to remember that we'd only been married two years. Okay, I'd seen astonishing changes in Gerry's personality in that time, but I could understand why. She'd been through a traumatic time, having to leave the BBC, pull up her roots, and come and live in the country with me. It wasn't the way we'd planned to lead our lives. Maybe I was being naive, but I was convinced that the woman she had become wasn't the real Gerry. She needed more time to adjust to being an ordinary human being instead of a media figure." His eyes darted left and right, signaling a disclosure more profound. No one else in the canteen could have heard anything over "She Loves You." "This is going to sound dumb, but I sometimes felt as if some demon had taken possession of her. If I could have exorcised it, we might have saved our marriage. To come back to your question, I didn't talk to her about divorce because I didn't want to abandon her. The love we had felt for each other ought to have got us through the crisis."

"You still had blazing rows."

"Of course—she was bugging me at every opportunity."

"Did you kill her, Greg?"

"No."

Question and answer, straight out.

"Without premeditation, I mean."

"Ah." Jackman opened his eyes a fraction wider. "That's the bait, is it? Manslaughter, rather than murder."

"You've studied the terminology, then."

"I do read other things, besides Milton and Shakespeare. No, Mr. Diamond, I won't settle for manslaughter. I'm not settling for anything you suggest. If you want to stitch me up, that's going to be your mistake entirely. Don't expect me to conspire in it."

Diamond ground his teeth. For a moment he didn't trust himself to go on.

"Speaking of writers," Jackman added, "I think it was a character in a Joe Orton play who said that policemen, like red squirrels, must be protected. Your bushy tail could be at risk if you make a mistake over me."

How it had happened so swiftly, Diamond was uncertain, but there was no denying that the interview had been turned around and he was on the defensive now. An unpleasant suspicion crept into his mind that this smartmouthed professor knew about the Missendale case. Maybe the thought was timely; the temptation to pound the truth out of him had to be suppressed at all costs.

Instead he swallowed his pride and turned for support to the men in white coats. "You can't buck the lab reports. If you killed her, the forensic evidence will stitch you up, as you put it, not me. Your blood, fingerprints, the samples from your car. I'm willing to wait a few more hours."

"What does my car have to do with it?"

"The body must have been transported to the lake by some means." He thought as he heard himself saying these things, I'm losing my grip. I was supposed to be charming the truth from him, not scaring him rigid.

"I'm allowed to have fingerprints on my own car," Jackman said, frowning.

"Yes, but if, for example, some human hair was found in the trunk and proved beyond doubt to have been your wife's, you would have some questions to answer."

Jackman looked dubious. "Can they identify hair like that?"

"It isn't the hair itself," Diamond backtracked. "It's the microscopic particles of skin attached to the roots."

"*Did* they find any hairs?"

"They're very assiduous. They find all sorts of dust and debris."

"You *are* going to stitch me up."

"You should stick with Milton and Shakespeare, Greg. You're way off beam."

Jackman said defiantly, "You have a hunch that I killed her, and you won't let go."

The whole tone of the conversation had changed irreversibly. Diamond shook his head slowly for a measured interval, conveying the message that he had more than a hunch, infinitely more.

Jackman said, "How do I convince you that you're wrong?"

"You begin by explaining why you waited almost three weeks before notifying us that your wife was missing."

"I should have thought that was obvious."

"Not to me."

"I wasn't surprised to find she'd gone. She'd stolen the Jane Austen letters and was unwilling to face me with the truth."

"Where did you think she was?"

"With some friend or other. She wasn't short of bolt holes."

"Did you phone around?"

"I tried the obvious people and got nowhere. It was quite possible that she'd asked them not to tell me anything."

"But you didn't report to us that she was missing. You didn't even report that the letters were missing."

"Because I wanted to deal with it myself," Jackman insisted. "I was certain that she'd taken them. If I ran straight to the police and branded her as a thief, what was that going to achieve? I didn't want the story getting to the newspapers." His answers were sounding plausible, disturbingly plausible.

"How *did* you deal with it—apart from phoning her friends?"

"I thought she might try to get the letters valued, so I made inquiries at auctioneers and dealers in the West Country as well as London. Again, I drew a blank."

"Let's get this clear," said Diamond. "You're telling me now that you expected her to sell the letters? You told us earlier that you thought she must have taken them out of malice."

Jackman nodded. "That was my first assumption. I didn't think their cash value was of any importance to

Gerry. She wasn't short of funds, so far as I was aware. Then a few days after she'd gone, her bank statement arrived. I opened it in hopes of getting some clue to her whereabouts. She was overdrawn almost three thousand pounds."

"Overdrawn?"

"I found her credit-card statement and she was carrying a fifteen-hundred-pound debt there. She'd run right through her money."

"How?"

"Most of it was signed out to cash amounts. She was borrowing money on the credit card, which is plain stupid at the rates they charge."

"Yes, but what would she have spent so much money on?"

Jackman lifted his shoulders in a gesture of uncertainty. "Living it up with her so-called friends."

"Running through a fortune?"

"I don't know if you could call it a fortune. I had the impression she was very well off when we met. The television money was good, and there were plenty of extras."

Footsteps clattered on the tiled floor. One of the constables from the incident room crossed the canteen and put an end to the conversation by telling Diamond that he was wanted urgently on the phone.

"Who is it?"

"Inspector Wigfull, sir."

"From Bristol?"

"Yes."

"Bloody better be urgent. Wait here with the professor. I'll be back shortly."

Cursing Wigfull under his breath for having the gall —he was damned certain—to check up on him, he snatched up the phone when he got to the interview room. "Yes?"

"Mr. Diamond?" John Wigfull's voice was tense.

"Who else?"

"I just spoke to the Plato couple. They told me something I think you ought to know right away, sir. On the day Professor Jackman last saw his wife—the Monday—she phoned the Platos sometime between ten and ten-thirty."

"In the morning?"

"You see the point, sir? If Jackman caught the eight-nineteen to London, as he claimed, and then went on to Paris, he couldn't have killed her. She was alive after he left. Mr. Diamond—are you there?"

Diamond dropped the phone without answering. He shouted across the room, "Sergeant Boon!"

"Sir?"

"Did you check the professor's movements as I asked?"

"Yes, sir."

"With what result? Come on, man!"

"It all checks out, sir. He saw Professor Dalrymple at University College, London, sometime before eleven on September eleventh and he was on the 1410 Air France flight from Heathrow to Paris."

For a moment Diamond had the look of a deflating balloon. Then he managed to say in a small voice, "Have a car at the back door directly. The professor is going home."

6

THE FIRST FROST. People had talked all summer of the damaged ozone layer and the greenhouse effect, unable to accept that weeks of steady sunshine were possible in the English climate. Now normality was restored. On this chill morning the geraniums in the window boxes of Bath had a wan, defeated look that Peter Diamond noted with a cynical eye as he waited in a traffic queue on his way up Manvers Street toward the police station. This year the Parks and Gardens Department had spared no effort in trying to wrest the title of top floral city from Bath's main rival, Exeter. Every sill, ledge, and surface had been stacked with pots, even the roofs of the bus shelters. Not a lamppost had been without its hanging basket. Such enthusiasm! Such commitment! To no avail; Exeter had retained the title. Bath's abundant flowers were losers.

Diamond, too much the policeman to take a few wilting geraniums as his text for the day, still wished someone would cart them away.

The bus ahead slowed as it approached a stop. Diamond moved out to pass it, only to discover that the entire line of traffic in front had stopped. Not a promising start to the day, stuck out there, obstructing the opposite lane. Fortunately someone behind flashed his headlights and backed a few yards. Decent of him. Diamond shunted back into line and looked in the rearview mirror to see who the Good Samaritan was. A fellow in a Toyota. Big mustache, wide grin. John Wigfull, of all people. Probably thinking what a dumbo his superior was for failing to notice that the bus was one of the bright yellow open-top double-deckers for tourists. Every kid in Bath knew that the city tour buses didn't use the regular stops.

He switched on the radio, and after the crackle as the automatic aerial went up (he hadn't wiped it clean for weeks), he heard the news reader saying, "Detectives are today expected to step up the hunt for the murderer of Geraldine Snoo, former star of the long-running BBC television serial *The Milners*, whose unclothed body was recovered from Chew Valley Lake this weekend. She was identified by her husband, Professor Gregory Jackman, of Bath University, who is understood to have given the police—"

"—a pain in the bum," Diamond muttered as he switched off.

The bus ahead started moving again, giving the full view of its back end. To underline its commitment to tourism, the company had given names to each of the buses, chosen from the city's illustrious past. Diamond had just noticed what this one was called. It was the *Jane Austen*. Much more of this and he would feel that the gods were mocking him.

Almost too late, he spotted the entrance to the police station and spun the wheel violently without giving a signal. A good thing it was only Wigfull who was following.

Neither man referred to the incident when, soon after, they were joined in Diamond's office by Halliwell, Croxley, and Dalton. A crime conference, so-called; let no one suggest that the murder squad was up a gum tree. Up a ladder was more like it—that stone ladder on the front of the Abbey, clinging rigidly to their positions. And now four rising detectives had better chip in some ideas, and fast.

Diamond decided on a low-key opening. "More forensic reports . . . for what they're worth," he told them first. "The men in white coats are still hedging over the date of death, but September eleventh looks the strongest bet. She was certainly dead before she got into the lake—as if we didn't know. And asphyxia remains the most likely cause of death. Damn all there." He snatched up a second sheet. "This is the report on the cars, Jackman's and the victim's. No indication that either was used to transport the body. No significant traces or fibers. Either the murderer was useful with a vacuum cleaner or we're looking for another vehicle." Muttering, he turned to a third lab report. "Blood groups. The victim was Rhesus Positive O and so was her husband. You'll recall that someone found traces of blood on the quilt. They proved to be too minute to analyze in preliminary tests."

"The heat's off the prof, then," Keith Halliwell observed, and must have wished he hadn't after the glare he got from his superior. He doubled his rate of chewing. Everyone on Diamond's murder squad needed some recipe for survival; young Halliwell's was to fantasize that he was a case-hardened New York cop. He was never seen in anything but leather and denim.

Diamond returned his eyes to the sheet of paper in his hand. "It says here that the blood sample on the quilt has been sent for DNA analysis—genetic fingerprinting—which ought to please the press boys, if no one else."

This prompted Croxley, usually the most reticent of the DIs, to speak up in the name of science. "It is an infallible identity test."

"And bugger all use to us unless we find a suspect with a matching profile," snapped Diamond.

Croxley turned pink.

Halliwell rashly tossed in a suggestion in support of Croxley. "Okay, so if they get a profile from the blood on the quilt, we keep sending in blood samples until we get a match, like they did for that rape-and-murder case in the Midlands."

Mercifully, Wigfull beat Diamond to the draw. "Come off it, Keith. If you're talking about that case in Leicester, there isn't a chance in hell of us mounting a similar exercise. The police up there were working within quite narrow parameters—looking for a male, between seventeen and thirty-four, in three small villages, about four and a half thousand men—and that took months to complete. We don't even know the sex of our killer."

Dalton said, "The reason they finally caught the bloke was that somebody talked. He fiddled the test. Persuaded some other berk to take it for him."

"If you've quite finished," Diamond said morosely, "I wouldn't mind talking about the case in hand. I may be an incurable optimist, but what I propose for this morning is a brainstorming session."

That silenced them all.

He took his time measuring the effect of the announcement before resuming. "First, let's have an update. Yesterday evening's interviews. Mr. Dalton, would you report?"

Dalton, who was responsible for the computer backup, stared in horror. "We haven't processed them yet, sir."

"Why is that?"

"It's too soon."

"I thought this all went on computer." Diamond glanced about him as if in need of advice, really just taunting the hapless inspector, who was so desperate to impress that he made an easy target. "We have umpteen thousand quids' worth of hardware in there. Why don't we have a printout in front of us?"

"The data has to be keyed in first, sir."

"You don't have to hammer us with jargon. I thought the main advantage of using the blasted things was to speed up the investigation."

"It is, Mr. Diamond—but the input is a manual function."

"Skip it, then. I've already cast an eye over the reports myself. I found nothing remarkable"—he paused —"with one notable exception."

For a moment it seemed as if no one was willing to provide Diamond with the cue he wanted. Then Inspector Croxley found the silence too stressful. "What was that?"

Diamond announced in a throwaway tone, "As a result of one of the interviews, we have learned that Geraldine Jackman was still alive on the morning of Monday, September eleventh. She made a phone call. John, be so good as to repeat what you learned from Mr. and Mrs. Plato."

"Well, it appears that—"

"No," Diamond interrupted him. "Facts, if you don't mind, not appearances."

A ripple of tension showed in Wigfull's jaw as he made another start. "Mrs. Valerie Plato told me that she took a call sometime between ten and ten-thirty. The caller claimed to be Geraldine Jackman."

"Is there any doubt?" Diamond pounced on the possibility.

"Not so far as I'm aware, sir," Wigfull said tightly. "But I don't know for a *fact* that the voice on the phone was Geraldine's. I have to take the Platos' word for it."

"Go on."

"She asked to speak to Roger, the husband. He was at home that morning. Roger Plato came to the phone, and his wife remained in the room. At this point, with your permission, sir, I should like to refer to my notes."

Diamond couldn't be certain whether this was deliberate sarcasm. Nobody was so foolhardy as to smile.

Notebook open, Wigfull continued, "Mrs. Jackman stated that she was sorry to be a nuisance, but she needed some help. She said there had been a spot of bother with Greg—Professor Jackman—and she needed to get away from the house for a few days, to clear the air, as she put it. She wanted to know if she could come and stay with the Platos. Well, Valerie Plato was at her husband's side and she made it very clear that she wasn't having that woman under her roof."

"Why not?" Halliwell asked. His ignorance was excusable. As the least experienced officer, viewed with suspicion for his quasi-American style, he had been delegated a series of doorstepping jobs that had kept him out of the incident room all week.

"Plato had been knocking around with her," Wigfull answered.

"Is 'knocking' the operative word?"

"Valerie Plato thought so. Roger strongly denies it."

"With a name like his?"

"Actually I believe him," said Wigfull. "I questioned him separately. He said it wasn't that serious, just a pairing-off because their respective spouses didn't usually go to the parties. He said Gerry Jackman wasn't looking for a lover."

"Maybe Valerie Plato sized it up differently."

Diamond said irritably, "We could spend the rest of the morning saying maybe. Get back to the phone call."

"That was it, really," said Wigfull. "Plato told Gerry Jackman it wasn't convenient for her to come and stay, and she rang off."

"In an angry frame of mind?"

"Apparently not. She must have guessed she was on a loser when Valerie picked up the phone first."

"And that was all she said about the row with Jackman, that she'd had a spot of bother and wanted to get away from him to clear the air?"

"Yes. She didn't sound unduly distressed, according to the Platos."

"Did she phone anyone else after that? What did we get from the other interviews last night?" Croxley asked in his west of Ireland accent.

"Bugger all," said Diamond in the less lilting sound of south London.

"So the call to the Platos was the last evidence that she was alive?"

"The last we have." Diamond spread his hands, inviting contributions.

An uneasy silence. If brains were storming, the lightning was slow to strike.

He scanned the faces. "In that case, gentlemen, in the absence of anything more brilliant, it looks as if we're forced to fall back on the Diamond method of investigation—good, old-fashioned knocking on doors. "Get your lads out to Widcombe, Halliwell. I want reports on everything and everybody seen in the vicinity of John Brydon House on Monday, September eleventh. Check the neighbors, the milkman, the newspaper boy, the postman. Got it?"

"Sir."

"Well, what are you waiting for?"

Halliwell left the meeting fast, no doubt with a sense of relief.

"And now what else?" Diamond demanded of the rest of his team.

"I could be out of order here, sir," Dalton guardedly prefaced what he was about to suggest, "but I think it's worth finding out how Valerie Plato spent the rest of that day. Rightly or wrongly, she seems to have been suspicious of Gerry Snoo's intentions, this famous television star making a pitch for her husband. The call could have made her pretty desperate when she heard Gerry openly asking to move in with them."

Diamond turned to Wigfull. "He thinks the Plato woman is a suspect. What do you say to that?"

"It's not impossible. She's the quiet type, reasonable looking, but not what you'd call glamorous. She *may* have panicked in a fit of jealousy, I suppose."

"Does she have an alibi?" Dalton asked.

"Does she have a car?" said Diamond.

"A car, yes. A Volvo. Being in the property business, they're quite well off. He drives a Rover. As for her alibi, they were both at home until about one, and then Roger left to do a valuation. Valerie went shopping in the afternoon."

"No alibi," said Dalton.

"Hold on," said Wigfull. "If she went shopping, presumably people in the shops will have noticed her."

"And if she went to a supermarket?"

"She may have kept the till receipt."

Dalton shrugged and withdrew from the discussion.

"How was she when you spoke to her?" Diamond asked Wigfull. "Did she appear nervous?"

"Not particularly. Reserved."

"And the husband?"

"He was more jumpy, but then he would be, with his wife at his side, thinking he was lying about the relationship."

"Did you get the impression that they'd had a row about it?"

"I'd put money on it."

"And yet you seem to be playing them down as possible suspects."

"Yes, sir. But you might want to talk to them yourself."

"Thank you for that advice, John," Diamond said with sarcasm. He leaned back in the chair and rested his palms on his stomach, as if to measure the span. "Gentlemen, I don't mind telling you I am not exactly blown away by your—em—input."

Doggedly, Wigfull defended his corner. "I believe the Platos told me the truth, sir. It's worth pointing out that their statement fits in with Professor Jackman's."

"Go on."

"It supports what Jackman told us about the Jane Austen letters that went missing. If Geraldine did take them, as he suggests, she wouldn't have wanted to face him on his return from Paris. So it's not surprising that she started phoning around for some place to lay up for a while."

"A bolt hole."

"Well, yes."

"Jackman's term, not mine," Diamond explained. "He told me last night that she wasn't short of bolt holes. That's the reason he gives for taking so long to report her disappearance. He assumed she was still alive until he heard about the body in the lake."

Dalton remarked, "The sixty-four-thousand-dollar

question is what happened after the Platos gave Mrs. Jackman the brush-off. None of the other friends appears to have heard from her."

"Unless one of them is lying," said Croxley.

Diamond screwed his face into a look that overlaid curiosity with a glare. "What is that supposed to mean?"

"Well, sir, that the next person she called on the phone was her murderer. Someone who offered her sanctuary and then killed her."

"What for?"

Croxley seemed unable to supply a plausible motive, so the irrepressible Halliwell suggested, "For the Jane Austen letters. She must have taken them with her."

"Killed her for a couple of letters?"

"They were worth a bit."

"Over ten thousand, by Jackman's estimate," Diamond admitted. "But these people Geraldine was keeping company with weren't complete idiots. They would know the dangers involved in trying to sell letters as rare as these. I don't buy it."

"Even so," Wigfull quietly put in, "it might be sensible to alert the dealers in antique letters. There can't be so many."

He was rewarded with a glacial stare from Diamond and the terse instruction, "Do it, then."

"If it were me, I'd take them to America," said Dalton. "Get a better price."

Diamond was shaking his head. "I'm not convinced that the letters provide a credible motive. I'm not even totally convinced of their existence."

"You think the professor is lying about them?"

"He was evasive."

"About where they came from?"

"Yes."

Dalton shrugged. "So let's put the heat on him."

Diamond flapped his hand dismissively. "Too late for that."

"There is another way of checking whether these letters exist at all," Croxley was emboldened to say, "and that's by getting a statement from the American, Dr. Junker. Isn't he supposed to have examined them?"

"Junker." Diamond snapped his fingers. "Yes—I'd written him off, thinking he was still touring in Europe. He should be back in America by now. We'll try and raise him. Which university does he teach in?"

"Pittsburgh," answered Wigfull.

"We'll call him at once."

"I wouldn't, sir," said Wigfull.

"Now what's the problem?"

He'd taken out a pocket calculator. "The problem is that now is five-ten A.M. over there."

7

DIAMOND'S CALL to Dr. Louis Junker was connected shortly after 3 P.M. He used a speaker phone so that Wigfull and Dalton, who had joined him in the office, could hear the responses.

"Who is this?" the voice from Pittsburgh asked.

"Detective Superintendent Peter Diamond, from Bath, in England. You won't know my name, sir."

"That is correct."

"I'm inquiring into the death of Mrs. Geraldine Jackman, of Brydon House in Bath."

There was an understandable pause. The three detectives waited.

"Mrs. Jackman . . . she's *dead?*"

"Sadly, yes."

"Greg Jackman's wife? Dead?"

"Her body was recovered from a reservoir. It appears that she was murdered."

"Murdered?" The voice climbed an octave. "You can't possibly mean this."

"She was last seen alive on Monday, September eleventh. I understand that you were a guest of Professor Jackman at Brydon House at about that time."

"September eleven? Let me collect my thoughts a

moment, will you? No, I left for Paris on the previous day. . . . Now listen, Mr. . . . em . . ."

"Diamond."

"Mr. Diamond. I know nothing about this, nothing. It's a total shock to me."

Diamond boomed reassurance down the transatlantic cable. "Dr. Junker, there's no suggestion that you are implicated in Mrs. Jackman's death. I am simply hoping that you can help me to piece together the events of that weekend. Do you mind?"

There was a silence sufficient for Dalton to murmur flippantly to Wigfull, "He's calling his lawyer on the other phone."

Junker's voice started up again. "If you really think I can help, I'll do what I can. I'm still trying to comprehend this. Is Greg okay?"

"Professor Jackman is fine."

"The last time I saw him was in Paris. He flew out to talk to me. Which day did you say she was killed?"

"I said she went missing on Monday, September eleventh."

"That Monday? Oh, my God . . . that was the day he met with me in my hotel—late. It must have been around eleven in the evening. He told me he flew out in the afternoon. Look, if you're putting the heat on Greg Jackman, I think you should tell me. He was very good to me. They both were."

Junker was a fast talker, and disembodied words in an unfamiliar accent can be difficult to take in. Diamond had a tape recorder running and he could analyze the responses later. He still needed to conduct the interview effectively, to a structured pattern of question and answer.

"Dr. Junker, nobody has been charged with this murder, if that's what you're suggesting. I'm simply asking for your help to establish some facts about the weekend prior to Mrs. Jackman's disappearance."

"Whatever you want."

"Thank you. Let's take it from when you first got in touch with Professor Jackman."

"That was back in July. We hadn't met before this summer. I wrote him when I heard about the Jane Austen exhibition he was putting on in the city of Bath. The nineteenth-century novel is my principal field of study. It so happens that I'm currently writing what I hope will become the definitive biography of Jane Austen. Do you need to know my background?"

"Not at this stage, sir. So you decided to come over?"

"In point of fact, I was coming to Europe on vacation. I adjusted my schedule to take in Bath to visit the exhibition, and Greg Jackman was kind enough to invite me to his home for the weekend."

"I believe he was at Heathrow to meet you."

"That's correct. This was on that Friday. Unfortunately there was some technical trouble with the airplane and the flight was delayed for hours. It was heroic of Greg to wait so long. I recall that we landed at four-ten in the afternoon, almost seven hours late, and I didn't expect to see him, but he was there to shake my hand as if it was still only nine in the morning. Then we drove along the freeway to Bath. We stopped someplace for a sandwich. I couldn't tell you where."

"Doesn't matter."

"The trip took about two, two and a half hours and we talked about his work and mine, as I recall. My memory of that evening is a little disordered. I was bushed, to be frank with you. I guess it was around seven-thirty when we finally reached Brydon House, and I had been traveling a long time. Gerry—Mrs. Jackman —came out to meet me. She was a dream, beautiful, just beautiful. There's no other word. Did you know she was a television actress? She was all ready to cook for me and I had to tell her that I was too tired to wait for a full meal, or to appreciate it, so she fixed me a sandwich and coffee. Greg went off to another room. He had some late calls to make about the exhibition. The poor guy hadn't figured on spending most of that day at the airport. Well, after I had eaten, Gerry showed me to my room and I took a shower."

Now that he had gotten over his reservations about talking to the police, Junker was proving to be a witness with copious recall, almost too copious.

Diamond said, "Dr. Junker, if nothing else of importance happened that evening . . ."

"But I haven't told you about the caller."

"The what?"

"The caller. Someone who came to the house—right?"

Diamond gripped the arms of his chair and sat forward. "I understand. Please go on."

"This was how I got to hear about the Jane Austen letters. The shower revived me a little and I put on a change of clothes and went downstairs, figuring that if I could stay on my feet a couple of hours more, I would adjust to your English time and beat the jet lag. When I got down, I heard Greg's voice from a room at the front of the house, so I looked in there. He had somebody with him and it wasn't Gerry. A short woman with brown hair. They were standing over a table examining a document. I apologized for interrupting, but Greg called me in. It was obvious that he was fired up about something because he forgot to introduce me to the lady. He said, 'Louis, you came at just the right moment. Feast your eyes on these!' Right off, I saw the reason for his excitement. Believe me, my heartbeat tripled. We were looking at two original letters in Jane Austen's hand. No question."

Diamond listened impassively, avoiding Wigfull's eye. Having repeatedly questioned the existence of the Jane Austen letters, he could expect some gloating looks from that quarter. Not that he cared much. A good detective took nothing for granted.

Junker plunged into a description of the letters so detailed that it was unrealistic to harbor doubts any longer. Both had been penned in September 1799, to Mrs. James Leigh Perrot, Jane's aunt, at the Warden's House, Ilchester Gaol, where the accused lady was awaiting trial on a charge of shoplifting. They were written from Steventon, and signed "Yr affectionate niece,

Jane." The first had apparently been written in support of an offer from Jane's mother to send her two daughters to reside with the Leigh Perrots (Uncle James had joined his wife in captivity) in the Warden's House until their ordeal was over. Jane's "chief wish" was that her aunt and uncle "might be persuaded to ease the desolation of this undeserved confinement" by sharing the experience with their loving nieces. The second, written after the offer had been welcomed, but declined, nicely complemented the first. Jane had not been able to suppress her sense of relief. It was lighter in tone and more spontaneous, short, but gossipy, and altogether more typical of her letter-writing style.

"Of course you have to guard against forgeries," Junker went on. "I'd bet my last dollar that these letters were genuine. The style, the handwriting, all of it was so right. Even the spelling. Jane had an endearing blind spot about the word 'believe,' quite often reversing the 'i' and the 'e,' and it cropped up in the second letter."

By now the three detectives, agog to discover the identity of the donor of the letters, had heard more than they cared to know about Jane Austen's style and orthography.

To nudge the conversation in the right direction, Diamond said, "A generous gift, then?"

"Amazing. Did I give you a physical description of the letters?"

"Thanks—but I can get that from Professor Jackman. What interests me more is the woman who was in the room that day. Had she found the letters herself?"

"So I was told."

"You said you weren't introduced."

"Not when I first came in. Greg was just too excited to notice. He did the honor later. Her name—I think I have this right—was Mrs. Didrikson."

Dana Didrikson.

One mystery solved. This time Diamond's eyes locked with Wigfull's.

Intriguing possibilities opened up. Gregory Jackman's refusal to reveal the name—allegedly because his benefactor wished to remain anonymous—was open to new interpretations now.

"Did you catch the name?" the voice from Pittsburgh asked.

"Yes. I've heard it before, in another connection. Tell me, did the gift of these letters come as a total surprise to Professor Jackman?"

"I'm sure of it. He was jubilant. Who wouldn't have been?"

"Mrs. Didrikson must have been excited, too."

"I wouldn't say so."

"No?"

"I don't know the lady, but I'd say she was pretty cool about the whole thing. She didn't say much at all."

"She must have told him where they came from."

"She already had, before I stepped into the room. I heard the story later, how she had tracked down the letters through some dealer in postage stamps."

"Do you think she knew their value?"

"Sure. She knew they were worth a bundle. I said in her presence that I was certain they would fetch a high price at auction. The weird thing is, it had no appreciable impact on her. I got the impression that she just wanted to hand them over and get the hell out of the place. Greg talked about giving them back to her when the exhibition was over, but she insisted they were a gift —a gift to him personally. Apparently this was her way of thanking him for some action of his in rescuing her son from drowning. Does that make any sense to you?"

"It fits the story we have."

"Right. Well, by now I was beginning to sense that I shouldn't be there. Greg needed to talk this thing through with her. I mean I have no idea what the lady's personal circumstances were, but she was parting with an extremely valuable item. I edged diplomatically toward the door, meaning to leave them to work things out. Just then the door opened and Mrs. Jackman walked in. No, that's an understatement. She made an entrance like she was the star guest on a talk show. She was reeking of expensive perfume and dressed in a skin-

tight black gown that reached to the floor. This was the
lady who only a half hour before had been wearing a
check shirt and faded blue jeans and had fixed me a
sandwich. Okay, I thought, maybe they're planning to go
out for dinner, even if Greg is still dressed in the casual
clothes he wore to the airport. Anyway, he greeted her
warmly and told her about the letters. She and Mrs.
Didrikson obviously knew each other, but there was a
chill between them from the beginning, and things
didn't warm up much when Gerry Jackman gave the
letters one quick glance and commented that she would
never understand why people bothered to collect musty
old things like that when they had no literary merit
whatsoever."

"Was she trying for a reaction?"

"That was the way I read it. Actually, she didn't get
one. Mrs. Didrikson didn't say a word. Greg tactfully
attempted some kind of counterstatement, and I backed
him up as well as I could, whereupon Gerry stepped
really close to me—practically toe to toe—gave me a
sexy look, and asked me what was big on Broadway just
now. She was blatantly upstaging Mrs. Didrikson. I felt
extremely uncomfortable. I answered her truthfully that
I didn't live in New York and didn't keep up with the
theater. She persisted in engaging me in conversation to
the exclusion of the others until Mrs. Didrikson made it
clear that she wanted to leave. Then Gerry broke off
what she was saying and suggested to Greg that he take
Mrs. Didrikson out to dinner."

"That evening?"

"Yes, to thank her for all the trouble she'd taken to
find the letters. I didn't know what game Gerry was
playing and I still don't. Greg said that he couldn't
abandon me, his houseguest, on my first evening, to
which Gerry said she'd enjoy entertaining me. Dressed
like that—she and I alone in the house—can you imagine?"

"Did he take up the suggestion?"

"No. Mrs. Didrikson scotched it by saying she was
busy that evening. He saw her to the door. In fact, he

went out to the driveway with her, I imagine to have some private words. I was left with Gerry long enough for her to run a finger down my backbone and say that she couldn't be blamed for trying." Dr. Junker coughed nervously. "Jesus, I'm an academic, Mr. Diamond. I wear thick glasses and I'm forty-six years old. I have a receding hairline and a larger-than-average nose. I'm not accustomed to attractive women making passes at me. No one makes passes at me. In my position, what would you have done?"

Interesting as it might have been to have heard Diamond's answer, he refused to supply it. Instead, he asked, "Are you telling me that something happened between you and Mrs. Jackman? Is that what you're saying?"

"No, sir! I'm saying that I didn't take up the offer." After the strong denial, Junker's voice changed to a discernible note of regret.

"I imagine it wouldn't have been easy, with Professor Jackman around."

"You think she didn't mean it? That she was putting me on?"

"How can I say?" answered Diamond, his patience running out. "I'm a policeman, not a shrink. What happened next?"

"She poured me a drink. Then I heard Mrs. Didrikson's car move off and Greg came back. We spent some more time studying the letters. Quite properly, Greg decided they needed authenticating before he put them into the exhibition. The earliest he could arrange it was Monday. God, I wish I'd had the good sense to photograph them. You haven't found them, I suppose?"

"No."

"That's too bad."

"And after you'd finished your drink, Dr. Junker?"

"I went to bed. I slept. Boy, did I sleep! I came to around eleven next day. When I went downstairs, Greg had already left for the exhibition."

"You and Mrs. Jackman were alone, then?"

An uneasy laugh came down the line. "True, only

she wasn't acting up like she had the night before. She was curiously different toward me. Kind of friendly, but in no way suggestive. She drove me to the Assembly Rooms for the opening ceremonies and stayed with me the whole of the afternoon—which must have been insufferably boring for her. The exhibition, I mean. I photographed almost every item. To give Greg his due—it was a terrific show."

"Did you have much conversation?"

"Sure."

"Did you learn anything of interest about Mrs. Jackman, her problems, her plans?"

"Sorry," said Junker. "We kept off personal matters. After my experience the previous night, I figured it was safer to stick with the nineteenth-century novel."

"Did you meet anyone? Any of her friends, for instance?"

"A couple of guys from the English Department who wanted to talk to me about a piece I wrote for the *Times Literary Supplement* a while back, that was all."

"Nobody who knew Mrs. Jackman?"

"Plenty who recognized her. She must have signed her autograph a dozen times. I don't think she met anyone she already knew. She told me her friends weren't the book-reading sort."

"That was probably true. Did you mention the letters to anyone?"

"No way. Greg and I had agreed to say nothing about them to a living soul. In the academic world, you keep a hot property like that under wraps until you're one hundred percent certain."

Diamond continued to probe as Junker continued his account of the day, but the story that emerged was substantially the same as he had gotten from Jackman: The pub meal after the exhibition had closed for the day. The decision to retire early. Next day, a quiet morning with the Sunday papers in another pub.

"Just you and Professor Jackman?"

"Yes. The lady was still in bed, or so I understood."

"Then this was the first opportunity Jackman had

of speaking to you alone since the episode on the Friday evening?"

"Correct."

"Did he refer to it?"

"Briefly. He tried to make some kind of apology and I said it wasn't necessary. He said Gerry had these unpredictable phases. I shrugged it off with some chauvinistic remark about women in general. That was all. We returned to the house after lunch, and pretty soon after, it was time to leave. Gerry was downstairs to wish me good-bye. She acted normally, we shook hands chastely, and that was the last I saw of her. Greg drove me to the station in time to catch the London train. Next morning I was due to visit with a professor at University College."

"Dalrymple."

"You're well informed. Actually, I had to cancel. When I booked my flight to Paris, I didn't realize how far out of town Heathrow is. There was no way I could fit in Edgar Dalrymple and catch my flight." Junker paused. "You want to know about my meeting in Paris with Greg?"

"If you please."

"It won't take long. I went out for a meal Monday and when I got back I was amazed to see him standing in the lobby of my hotel. He told me the Jane Austen letters were missing and asked if it was possible that I'd taken them by mistake. You can imagine how I felt. It was obvious what he was thinking. I hadn't disguised my envy when those letters had dropped into his lap. Now it looked like I'd abused his hospitality by stealing them. Mr. Diamond, I assure you that I hadn't—and there's no way I could have taken them in error. We searched my things together. My luggage, my room, everything. I believe I convinced him finally that I didn't have them. He said Gerry must have taken them out of spite. No one else knew about them. I had to agree with him. I said maybe she resented the fact that another woman had given him this unique present. It could help to explain why she'd behaved so oddly at the time."

"What did he think of your theory?"

"Not much. He said these histrionic scenes were pretty common. I guess he was more concerned about recovering those letters than trying to analyze his wife's behavior. We parted in a civilized fashion. He promised to call me if the letters turned up. I said I might see him at breakfast, but in the morning he checked out early. I heard no more from him."

By means of sign language, Diamond invited Wigfull and Dalton to pass him any questions they might want to put, but they shook their heads. He wound up the conversation and ended the call.

Nobody moved.

"Why the mystery?" said Wigfull after an interval. "Explain."

"Mrs. Didrikson. Why didn't Jackman tell us it was Dana Didrikson who supplied him with the letters?"

"Are you looking for an answer," said Diamond, "or do I sense that you have it ready?"

Wigfull spread his hands to show how obvious his conclusion was. "He's shielding her. He knows she killed his wife and he's shielding her."

"Not too successfully," commented Diamond.

"He expected it to come out, but he didn't wish to point the finger."

"Why not?"

"Because he doesn't really blame her. He thinks she deserves to get away with it. It's not impossible that he loves the woman."

Diamond's surprise at this confident analysis was surpassed only by his disbelief that it should have come from Wigfull, the plant from headquarters. He didn't object to anyone on the squad going for broke with some blinding theory . . . but *Wigfull*. He could only assume it was a rush to the head, a momentary loss of concentration, and he actually warmed to the man for showing that he was human. "John, I'd like to hear more. What could Mrs. Didrikson's motive be?"

"Infatuation."

Diamond glanced toward Dalton, who was preserving a statuesque neutrality.

"It's the classic setup," Wigfull said in support of his theory. "She's a single parent, not too well off, working her butt off to keep her kid in a private school. Jackman is the white knight, the fearless, good-looking fellow who rescued the boy from the jaws of death. She finds out he's a professor, loaded, with a big house and a wife who is not only making his life a misery, but actually tried to kill him. Dana sees him as the solution to all her problems, if he'll ditch the wife. Inconveniently, he won't. He's so chivalrous, so loyal a husband, that he hasn't any plans for a divorce. So . . ." He climaxed his argument by drawing an extended finger across his throat, not a mime that fitted the facts, but sufficient to make the point.

"We'd better talk to her," said Diamond, reserving judgment.

"Would you like to leave it to me?" Wigfull asked.

Diamond grinned. It wasn't a generous grin.

8

HARSH WORDS were spoken in Diamond's BMW when he missed a vital turn because Wigfull, navigating, was too late in pointing it out. Wigfull said in mitigation that Mrs. Didrikson's address (which they had gotten from the phone book) happened to be situated between Widcombe and Lyncombe in the section of the map that lay along the centerfold and was not quite aligned after a repair with adhesive tape. In spite of the difficulties, he was confident of finding another way through. Diamond, sensitive to the charge that he was an inept map restorer, shifted the attack by commenting that the road Wigfull had gotten them into had not been built for the modern automobile. He'd never liked these hills south of the city, their pitted roads lined by uncompromising stone walls ten or fifteen feet high, overhung with dreary evergreens.

Wigfull stayed silent until the next problem arose. Unable to make a U-turn, they were obliged to take a route up a steeply inclined lane with a passage so narrow that it ought to have been designated one-way. As proof that it was not, they met a Post Office van making its way down and were forced to reverse. At the second try, they got three-quarters of the way up before another vehicle appeared at the top, a red Mini, small, yet sufficient to obstruct the way. In common courtesy, the driver should have given way and backed up. He continued to advance, however, with his headlights on full beam.

"You know what they say in traffic division," said Diamond. "Always watch out for the ones wearing hats and driving red cars. This looks a prize specimen." He stopped the car.

"I'll handle it," Wigfull volunteered, unfastening his safety belt. The atmosphere was improving in the BMW now that they were united in the face of a common nuisance.

Diamond took a second look at the driver, who had also come to a halt. "No. Leave him. He's ninety if he's a day, poor old codger. Probably forgotten how to get into reverse."

"In that case he shouldn't be on the road."

Wigfull plainly felt that the sympathy was misdirected. He'd taken plenty of stick; why should some inconsiderate old man get away with it?

"Something tells me to let this one alone, John," Diamond told him, turning in his seat and starting to back down the hill.

"Bet you wouldn't have done this in London," Wigfull commented.

"You're right. I've gone soft as a cider apple since I came down here."

"I hadn't noticed."

At the foot of the hill, the old man in the Mini revved powerfully and passed them, recklessly removing his hand from the wheel to raise his hat.

"You see?" said Diamond. "Politeness breeds politeness."

Their third attempt was successful. They turned right at the top, negotiated two tight turns, and found the name of the street chiseled into the wall. High above the street level was a terrace of six small Georgian houses set back from the road, each with its own iron gate. The Didrikson house was the second. Like the others, it was in need of cleaning, stained most heavily below the cornice and sills. They drew up outside and toiled up three sets of stone steps to a front door painted royal blue.

"Someone's in," Wigfull said.

"Good—I wouldn't want to make this trip too often."

Their knock was answered by a boy in the gray trousers, white shirt, and striped tie of one of the more exclusive schools in the area—presumably the lad Professor Jackman had pulled out of Pulteney Weir.

"Hello, son," Diamond hailed him. "Is your mother in?"

This amiable greeting was answered with, "We don't buy anything at the door." The boy could have been any age from twelve to fourteen, at that stage of life when the features grow out of proportion and the look on the face expresses resentment at the process—or at the world in general.

"We're from the police," said Diamond.

"Where's your warrant?"

"What's your name, son?"

"Matthew."

"Matthew what?"

"Didrikson."

"Well, Matthew Didrikson, do you ever watch *The Bill?*"

"Sometimes."

"You want to pay more attention, then. We don't have warrants unless we're searching a place. We just want to see your mum. I'm asking you again. Is she in?"

"She goes out to work," said the boy.

"We'll come in and wait." Diamond stepped forward.

Momentarily the boy blocked the doorway in defiance, then took a step back as Diamond put a huge foot over the doorstep.

Wigfull, behind him, had spotted a movement along the hall. "Someone's going out the back!" he said.

"Grab them."

In the first stride of the pursuit, Diamond was

stopped by a vicious kick in the groin. As any ex–rugby player would, he reacted to the swing of the foot by attempting to swerve, with a simultaneous jackknifing action. The movement would have saved him if he had not acquired so much extra poundage since giving up the game. His agility was unequal to the intention. True, the impact might have been more damaging had Matthew Didrikson been wearing leather rather than rubber. It still felt like being impaled on a heat-seeking missile and savaged by a Rottweiler at the same time. And the boy followed it up by making a diving grab for Diamond's thigh.

Acting on instinct now, Diamond pushed him away and pitched forward onto his hands and knees, bellowing in agony. Somewhere behind him, the boy thudded against the wall.

The pain was extreme. Numbness would take over eventually, Diamond promised himself. Could he wait that long?

His eyes were shut tight. Through his groaning, he heard Wigfull's, "Leave it to me." It was a superfluous offer.

By degrees, the pain spread and became less intense. Diamond opened his eyes. They watered copiously. Just as well, he told himself grimly, because he doubted whether the organ intended for watering would ever function again. He looked around for the juvenile delinquent who had maimed him. Prudently for his survival, Matthew Didrikson had fled through the front door.

With the help of a table leg, Diamond succeeded in hauling himself off the floor. In a fair imitation of a sumo wrestler charging his opponent, he lurched a few steps and found a chair. There he sat, conscious of nothing but the fire below. How long he was there, he neither knew, nor cared.

"You all right, sir?"

He looked up.

The fatuous question came from Wigfull.

"Do I look all right?" Even the vibrations of his own voice gave him pain.

"It was obviously Mrs. Didrikson I saw," Wigfull informed him. "I didn't catch her, unfortunately. The house backs onto another street. She ran through the yard and drove off in a black Mercedes. I got the number."

"So what do you want—a pat on the back?"

"I suppose you don't happen to have a personal radio on you?" Wigfull ventured.

"What would I want with a bloody bat phone?"

"We could put out a message."

"There's a phone on the table beside you," growled Diamond. "Come on, man!" With that, he began to feel marginally better.

Wigfull got through and ensured that the motor patrols would be alerted. "In that fast car she's probably heading for the motorway," he said when he had finished. "They'll pick her up in the next hour with any luck." He continued to fuel his optimism. "Well, we're quite a bit further on, funnily enough. The lady does a bunk and confirms herself as the number-one suspect, in my book, anyway. She's going to regret this. Look, would you like me to see if I can find some sort of painkiller?"

"The first sensible thing you've said," Diamond told him.

A short time later, he lowered himself gingerly into the passenger seat of his car. The codeine Wigfull had found in the bathroom was beginning to work. Wigfull closed the door gently on him and walked around to the driver's seat and got in.

Then gave an embarrassed cough.

What's the matter with him now? Diamond thought.

"The keys."

"Why didn't you think of it before? Why didn't I, come to that?" Nothing is so awkward as fishing in your pocket when you're seated in a car, or as perilous, when you're sore down there.

It was an effort and a pain, but Diamond prized them out and handed them over and they drove off. He didn't offer to map-read. It was up to Wigfull to remember. They took the two sharp turns and then steered left to the top of the narrow hill that had caused such problems on the way up. Wigfull stopped the car.

"Not again."

The way down was obstructed.

Diamond started to laugh. It was ridiculous to do so, because every movement gave him a spasm of pain, but he couldn't prevent it. He shook with laughter.

The car halfway down the hill was a stationary black Mercedes—stationary because it had met another vehicle coming up. They were fender to fender, quite literally. The vehicle the Mercedes had hit was a red Mini with the headlamps full on. The driver, familiar in his trilby, had gotten out and was standing beside the cars examining the damage. There was a figure still seated in the Mercedes.

"Can't be too serious if his lights are still working," said Wigfull. "I'll trot down and see."

Diamond got out and hobbled after him. This was going to be worth the discomfort.

9

THE DAMAGE to the vehicles was slight, no more than a flaking of paint from the Mercedes and a small dent in the fender of the Mini. But it was enough to provide a pretext. Having established that neither driver was injured, Wigfull solemnly took particulars from the old man—a retired doctor—who owned the Mini, while Diamond opened the door of the Mercedes, introduced himself, and asked the woman inside to hand him the key.

"Thank you. Now would you move across to the other seat?"

She obeyed, her hands trembling as she put them out to support herself.

"Sure you're all right?"

"Yes."

He lowered himself toward the driver's seat, then realized just in time that he wouldn't fit. The level of the seat had been raised by two squares of foam rubber, leaving so little space below the steering wheel that it would have courted disaster to squeeze the already suffering portion of his anatomy under there. "I'll have to move these."

She shrugged her consent and he managed the maneuver at the second try.

"You're Mrs. Dana Didrikson?"

"Yes." Her face had turned the color of skim milk, accentuated by the brown hair that framed it. A neat, finely shaped mouth and dark, intelligent eyes that now had a hunted look. Without it, Diamond might have guessed that she was a teacher or a social worker.

Capable of murder? he asked himself as he said aloud, "Would you care to tell me how this happened?"

"I was driving too fast. It wasn't his fault. I thought I'd stopped in time."

"Why the hurry?"

She let out a sigh that said this was playing games because they both knew the reason. "I was trying to escape."

Simple cause and effect. Naturally she'd hurried because she was trying to escape. From her impassive manner, she might have been talking about the weather.

Diamond couldn't match her composure. He quivered. The adrenaline coursed through him. The breakthrough was happening. All those miserable hours by the lake, in the caravan, on the phone to Merlin, at case conferences, watching the pesky computer screens, teasing out information from the professor—were about to be rewarded.

His throat had gone dry. He dredged up the one word that mattered. "Escape?"

"Out of the back of the house. Didn't you see me?"

"We saw you."

"Well, then." More words, apparently, were superfluous.

Not wishing to say one syllable that might discourage her candor, he kept to practicalities. "Your car was parked at the back, I take it?"

She nodded. "I got in and drove too fast. What's going to happen to me?"

"We're going to require a statement. Would you wait here, please?" He hauled himself out of the seat and approached Wigfull, who was still going through the motions of questioning the elderly Mini driver. "Reverse the Mercedes, John. She's willing to cough the lot, I think."

The old man said at once, "If she's admitting responsibility, I'd like it noted."

"Thank you for drawing it to our attention, sir," said Diamond. "An officer will come and see you in due course." He returned to the Mercedes and got into the backseat, behind Dana Didrikson. "Back to the house," he told Wigfull when he got in.

At the top of the hill, he transferred to his own car and drove the short distance, and somehow his soreness was less disabling now. Wigfull followed in the Mercedes and they parked both cars in front of the Didrikson house.

The door stood open as they had left it. Sensing that a second escape attempt was unlikely, Diamond allowed Mrs. Didrikson to go in first. She called out a name.

"If that's your son you're calling," said Diamond, "he went out through the front as we came in."

She said, "He had no reason to run off." More loudly, she called, "Mat, are you there?"

Wigfull explained, "He attempted to stop us from entering, ma'am. We could charge him with obstruction and assault. He caught Mr. Diamond well and truly."

She said with contempt, "He's just a schoolboy."

Diamond signaled to Wigfull not to pursue the matter, a fine instance of altruism in the line of duty. "We'll be wanting to interview you at some length, Mrs. Didrikson."

"Here?"

"Down at Manvers Street. It's late already. You might wish to put a few things in an overnight bag."

"You want me to come to the police station? Can't you talk to me here?"

"That won't be possible."

"What about Mat? I can't leave him alone all night. He's only twelve, you know."

Diamond assured her that the boy would be taken care of. The Abbey Choir School had a house in Lansdown Road for boarders. While Mrs. Didrikson, accompanied by Diamond, went upstairs to pack her bag, Wigfull spent some time on the phone arranging for a patrol to find the boy and drive him to the school to spend the night there.

Dana Didrikson's bedroom revealed little about the character of its owner, unless it was that she was tidy-minded and self-effacing. Painted walls in the magnolia shade so popular with decorators. Fitted shelves, wardrobes, and a double bed. Freestanding dressing table. A wall-to-wall carpet in a neutral stone color. And matching curtains. No pictures, photos, books, stuffed animals, or discarded clothes. Perhaps the reason why it so resembled a hotel room was that Mrs. Didrikson's work as a chauffeur allowed her little time for anything but sleeping there.

She took a bag from the top shelf of the wardrobe and put in a few things. "Now may I pack a bag for Matthew?"

Diamond gave his consent. He could hear Wigfull still on the phone downstairs.

They had to go up another flight to the boy's room, which had a more lived-in look. Cardboard birds and bats, made from modeling kits, were strung from the ceiling. Pop posters adorned the walls and socks and record sleeves were scattered about the floor. An unfinished chess game stood on the top of a desk. Decisively more lived-in, not least because its occupant was lying on the bed behind the door.

"Mat—I thought you were out," his mother said. "I called out and you didn't answer."

He was on his stomach leafing through a comic, only his dark hair visible. He didn't look up.

"Mat—do you hear me?"

Still without turning to look at her, the boy said, "They're the fuzz. They knocked me over and forced their way in. I asked them for a warrant, but they took no notice."

"Knocked you over?"

Diamond explained, "I pushed him aside when he aimed a kick at me."

"Against the wall," Matthew stated vehemently. "You bashed my head against the wall and knocked me over. What do you want, anyway?"

"Your mother is going to give us some help with a matter we're investigating," Diamond said, expressing it more sensitively than he thought the kid's attitude deserved. This looked a prime example of a boy in want of a father's authority and playing hell with his hapless mother. He went out to the landing and called downstairs, "John, the kid's up here. He was here all the time."

Back in the boy's bedroom, Mrs. Didrikson was explaining to her son why it would be necessary for him to spend a night at school. Matthew made an unsuccessful appeal to be allowed to remain alone in the house, then turned his back on everyone and went back to his comic. His mother packed a bag for him, watched indulgently by Diamond, who felt a stirring of pity for the kid, in spite of everything. One night as a boarder was likely to be an underestimate.

PART FOUR

Dana

1

THIS IS ABOUT what happened to Geraldine Jackman, isn't it? You want to know how I got involved with the Jackmans. I'm willing to talk about it now, if you'll let me tell it in my own way, but this is going to be quite an effort for me. I'm not one of those twittering women who broadcast their life stories to everyone in the supermarket queue. By nature I'm a private person, which sounds like a way of keeping people at a distance and often is, but I wouldn't describe myself as shy. It's more true to say that it doesn't come naturally to me to confide in anyone else. As a result, I'm sometimes accused of being unfriendly, or standoffish. I constantly struggle to break out of it because, believe me, when you're a single parent, you have to speak up for yourself and your child.

After Sverre, my former husband, left me three years ago, I drove taxis, and you might think that was a peculiar way for a social misfit to earn a living. Actually it was my salvation. I learned to put up a front and shelter behind it. I could hear myself playing the part of the taxi driver and saying these mundane things about the traffic and the tourists and what I'd just heard on the radio, knowing all the time that the real me was a million miles back from the action. None of it touched me personally. But this situation is another thing altogether. Blood from a stone.

All right, let's plunge in. At the time I met the Jackmans I'd given up the taxi driving. I had a job as chauffeur with Mr. Stanley Buckle, the managing director of Realbrew Ales. That's how I got to drive the Mercedes. It doesn't belong to me.

I was offered the job by Mr. Buckle himself one evening when he used my cab for a trip from Bath to his home in Bristol. On a few previous occasions he had been my passenger and I'd got into conversation and found him pleasant enough, with just a suggestion of the mild flirting a woman cabbie gets from middle-aged males. Nothing I could take exception to. At that time I didn't know he was the Realbrew boss. I had a vague idea he had stakes in several businesses in Bath and Bristol, and of course I'd seen his beautiful house overlooking Clifton College, so I was pretty certain he wasn't stringing me along when he offered me the job. At the end of the ride, he simply asked me how much I took in fares in a good week and offered to match it with a regular salary in return for a six-day week and no nights. I would be allowed to use the company car whenever I wished, as long as I kept an accurate log of mileage.

I didn't hesitate. The taxi driving had been a living, but it was a treadmill. Until that evening, I'd seen no possibility of escape.

Of course you know about my son's fortunate rescue from drowning last July. You'll have heard about it from Greg—Professor Jackman. That was one of the most horrible days in my life, and not just because of what happened to Mat. I was in trouble with the police before I even heard about Mat. Not here in Bath, or you'd have known about it, wouldn't you?

I'm sorry. This doesn't sound very coherent, does it? I'd better tell you exactly how that day turned out, because it all links up with what happened later on.

Early in the morning, Mr. Buckle rang me. He

needed the car, so would I drive over to his house at Clifton by 9:00 A.M.?

This usually meant that he was making a business trip to London and wanted to be ferried to Bristol Parkway in time to catch the train; the intercity service was a full hour quicker than a belt along the motorway. But when I arrived at the Buckle residence that morning, I had to revise my ideas. It was building up to be a really hot day, by the way. Not a cloud in the sky. The Filipino maid escorted me to the rear of the house, where my boss, flaunting a straw hat, powder-blue shorts, and mirror sunglasses, was stretched out on a lounger beside the swimming pool. The only concession to business was a cell phone within arm's reach on the paving. He waved me toward a metal chair.

Mr. Buckle was in a mood to match the weather. He apologized for bringing me out so early and offered me a fresh grapefruit juice. Then he asked me if my son had got his Common Entrance result yet.

I told him Mat wasn't taking the exam until next year when he'll be thirteen.

He said, "In that case, take a tip from me, Dana. Give him a rest from books now. Let him get out and enjoy the summer."

I nodded. Men are always giving me advice I don't ask for, as if male solidarity requires that Mat doesn't end up as that reviled creature, a mother's boy.

With that off his chest, Mr. Buckle pitched his voice lower. "The reason I asked you to come is confidential." To reinforce the point he tapped the side of his nose. "Family jewels, right?"

I shaped my mouth into and "O" that was meant to imply that I understood without agreeing to anything.

"Far be it from me to lead young ladies off the straight and narrow," he confided to me with a wolfish grin. The irony was that he was right. Charmian, the tigress he lived with, would claw out his vitals at the swerve of a roving eye. She'd made that very clear to me the first time we had met. "What I'm proposing is rather naughty," Mr. Buckle went on. "You're a Realbrew driver, and the Merc is a Realbrew car, but I have other stakes in business, as I'm sure you know. I want to borrow you for the day, so to speak. There's a small consignment of goods awaiting collection in Southampton. All my regular drivers are spoken for. Would you be an angel on this occasion and help me out?" His eyes uplifted in appeal reminded me of one of those dogs pictured on collecting boxes for animal charities. "It is extremely urgent."

I hesitated. If he had given me my orders straightforwardly, I wouldn't have thought twice about them. The way he'd asked made me suspicious. In view of his life-style I'd sometimes wondered if all of his activities were strictly within the law. The last thing I wanted was to get drawn into some racket. "What exactly is it?" I asked.

"Teddy bears."

After an interval to be certain that I'd heard correctly, I said, *"Teddies?"*

"Eight hundred teddies made in Taiwan. Very small. About this size." He made a space between the thumb and forefinger of one hand. "They don't weigh much at all. They're in four cartons that will easily fit into the car."

An alert was sounding in my head. My brain hammered out possibilities like a teleprinter. Southampton docks . . . import license . . . dangerous toys . . . hidden drugs . . .

"The paperwork is all in order, if that's what you're thinking about," he said to reassure me. "You just show the pass I'll give you, Dana, collect them from the warehouse, and bring them back here. Well, not here. There's a garage in Whiteladies Road. I'll give you the key."

"May I ask what the urgency is, if it's just a load of teddies?" I inquired, trying to sound merely curious.

He spread his hands as if it were obvious. "Come on, you must have heard of the big charity day at Longleat House. The Teddy Bears' Picnic, this Saturday. Every bear of any distinction is there. Hundreds of teddies.

And children, of course. I've been asked to supply these minibears for souvenirs, and I can't let the kiddies down."

"Oh." I could almost hear that song about the teddy bears' picnic. Suddenly I felt extremely foolish.

And Stanley Buckle was grinning.

I agreed to make the delivery, of course.

I was on the A36 approaching Warminster when I was stopped. The trip had gone smoothly enough until then. I had found the warehouse in Southampton docks without difficulty, signed for the teddies, and loaded the four cartons into the back of the Mercedes. I'd traveled some forty miles on the return and was through Heytesbury when I noticed a red car following me. At one stage I moved over, but they made no attempt to overtake, so I accelerated a little because I didn't like being tailgated. A mile or so further on, I looked in the mirror again and saw a blue flashing light on the roof of the pursuing car. It hadn't been there before. The two men inside weren't wearing police uniforms so far as I could make out, but they were flashing their headlamps like crazy, so I stopped at the next lay-by, and so did they.

I wound down the window.

The man at the car door told me he was from the police. He held up an identity card that looked official. He told me to turn off the engine and remove the key.

I obeyed, and the conversation went something like this.

"Did you know you were exceeding seventy miles an hour just now?"

"I wasn't aware of it."

"Do you know the limit, miss?"

"Sixty on this stretch."

"Where are you traveling?"

"Bristol. I've come from Southampton."

"Business?"

"Yes." As I spoke I thought of the packages in the trunk.

He asked for my name and some form of identification. Then he asked the nature of my business. I described myself as a driver. There was a horrid sense of inevitability about the whole thing. I was asked to step out of the car and somehow I knew it wasn't to be breathalyzed.

The second man had gotten out of the red car and walked over to join us. He showed me his identification. He was a detective inspector.

"Is the boot locked, miss?"

"I believe so."

"Would you unlock it, please?"

I obeyed and pulled up the lid.

The four cartons lay there. I thought of my boss at leisure beside his pool while I went through this ordeal. If they found something and charged me, I would bloody well see that Mr. Buckle took the rap. There might be honor among thieves, but I was no thief. Nor did I knowingly have possession of whatever items of contraband might be in those boxes. I would lose my job, but that would be less of a disaster than acquiring a criminal record.

One of the policeman asked, "What's in those, miss?"

"Teddy bears," I said, trying to sound convincing. If I was going to plead not guilty, it was vital to stick to the story I'd been fed.

Glances were exchanged. The first said, "What did you say the name of your firm is?"

"You didn't ask me. It's Realbrew Ales Limited, but I was asked to collect the teddies as a personal favor to my boss."

"Personal. He likes bears, does he?"

I explained about the picnic at Longleat.

"I think we'd better have a look at these teddies. Would you mind opening one of the cartons?"

Squirming on the hook, I said, "They don't belong to me. I require some authority."

The inspector nodded. "You can tell the owner we

identified ourselves as policemen and asked for your cooperation. I take it you're willing to cooperate?"

I was handed a penknife. The pulse was still thumping in my head. I cut a line along the tape that sealed the lid.

"Remove the packing, miss."

I lifted aside a layer of foam rubber—and a tremor of relief ran through me as I saw twenty-five small yellow teddy bears in five ranks lying on a bed of polystyrene.

The police insisted that I lift out each layer of bears until they had seen the entire contents of the box. Two hundred bears. Then they asked me to open the other cartons. There was nothing to be gained by protesting; clearly they expected to find something. I felt the same flutter of nerves at each layer, but rank after rank of teddy bears gazed innocently up at me until the entire consignment had been checked.

The inspector picked up one of the bears and turned it over, examining it minutely. He and the other policeman withdrew a few yards and conferred. I watched them twist the teddy's head and limbs. The inspector gave it a shake and held it to his ear. He put it to his nose and sniffed it. The whole thing would have been laughable if I hadn't felt so intimidated by their suspicion.

Whatever they'd decided, it required some authority, because the inspector went to their car and used the two-way radio.

I tried to contain my anxiety by busying myself repacking the cartons until the policemen approached me again. The inspector handed me the teddy bear.

"In view of the way you have cooperated, I won't be reporting you for exceeding the speed limit on this occasion, miss, but take this as a serious warning. The limit is for your own protection as well as that of other drivers." He said nothing about the bears.

I murmured something suitably contrite.

The pair of them returned to their car and drove away.

•   •   •

Mr. Buckle was still beside the pool when I returned to
his house. He had turned the lounger the other way to
stay facing the sun and his skin looked as if it might be
sore later. He wasn't alone. There were two other
middle-aged fellows in shorts playing cards under an
umbrella beside the pool. They didn't look up. A third
man was swimming lengths with a slow breaststroke,
and I had to look twice at his long hair, fanned on the
water, before deciding that it wasn't white, but pale
blond. He glanced across and assessed me in the way
that men do. Apparently I wasn't worth even a passing
nod.

My boss was asleep. I had to say his name twice.
Then he stirred and asked me what time it was.

I told him and asked if we could speak privately, to
which he said there was nothing he couldn't discuss in
front of his friends.

So I told him what had happened on the road.

He paid close attention and didn't interrupt or
comment.

"I think I'm entitled to know what it was all about,"
I said in conclusion, and it was more of a demand than a
request.

He rubbed the back of his neck. "All this is a puzzle to me, Dana. Did they mention my name at all?"

"No."

"That's the way they work, of course. You commit
some minor traffic offense and they throw the book at
you. Did they test your tires and brakes?"

I shook my head. "Didn't I make that clear? They
weren't interested in the state of the car."

"Well, it's nearly new. They could see that," he
said, "so they tried to get you on something else. You
did well to keep your cool, my dear."

Still sure that I had been duped in some way, I
went so far as to say, "I think they were acting on a tip.
They seemed so sure of themselves."

He didn't seem impressed. "I doubt it," he told me

firmly. "It's their mentality. They see a big shiny Mercedes and they think it must be part of some scam. You'd better get used to this sort of thing happening, or drive more slowly."

"You sound like one of them."

He grinned, and asked if I would care for a swim. He could find me a two-piece if I wished. "Or just the one piece, if you feel inclined," he added.

He was playing the philanderer again. Presumably Charmian was out for the afternoon.

I made some excuse and was about to leave when he remembered that there was a phone message for me. Would I call the switchboard at the office urgently? He handed me his phone.

And that was how I learned that my son had been taken to hospital.

2

YOU CAN IMAGINE the turmoil I was in. Anita, the switchboard operator at Realbrew, broke it to me as gently as she could, saying that apparently Mat had been taken to the Royal United only as a precaution after falling into the river, but when you get news like that about your own son, you immediately put the worst construction on it. You think everyone is glossing over the seriousness of what has happened so as not to panic you.

Horrific possibilities filled my head while I was driving at high speed to the hospital, putting my license and my livelihood in jeopardy. Things are never as straightforward as people would have you believe. Matthew was my only child, my entire family. I parked the car in the bay outside the emergency room, ran up to the entrance, took a deep breath to control myself, walked in, and announced who I was.

The receptionist gave me one of those plastic smiles that are supposed to ease the strain in emergency rooms and told me that Matthew was being examined by Dr. Murtah. I asked if he was injured in any way, and she wouldn't tell me a blessed thing, except to take a seat. Oh, and I remember that she half turned away and then took a second look and asked if she had seen me before.

I simply hadn't the mental energy left to remind her that I worked for Realbrew and had brought in a man whose arm had been fractured on the production line the previous week.

I went to a seat in the front row and rubbed the backs of my arms. The gooseflesh wasn't because the place was cold. This was July, remember. I'm often accused of taking life too seriously. No use protesting that I like a good laugh; as I told you, I'm guarded in my reactions to all but the closest friends. That's no bad thing. Anyone who drives for a living has good reason to treat the rest of humanity as wolves and vampires.

Presently, a white-coated man came over to me. He introduced himself as Dr. Murtah and invited me to follow him. As we went through a swing door, he announced in the rather formal speech that Asians use that the young fellow—meaning Mat—should be none the worse for his misadventure. There was superficial grazing. And he'd had a jab in his backside. Dr. Murtah had thought it wise to give him a precautionary shot of penicillin in case of infection.

He asked me whether Mat often played by the river, and I answered truthfully that I'd had no idea he was there. I could only assume he must have been playing truant from school.

"He is a scholar at the Abbey Choir School, he tells me."

"Yes. A day boy."

"Far be it from me to interfere, Mrs. Didrikson, but when all is said and done he seems a good lad. We don't want a repeat of this misadventure. If I were you, I would ask your husband to read him the riot act. I wouldn't chastise him this time. He had a pretty unpleasant physical shock. However, I would leave the young tearaway in no doubt."

"I understand." I didn't say I was divorced. "Thank you for attending to him, doctor."

He waved me into a cubicle and left me with Matthew, a distinctly chastened young tearaway sitting up on an examination couch.

"Mum." Mat's eyes glistened.

I went to him and held him a moment, not saying a word. I didn't trust my tangled emotions.

He said, "I'm—"

I put a hand over his lips. "Later. We'll talk about it later. Not here."

He said, "They lent me this dressing gown. My clothes are still wet."

"Doesn't matter," I told him.

A nurse came in and asked if we had any transport, and I confirmed that we had. She told me Mat had better wear the dressing gown and sandals home, and I promised to return them later.

I tried to let the practical arrangements fill my mind. I stooped to help Matthew get his feet into the sandals, but he put his hand to them first. He didn't want to be mothered, you see. When he stood upright I was reminded that he was an inch or so taller than I—at twelve years old. It's curious how the relationship has altered since he gained that extra height. It's so easy to fall back into the old ways and treat them as babes in arms.

As we passed through the swing doors again, the receptionist stepped forward with a form in her hand and asked me to fill in a few details. She said it had to be done, and it wouldn't take a minute.

It was just a matter of my name and address and Matthew's date of birth and the name of our GP. While I was filling it in, I was surprised to overhear Matthew in conversation with someone. I looked up and saw him by the tea trolley with an overweight girl with cropped blond hair and large earrings. She was wearing a blue linen coat, unbuttoned, over a red T-shirt and white jeans, and at first it appeared that she was in charge of the trolley. Then she and Matthew came away from it carrying cups and I realized that the coat wasn't a uniform. It was part of her ensemble.

I went over to them. "I thought you'd appreciate a cuppa," the girl explained with a dimpled smile. "Shall we sit down for a minute? How about the back row, Matthew?"

It crossed my mind that she was possibly something to do with the almoner service. I was handed a paper cup. "Thank you, but I don't think I know you."

"You may have heard of the name," she told me. "Molly Abershaw."

I hadn't. I didn't know it and I hadn't seen her before. The remark smacked a little of self-importance, I thought.

"You want to get home, I know," she told us both, "and I shan't keep you longer than it takes to drink the tea. Did you want a biscuit, by the way, Matthew? I always forget to ask. I have to watch the calories myself."

I'm repeating what she said, more or less, because it gives you an insight into the sort of person Molly Abershaw is, and she had a big influence on what happened. You must have come across her sort, with the cheek of old nick, brazenly going up to people as if they were the oldest of friends.

Matthew had the good sense to refuse the biscuit.

"This is such an exciting story," Molly Abershaw insisted on telling us. "I was out at Bathford when I got the call. I really broke the speed limit on the A4. I was thinking if I don't watch out I'll be in the news myself. It's so important to be first on the scene. My photographer is on his way. We'd like a shot of you, Matthew."

"You're a reporter?" I said, hearing the disfavor in my own voice.

"Didn't I say? The *Evening Telegraph*. You don't mind, do you? A rescue story is such a joy to write when we so often deal in tragedy and disaster."

I told her curtly that we'd rather not have anything in the newspapers.

"Mrs. Didrikson," she protested, "it's unavoidable. If we don't run the story, the other papers will. It was a major incident by local standards. We won't print distortions, I promise you. That's why I'm talking to you, just to verify the facts. *Do* say you'll answer my questions."

"What's the point?" I said, looking for somewhere to get rid of the tea. "I wasn't even there. I know less about what happened than you do."

Matthew added in support, "And I don't remember much."

She was very persistent. "Listen, I'm not trying to harass you," she said. "I just need to check the essential facts. I don't even know yet whether there's a 'c' in your name."

"There isn't," I told her.

"It's unusual."

"I'd rather not prolong this."

Instead of taking this as a rebuff, she dipped into her handbag and produced a notebook. "All right. Just the essential facts. How old are you, Matthew?"

Matthew glanced toward me to see if he should answer and I gave a nod, foolishly telling myself that we might get rid of her after she'd taken a couple of notes. "Twelve."

"And you were playing by Pulteney Weir. With friends?"

"Yes."

"How many?"

"Two."

"Who were they?"

"I don't want to get them into trouble."

"Why—did they push you in?"

"No, I fell. I walked along the edge and tipped over."

"And nearly drowned, I gather."

"I don't know much about it."

I stood up. "There—that's all the help we can give you. Now, if you'll kindly allow us to pass, I want to get my son home."

"But we haven't covered the rescue yet."

"You heard what he said. He doesn't remember."

"You *must* remember the man who saved you, Matthew. You saw him when you opened your eyes."

"Yes."

"Did you find out his name?"

"No. He was dark and he had a mustache."

"What sort of mustache?"

Matthew put both hands to his face and traced his fingers from under his nose to the edges of his mouth. "Like this."

"Mexican style?"

He nodded. "He was wearing a striped shirt and tie."

"Smartly dressed, then. A young man?"

"Not very."

"Middle-aged, would you say? Over forty?"

"Not as old as that."

"Did he say anything to you?"

"He was talking to Piers mostly."

"Your school friend?"

Matthew let out a short, troubled breath. "Please don't put his name in the paper. We were supposed to be in school."

"You were playing truant, then?"

I just had to assert myself. "I don't think this is a matter for the papers," I told her. "It's up to the school to deal with it, and I'm sure they will. Come on, Mat." I made a move toward the door.

"I wish our photographer had got here," said Miss Abershaw. "I can't ask you to wait."

"No, and we wouldn't."

She walked with us out of the emergency room and offered to drive us home.

I told her we had transport.

I looked along several lines of cars gleaming in the sun, trying to remember where I'd left the firm's black Mercedes. I had been in such a distracted state when she arrived.

"It's over there," said Matthew, pointing.

Miss Abershaw was still standing beside us. "You drive a Mercedes?"

Matthew came out with, "My mother is a chauffeur."

I said bitterly, "Yes, put it in your notebook. Do you want the mileage as well?"

"I was only thinking that we all have to work for a living," she commented, almost as an apology.

I hesitated as she felt for her keys. Do you know, the remark got through my defenses? The girl's persistence had annoyed me, but a voice inside told me that she was doing a difficult job. She'd been sent by her editor to cover this story. It was not far removed from my own line of work, my boss, Stanley Buckle, sending me off to meet important clients at Bath or Bristol railway stations. Some of those VIPs turn out to be pretty unfriendly. I said, "I'm sorry. It's been a hell of a day."

"Do you think if Maxim, our photographer, called at your house in an hour or so, he could get a picture?"

I got into the car, picked up a card, and scribbled our address on the back.

She said, "Thanks. I really appreciate it. Will your husband be at home?"

"I'm divorced."

Matthew spoke up and announced, "My dad played chess for Norway."

I closed the door and started the engine. When we had driven out of the hospital gates, I told him, "You didn't have to say that, about your father."

"It's true. I'm proud of him."

I didn't say any more.

3

MATTHEW stayed out of school the next day, but not because of illness. I decided he should have a day's grace before he was called to his headmaster's study. It was almost the end of term, anyway. You know the Abbey Choir School, of course. There's the prep school which Mat attends, and the main school for boys of thirteen and upward. He won't start there for another year. They take Common Entrance in the year of their thirteenth birthday, and his will be February. The high fliers go on to some of the best public schools in the country, but the majority just move up to the senior school. The prospectus makes a big thing about traditional values. Parents have to sign a form allowing their boys to be "chastised" for misbehavior. It's supposed to be the right way of encouraging respect and loyalty and most parents seem to accept it. Truancy leads inevitably to a slippering.

I was educated at a comprehensive, a large one, and I must confess that I find the private-school methods quite alien. I've agonized over whether I'm right to keep Matthew at the school. Yet three years ago, when he was nine, I pleaded with the head to admit him. It was at the time when Sverre had just deserted me. At that low point in my life the prospect of bringing up a son unaided terrified me. I'd failed completely in all my relationships with men—my beer-swilling father I grew to despise, the brothers I treated as rivals and still do, and the husband who gave me up not for other women, but for *chess*—so what right had I to raise a son to manhood?

Well, I tell myself that the school is a male institution and Matthew is learning to live among men, supported in the complexities of growing up. That's the justification, and now he's in the choir and everything, I doubt if I'll move him. And I've worked damned hard to scrape together enough to pay the tuition.

I'd be happier if I really believed in the system. I accept that Scripture and church music must play a prominent part in the curriculum of a choir school, and that Latin has to be obligatory, but why does everything else have to be treated in an old-fashioned way? In English they spend hours on clause analysis. The reading list ends at Dickens. The maths master bans calculators from the classroom. Games seem to consist of learning to hold a cricket bat correctly. You don't have to be an educationist to see that there is too much cramming. And the use of corporal punishment is repellent. That's my opinion, anyway.

Surprisingly, Matthew has never asked to change schools. The only thing that he takes strong objection to is singing at the occasional Saturday wedding in the Abbey, obliging him to give up part of his one free day in the week. Otherwise he hardly ever complains. This truancy (at my school it was known more uncouthly as "bunking off" and I did it often) was a new development, unless he had been remarkably clever in covering it up.

When I asked him about it, he dismissed it lightly. Without looking away from the television, he said, "Mr. Fortescue was away on jury service, so our form was sent to the library. Three of us decided to go for a dip. That was all."

"You picked a dangerous place for a swim, Mat."

"We didn't swim. We were messing about in the water."

"Whatever it was, it was dangerous. Why did it have to be you who went along the weir? Why not one of the others?"

"They dared me."

"Oh, Mat!"

He turned his face toward me, ran his fingers through his hair, and said on a note that signaled something of significance, "Ma."

"Yes?" I had ceased to be "Mum" recently. I took it as a sign of Mat's wish to appear more mature. At the hospital he'd forgotten about this, but now he was the young man again.

"I'm sorry I caused all this trouble. It won't happen again."

I hadn't been looking for an apology. I just wanted to reach out to him. I said, "You're not alone in doing stupid things. I've done them. Everyone has, at some stage."

He stared at me in surprise. "He said that."

"Who?"

"The man who got me out. He said almost the same thing as you just said. He used the word 'daft'— 'daft things.' He said sometime in our lives we all do daft things. Something like that."

I commented that he sounded a nice man, adding that I wished we knew who he was so that we could thank him. Apart from anything else, his clothes must have been ruined.

Matthew said, "It's funny that you should say the same thing."

"I suppose it is."

"We ought to find out who he is. I think I'd like to meet him again."

"Well, I can't think where he would have gone in a set of wet clothes," I told him. "Maybe he went to the taxi rank by the Abbey. Tomorrow I'll ask the fellows I used to work with."

I turned up the sound on the television. Talking about the incident was difficult for both of us.

I was greeted warmly at the Abbey rank next morning, and there was the inevitable teasing from the drivers about the Mercedes and my supposedly up-market status. At the first opportunity I asked about yesterday's incident. Nobody remembered a fare in wet clothes, but several of the fellows had early copies of the evening papers. I was handed the *Telegraph*. Prominent on the front page was the picture of Matthew under the headline SHY HERO IN WEIR RESCUE.

I read Molly Abershaw's article and had to admit that the story was broadly correct. I didn't remember a rather pious-sounding quote attributed to me, but the gist of it was true. Mat and I *did* want to trace the man who had gone to the rescue and thank him personally.

I handed back the paper and asked the drivers to let me know if they heard anything.

My visit to the taxi rank made me nearly forty minutes late for work. When I got there, I slammed on the brakes at the sight of another black Mercedes parked in the space reserved for the chairman. The company owned two such cars, one for me to drive, the other for Mr. Buckle's exclusive use. Wouldn't you know it! My boss's appearances at the Bathford site were pretty few and far between, and he was never usually in so early. In my fatalistic mood, I knew before talking to Simon, the office supervisor, that Mr. Buckle had left word that he wanted to see me as soon as I reported for work.

Stanley Buckle bought a controlling interest in Realbrew in 1988, when it was on the point of collapse after years of ineffective management. He invested heavily in a new plant and brought in a new team to run it, and already it looks as if the firm's decline has been halted.

Upon joining Realbrew Ales, I learned that Mr. Stanley Buckle isn't everyone's idea of Santa Claus. He sacked half the existing staff when he took over, and several others have gone since for various shortcomings. Being summoned to his office isn't reckoned to be a promising way to start the day.

I tapped on the door and went in, prepared to be penitent—if necessary, to plead for mercy, offer sackcloth and ashes, anything . . . I needed this job. I couldn't afford to go back to taxi driving. I'd sold my cab and the money had gone on a dozen essential things.

So it was immensely reassuring that Mr. Buckle smiled as he looked at me over his half-glasses. Dressed as usual in a dark pinstripe that must have been Italian and outrageously expensive, and with the customary red rosebud in his buttonhole, he was giving out a distinctly roguish message for the time and place. He stepped around the desk and approached as if to embrace me.

The thought raced through my brain that if this was the price he wished to exact for my late arrival, I'd better settle for it. Physically, he was not exactly my fantasy lover, but this need not amount to any more than a token smooch. He reached out and grasped my upper arm, pulling me firmly toward him. Then, against all expectation, he pressed his hot hand against mine and shook it.

"Congratulations, my dear!"

My confusion must have been starkly obvious.

"Upon your boy's fortunate escape!" he explained. "I read it in the paper. Miraculous! I spotted the name. Unusual name, yours. But I couldn't be certain until I saw the reference to Realbrew."

That was what had pleased him: free publicity in the local papers. Saved by the power of the press!

He said, "How about some coffee? What this must have done to your nerves! Is the boy really none the worse?"

"He's fine," I assured him. "The reason I'm late—"

"Late!" Mr. Buckle cut in. "We didn't expect to see you at all after a ghastly experience like that. Are you sure you wouldn't like the day off?"

"That's very generous," I succeeded in saying, "but it happened the day before yesterday."

"Never mind. If there's anything we can do, just mention it."

That evening I got home after Matthew. He was watching TV and eating baked beans on toast. I didn't inquire what had happened when he'd reappeared at school; he must have had enough humiliation.

"There was a phone call," he told me. "That jumbo-sized reporter, Miss Abershaw."

I sighed, partly in annoyance at Molly Abershaw and partly in her defense—against masculine insensitivity. "Mat, she can't help her size. What did she want this time?"

"She asked if I could remember anything else about the man. She said she would call back when you got in. She *could* help her size if she dieted."

"What exactly did you say to her?"

"There was nothing much I could say. I mean it isn't as if he had a safety pin through his nose. He was just an ordinary bloke with a mustache. I told her that."

I asked him tentatively if he had any homework.

He switched off the TV. "Plenty actually. The usual Latin vocab. And old Fortescue has given us a pig of a history project. We've each been given a street in Bath and we've got to write its history."

"What's yours?"

"He really planned this. He said as I was given the kiss of life I should have Gay Street. It got a cheap laugh, of course."

"Some of those masters are no better than the boys they teach. What are you supposed to do tonight?"

"Draw a large plan of it. We've got to show every building. Then tomorrow we start trying to find out when everything was built and who lived there and all that stuff."

"It sounds more interesting than Latin verbs," I said by way of encouragement.

The phone rang.

Molly Abershaw. She asked if I had seen the paper.

"Yes, I did," I admitted in a tone that surrendered nothing.

"And did you like it?"

"Like it?" I said. "I wouldn't put it as strongly as that. We're not accustomed to being in the newspaper, as I'm sure you must appreciate. But we can't complain. You kept to the facts of what happened. My boss was pleased you mentioned his company by name."

"Just out of interest, I was wondering whether you found out any more about the man who saved Matthew's life."

"No," I told her. "Nothing else. I've been asking around, but with no result. That quote you attributed to me in your report—the one about wanting to thank him personally—I really meant it."

Now the voice became more animated. "That's why I wanted to talk to you, Mrs. Didrikson. I've got this idea for a follow-up. I thought we might run a 'Find the Hero' piece, appealing to our readers to help."

"I see."

"You don't sound too overjoyed."

"To tell you the truth," I said, "I thought there wouldn't be any more in the papers."

"But you said you'd like to find him."

"Well, yes."

"This is as good a way as any. What I would like from you is another quote to say how keen you are to find this man."

"Obviously I am. He put his own life at risk and saved my son. We'd dearly like the opportunity to say how grateful we are, but—"

"Great. And Maxim would like to take a picture of you and Matthew together. He can do it first thing tomorrow if you like, before Matthew leaves for school."

"That would be early. He leaves at eight-thirty."

"No problem. Maxim will be with you soon after eight. And Mrs. Didrikson . . . ?"

"Yes."

"Would you mind asking Matthew the names of his two friends? I'm hoping that they might remember some detail that would help us find the man."

I was wary. "I'm not sure about that. Couldn't we keep the boys out of it?"

"I just want a word with them. I'm wondering if between us we can get a description good enough to publish an artist's sketch of the man."

"The police do that to identify criminals," I pointed out.

There was a moment's silence, then: "I hadn't seen it that way, and I doubt if our readers would. Anyway, I would like to hear from those boys. They can talk to me on the phone tomorrow. Do you have our number? It's on the back page of the paper."

I said that without making any promises, I would speak to Mat about it.

"Fair enough. And of course if Mat should remember anything else, I'll be delighted to hear from him."

"I'll tell him." I put down the phone. It was a strain being subject to so much interest. I had some sympathy with Matthew's rescuer if he wanted to remain unknown.

4

ON FRIDAY EVENING Matthew came into the kitchen and opened the fridge. I asked him what he was hoping to find.

"Some of that custard," was his answer.

"You're an optimist," I told him. "You had the last of it yesterday. There's ice cream in the freezer if you're really desperate. What have they given you for homework this weekend?" Time always seems to be so short that my conversations with my son are reduced to this sort of exchange. I don't like playing the overanxious mum, but that was how it must have seemed to him, and it certainly seemed so to me. At his age, he doesn't often want to share his thoughts, so we keep to the practicalities, and homework is inescapable.

He told me he'd been given a Latin translation to complete, a Scripture reading for a test on Monday and—I quote—"that sodding history project."

"*Matthew.*" I'd heard much worse language when I was driving taxis, but from my own child it was wounding. "What exactly are you objecting to?"

"We're supposed to find out the famous people who lived in the street and write something about their lives. It's easy for Piers. He was given the Circus, and there are plaques with the names up. I'm stuck with Gay Street, worse luck."

"Well, you must do some research. That's the point of the exercise, I expect."

"Research?"

"Don't be so dumb, Mat. There must be books you can look up."

"Where?"

"The library, for a start."

"You've got to be joking."

"Not the school library. The public library. We'll go tomorrow. I'll show you where to look."

"What time tomorrow? You work Saturdays."

"I can't say just now, love. I'll try and make time."

He gave me a look that said he didn't have much faith. Then he turned his back on me and slouched into the back room. I heard him switch on the TV. I felt the tension in my neck and shoulders. If I couldn't spare the child enough time to help him with his homework, what was the point of it all? And my sense of despair wasn't helped by Mat's ungraciousness. I have to remind myself repeatedly that his behavior is normal in an adolescent. He hasn't acquired the maturity to cope with his hormones—if they ever do. His father's example is no encouragement.

There was a sudden shout from the back room of, "Ma, come here."

It riled me. "You don't speak to me like that, Matthew."

"Quick."

The urgency in his voice galvanized me. I found Matthew on his knees in front of the television set with his finger against the screen.

"That's him!"

"Who?"

"*Him*—the man who saved my life."

On the screen I glimpsed a dark-haired man with a mustache, and then the camera moved on to other things, the interior of some lofty room with pillars and chandeliers. Then a young woman in a blue shirt was shown asking a question.

Matthew said, "They'll show him again."

"Who is it?"

"I don't know. I just switched over."

The woman on the screen was asking some question that involved Jane Austen.

The man's face appeared again, responding confidently, spacing his words in a way that suggested he was used to being interviewed. There was an amused glint in his eyes, as if he found the whole subject faintly ridiculous.

"That's him—with the mustache," my son insisted.

"Thousands of men have mustaches like that."

"I know."

"It can't be the same man, dear."

"Why not? It is."

"Out of all the faces you see on television? This program could be coming from Scotland, for all I know. Anywhere."

"Ma, this is Channel 1. *Points West.* If you shut up and listen, we might find out his name."

The man on the screen was saying, ". . . in *Persuasion,* she wrote of the public rooms having to take second place to what she described as 'the elegant stupidity of private parties.' A touch of sour grapes there, I suspect. She didn't get the invitations she would have liked. These parties, or 'routs,' as they were called, were pretty wild affairs for their time, free from the rules and conventions that operated in the Assembly Rooms. So the numbers attending the balls were thin. In one of her letters, Jane writes of being cheered up when scores more people arrived at the Rooms after the private parties broke up. Can you picture her sitting here drumming her fingers on the chair arms while she waits for the action?"

I said, "He's talking about Bath."

"So the pattern of social life was changing?" said the interviewer. "Poor Jane missed the best years here."

"Yes, by the time her family got here, Bath was

socially on the skids. Brighton had taken over as the fashionable place. The Prince of Wales preferred the seaside air, so everyone of note started going down to Brighton instead."

The interviewer turned toward the camera. "And the Assembly Rooms began to be put to different uses. Professor Jackman, thank you. An exhibition about Jane Austen in Bath is being organized by Professor Jackman here in September. To take up the story of the Rooms in more recent years—"

Matthew turned down the volume. "See? That's who it was," he said elatedly. "His name is Jackman."

"But that man was a professor."

"So what? He still got me out of the water. Ma, we've got to thank him properly."

"We'd look awfully silly if you were wrong."

"I'm not."

"Mat, it's easy to make a mistake. People look different on television."

"*He* didn't." He pressed his lips defiantly together. "Don't you want to find him?"

I hesitated. This threatened to become an issue between us. It could easily be settled. "Of course I'd like to find him, if this is the right man, but I'd like you to see him properly before we approach him, not just on television. I wonder if he's in the phone book."

Matthew went to fetch it.

Any lingering suspicions in my mind about the consignment of teddy bears had to be shed on Saturday morning. Mr. Buckle asked me to deliver them to the Women's Institute tent in the grounds of Longleat House in time for the Teddy Bears' Picnic. The wild theories I had concocted in the small hours that some of the bears were stuffed with heroin or diamonds looked pretty silly now. And my boss was looking smug.

He hadn't finished with me, either.

"Little lady, I keep reading about you in the papers. Did you see the *Telegraph* last night?" He handed me a copy. "Page four."

I turned to the page and saw a picture of myself with my arm around Matthew below a headline, HELP US FIND OUR HERO. I just said, "God!" and didn't read on.

"I hope this fellow will turn up soon," Mr. Buckle remarked.

"Thanks."

"If by the start of next week, say, he's still not found, I propose to offer a reward of a hundred pounds for anyone who can name him."

I swallowed hard, not liking the idea one bit. Probably it was my boss's way of compensating me for the hassle I'd had from the police over the teddy bears. "That's generous," I said in a way that was meant to show appreciation without much enthusiasm.

He missed the subtlety entirely. "Not at all," he said. "A gesture like this will do no harm to the firm's reputation."

"What I was going to say is that I'm not sure if a reward is appropriate. Rewards get offered for information about bank raids and burglaries."

"And lost pets," he said. "I see no difficulty."

I didn't question his logic. Instead, I said, "Don't think I'm ungrateful, Mr. Buckle. I just don't want this man to feel hounded. He may prefer to remain unknown. He's entitled to his privacy, if that's what he wishes."

"Fair point," he conceded. "Who knows, he might have a reason not to have been in Bath that day."

"True."

"We all like to slip the leash occasionally, wouldn't you agree, Dana?"

I answered evenly, "In my case, it doesn't apply. But I'm not ungrateful for your offer—I mean the offer of a reward." I left on my errand.

I made sure when I collected the four cartons from the garage that no one had disturbed them since I had deposited them there. To be completely certain, I checked that all eight hundred bears were present. Then

I drove down to Longleat and handed them over to the WI for distribution to the children. It was all done by 10:30 A.M.

Having made such good time, I felt justified in slipping the leash—although not quite as Buckle had meant —to keep my promise to Matthew. I picked him up at home and we drove up Bathwick Hill in search of an address called John Brydon House. The owner, according to the phone book, was the only G. Jackman resident in Bath. I faintly remembered having driven past a house of that name on some occasion, but I wasn't going to make demands on my memory now.

I told Matthew, "I'm making no promises. We'll just find the house and park the car somewhere near and see if he's about."

"Suppose he doesn't come out?"

"Then we'll have to think of something else."

"You mean knock at the door?"

"Don't keep on so, Mat. I told you I'm making no promises."

Really he was right. The proper course of action was to call at the house. Trying to sneak a sight of the man without his knowledge was underhand, but I know how unreliable my son can be. He fantasizes. From the days when he first strung words together he peopled the streets of Bath with goblins, aliens from outer space, pop stars, and characters from soaps. Although he has lately been more restrained with his sightings, I still thought it would save blushes all round to let him get a look at Professor Jackman from a safe distance before we attempted to introduce ourselves. I was pretty sure in my own mind that Mat would be forced to admit to a mistake.

We turned left and drove slowly for some minutes looking at the names of houses. Presently the street took on a more countrified look as the spaces between the plots increased. John Brydon House came up on the right. Matthew spotted the name on the gatepost a moment before I did.

I drove the Mercedes fifty yards or so further and

stopped out of sight of the house, which was set back from the road in its own grounds. More gray than the local limestone, and extensively covered in ivy, it was neither Georgian nor modern; Victorian or Edwardian was my guess. A maroon Volvo stood on a wide, semicircular drive.

"A-OK, chief," said Matthew, slipping into one of his cops-and-robbers roles. "Shall we stake out the joint?"

I wasn't equal to that kind of wit. "Someone is at home, apparently. We'll walk slowly past."

We got out and followed the line of the drystone wall that fronted the drive, trying not to stare at the house too obviously. Where the wall came to an end we paused beside an overhanging pyracantha bush that formed a useful screen, with a narrow view of the house and drive.

Matthew asked, "Want to walk past again?"

"I think we'll stand here awhile."

"There's a path down there. If we cut through to the field, we could see the back of the house. He might be gardening."

"Don't agitate," I told him.

Matthew gave a shrug and hoisted himself onto the wall and sat bouncing his heels off the stones. Somewhere above us a blackbird warbled. It was good to hear. Bird song is rare in my life.

Matthew said casually, as if to fill in the time, "Mighty Molly gave us a bell last night."

This time I didn't pull him up for insulting one of my own sex. "You didn't tell me. What time was this?"

"Quite late. When you were running your bath. I told her you couldn't come to the phone."

"What did she want this time?"

"Same as before. Did we have any news. She said quite a lot of people phoned the paper after she printed some stuff about wanting to find the hero. Some of them were watching when I was rescued. She said they described the man for her, but not one of them recognized him. I told her I could. I told her he was on the television."

"Oh, Mat!"

He folded his arms and stared at the sky. "What's bugging you now?"

I felt like wringing his neck. "You told her that? Did you give her Professor Jackman's name?"

" 'Course I did."

"You great ninny! Suppose you made a mistake."

"I didn't. I keep telling you."

"Mat, would you look at me when I'm talking to you? You don't say things like that to the papers unless you're one hundred percent sure, and even then it isn't always wise to talk to them."

"Why? We're not ashamed of anything. She was bound to ask me if I had anything else to tell her. Did you want me to tell a lie?"

"You could have told her . . . oh, what does it matter now? What are we doing skulking behind this bush if the whole thing is public knowledge?"

"It was *your* idea to come here," Matthew pointed out ungratefully. He jumped down from the wall. "Shall we call at the house, then?"

"I think we must. She will have phoned him by now, I'm sure of that. And Matthew . . ."

"Yes?"

"Leave the talking to me."

"Be my guest."

Mat's condescension stung me. I sensed an assumption of male superiority in the remark. It had gotten through to me in almost everything Mat had said this morning. It came from the school, I was convinced. I couldn't allow it to take hold. I was mother and father to him and I needed his respect. So I grasped him by the sleeve of his blazer and told him firmly, "If you give me that kind of lip, young man, you'd better find someone else to dig you out of messes like this, because you're going to lose my sympathy here and now."

His eyes widened and suddenly he looked very childish. "Sorry, Ma."

Saying, "Come on. Let's get it over with," I stepped out toward the house.

We had not even reached the entrance when Matthew said, "Someone's coming out."

I glanced over the wall and saw a man on the porch.

"That's not him!" Matthew said in a stage whisper. "Ma, that's not him."

I saw for myself that the man now moving briskly and with a bit of a swagger toward the Volvo in the drive was nothing like the professor we'd both seen on TV. This was a hunk of muscle and sinew not much over twenty, with swept-back straw-colored hair and no mustache. He was in a cornflower-blue short-sleeved shirt, white jeans, and white sneakers. Some flicker of memory led me to think I'd seen him before in different surroundings. Generally when I recognize people they turn out to have been fares in my taxi, but you know how it is when your brain can't place someone. Mine was telling me this handsome young buck had never been in my taxi. I'd seen him in some other setting. I placed my hand over Matthew's wrist. "We'd better leave it a few minutes. We'll walk past."

We had not taken a couple of steps when a scene of pure melodrama unfolded. From the still-open door of the house came a voice in shrill protest: "You can't walk out on me, for Christ's sake! Come back!" Then a woman with long, loose red hair appeared in the porch and dashed after the man, catching up with him as he opened the car door. She must have been some years older than he, with a face that was still pretty, yet with a strained, stretched look to the skin.

All this happened as Matthew and I passed the front of John Brydon House. I didn't like to take too obvious an interest, particularly as the woman was barefoot and wearing a pink silk dressing gown open to the thighs. I need not have troubled. The actors were too caught up in the drama to care who was watching. The woman reached out and got a grip on the gold chain at the man's throat. She was trying to prevent him from getting into the car. She cried out, "Don't go, Andy, you can't do this to me! Come back in, please, please! What do you want me to do, get on my knees and beg?"

The man called Andy didn't answer. He was prizing her fingers one by one from the chain as if he didn't want to risk snapping it by thrusting her away from him. Meanwhile she clutched a mass of his blond hair with the other hand, but that didn't appear to trouble him. Having succeeded in saving the necklace, he gripped her wrists, forced her to her knees, and then toppled her off balance with a light, contemptuous push. She cried, "Bastard!" as her shoulder made contact with the gravel, but a stronger shove could have made it a lot more painful.

By the time the woman was on her feet again, Andy had gotten into the car and slammed the door. He started the motor. She drummed her fists on the window and cried, "Andy, I didn't mean that!" The Volvo crunched on the gravel, swung into the road, and headed toward Bath. The woman ran as far as the entrance and watched it go. She was sobbing.

Matthew and I had raised our walking pace from a stupefied shuffle to a quick march toward our own car, which was fortunately parked in the opposite direction from the route the Volvo had taken. We got in and closed the doors.

"Who do you think they are?" Matthew asked.

I told him I hadn't the faintest idea.

"It's the right house."

"I know. Phone books aren't always up to date. Maybe your professor sold it to these people and moved somewhere else. Anyway, I don't propose to knock on *that* door."

"What was she shouting about?"

"It's none of our business. Something private."

"Like sex, do you mean?"

"Matthew, that's enough."

"She wasn't wearing anything under that dressing gown. Was she a prostitute, Ma?"

"Don't be ridiculous." I started the car.

"I was only asking. You hardly ever talk to me about sex."

Liberated youth! At his age, I almost died of shame when my mother told me what to expect—without once mentioning the reproductive organs by name.

I reversed the car and drove past the house. The woman had gone and the front door was shut. We drove down into Bath and parked in one of the spaces opposite the Orange Grove. I was glad to have the distraction of the other promise I'd given to Mat—the visit to the local history section in the central library. I took him downstairs and we passed a quiet half hour taking books off the shelves and looking for references to Gay Street. We discovered it was named after someone called Robert Gay, who owned the land on which it was built. "Big deal!" said Mat. But we managed to compile a list of former residents and visitors that included John Wood, Tobias Smollett, Josiah Wedgwood, Jane Austen, and William Friese-Green. Matthew wrote down the names and said he hadn't heard of any of them.

"You've got to find out. That's the purpose of the exercise," I told him, trying to generate some enthusiasm. "We'll walk to the reference library now and I'll show you where to look."

I left him making notes from the *Dictionary of National Biography* and went to buy a fresh parking card. When I got back to the car, a large, familiar, and not-too-welcome figure was waiting beside it.

Molly Abershaw greeted me by saying that the fellows on the taxi rank had spotted my car and suggested that I wouldn't be long in returning to it. Today she was in a multicolored poncho that she had probably bought from the Latin American craft shop. "I thought you'd like an early copy." She handed me an *Evening Telegraph.*

The main story was headed PROFESSOR'S RESCUE PLUNGE. I read it rapidly. Clearly Mat and I could have saved ourselves some trouble if we'd picked up a telephone instead of peering over the wall of John Brydon

House. Professor Jackman was confirmed as the hero of
Pulteney Weir.

Molly Abershaw beamed and said, "I must admit
I'm quite proud of it. This has been my story from the
beginning. It's really satisfying when you can follow it up
like this."

"So you spoke to the professor yourself?"

"After Mat put me on to him, yes. He's a bright
lad."

"Do you mean Mat?"

Molly Abershaw quivered with amusement. "Both,
I assume, but I did mean Mat, yes." It was clear from
the way she continued to smile that she had something
else to raise. "You didn't mind me speaking to Mat?"

"How could I object?" I said reasonably. I refused
to be lured into saying anything controversial. "He answers the phone if I'm out."

"Very capably, too. Most kids his age speak in
monosyllables. I'm sure the school makes a difference."

"Possibly." I was wary. I didn't want the school
mentioned in the paper again and nor did Mat.

"May I ask, will you be going to see Professor Jackman to thank him personally?"

This was where Mat would have blurted out a
graphic account of the incident at John Brydon House.
Thanks to Mr. Fortescue and his history assignment,
however, the press was denied a salacious story. I answered with well-chosen words, "We'll find some way of
expressing our thanks, certainly."

"I knew you would, and I can arrange it for you."

"Oh, that won't be necessary," I said quickly.

"You do want to meet him?"

"Yes, but—" My poise was gone.

"Shake his hand and all that?"

"Well, I expect so."

"He's going to be at Waterstone's bookshop tomorrow. There's a signing by Ted Hughes and all the local
literati are invited."

"I couldn't possibly go."

"Why not? It's open to the public. That's the point

of these parties. It's all about selling books. You and Matthew can sidle up to the professor and have a quiet word with him over a drink. Much easier than calling at his house or going up to the university."

I wavered. It did sound painless.

Molly Abershaw added, "And Mat won't have to take any time off school."

"He's quite busy with services on Sunday."

"In the afternoon?"

I conceded that on balance no better opportunity was likely to present itself for expressing thanks to Professor Jackman. Fickle creature that I am, I found myself wondering what to wear.

"I'll probably see you there, then," said Molly Abershaw.

5

THAT SUNDAY LUNCHTIME, Waterstone's bookshop in Milsom Street was teeming with people wanting a glimpse of the Poet Laureate, or his autograph. Just out of the crunch, Mat and I were at a temporary standstill between the fantasy and crime sections. We were keeping watch for another distinguished man.

Mat, under heavy protest, was in his red-and-white-striped school blazer, gray trousers, white shirt, and tie. I'd told him he couldn't turn up to an occasion like this in his usual Sunday choice of T-shirt and jeans, which the choir wore under their cassocks at the Abbey services. He'd grumbled to me that if any of his form mates spotted him walking up Milsom Street in school uniform, his life would be hell next time he saw them. I'd pointed out that I could expect some flak myself from the taxi drivers if they saw me in a skirt.

"That's him!" Matthew said suddenly.

"Where?"

"In that group on the far side, close to the books."

"There are books all around us."

"Against the wall, under the fiction notice, just in front of the woman with the green hat. He's with the tall black man and that bald man with a bow tie."

"Is that him?" I said. "I imagined he was taller when I saw him on the television."

"That's him, all right," Matthew insisted. "He *is* quite tall."

"Well, yes. It does look like him. You're right."

Professor Jackman was talking animatedly to the people with him. With the black mustache and darting eyes and the hands vigorously reinforcing what he was saying, he looked more like a gondolier haggling over a fare than an academic. A communicator, obviously. No doubt his lectures were worth attending. I found myself wanting to get closer to hear what he was saying. Yet I was petrified by the prospect of interrupting him to introduce my son and myself. His reaction was impossible to predict.

Matthew, too, shrank from seizing the opportunity now that it had come. "His hair is standing up more than when I saw him," he said to me, blatantly marking time. "Of course, it was wet. And he wasn't wearing a jacket."

"That one is tailor-made, by the look of it," I murmured. "He must be hot."

"So am I," said Mat.

"There's a woman serving orange juice over there," I said. "Shall we see if it's for everyone?"

We'd not moved a couple of steps when I felt my arm touched and held. The air was warmer and there was a clank of metal jewelry. Molly Abershaw had found us.

"You're heading in the wrong direction, my loves. He's over there. My, you're looking smart, Mat. Come on, I'll introduce you."

She cleared a route across the room, with Mat and me following like foot soldiers after a tank. The group around the professor was still listening keenly to his conversation.

"Professor Jackman?"

"Yes?" He turned, eyebrows raised at being interrupted in midflow.

"My name is Molly Abershaw. We spoke on the

phone yesterday morning. I'm from the *Evening Telegraph.*"

The muscles at the edge of his mouth tightened. "I
thought it was agreed, Miss Abershaw, that I don't have
any more to say to the press."

The tank might have stopped advancing in one
sense, but in another it trundled on. "Relax, professor.
I'm not asking for a statement. I just want to introduce
somebody to you—well, it's more of a reunion than an
introduction, in point of fact. Remember young Matthew?" She placed her hand on Mat's shoulder as if
there might be some uncertainty in identifying him.
"You can say your piece, Mat."

Before Matthew opened his mouth, Professor Jackman said tersely, "There's no need."

"This is his mother, Mrs. Didrikson," said Molly
Abershaw. "They've come here specially to meet you."

The bald man with the bow tie said, "What's this,
Greg—your past catching up with you?"

Molly Abershaw took a tighter grip on Matthew's
shoulder and pushed him closer to the professor, saying
at the same time, "Stand back, Mrs. Didrikson."

Then a fresh voice said, "Professor, would you look
this way, please?"

A camera flashed.

It was unexpected by everyone except the photographer and Molly Abershaw. In the mass of people I
hadn't seen a camera until that moment. I was furious.
The whole thing had been set up like an ambush and
Mat and I appeared to be parties to it.

Professor Jackman said, "What the hell is going
on?"

"Hold it like that. One more," said the photographer, a tall and bearded youth in a pink shirt.

The professor moved fast. He stepped forward,
reached across the bookcase that the photographer was
standing behind, grabbed him by the wrist, and told him
to open the camera and expose the film.

"I can't do that."

"If you can't, I will." He forced the hand and camera upward.

"You'll damage it!" the photographer said.

"Do it, then."

Molly Abershaw said, "Hey, you've no right—"

"Correction," the professor said without relaxing his grip. "*You* had no right. Bloody nerve you people have got. This is a party for Mr. Hughes, not a football match."

Heads were turning and conversation had ceased around us.

"All right, let go of my arm," said the photographer.

Professor Jackman released his grip.

The photographer pulled the release to open the camera.

"Take out the film and give it to me," the professor ordered. "Yes, I want the film." He pocketed it and turned away, looked at some people, said, "Incident closed," and returned to the group he had been in conversation with.

He had his back to us. I couldn't possibly speak to him now, nor could Matthew. I was mortified and angry, more for Mat's sake than my own. It was a horrid outcome to Mat's decent wish to express his thanks, and Molly Abershaw was to blame. Not the professor. His angry reaction was understandable. We had been cynically used, all of us.

I glared across to where Molly Abershaw was conferring with the photographer.

"Leave it, Ma," said Mat.

He was right. There wasn't any point in another scene. We left it.

PART FIVE

A Pain
in the Head

1

IN MANVERS STREET POLICE STATION, Diamond handed Dana Didrikson a mug of coffee and told her that a message had just come through about her son. Young Matthew had been delivered to his school boarding-house by a police patrol and they had left him watching the *Benny Hill Show* with some of his friends. "So now you can relax," he told her with a slight smile that conceded the absurdity of the suggestion, even if it was kindly meant.

She didn't respond, except to pass a slow glance around the interview room, its acoustic walls stained with coffee, cigarette burns, hair grease, and undetermined substances. Over the past hour she had given a fair impression of a cooperative witness, recalling her first encounters with the Jackmans in a frank, dignified manner, as if the escape attempt earlier in the evening had never happened, and it had always been her prime intention to talk to the police. Looking at her childishly small left hand as it rested quite flat on the wood table, apparently free of tension, Diamond was encouraged to think that Dana Didrikson was at peace with herself. Was it too much to hope, he wondered, that she had now resolved to confess to the murder and would presently explain in her unruffled style exactly how and why she had done it?

"Shall we go on?" he said, impatient to bring the interview to its climax.

Another tape was switched on, and John Wigfull, observing the letter of the law as usual, went through the ritual of assigning it with its number and stating the time and date.

"Let's take it from the party at Waterstone's, then," Diamond cued her. "You were obviously embarrassed by what had happened there."

"Mortified." She shook her head, remembering, and then explained how later that same day she had plucked up the courage to phone Jackman at home. He had been out, and Geraldine had answered, been perfectly charming, and invited her over the same evening to a barbecue. It had seemed a good opportunity of speaking to the professor, without any obligation to stay for long. Better still, when she had gotten there, she had been met outside by Jackman himself. He had suggested driving to a pub and over a couple of drinks they had ironed out all the misunderstandings.

Wigfull chose to comment, "So you two got on well when you were one-to-one?"

She declined to answer, and no wonder. Wigfull's interruption, in Diamond's estimation, was about as well judged as three cheers at a funeral. This wasn't the time to probe her relationship with Jackman—not when she was just getting into her narrative stride again.

Leaving a distinct pause as the remark sank away, Mrs. Didrikson continued, "He told me about the exhibition he was organizing in honor of Jane Austen, and the problems he was having collecting exhibits. Somehow the talk led on to Jane Austen's aunt, who was had up for shoplifting in Bath. Greg told me the story and funnily enough that rang a bell in my head, although I said nothing at the time. Oh, and he generously said he'd like to meet Mat again. He offered to take him swimming in the university pool."

This time Diamond himself interrupted her, flagrantly doing the very thing that had caused him to glare at Wigfull. "Tell us about Jane Austen's aunt."

"The shoplifting episode?"

"No. The reason it rang a bell."

She took a sip of coffee first, and still the hand was remarkably steady. "Well, you have to know that her name was Mrs. Leigh Perrot. I think I told you about Mat and his history homework, and how I took him to the library to look up the famous residents of Gay Street."

"The aunt lived there?"

She shook her head and betrayed some slight irritation. "I'm trying to tell you, if you'll give me a chance. We started in the local history section in the basement at the main library, as I mentioned. The shelves were stuffed with books about Bath and Bristol and the towns round about, as you would expect, and while we were looking along the titles, my eyes lighted on one that looked as if it had strayed from the zoology section. At a quick glance, I thought the title was *In Search of the Parrots.* When I picked it up, I realized my mistake. The word was *Perretts,* and it was by a George Perrett, a local man who had written this book about his family history. It didn't help our Gay Street researches, so I returned it to the shelf, but later, when Greg told me the story of Mrs. Leigh Perrot, I decided to go back to the library and have a closer look at the book. It was just possible that I might discover something of interest to him—and I thought how marvelous it would be if I could find out something he didn't know, something that might be of use in the exhibition, just as a mark of thanks for rescuing Mat."

"You didn't say anything to Professor Jackman at the time?"

"No, there was no certainty that the book would mention Mrs. Leigh Perrot." And then Dana Didrikson pressed her hands together, locking her fingers tightly, slipping the reins of her composure as she recalled the moment. "But it did," she said with satisfaction. "Tucked away in the middle was a paragraph pointing out that many of the Perrett family weren't considered worthy of mention in the various archives and what a pity it was that they had been so law-abiding, or they might have rated a mention somewhere, *like a certain Mrs. Leigh Perrot,* who had been tried at Taunton in 1800 for shoplifting. The name leaped out at me. It had to be Aunt Jane! And—even more exciting—the author added that there was a bundle of papers in the Wiltshire County Record Office containing an account of the trial and a letter signed by one of the Leigh Perrot family."

"The Wiltshire CRO. That would be Trowbridge," Wigfull put in stolidly, just to air his erudition, so far as Diamond could judge.

Thankfully Mrs. Didrikson was too hyped up by the memory of these events even to pause. She went on to describe how she had gone to Trowbridge at the first opportunity and put in her application for the papers. "To be honest, it was quite an anticlimax when they were put in front of me. The letter had been written by someone called John Leigh Perrot, and when I eventually deciphered the handwriting, I found nothing of interest. And the account of the trial was very dull. I had a word with the assistant there, just in case they happened to have anything on file about Aunt Jane. He looked through a card index and consulted a computer, and found nothing. I was about to give up when one of the more senior people, an archivist, I think, came over and asked which name I was researching. I told her and she looked up the details of the acquisition of the papers I'd seen. She said one of her colleagues had been involved. Well, to cut it short, she made a call and this person on the end of the line was able to confirm that quite a stack of Leigh Perrot family letters had been offered for sale to the record office back in the 1960s, or whenever, and they had taken only a representative sample. Whoever had dealt with it had been unaware of the connection with Jane Austen. But they had the name of the man who had offered the letters, a Captain Crandley-Jones, from Devizes."

"And you traced him?"

"Eventually. It took longer than I hoped. He wasn't in the phone book."

"Meanwhile Professor Jackman had no idea you were on the trail of these letters?"

She shook her head. "I didn't say a thing about it. It might so easily have come to nothing."

"Then you contacted this man in Devizes?"

"His son-in-law. The captain had died, but I was given the address of his executor, the son-in-law, who lived on the Isle of Wight. I wrote to him and heard nothing for over two weeks. I thought the trail had gone cold, and of course there were only a few days left before the exhibition opened. Then one evening in the first week in September he phoned me. He said he'd been going through the captain's papers, and he'd found a receipt for the sale of a collection of sixty-three Perrot family letters. Sixty-three! The purchaser had been a stamp dealer in Crewkerne, named Middlemiss. He'd bought the lot in 1979 for a hundred and fifty pounds. Naturally I drove down there the next day, and this time I was in luck—more luck than I could have dared to hope for. Mr. Middlemiss still lived at the same address, and he still had the bulk of the Perrot letters. He'd bought the collection because some of the letters bore early postage stamps, which he'd sold at a good profit, I gathered. Then he'd put the rest into a box file and hadn't touched them since. He brought out the box and let me examine the contents." Mrs. Didrikson squeezed her eyes shut for a second. "I can't begin to convey the excitement I felt going through those dusty old letters. They were in various hands and I suppose they covered a period of about eighty years. Some of them had squares cut out, where postage stamps had been. Fortunately the ones that interested me would have been written before stamps came into use, whenever that was."

Like the bright boy in school, Wigfull supplied the date: 1840.

But Dana Didrikson was too gripped by her story to notice. "Imagine how I felt when I found two short letters dated as early as 1800, addressed to Mrs. James Leigh Perrot, at the Warden's House, Ilchester Gaol, and signed 'Yr affectionate niece, Jane.' I'd struck gold."

"Did Middlemiss realize their significance?" Diamond asked.

"I'm afraid I didn't tell him."

"Naughty."

She took it as a serious rebuke. "I could never have afforded the price he'd ask. As it was, he wanted thirty pounds for them, and he thought I was just researching my family history. I paid cash and left. Was that dishonest?"

"No, it's fair game," Diamond commented. "The first rule of the open market: An object is worth no more and no less than your buyer is willing to pay for it. He was pitting his knowledge against yours. You were smart enough to know it was worth a bit and he didn't. You'd have been a fool to enlighten him. You needn't lose any sleep over it, except that you could probably have knocked him down to twenty-five pounds. They expect you to haggle."

"I know—but I couldn't have stood the suspense."

"So you got out fast."

"And drove home picturing the moment when I would hand them over to Greg."

"You were still in touch with him at this time?"

Mrs. Didrikson hesitated, gripped the edge of the table with both hands, and eased back, as if she sensed a trap in the question. "I'd seen him on several occasions when he took my son swimming."

"And to the cricket and the balloon festival," Wigfull prompted her with sledgehammer subtlety.

That did it: frigidly, she remarked, "You seem to know everything already."

After an uncomfortable interval, Wigfull attempted to repair the damage. "What I meant was that Professor Jackman went out of his way to be kind to your son."

"Well, yes," she conceded.

"Which gave you even more reason to make him a present of the Jane Austen letters."

Diamond asked, "When did you hand them over—the same evening?"

Again she paused before answering. Her fluency had gone and Diamond knew who to blame. "Not that evening," she answered eventually. "A couple of days later."

"On the eve of the exhibition, I heard," said Diamond. "What made you leave it so late?"

More unease showed in the way she grasped at her hair and flicked it off her shoulders. "I, em . . . When I got back from Crewkerne, there was, em . . . an ugly scene with Geraldine Jackman. To my utter amazement, she was in my house, sitting in my living room drinking coffee."

"Alone?"

"No. What happened was that while Mat was swimming with Greg up at Claverton, somebody phoned the Jackman house from Chawton—that's the cottage in Hampshire set up as a kind of Jane Austen museum—to say that permission had been given for Greg to borrow several extra pieces for his exhibition. Understandably, he was keen to go down to Chawton straightaway, so he asked his wife to run Matthew home in her car, which she did. Out of politeness Mat thought he'd better invite Geraldine in for a coffee, and she accepted like a shot, which explains what I walked into. What I cannot explain is the vicious and quite unprovoked attack that woman made on me almost the moment I stepped into my own living room."

Diamond briefly locked eyes with Wigfull in case he was moved to interrupt again. "A physical attack?"

"No, I don't mean she hit me, but the force of it was almost physical. This was the first time we'd actually met, you understand. We'd spoken on the phone some weeks before when she invited me to her party and she'd sounded quite charming. I couldn't believe this was the same woman. In fact, I didn't know who she was for a moment. She just bombarded me with abuse."

"What sort of abuse?"

"Do I have to repeat it?"

"Everything you can remember, please."

Dana Didrikson fingered her hair again and looked down into the coffee mug, speaking in a low voice. "She began by asking me who I thought I was kidding by driving around in a Mercedes when I was really the town bicycle."

Wigfull asked, "The what?"

"For Christ's sake, John." Diamond rounded on him. "Carry on, Mrs. Didrikson."

"I was more surprised than offended. I asked who she was and she said she happened to be married to the man I was currently humping. This was in front of my son, a twelve-year-old." She looked up, her face creased in distress at the memory. "Can you imagine? I asked him to leave the room. Poor child, he looked blitzed. And before he was through the door she launched into an accusation so twisted in its logic that I couldn't believe she meant it. She said I'd used Matthew as bait, to catch her husband. Having discovered that Greg was childless, I'd dangled Mat in front of him—those were the actual words she used—knowing how much he wanted a son of his own."

"What did you say to that?"

"The truth—that she was talking bloody nonsense and I'd never slept with her husband. Then of course she did her best to justify her crazy notions by bringing up the times I'd invited Greg in for coffee after he'd brought Mat home from the pool. I mean, a coffee and a biscuit in my kitchen isn't grounds for divorce, and I told her so. But in Geraldine's eyes everything was part of this web I'd spun—the swimming, the days out, the drink I'd bought Greg in the Viaduct—someone had seen us, of course. There was no shaking her. In the end I just stopped protesting and let her carry on in the hope she'd get it all out and go. That's what happened. She hadn't come to listen to my point of view. She just wanted to let off steam, and by God, she did. Finally she stormed out."

"She didn't actually threaten you, or make some kind of ultimatum?"

"No, it was just a torrent of abuse."

"How did you feel at the end? Bloody angry, I imagine."

"Dazed is more like it. Reeling. The first thing I did was talk to Mat and tell him that the woman was obviously unhinged. He apologized for letting her into the house, but she had been perfectly agreeable until I showed my face. That's how it is with that kind of madness. Ninety-nine percent of the time they seem perfectly sane."

Diamond nodded.

"Just in case Matthew was tempted to believe any of her crazy claims, I gave him a solemn promise that they were all untrue. We agreed that Greg had a terrible problem with a woman like that on his hands. I told Mat that after what had been said I didn't think he should go swimming with Greg again."

To Diamond's ear, this struck a note of bathos, but he treated it solemnly. "How did he take it?"

"Manfully, for a kid of his age. Oh, he couldn't see the sense in it at first. After all, Greg had been like a second father to him through the months of July and August. So it was a wrench. I had to point out that Greg himself would be bound to put a stop to the swimming in view of what Geraldine was saying."

"Did he see the point then?"

"Yes."

All of this had given Diamond some vital insights. The incident may not have provided a direct motive for murder, but it had clearly struck deep into Dana Didrikson's psyche. Not only had her moral conduct been under attack, so had her integrity as a mother, and that was enough to goad any woman dangerously. Even this long after the incident, a feral outrage had shown in her eyes and voice as she spoke of Geraldine Jackman.

He steered her back to the main line of inquiry. "And you had another problem on your hands—the Jane Austen letters."

"Now do you understand why I didn't hand them over the same evening?"

"But you did eventually."

"Yes. After a couple of sleepless nights. I thought why should I let that pathetically jealous woman deprive Greg of the satisfaction of owning those precious letters? They were of no use to me, but in his hands they were sure to make a stir in the literary world. They would guarantee the success of his exhibition. After the tremendous risk he'd taken to save my son, I'd have to be an absolute wimp not to face another roasting from Geraldine. So on that Friday evening, the night before the opening, I steeled myself to call at the house."

"You could have posted the letters, surely, and avoided seeing Mrs. Jackman?" said Wigfull.

"They were too precious to put in the post. Besides, there wasn't time."

Diamond commented with more understanding, "And I daresay you wanted to see his reaction when you produced them."

The corners of her mouth curved, confirming that he was right. "If I'm honest, yes. I phoned first, to make sure he was going to be there, merely telling him I had something I wanted to give him, and would it be convenient if I came over right away. And I took the opportunity over the phone to thank him again for his kindness to Mat and me, and to make clear that I'd decided that the swimming sessions must come to an end."

"Did you say why?"

"I think he knew. No doubt Geraldine had told him her suspicions. She wasn't noted for being reticent. Anyway, he didn't press me. And when I got to the house, it was Greg who opened the door, much to my relief, of course. And when I showed him the letters in the front room, oh, it was a terrific moment! I was *so* pleased I'd come. He was over the moon. He made me tell him exactly how I'd tracked them down, every detail. And then a man I didn't know came in, an American."

"Dr. Junker."

"That was the name. He seemed to be an authority

on Jane Austen, and when he saw the letters, he was agog with excitement. He was confident that they were in Jane's hand. So when Geraldine Jackman made an entrance a few minutes after, she didn't get the attention she felt was hers by right. She acted just like a spoiled child."

Fascinating as it was to listen to a fresh point of view on an episode that was becoming familiar, Diamond fixed his mind on the facts as he continued to listen, rather than looking for insights into character. Dana Didrikson's account corresponded impressively closely with what Jackman and Junker had said. She had noticed Geraldine's blatant passes at Junker and she repeated that lady's mischievous suggestion that Jackman should show his gratitude by taking her—Dana—out for a meal.

"Just for the record, you made no arrangement to visit the house again?"

"Didn't I make that clear?" she said. "I was ending our association with the Jackmans."

"And did you?"

"Yes." She leaned back, fatigue showing in her brown eyes. "That's it. I've nothing else to tell you."

Diamond studied her, uncertain for a moment whether she had spoken out of mischief or defiance. "You mean you need a break now?"

"No," she said. "That isn't what I mean."

"Come now, Mrs. Didrikson," he said gently. "There must be more to come. We know there's more."

Her eyes may have given a clue that he was right, but she wasn't willing to admit to it. "Am I under arrest, then?"

"Not up to now."

"In that case I'd like to leave."

"In that case," said Diamond, "I shall be forced to arrest you."

"For what?"

"Driving without due care and attention will do."

"That's absurd."

"Sorry. You're nicked, Mrs. Didrikson."

"What does that mean?"

"It means we can detain you for twenty-four hours, or thirty-six, if I so decide."

Her lip quivered. "But I'm expected at work tomorrow. My boss relies on me to drive him about."

"He'll have to use a taxi, won't he?" He looked toward Wigfull. "Stop the tape there. We'll need a fresh one shortly."

2

————————

"BEFORE we go back, John . . ."

"Yes?"

"A word."

Wigfull, eyebrows arching above that comic-opera mustache, appeared to have no idea what was on Peter Diamond's mind. Leaving Dana Didrikson in the interview room to mull over what she had so far failed to disclose, the two detectives had busied themselves independently for twenty minutes or so, Diamond at his desk, Wigfull at a phone in the incident room. They now faced each other at the top of the stairs.

Diamond came to the point. "We're at cross-purposes in there. I get her going and you keep gumming up the works."

"Such as . . . ?"

"You know damned well what I mean."

"If you have a complaint about me, I'd rather you specified exactly what it is, Mr. Diamond."

How typical of his whole nitpicking approach, Diamond thought in a spasm of anger he had difficulty in containing. "It's more fundamental, John. You and I are not on a wavelength. You're basically hostile to the woman and it shows."

This was received with a cold stare. *"I'm* hostile? *She* tried to avoid arrest."

"That doesn't mean we have to come down hard."

"Great," muttered Wigfull, plainly implying that this kind of talk from the man who had put Hedley Missendale away didn't cut much ice.

Diamond would not allow himself to be deflected. "Look, the object is to get at the truth."

"Yes, and the truth is that she was besotted with Jackman and murdered his wife."

To Wigfull, it was all so obvious.

"You could be right, but there's still another dimension to this," Diamond told him.

"The sob story, you mean?"

"I can't say. There's definitely more to come, if we give her a chance to tell us."

"In other words, you want me to button my hairy lip."

The note of self-mockery was a concession, a step back from cold-eyed hostility, and Diamond acknowledged it with a grin. "The chance of that has gone. She's dug a bloody trench for herself. We've got to move in, but to a purpose. In my judgment, she won't respond to threats."

"Okay, I said I'll shut up."

"No, I want you to chip in. I need your command of the details. That's how we'll tackle her, with the truth, testing her story with the facts we know to be true, you and me, John, working as a team."

This earned a grudging nod from Wigfull, and a sharp inquiry as to what line the questioning was to take.

Diamond was equal to it. They would begin by suggesting to Dana Didrikson that she had been at the Jackman house on the day of the murder. Whatever her response, they would commit her to an account of her movements on that Monday. Only when they had gotten a full picture of her day would they probe her motives or point to inconsistencies. It was the structured interview so beloved of training-school instructors, and

Wigfull couldn't fault it. Diamond added, to bring a human dimension to the exchange, that all this would be at great personal cost because his wife Stephanie was using the late nights as ammunition in her campaign to have her kitchen modernized. She was serving him burnt offerings nightly.

"You should get her a microwave oven," Wigfull advised him.

"I don't trust them."

"They're part of the new technology. I wouldn't be without ours."

"That figures," said Diamond, prepared to believe that Wigfull's home was indistinguishable from an electricity showroom.

"Maybe you saw me on the phone just now," Wigfull went on. "I wasn't calling my wife. I don't, now that we have a microwave." While Diamond was pondering the cause and effect behind that, Wigfull added casually, "As a matter of fact, I was phoning Mrs. Didrikson's employer, Buckle."

"What for?"

"I told him she wouldn't be in to work tomorrow."

"Wasn't it a bit late for that?"

"I got him at home."

"I see." Slightly put out, but wary, Diamond started walking toward the interview room. "She'll be grateful, I'm sure."

Behind him, he heard Wigfull raise his voice to say, "I didn't do it out of the goodness of my heart, Mr. Diamond. I asked him if she reported for duty on Monday, September eleventh."

He wheeled around.

Wigfull was looking as smug as a cat in the best chair. "And she didn't. Buckle checked his diary. She took the day off. She wasn't at work on the day of the murder." He spaced the words like an actor in a radio serial rounding off an episode. It demanded a burst of music.

Diamond wasn't moved to supply any. He merely nodded his head.

"You knew already?" Wigfull piped in disbelief.

Diamond answered in throwaway style, "The statements are in from the door-to-door lads. I've just been through them. A woman in a black Mercedes was seen turning into the drive of John Brydon House shortly after eleven-fifteen."

It was a much better payoff.

She had her back to the door when they returned, a slight, tense figure staring out of the window at the lights of Bath, arms crossed in front of her. Diamond was moved to think how little he'd learned of this woman's character in the two or three hours so far of question and answer. Part of the difficulty was that she'd obviously rehearsed her story in her mind, knowing that sooner or later the police would catch up with her. The smoothness of the performance had given few insights, save for those bursts of waspishness at Wigfull's interruptions toward the end. Admittedly she had projected a strong sense of moral obligation, whether toward her disagreeable son, her shady boss, or the knight in shining armor, Professor Jackman, but how much of that was window dressing remained to be discovered. One other point Diamond had noted: the still-potent sense of triumph in her account of the quest for the Jane Austen letters—letters that looked increasingly like the spur to murder.

"Shall we resume?" he said.

"I've nothing else to tell you." She need not have spoken. He could read the defiance in the set of her shoulders.

He nodded to Wigfull to run another tape and speak the preliminaries. When it was done, he reminded her of the formal caution before saying, "We've just had some information about you, Mrs. Didrikson."

All this had no appreciable effect.

"We know you visited Geraldine Jackman on the day she was murdered. You were seen."

This time a tremor of shock went through her,

which she tried to convert into the action of rubbing her arms.

Diamond concluded his statement. "So there must be something else to tell."

Wigfull said, in his new, nonaggressive guise, "Why don't you sit down?"

She half turned and looked over her shoulder, indecisively, then walked to the table and took her place opposite Diamond, her eyes glazed, as if too much was going on in her brain for it to interpret what she was seeing.

"You do admit going to the house?" Diamond put to her.

She dipped her head in what may have been meant as a positive response.

"Why?" Diamond asked, already departing from the structured interview he had proposed. "Why did you go there?"

She spoke in a whisper too low to register on the recording equipment. "To ask her to hand over the letters."

"Geraldine?"

She nodded, and said a little louder, "I was sure she had them hidden in the house." Her eyes began to function intelligently again. "It was obvious that she must have taken them."

Wigfull asked, "How did you know they were missing?"

"Greg phoned me early that morning, about half-past seven. He believed Dr. Junker had taken them. He was going after him, on the train to London."

"But why should he have told you about it?"

"He was sure Geraldine would call me out of spite, just to gloat. He didn't want me to hear it from her."

On rapid reflection Diamond decided that this explanation was plausible. It was reasonably consistent with Jackman's suspicions of his wife.

"And did Geraldine call you?"

"No." Mrs. Didrikson leaned forward, her dark eyes intense. "Which makes it even more certain that she had the letters herself. Greg was mistaken. I was positive she had them." She used the word "she" with unconcealed contempt, with a passionate dislike that had not been expunged by the killing. The animus between the two women must have amounted to more, far more, than the events so far described had justified.

Diamond knew he was in danger of being sidetracked, and this time he kept to the record of what had happened on the fatal Monday. "So what did you decide to do about it?"

"I didn't do anything at first. I waited some hours. It really got to me, that she could be so bloody-minded. I was in such a state that I phoned my boss and made some excuse to get off work. About eight-thirty I drove Matthew to school and did some shopping in Bath. Had a coffee in one of those places by the bus station and did some thinking. While I was sitting there, a phrase came back to me, something Geraldine had said when I handed the letters over to Greg. She tried to rubbish them. She called them musty old things with no literary merit."

A detail, Diamond noted, that they had heard almost verbatim from Dr. Junker. Dana Didrikson hadn't previously mentioned it herself.

"You *must* understand the appalling thought that came to me," she said, scanning their faces for a sympathetic response. "She wouldn't think twice about destroying those precious letters. She would put a match to them rather than admit to Greg that she'd hidden them out of spite. It was up to me to stop her. It mattered more that she was stopped than any misgivings I had about crossing swords with her again."

"So you drove up to Widcombe?"

"Yes."

"What time?"

"When I got there? I suppose about half-past eleven. Maybe slightly earlier. I rang the doorbell. Got no answer. Assumed she was out. Walked around the side of the house to see if by any chance a door was open. And the back door was." She paused and stared at the back of her right hand, as if the memory was too taxing on her nerves to continue.

"So you let yourself in?" Diamond prompted.

"Yes."

"And?"

"I called out. Called her name several times. Got no reply. Decided to make a search."

"Go on."

"Starting with the bedroom. If I'd been in her position, that's where I would have hidden them. So I went upstairs and called her name once more in case she hadn't heard before. I located their bedroom and looked inside. She was there."

"What?"

"In bed. She was in the bed."

Diamond kept his eyes on her.

It seemed that Dana Didrikson couldn't bring herself to say that Geraldine had been lying dead, but it was implicit in the way she had spoken. That was what she had intended to convey.

Diamond's first response was to treat it as another attempt to cut short the questioning. He didn't believe her.

Nor, plainly, did Wigfull. "Are you serious?"

She answered, "I'm telling you what I saw." She had removed her hands from the table, but beneath it she was pressing them together with such force that her head and shoulders trembled.

"Mrs. Didrikson," said Diamond, "for the record, I must ask you to state your meaning clearly. You said she was in the bed."

"Yes."

"And . . . ?"

She whispered, "Dead."

"You're certain?"

"I didn't imagine it."

"You'd better describe what you saw."

She took a long breath. "She was lying face upward. Her eyes were open and seemed to be staring at the ceiling until . . . until I saw that they didn't move.

Her face was a dreadful color, as if she'd put on a face pack. Her lips were blue."

Lividity, notably of the lips and ears, is a sign of asphyxiation. "Did you touch her, feel a pulse or anything?"

"No. She'd gone. It was obvious."

Painstakingly, as if they accepted every word of her story, they got her to describe the scene. Diamond had laid the ground rules: they would test the facts she gave them, and this was the method, inducing her to talk, suppressing their skepticism until the right opportunity came.

The body, she told them, had been lying diagonally in the bed, the congested and livid face at one edge, the auburn hair tousled, some of it below the pillow that lay beside the head in the normal position. Both arms were under the pale green quilt. Mrs. Didrikson had not disturbed the bedding, nor touched the body, but enough of the shoulders were visible for her to see that it was clothed in a white sleeveless nightdress. She had noticed no scratches on the flesh.

The bedroom itself had revealed no obvious signs of a struggle except an empty glass tumbler lying on its side on the bedside table nearest to the corpse. The second bed had a matching quilt folded back on itself, and she thought she remembered a man's pajama trousers lying across the pillow. She had not looked into either of the dressing rooms. The door to the bedroom had been open and the sash window partly raised. The curtains had been drawn back, giving abundant light.

"What did you do?"

"I thought I was going to faint. I went to the window and took some gulps of fresh air. Then I fled the room without looking at her again. I think I drew some water from the tap in the kitchen. I was functioning like a robot, as if it wasn't me."

Diamond couldn't allow this to pass. "Explain."

"I suppose what I mean is that I was on autopilot."

Wigfull said eagerly, too eagerly, "Not responsible for your actions?"

She glared at him. "You're trying to trap me, aren't you?"

It was left for Diamond to provide reassurance. "We're trying to understand you, Mrs. Didrikson."

"Haven't you ever been shocked rigid?" she said. "Don't you see that I'm trying to explain what it means to be in shock? I knew what I was doing throughout, if that's what you're asking. I felt stunned by what I'd seen."

"And after you drank the water?"

"I left."

"The way you'd entered—by the back door?"

"Yes. I made my way back to the car and drove home."

"And then?"

"Had some brandy, I think."

"What time was this?"

"I can't remember exactly—sometime between twelve and one."

"Would your son remember?"

"No. He has school dinners."

"So what did you do next?"

"Sat and thought for a bit. Then put on the television to try and shut out the image I had in my brain."

"You didn't report what you'd found?"

"No."

"Not that afternoon, or the evening, or the next day, or ever. Why not? Why didn't you notify us?"

She was silent.

"Did you discuss it with anyone at all?"

She shook her head.

Diamond rested his hands on the table and drew himself up in the chair. "You'll appreciate that it doesn't reflect too favorably."

Still she made no comment.

"See it from our point of view," he suggested to her. "When we called on you this afternoon, you ran out of the back door. When we caught up with you and asked you to help us, you told us a certain amount and tried to have us believe that it was all you knew. You only admitted going to the house on the last day Mrs. Jackman was seen alive because we told you your car had been seen there. And now you ask us to believe that you found her dead and for some undisclosed reason decided to do nothing about it. It isn't good, Mrs. Didrikson. In fact, it stinks."

Ripples of shock or tension disturbed her cheeks. Her lips remained tightly compressed.

He tried repeating the case against her, demanding explanations, but she refused to speak at all. At his side, he could sense Wigfull's impatience with the procedure. The man was agitating to try the theory he'd been nursing all day.

It couldn't be less productive than the last ten minutes, so Diamond gave him a nod.

Wigfull said without preamble, "Let's face it, Mrs. Didrikson. You and Jackman are lovers, aren't you?"

It rocked her. "No!"

"What's wrong? He was unhappily married. You're divorced. You met by chance, found each other attractive, and did what millions of people do."

"That isn't true," she said vehemently. "There was nothing like that."

"No sex?"

"No."

"Come on, Dana, we're grown-ups."

"You're wrong," she insisted. "We never did anything like that. Never. Not even a kiss."

The way she spoke the last four words revealed more than she had meant to. Wigfull paused a moment and suggested with a knowing smile, "But you wouldn't have minded a kiss."

She reddened and said, "This is intolerable."

"But true?"

"I've given my answer."

"Fair enough, you say you didn't sleep with him."

"And it's the truth."

"I hope everything you tell us is the truth. Let me suggest something else to you. You thought the Jane Austen letters would please him."

"What's wrong with that?"

"You went to no end of trouble to acquire them. In your heart of hearts, didn't you hope to rise in his estimation?"

"I may have done," she conceded.

"The letters weren't just a way of thanking him for saving Matthew's life. They were a bid for his affection."

"That wasn't why I did it."

"But that afternoon when you drove home from Crewkerne with the letters in your car, you must have fancied your chances a little bit, Dana. Am I right?"

Again the color rose in her cheeks.

"You're entitled to your private fantasies," Wigfull pressed on. "No one can blame you for that."

With an intake of breath that sounded very like a hiss, she answered, "Even if I did, it's not what you were saying a moment ago."

"But it's broadly true?"

"I wouldn't say broadly."

"Marginally, then?"

"I suppose so."

Wigfull had scored a useful point, and he wanted more. "And you came home to Geraldine and a right old rollicking. She accused you of—what was the word? —humping her husband, which wasn't true, and she brought your son into it, which infuriated you. More to the point, she scotched those romantic thoughts of yours, however marginal they may have been, and made it impossible for you or Matthew to go on seeing Professor Jackman. You were in two minds about what to do with the letters."

The more Wigfull steamed on, the more Diamond felt that he was fitting the theory around insufficient facts. From the way Dana Didrikson had conducted herself so far, she wasn't about to break down and confess. She would stonewall all night, if necessary. They needed stronger evidence. With commendable restraint, he let the monologue run its length and listened to Dana Didrikson's firm denial. Then, while Wigfull recovered his breath, Diamond asked her if she wouldn't mind having her fingerprints taken and submitting to a blood test in the morning.

She agreed, whereupon Diamond called an end to the interrogation for that day.

Outside, Wigfull was generous enough to admit that he had been overeager, and the forensic backup was necessary. "We must also have her car checked for traces."

"Yes. I intend to ask her for the keys in the morning."

"No need." Wigfull felt in his pocket and dangled a key ring a foot from Diamond's nose. "I drove it last, remember?"

Smart-arse, Diamond thought.

3

_____

HE AWARDED HIMSELF a lie-in until eight the next morning, followed by a decent breakfast—and why not? His presence wouldn't be required first thing in Bath. The fingerprinting and the blood test were laid on for 8:30 and the car was due to be taken away for forensic examination at about the same time. Meanwhile Wigfull could play at being chief of the murder squad for an hour.

So a fortified Peter Diamond drove into the city at an hour when the sun was high enough to pick out all of the tiered ranks of Georgian housing in the familiar, yet still-spectacular view from the slope of Wells Road, the gleaming limestone terraces topped with slate roofs as blue gray as the backcloth of Lansdown. In the foreground, the castellated railway viaduct with its Gothic arches contrived to blend into the scene, dominated from this view by the pinnacled tower of the Abbey beyond it and softened by patches of gold and copper foliage. A day when Diamond was almost willing to forget that the backs of most of the elegant streets and crescents were eyesores of blackened masonry abandoned for two centuries to the ravages of the weather, builders, and plumbers. Almost, but not quite. The policeman in him couldn't overlook the hidden side, just as he never took the citizens of Bath entirely at face value.

He hoped that cynicism hadn't taken permanent root in his character. He preferred to think of it more positively, as professional discernment. Experience had taught him that you cannot discount anyone as a possible murderer. Faced with a model of innocence, a bishop or a flower arranger, you needed to be that much more alert, to guard against slack thinking. The Jackman case demonstrated the principle neatly. Who but a case-hardened policeman would be willing to believe that a professor from the university could be drugged and almost incinerated by his paranoid wife, and that a respectable working mother would suffocate the obnoxious woman and dump the body in a lake? Actually, if pressed to charge Mrs. Didrikson on the evidence so far, he would balk. Certainly she had been evasive and obstructive, but he remained less sure than Wigfull of her guilt. She had discredited herself with her evasions, and now some evidence was needed. By the end of the day he expected to have it from the forensic lab. And at the end of the day he would be sorry; he had a sneaking regard for the woman. Perhaps in the last analysis there *was* a dash of the romantic in him.

Then his spirits took their usual downward lurch at the sight of the four-square institutional-looking building wedged between the Baptist church and the National Car Park. The best you could say for Manvers Street Police Station was that it was one of the few buildings in Bath that looked no worse from the rear. Inside, it was typical of penny-pinching postwar architecture, drably functional and fitted with cheap wood and strip lighting, a workplace where you needed to make a conscious effort to start the day cheerfully. His "Grand day out there, isn't it?" drew no response from the men on duty, which was understandable, yet worrying. He wasn't used to being ignored and there sprang into his brain a suspicion that everyone else in the place knew something to his discredit and didn't wish to give him the bad news. The sergeant at the reception desk suddenly started leafing through the phone book and the computer operators in the incident room appeared mesmerized by their screens. All this was threatening to become a chapter out of Kafka until he caught the eye of Croxley and asked what had happened to Wigfull and was stutteringly informed that he was with the assistant chief constable. Mr. Tott had appeared without warning at 9:00 A.M. and asked to see Diamond. Soon after, Wigfull had been called upstairs. It was now 9:48.

The obvious assumption, Diamond reassured himself, was that the official copies of the Missendale report had arrived, and Mr. Tott was obliged to hand him one in person. If that were so, there should be no sweat. His own belated appearance need not be an embarrassment; he could supply a hundred reasons for being elsewhere in the course of duty. But he still didn't fathom how Wigfull came into it. And it did seem odd that the Assistant Chief Constable was acting as a delivery boy.

He went up to the carpeted meeting room on the top floor where Mr. Tott installed himself on his rare visits. The girl posted as sentinel in the outer office asked him to wait. If John Wigfull was making some excuse on his behalf, it was a protracted one. A further ten minutes passed before the door opened and Wigfull emerged. On seeing Diamond, he gestured with open hands and a lift of the shoulders that he was powerless to influence whatever was going on. Before Diamond could ask what it was about, the Assistant Chief Constable appeared in the doorway and crooked his finger.

"Shut the door behind you."

Ominously there was no invitation to be seated. Mr. Tott, in uniform today, all braid and silver buttons, positioned himself at the far end of the oval table. On its surface were a cup and saucer, two biscuits on a plate, Mr. Tott's peaked cap and his white gloves, but no copy of the Missendale report. He seemed unwilling to speak. In fact, he looked immobile, a wax figure in a costume museum, "Assistant Chief Constable circa 1910." Diamond wondered fleetingly whether it was a sign of incipient paranoia if you believed you were being persecuted by men with ridiculous mustaches.

He decided he had better apologize for being unavailable earlier.

The substance of what he said was ignored, but it did induce an utterance from Mr. Tott. "I gather from Inspector Wigfull that you expect to charge the Didrikson woman with the Jackman murder."

"It's possible, sir."

"*Possible?* You put it no higher?"

"Not until I have the lab reports."

"But you held her overnight?"

"Yes, sir."

"And she is still downstairs?"

"I believe so."

This encounter was markedly less friendly than their previous one. Mr. Tott let out a troubled gust of breath and started pacing the section of floor at the far end of the room. "You'd better tell me precisely what happened when you arrested her. I've already had Wigfull's account, you understand."

"Is something up, sir?" Diamond asked in the hope of finding out what this was about before he committed himself. Clearly something *was* up.

"I am waiting, Superintendent."

A lapse in procedure? he asked himself as he outlined aloud what had happened. Some pettifogging breach of the Police and Criminal Evidence Act?

When he had finished, Mr. Tott said, "The boy."

"Matthew?"

"Yes. He tried to stop you from entering the house?"

"We wanted to speak to his mother, as I explained."

"And he challenged your right to go in?"

"He did more than that. He put in the boot, sir."

"A twelve-year-old?"

"He caught me where it hurts most."

"So you retaliated?"

Abruptly, with petrifying certainty, Diamond saw the drift of this cross-examination. "That isn't what happened, sir. He was clinging to me and I pushed him away, as I described to you."

"What you neglected to say is that he hit the wall."

"It was a very narrow hallway, sir."

"Do you deny that he was thrown against the wall, and hit it headfirst?"

While his mind leaped ahead, picturing dire possibilities, Diamond tried to cling to the facts. "He couldn't have been badly hurt because he got up and ran off."

Mr. Tott uncharitably allowed the remark to stand for as long as it took Diamond to modify it.

"He wasn't hurt—was he?"

In a voice as dry as antique tapestry, Mr. Tott said, "He was admitted to hospital last night, as an emergency."

"Hospital? Whatever for?"

"He blacked out. The school quite properly called the emergency number. It seems that concussion has been diagnosed." Mr. Tott gave out the information routinely, as if he were a hospital spokesman. Routinely and unsparingly.

"He was all right when I saw him last," Diamond said, conscious how feeble this sounded. "Conversing normally, quite relaxed."

"The effects aren't always immediate," commented Mr. Tott, and then continued with the bulletin. "They are taking X rays, in case the skull is fractured. It's too early to tell if there is permanent damage."

The whole thing was so incredible that Diamond wanted to ask if anyone had considered whether the boy was playacting, but he checked himself. Such a suggestion was most unlikely to ease his predicament. Mr. Tott was taking it seriously, and Mr. Tott wouldn't take kindly to being duped.

Instead, he confined himself to a defense of his own actions. "If the kid did crack his head on the wall, it was accidental. He kicked me in the privates first and then made a dive for my leg. All I did was push him away. John Wigfull saw it. He was right behind me, sir."

Mr. Tott shook his head. "That's where you're mistaken. Inspector Wigfull didn't see it. His attention was directed to Mrs. Didrikson. He had just caught sight of her making her getaway through the back of the house. He wasn't looking at you or the boy."

Thanks a bunch, John, Diamond thought bitterly. Any brother officer with an ounce of loyalty would have given me some backing. Wigfull *knew* there was nothing deliberate in the handoff.

"Whatever the rights and wrongs of it," Mr. Tott said in a cold, judicial tone, "I have to consider the way it could be interpreted by others, outside the police. I mean the school and the parent. This morning I took a pretty irate call from the boy's headmaster."

"Oh, no!"

"The school had not been informed that the boy had received a blow to the head."

"It wasn't a blow, sir. Nobody struck him."

"I'm not here to argue terminologies, Diamond. This is too serious for that. The headmaster registered a complaint and he assumes—not without reason—that Mrs. Didrikson will wish to do the same." He tilted his head back a fraction, signaling a significant statement. "In the circumstances, I have asked Wigfull to take over the investigation into Geraldine Jackman's death. With the acting rank of chief inspector."

"What?" Diamond's skin prickled and a pulse started thumping in his head.

"I'm relieving you of your command, pending a possible inquiry into your conduct. I have no option. What has happened may already have undermined our case against this woman."

Even the semblance of respect cracked now. "This must be fairyland. It's bloody fairyland. I don't believe it."

"Have a care what you say, Superintendent."

But Peter Diamond was in no frame of mind to care anymore. "Too late for that, Mr. Tott. I've got your number now. I know what this is—your golden opportunity. You're terrified of my record. All that horseshit about no blame attaching to me from the Missendale inquiry and you hit the panic button at the first whisper against me. It suits your book beautifully. Your stooge was sitting in, waiting for me to screw up, and now he takes over. Well, I just hope he delivers. You bloody deserve each other. As for me, I'll save you the trouble of an inquiry. I'm quitting. You have my resignation."

After which, he had nothing else to do but walk out and down the stairs.

4

_____
.

TOO ANGRY to speak to anyone, he left the building and
crossed the street, only to realize that even the timing of
his exit was ill judged, for the pubs wouldn't be open for
another hour. He started walking, past the bus station
toward Stall Street, telling himself that by degrees the
anger would recede. He didn't regret what he had said.
Every word had been justified, and if he had expressed
it more diplomatically, he would still have been there
trying to find an exit line. All right, he could be called
impetuous, wrongheaded, and insubordinate, but he still
had balls. To have capitulated to Tott, allowing himself
to be sidelined, excluded from the murder squad, con-
demned to see out the rest of his career from behind a
desk, would have been emasculation.

Regrets? None that would cause him to reconsider.
He hadn't been long enough with Avon and Somerset to
make strong friendships. And—it was no less true because he beefed about it so often—his job satisfaction
had been in steep decline in recent years. The scientists
were taking over CID work. The great detectives of the
past—the idols of his early years in the force, like Bob
Fabian, Jack du Rose, and "Nipper" Read—now
seemed as remote as dinosaurs. They were honest-to-
God detectives. They'd have been hamstrung by the

paraphernalia of modern technology—computers, cell phones, photofits, police programs on television, ultrasonic surveillance, and genetic fingerprinting. Maybe he was rationalizing what had just taken place upstairs, but he didn't see how he could have lasted much longer in the modern police. He'd chalked up some modest successes over the years. Pity he was denied the satisfaction of clearing up the Jackman murder. Yes, that was a genuine regret.

His biggest concern was the shock this would be for Stephanie. Poor Steph was going to hear it cold. If *he* was stunned by the suddenness of his going, how much worse would it be for her? At least he'd been there at the time and brought it on himself. Steph hadn't been given the slightest warning that this would happen. Her world was about to cave in and she was likely to cave in with it. Even after the shock subsided, she would sink into a deep despair about the mortgage and the bills and the cost of staying alive. He would deal with those things as they happened, but Steph was a born worrier.

On his right as he made his way up Stall Street was an electricity showroom, and the sight of all those appliances in the window gave him a thought. As impulsively as he had quit his job, he marched in and asked to see the microwave ovens. Big enough to cast aside his principles in an act of mercy, he decided to go for broke, selected the one with the biggest display of controls, and paid for it by check. They promised to deliver it to Mrs. Peter Diamond the same afternoon. That, he told the salesman, would be the good news.

Coming out, he continued past the colonnaded entrance to the baths and came to the Abbey churchyard, his lunchtime haunt in summer. At this end of the year there were fewer tourists, so he had a wooden seat to himself. Only the pigeons remained in any numbers, and they converged on him at once, too single-minded even to coo as they searched the flagstones by his feet for crumbs. Then a loose dog, a black retriever, came running from the direction of Abbey Green, and the pigeons took flight. Diamond watched their whirring ascent. They formed into a tight flock within a moment of taking to the air, and when they had wheeled out of sight behind him, he was left gazing up at the Abbey front, those stone angels perpetually trapped on the ladders. The consoling thought came to him that he could stop identifying with them now. Just as he started to look away, something strange made an impression on his vision, demanding a longer inspection. He squinted up at the stonework. He had spotted a feature of the carving he had never previously noticed. It was not a trick of the light, nor a failing of vision. One of the angels—the third from the top—wasn't sculpted in the attitude of climbing, but was upside down. No question. That angel was coming down headfirst.

He couldn't summon a grin, but he nodded and said, "You and me both, mate."

He didn't, after all, make straight for the nearest pub. Apart from the bitterness he felt toward Tott, something else rankled—his strong suspicion that the whole thing had been founded on a deception. He didn't believe Matthew Didrikson had blacked out. It couldn't have been more than twenty minutes after the alleged incident in the hall that he'd seen the boy lounging on his bed, not in the least distressed, doing his best to convince his mother that what had happened amounted to deliberate assault by the police. In his rugby-playing days, Diamond had seen a number of genuine cases of concussion, and not only had the effects been immediate, but the victims hadn't been able to recall the events immediately before they were hit. If the kid *was* shown to be faking, Diamond still couldn't turn back the clock and get his job back: he accepted that. But a disturbing possibility was beginning to dawn on him. His sudden resignation might be interpreted as an admission that the boy *had* been treated violently. Taking the worst possible scenario, he might find himself being sued for assault, facing ruinous damages. And it was too late now to turn to the police for support.

In this somber cast of mind, he resolved for his own protection to find out the truth about the Didrikson boy's condition. Back to Manvers Street, then, to collect the car and drive along the Upper Bristol Road.

He had no qualms about showing his police identity to the woman in reception at the Royal United Hospital. Matthew, she told him, had been moved out of casualty into a general ward. There, the ward sister confirmed that the boy had been X-rayed and they were waiting for the results. He had not suffered any further symptoms of concussion since being admitted and, yes, he was well enough to receive a visitor. In fact, some people from the school had been in earlier.

She pointed out the room where Matthew was supposed to be, but Diamond didn't find him there. He tracked the boy to the day room, where he found him watching television, a cigarette drooping from his mouth, supplied, presumably, by the only other occupant of the room, an old man who had fallen asleep in his chair with an ashtray in his lap.

It wasn't Diamond's job to issue a health warning, so he asked without a hint of disfavor, "How are you doing?"

"I might be going home this afternoon." Matthew had the trick of speaking without removing the cigarette. His gaze didn't shift from the television screen. He was in a gray hospital dressing gown, slumped in a low, steel-frame armchair, his slippered feet supported on a coffee table, hands clasped behind his head.

"You're obviously feeling better, then."

"Mustn't grumble."

"No more blackouts?"

Matthew swiveled his head enough to take in Diamond without otherwise altering his position. "It's you. Did they send you to check up?"

"They can phone the sister if they want," Diamond pointed out by way of a denial. "You must like this place."

A wary look passed across the brown eyes. "Come again?"

"It's the second visit this year, isn't it? You nearly drowned."

"That was yonks ago," the boy said scornfully. "They didn't keep me in."

"How's the swimming coming on?"

Matthew's eyes slid back to the television. "I had to quit doing it, didn't I? Mrs. Jackman kicked up a stink about it. She's dead now, serve her bloody right."

"Do you remember the day it happened?" As he spoke the question, he thought, This is crazy. Hardly two hours have passed since I chucked in the job, and here I am refusing to let go, hanging on to some chance remark by this bumptious kid in the hope of a new slant on the Jackman murder. Technically finished as a policeman, I can't let go. I'm continuing to function, like a headless chicken running around a yard.

"That was the day I went back to school," answered Matthew.

"Monday, September eleventh?"

"Mm."

"And your mother drove you there?"

"Yes."

"Before you left, do you remember the phone ringing?"

"Yes. It was Greg, for my mother. You probably call him Professor Jackman," he added with condescension.

"You don't recall what time he phoned?"

"Quite early. Well before eight. Ma was still in her nightie. She was hopping mad."

"What about?"

"The phone call. She'd only just given Greg some really valuable letters some famous author wrote hundreds of years ago and they were missing. Greg thought some American guy had swiped them and he was going after him."

"And your mother—what was her opinion?" Diamond asked.

"She was certain Mrs. Jackman had them."

"How do you know?"

"She told me when she was driving me to school."

"What time was that?"

"Half-eight. We have to be there by quarter to." He reached for the remote control and switched channels.

"Don't you like school?"

"It's full of little kids. I have to wait till next year to take Common Entrance. Then I'll just move up to the main school."

"If you pass."

"No problem. I'm in the choir."

Diamond had transferred to a grammar school at eleven and to his mind there was something wrong with a system that held back boys of Matthew's size and maturity. "Do you mind being driven to school by your mother—a big lad like you?"

"It's better than walking."

"You could take a bus."

"I'd rather take a Mercedes."

The remark confirmed how much emblems of status still mattered in school, any school. The boy's manner grated with Diamond, but he remembered his own adolescence well enough to understand the insecurity that lay behind it. Just as well, because the impulse to box the kid's ears—if only metaphorically—was strong, and a set-to would be disastrous. So with restraint—and curiosity unslaked—he concentrated on Matthew's memories of the day Geraldine Jackman had been killed. The choristers, he learned, had passed a dull morning in and around the Abbey vestry being issued with a clean set of robes; and in the afternoon the timetables and textbooks had been given out for the eight Common Entrance subjects.

"And was your mother there to meet you at the end of the day?"

"She never is. I get a lift with my friend's father as far as Lyncombe Hill. It's only an old Peugeot, but he's a schoolteacher, so what can you expect?"

"You're interested in cars, Matthew?"

"If you mean decent cars, yes."

"Ever tried driving one?"

"Give me a break—even if I had, I wouldn't tell one of the fuzz." The last word had more disdain for being spoken in the well-honed accent of a private education.

Diamond followed up the possibility he'd raised. The assumption behind it—that the boy had contrived to murder Geraldine Jackman himself, then transported her body to Chew Valley Lake and dumped her there—bordered on the absurd, but now that he had started, he might as well go on. "Some kids of your age manage to learn without going on public roads. It isn't illegal. I've heard of schools that give driving lessons on the premises."

"All we get is piano lessons," Matthew said, making plain his discontent.

"Maybe your mother—"

"You're joking, of course."

"She could take you somewhere quiet, like an empty beach or a deserted airfield."

"She won't even let me ride a bumper car at the fair."

It wasn't deception. It was the authentic protest of a frustrated child and the finish of Diamond's short-lived speculation. He had to dismiss the notion of Matthew at the wheel of the Mercedes or any other vehicle.

"Anyway, as soon as I'm old enough I want to get a Honda MT5," said Matthew.

"So you do fancy yourself as a driver?"

"It's a bike, you dingbat."

"Watch it, lad." The reproof sprang unbidden, and Diamond added more jocularly, "I might just mention cigarettes to Sister on the way out." Doggedly, he reverted to the original line of questioning. "That evening we were talking about . . . You didn't actually say if your mother was at home when you got back from school."

Matthew took a last drag on the cigarette and stubbed it out. "She was there."

"How did she appear?"

"What do you mean?"

"Her manner. Was it any different from other days?"

Matthew turned to look at Diamond again. "You think she did the murder, don't you?"

"Did she go out in the car that evening?"

"No."

"You're telling the truth, I hope."

"Of course."

Diamond said, "Let me put something to you, Mat. You might think that what you're doing is the best way to help your mother out of a tight spot, but it might not work like that."

Matthew flicked the television off and looked up. "What do you mean?"

"For a start, creating this diversion. The reason you're here in hospital. I don't believe you cracked your head that hard. I don't believe you blacked out. My first thought was that you were making a protest about having to spend the night at school."

"That's not true!" Matthew said vehemently.

"But now I think it wasn't selfishness. I reckon you did it for your mother's sake. You thought we'd stop questioning her if you were taken ill. We'd have to bring her to see you."

The boy was frowning. "Well, you will, won't you?" Once again, it was the child speaking.

"It isn't up to me, son."

The significance of what Diamond had just admitted went over Matthew's head. "My ma wouldn't kill anyone."

"If that's what you really believe, acting up as you did last night isn't going to help her."

"You *did* shove me against the wall. That was the truth."

"Yes," said Diamond, "and you kicked me in the goolies, but I didn't make a production number out of it."

Matthew grinned.

Given time, Diamond reckoned he could achieve

an understanding here, if nothing more. The bravado
was paper thin. Behind it was a kid pining for his father.

But they were interrupted by the ward sister. "Your
X rays are through, Matthew, and we can't find anything
amiss. I think we can safely send you back to school."

"Right away?"

She winked at Diamond. "After four, I think."

Steph took the news infinitely better than he'd expected.

"When the microwave oven arrived, I knew something ghastly must have happened. I'm glad you thought
of me. Of course, it's barmy getting me a present."

"Stupid."

"Not stupid. No, I won't have that. Daffy, if you
like, but I always knew you were daffy—well, ever since
that day you brought the donkeys to the Brownies'
camp." She smiled. "Not everyone appreciates you."

"Too true. I wasn't right for the job. I was an ogre."

"You're not a violent man."

"Tell that to Mr. Tott. Steph, let's face it, man management wasn't my strongest suit. I got by because I
drove people hard. No one was given any favors."

"That isn't bad management. After all, you weren't
running a playgroup."

He was forced to smile.

She said, "In your job it was no good trying to be
popular."

"No, but I had to command respect, and I'm not
sure it was there anymore. I should have kept up with
technology. I was the only one on the squad without a
pocket calculator. I still do mental arithmetic."

"I don't think you ever settled down in this place."

"It's not the place. It's the frustration. The top dogs
provide you with all these aids and expect you to be
super-efficient, but when all's said and done you're investigating people, dodgy people, dangerous people,
frightened people. And the villains are more sophisti-
cated than they would have been twenty years ago.
You've got to talk to them, get inside their minds and

tease out the truth. That's what I joined the CID to do. These days it's slide-rule policing. You have to justify the bloody hardware. Supposedly there's this infallible forensic backup, but they're understaffed, and the results take weeks, months to come back. Meanwhile what do you do with your suspect? The law won't let us hold him indefinitely. Is it any wonder that we try for confessions? All these cases of statements taken under duress that you hear about—it's the result of pressure—pressure in a system that isn't functioning properly." He sighed and shrugged. "Sorry, love. I didn't mean to unload it all on you."

"Better out than in," Stephanie commented. "But if you can face it, I'd like some help with my new piece of hardware. Let's see if we can work the microwave."

Together they cooked a passable meal of steamed plaice and vegetables in a miraculously short time. They cracked a bottle of Chablis and agreed that it wouldn't be wise for him to rush off to the job center in the morning. He would take a week off, do up the kitchen (which now looked too scruffy to house the microwave), and think about his future.

In the morning he wrote his formal letter of resignation.

5

ON THE FOLLOWING MONDAY the *Bath Evening Chronicle*'s main headline was GERRY SNOO KILLING—BATH WOMAN CHARGED WITH MURDER. The essential facts were few. Dana Didrikson, a thirty-four-year-old company driver, had been brought before the magistrates on a charge of murdering television actress Geraldine Jackman on or about the eleventh September last and had been remanded in custody. The proceedings had lasted only a few minutes.

With new priorities pressing, Peter Diamond turned to the Situations Vacant. He had to let go, he kept telling himself. The letting-go was briefly delayed by a mental picture of John Wigfull cock-a-hoop in the charge room at Manvers Street, but the hell with it, he thought—I've moved on.

Traditionally, ex-policemen looked for work with private security firms. All morning, he had worked through the Yellow Pages, trying his luck with what he had always thought of as Mickey Mouse organizations. Some of the names made him squirm as he spoke them. "Is that Secure and Sleepeasy?" "Somerset Sentry-Go?" The only result of this phoning—apart from all the metered units he'd used—was the discovery that his seniority didn't have the pull that he'd counted on. If anything, it was a handicap; the people he spoke to didn't see an ex-superintendent riding the vans or on foot patrol in the big stores, and they were unwilling to take him on as an executive. His experience with murder squads wasn't a recommendation for dealing with business clients.

The Yellow Pages also listed a number of detective agencies offering vast ranges of services. On inquiry they turned out to be one-man outfits run by retired police sergeants uninterested in taking on an ex-superintendent as sidekick.

In the next two weeks, he broadened the search, trying for office work of any description, and still got a series of rejections. Too many middle-aged men were touting for white-collar jobs, he was unkindly told, and had he thought of laboring? As this generally involved climbing ladders or wheeling barrows over planks, activities ill suited to a fat man, he didn't warm to the suggestion.

His luck changed in the last week in November. "I've been offered *two* jobs," he was able to tell Stephanie one Friday evening. "Two jobs that I am singularly qualified to perform."

"Two—that's marvelous!" she told him. "Are they safe?"

"Safe? I should say so! You know the new shops in the Colonnades, just off Stall Street? Well, they want a Santa Claus to rove around the precinct chatting to the kids and so on. Ho, ho, ho! All under cover. Three of us were interviewed and I got it on the size of my waist. I start tomorrow, for a limited season."

"Oh, Peter." Stephanie's face creased in dismay.

"What do you mean . . . 'Oh, Peter'?"

"I know jobs are thin on the ground, but . . ."

"But what?"

"A detective superintendent dressing up as Father Christmas?"

"A DS no longer," he reminded her.

"It's such a comedown."

"Not at all. Santa is a VIP to twenty percent of the population. The rest won't know me from Adam."

She sighed. "What's the other job?"

"Barman cum bouncer at the Old Sedan Chair, evenings only."

"Where's that, for pity's sake?"

"The new pub in that road behind the theater."

"Don't they get a lot of rowdies from the disco club?"

"That's why they need a bouncer, my love."

One evening he saw in the paper that Dana Didrikson had gone through the committal proceedings at the magistrates' court and had been sent for trial at Bristol Crown Court on the charge of murder. He turned to the sports pages and tried to interest himself instead in a report on Bath's crop of rugby international players.

He proved to be a popular Santa, in spite of the fact that he had nothing to give away except balloons stamped with the Colonnades logo. The role appealed to him and he filled it with a gusto and panache that had never characterized his police career. The awestruck faces of small children, eyes shining with anticipation, enchanted him. As a childless parent, he had never had much difficulty convincing himself that kids, like dogs, were in the main a nuisance. Now, behind the white nylon whiskers, he shamelessly played Dad.

One afternoon on the top floor of the Colonnades he saw Matthew Didrikson and a couple of friends playing some game that involved the glass-sided elevator that served the three levels of the precinct. The shop owner who had interviewed the would-be Santas had been sufficiently impressed by Diamond's police background to speak of the nuisance sometimes caused by boys of school age running about the concourse, but as Diamond had pointed out, a man in a Father Christmas outfit wasn't best placed to control rowdy kids. As it happened, Matthew and his friends weren't kicking cola cans about or bumping into old ladies. The worst that could be said about them was that they were monopolizing the lift. It was a slack time, early in the afternoon, and he decided to leave them to it.

Shortly after, they must have tired of the game, because they came over to poke fun at Father Christmas. No small children were about, no danger of illusions being shattered, so he submitted to the send-up, which was as bawdy as he expected from schoolboys their age—did he have a fetish for black rubber boots . . . or were stockings his hang-up? . . . and (pointing to the balloons) didn't he know what you were supposed to do with condoms?

They found their own wit so hilarious that there was a delay before Diamond's riposte got through: "If you want to know, I get my kicks from reporting shopping choirboys to their headmaster."

The glee changed abruptly to near panic. "He knows us!" Two ran off. Only Matthew remained, staring him out with his dark eyes and commenting, "I know that voice, and that's a naff disguise." It was serious criticism this time.

He was straight with the boy. He explained that he was no longer working with the police, and this was his job.

Matthew matched him in candor by admitting that he and his friends had slipped out of school for an hour. They were supposed to be rehearsing carols in the Abbey at four, and no one would bother about their whereabouts before then.

Diamond took the opportunity to ask something that had been on his mind since he'd read that Dana Didrikson was in police custody, charged with murder. "Where are you going to be over Christmas?"

"With Nelson—one of my friends. And his parents. I'm spending all the hols there."

"Kind of them."

"Nelson owed me one."

Diamond recalled what he had heard of the accident at Pulteney Weir. The boy who had flung the stick that had caused Matthew to slip had been called Nelson. A three-week stay wasn't bad compensation for one wild act of mischief.

Until hearing of this invitation, Diamond had assumed that the school would board Matthew somewhere during the holidays, perhaps at the house of one of the teachers. Quite an ordeal for any kid. Since their conversation in the hospital, Diamond's dislike of Matthew had lessened. He understood some of the reasons behind the brashness. If the truth were told, he had a strong streak of alienation in his own personality. In fact, his sympathies had shifted so far as to consider asking the boy over to their place for a day. He'd discussed it with Stephanie, and she had given her consent. She'd always liked kids. Now, after all, the offer wouldn't be necessary. Matthew would be better off with company his own age.

Matthew may have sensed the thaw. Revealing strains he would not have owned to in front of the other boys, he asked, "How long will she have to wait for the trial?"

"Your mother? Quite a few months, I'm afraid."

"Will she get off?"

Diamond hesitated, torn between honest opinion and comforting lies. "It depends on the evidence. Look, I think you'd better find your friends and get to that choir practice. Your mother has worries enough, without hearing that you're playing truant. Have a good Christmas, son."

The bar work each evening was grueling after a day on his feet parading the precinct. Thankfully there were intervals when he could shift his weight to a stool. The pub's clientele was mostly under twenty—taking breaks from the disco across the street—generally amenable, but out to impress and not always exhibiting youth in its most appealing form, thus providing a counterbalance to Santa's small clients during the day. Even the most winsome kids grew up into teenagers.

The weeks passed, and so did his stint as Santa Claus. He and Steph spent Christmas quietly. A card arrived from the CID lads, a somber scene of a decrepit old man dragging a yule log along a snowy lane. Maybe that was how they pictured him in his new life. They had all signed it, including Wigfull. And when he looked at the names—Keith Halliwell, Paddy Croxley, and Mick Dalton—they appeared remote, an indication, surely, that he *had* let go.

So much so, that one evening in mid-January he had to think hard before putting a name to the man in a black padded jacket who strolled into the Old Sedan Chair and said, "How are you? I was told I might find you here." A voice that was more Yorkshire than West Country. The penetrating eyes, broad face, and black mustache of Professor Gregory Jackman.

Diamond gave his barman's nod. "What can I get you, professor?"

"A cognac. Have one with me."

He turned down the offer with good grace, making clear that no other drink would tempt him. Whether the visit was out of curiosity, or had some ulterior purpose, a dignified aloofness recommended itself.

"I was told that you left the police," Jackman ventured after he'd taken a sip of the cognac. He'd picked an evening when the disco was closed, and a mere handful of drinkers were in, at tables some distance from the bar.

Diamond busied himself washing glasses, so Jackman provided his own comment on what had happened since they'd last met. "It's a bastard."

Without looking up, Diamond said, "I'm coping."

"I meant the fact that you jacked it in. That really sunk Dana."

"Leave it alone, will you?" said Diamond. "That's a closed book for me."

"It isn't for Dana. She's accused of a crime she

didn't commit. If nothing is done, she'll be sent down for life."

"You expect me to do something about it?"

"She needs help."

Diamond turned his back and reached for more empties. "That's the job of her defense lawyers."

"I've talked to her solicitor. She has no answer to the prosecution case."

Diamond plunged the glasses in the water. "She did it, then." If his indifference to Mrs. Didrikson's plight came across as callous, he was under no obligation to spare Jackman's feelings.

Some new people—a party of five Americans—entered the bar and stood by it settling the question of who should pay for the round and what they would choose to drink. Jackman was silent until they had been served their drinks and taken them to a table.

"You don't really believe she's a murderer," he said.

"What I believe or don't believe is of no more importance now than how I feel about the Channel tunnel or women priests," said Diamond. "I'd rather not prolong this, professor."

"Greg. You called me Greg when you were interviewing me."

Diamond sighed, unwilling to believe that a man of intelligence had been taken in by an interrogator's ploy.

"How *do* I get through to you?" Jackman asked.

"That isn't the question," Diamond said. "The question is what do you want from me? And the answer is that I have nothing to offer except a drink."

"You lived with the case for weeks. You did the groundwork. You must have come up with alternative theories, even if they were later set aside. That's how you can help—by suggesting avenues we haven't considered."

"We?"

"Her defense. I told you I'm in touch with her solicitor."

"Is that wise?" Diamond asked, intrigued, in spite

of his determination to remain uninvolved. "Surely the prosecution will be out to establish a relationship between you and Dana Didrikson. By actively taking up her case, you hand them a trump card."

Jackman ran his hand through his hair and down the back of his neck, where it remained. "I know. It's a dilemma. But I *do* care. I care passionately. Can I be frank with you? There's no relationship between Dana and me, not in the way it's generally understood. We haven't been to bed. We've never even talked in intimate terms. But over these difficult weeks I've come to regard her as someone . . . Oh, let's face it—I care about what happens to her. I want to get her out of this mess. And you're perfectly right. My involvement can only damage her now. God, I sound like something out of a third-rate Victorian novel."

Diamond felt the creeping unease that any man feels when another bares his soul. Up to now he'd thought of Jackman as the flinty academic, urbane and self-possessed.

Nor had the soul-baring finished. "And Dana has shown quite touching faith in me."

"In what way?"

"Ask yourself why she didn't call the police on the day she found Gerry's body. She came to the house and found her lying dead in bed. Anyone would have assumed that I'd murdered my wife, wouldn't they?"

Diamond answered with a neutral twitch of the lips.

Speaking in the partisan tone of a smitten man, Jackman went on, "She's incredibly good to me. Even after the body was found in the lake, she didn't come forward. When you went to interview her, she made a run for it. All very suspicious in the eyes of the law. But I'm certain she did it to protect me. She didn't want to be instrumental in getting me charged with murder."

"How did you know she made a run for it?"

"From her solicitor. He's got the police file with all the statements."

"In that case," said Diamond, "you're more up to date than I am. How much has she admitted?"

"Only that she went to the house and found the body."

"She's sticking to that?"

"Of course."

There was an assumption in that "of course." Diamond was expected to concur in Dana Didrikson's innocence. However, he remained unconvinced. Once or twice before he'd heard such rationalizing from men in love. Or guilty men.

"Has the solicitor discussed the forensic evidence with you?"

Jackman sighed and spread his hands in a gesture of helplessness. "It couldn't be worse. They've established that her car was used to transport the body. Particles of skin tissue and some body hairs were found in the trunk. The scientists proved by DNA analysis that they came from my wife."

To say that it couldn't be worse was no exaggeration. The case was buttoned up now.

Out of charity for the man's state of mind, Diamond softened his conclusion. "I understand your concern, professor. These days you can't buck the scientists. There was a time when forensic evidence gave rise to different interpretations. Each side had its own set of experts. But with genetic fingerprinting, it's cut and dried. Faced with evidence like that, I'd have charged Mrs. Didrikson with murder myself." Bloody ironic, he thought as he said it. Peter Diamond conceding infallibility to the men in white coats.

"Surely there's room for doubt," said Jackman. "What if someone else used the car?"

"You mean she lent it to the murderer? You'd have to ask her. She said nothing about it when I interviewed her."

"But would she? At that stage you didn't know the car had been used to move Gerry's body."

"Her lawyers will have to ask her, then. I wouldn't place too much hope on it."

Silence dropped between them as divisively as if the grille over the bar had been lowered.

Jackman hesitated, locked in thoughts of his own, staring down into the brandy glass and rotating the dregs of his drink. Finally he said, "That inspector who took over from you."

"John Wigfull? Chief inspector now."

"Yes. Don't get me wrong, Mr. Diamond, but one hears a lot in the press about wrongful convictions. From my observations of the man, he's highly ambitious. He seemed almost fanatically—"

Diamond cut in sharply, "Don't say it, professor. I'm not stabbing former colleagues in the back."

"I'm trying to account for the inexplicable."

"Obviously. Drink up, will you? I have some tables to clear."

An hour after getting to bed dog-tired, he was still actively engrossed in what he had heard from Jackman. Stupid. He had no desire to get involved again. Any assistance he gave the defense would be taken as sour grapes, an embittered attempt to get back at John Wigfull.

From all he had heard, the case against Dana Didrikson was unassailable now that the forensic team had linked her car to the crime. Jackman's doting support would only strengthen the prosecution's hand. The motive couldn't be spelled out more clearly if Jackman had chartered a plane and flown over the city trailing a banner with the words DANA LOVES GREG.

Yet he'd always felt that there was another dimension to the murder. Loose ends dangled tantalizingly. That strange business of the fire, and the question of whether Geraldine Jackman had really meant to kill her husband. Was she paranoid, as Jackman had asserted more than once?

Then there was the extraordinary scene Dana Didrikson and Matthew had witnessed in the drive of John Brydon House, when Geraldine had fought with the man she called Andy, apparently to stop him from leaving. Was Andy her lover, wanting out?

And why hadn't the Jane Austen letters turned up?

He must have fallen into a shallow sleep for a time, because when he woke, it was still only 1:55 by the clock, and he was repeating question and response in the kind of maddening litany that troubled sleep induces: "Who have I overlooked? Louis Junker, Stanley Buckle, Roger Plato, Andy somebody, Molly Abershaw . . ."

He sat up and thought, Why am I bothering?

Nobody else does, except Jackman.

Wigfull is sleeping the contented sleep of a man who has wrapped up a case.

Maybe I'll sit up a little longer and think.

6

_____

HE PHONED JACKMAN at the university the next morning—
disregarding his own judgment that it was unwise to get
involved. The slender possibility that Dana Didrikson
was innocent of murder impelled him to pass on an idea
that had come to him in the small hours. "Look, I've
remembered something that could possibly have a bearing on the case. I'm passing it on to you because I believe it might bring out the truth, but I don't want you
mentioning my name to the lawyers, or anyone else, do
you understand?"

"What is it?"

Jackman was too eager for Diamond's peace of
mind.

"You guarantee to keep me out of it?"

"Absolutely."

"It concerns Mrs. Didrikson's car."

"Go on."

"You said the forensic tests established that your
wife's body had been placed in the trunk of the Mercedes, right? The assumption is that Mrs. Didrikson drove
it to the lake. When I interviewed her some days ago,
she told me she had to keep a log of every journey."

"A log?" Jackman picked out the word and repeated it without yet understanding its significance.

"It was a company car. The mileage showing on the gauge had to be written in the book each time, even for private trips. Get hold of that log, and you can find out what use she made of the car on Monday, September eleventh and the days immediately after. If someone else used the car to transport the body from Widcombe to Chew Valley Lake, that's a round trip of thirty miles. It must show up in the figures."

"Jesus Christ, you're right!" Jackman paused and then, sensing a catch, said with less buoyancy, "But what if it doesn't show?"

"It has to. The only way a journey of that length could be wiped from the record is by falsifying the log—either inventing a trip to some other place, or making it appear part of a longer run. The point is, she would have noticed if there was a bogus entry."

"True."

"And if she falsified the log herself, it should be simple to check. One way or the other, you'll know."

"Yes." The enthusiasm was ebbing from his voice.

"Do you follow me, professor?"

"Thank you, yes. I'll be in touch."

"There's really no need." Some people are afraid of the truth, Diamond thought. He put down the phone and looked for something else to do. It was a problem having so much time to fill.

Almost a week passed before Jackman phoned the bar one evening at a moment when it was under siege from the disco clientele.

"Who is this?"

"Greg Jackman. I've blown it."

"What? I can't hear you."

"The mileage log. I've really screwed things up for Dana."

"Listen, this isn't a good time. People are lining up in front of me here."

"Shall I come over?" Jackman asked, his agitated state obvious in his tone.

"No, it's too damned busy." Diamond put his hand over the mouthpiece and promised two tattooed customers with punk haircuts that he would serve them directly. Then he told Jackman, "I'll be on the go until closing."

"Come to the house, then."

"When do you mean—*tonight?*"

"Thanks. I'll be waiting."

He'd meant to protest, not acquiesce. With so many people crowding the bar, he hadn't time to make himself better understood.

After the last customers had been persuaded to leave, and the doors were bolted, he thought of phoning Jackman again, then dismissed the thought. It wouldn't put the man off. The desperation behind the voice wasn't going to recognize that people were entitled to their sleep.

It was after midnight when he drove up to John Brydon House. Jackman came down the steps and put a hand on his upper arm like a despairing relative receiving the doctor on a visit.

"I really appreciate this."

Diamond's heavy evening had left him bereft of cordialities. He said grouchily, "I don't know why I came. I've damn all to tell you."

They went inside. The interior was cold. Presumably the heating had gone off and Jackman had been too distracted to notice.

"You'll have to forgive the state of the place," Jackman explained. "You people . . . Sorry, let me start again. The police left it in a hell of a mess and I haven't straightened it out yet."

"They must have been looking for the Jane Austen letters."

"They needn't have troubled. I already searched the house from top to bottom. My files are going to take months to sort out again."

The piles of books on the living-room floor and the pictures removed from the walls didn't trouble Diamond; he'd seen searches before. Authorized them. He picked up a replica Tang horse from an armchair, deposited it on the floor, and sat down heavily, still in his raincoat. "I'm not staying long."

"Coffee?"

"Let's get to the point. It's the car log, is it?"

Jackman nodded. "It's missing."

"It should have been in the car."

"Well, it wasn't. The police files contain no reference to it. I checked with Dana's solicitor. He said if it had been there, a copy would have been included in the file that was sent to the Crown Prosecution Service and made available to the defense."

"True."

"There's nothing—no reference to a log. Mr. Siddons—the solicitor—has spoken to Dana. She insists that she always kept the log in the glove compartment of the car."

"It was there the last time she drove the car?"

"The day you took her in for questioning." No imputation of malpractice was discernible in Jackman's words. His own conduct preoccupied him. "I was so concerned when I heard it was missing that I did the dumbest thing. At the time I didn't appreciate how damaging it could be. I went down to the police station and demanded to see Chief Inspector Wigfull. Did it off my own bat, without telling Siddons. I asked Wigfull if the police were holding the log."

Diamond winced. "That *was* unwise."

"I mean I didn't accuse him of perverting the course of justice, or anything like that. It was all very civilized. I told him Dana insisted the log had been in the car. He said it hadn't been found."

"John Wigfull wouldn't tell you that if it wasn't true," said Diamond in all sincerity. His former assistant was too much the police college man to sully his career with misleading statements.

Gregory Jackman drew no comfort from the assurance. He emitted a long, tremulous sigh that signaled more alarming depths in his confession. He was standing stiffly in front of a white, denuded bookcase like a convicted man lined up for mug shots.

"I made a blinding error by drawing it to their attention—handed a trump card to the prosecution. Siddons is incensed. He says they might have missed the significance of the bloody log. Now they'll seek to suggest that Dana destroyed it."

The gravity of what had happened came home to Peter Diamond. Almost certainly the disappearance of the log would now be used against Dana Didrikson.

He asked precisely what she had told her solicitor.

"She's adamant that she never took the log out of the car except on the last day of each month when it went in for checking at the Realbrew office. She always got it back the next day. She's telling the truth. I know it."

"Does she remember any discrepancies?"

Jackman shook his head slowly. "She doesn't. She says it was up to date. The last entry would have been the day you arrested her."

"Invited her for questioning," Diamond corrected him. "Was it all written in her own hand?"

"Yes."

"She's positive?"

"Utterly."

"So we must expect her to say so in court." He took a grip on the chair arms. "I'm not surprised your Mr. Siddons is busting a gut."

Jackman looked about him as if he wanted to pace the floor, a feat rendered unlikely by the chaos of books and ornaments.

Diamond, meanwhile, was searching his own soul. "I take a share of the responsibility," he admitted. "I started this hare."

And should have seen where it was leading, he went on to tell himself. Dana Didrikson would have been better off if the log had never been mentioned. The prosecution were sure to question her about it now, and the more she insisted that it had been properly kept, the stronger would be the implication that she had destroyed it.

A sense of guilt oppressed him, adding to his burden of self-reproach.

"I could do with a coffee after all, if you don't mind."

While Jackman was busy in the kitchen, Diamond brooded in the armchair. The probability was strong that Dana Didrikson was the killer, but to treat her guilt as a certainty was a cop-out. His interference had stacked the odds more heavily against her. If he could think of something to redress the balance, he had a moral duty to mention it.

Yet when Jackman returned with the coffee, nothing of comfort was said by either man.

At Realbrew Ales next morning, he started to expiate his error. "No," he told the receptionist, "I don't have an appointment. On a visit like this it isn't the practice to announce that we are coming. Kindly inform the managing director—Mr. Buckle, if that is he—that he has a visitor."

"I'll see if he's free. Your name, sir?"

"Diamond."

"And what shall I say you have come about, Mr. Diamond?"

"Taxation."

It worked. She mouthed an "Oh," pressed a button on the intercom, and spoke into it with her hand cupped over her mouth and her eyes on Diamond as if he were pointing a gun at her.

While waiting to be shown upstairs, he pictured the panic in the manager's office. From all he had heard of Stanley Buckle, his relationship with the tax authorities was likely to be precarious.

"You'll have to bear with me, old chum," were Buckle's first words when the confrontation came. "I'm supposed to be in Bristol for a meeting in twenty minutes, and you know what the bloody traffic is like."

He got up from behind his desk and shook Diamond's hand, clearly resolved to disarm the threat if at all possible. The hand was warm and damp. Shorter than Diamond had pictured him, neat-featured, with slicked-back, receding black hair, Buckle beamed benignly and gold gleamed at the edge of his mouth. His choice of clothes was about right for a wheeler-dealer with a spread of business interests—fawn-colored suit with brown shirt and a pale yellow silk tie that was probably called champagne-colored by the fashion house it came from. A rosebud was in his lapel.

"I won't detain you long," Diamond promised.

"Tax matter, is it?"

"It's not unconnected."

"Nothing personal, I hope?" A smile.

Diamond shook his head. He could be amiable, too. "Strictly business. I believe you have extensive business interests in the West Country, Mr. Buckle."

"That's putting it strongly," said Buckle. "I do a bit of importing in addition to my work here."

"Importing what?"

"Novelty goods, cheap toys—that sort of thing. I supply quite a number of toy shops and stationers with items from the Far East."

"Japan?"

"Hong Kong and Taiwan principally."

"You ship the goods over and distribute them?"

"Yes. It's concentrated in Bristol and Bath. I charge the Value Added Tax. It all goes through the books."

"Is it a good living?"

"I get by."

"I heard that you have a large house in Clifton."

"So what? There's no law against it."

With what he intended to appear as the air of an inspector, Diamond whipped a buff folder from the briefcase he was carrying. From it he produced the Guide to Value Added Tax that he had picked up that morning from the VAT office in Ham Gardens House. "You've studied this, Mr. Buckle?"

A wide, defiant grin. "Next to Charles Dickens, it's my favorite reading. Have a seat."

The seats—apart from Buckle's vast executive chair—were fashioned out of beer kegs. Diamond lowered himself onto one, and found it inadequate. "So you do your own returns?"

"Actually no, squire. I have an accountant. Want me to give him a call?"

"Not just now. I presume you keep tabs on the figures anyway."

"Figures in which sense?" Buckle punctuated this with a wink.

"The input tax. Mileage of all the vehicles in use by the company."

Buckle became more serious, adjusting the knot of his tie and trying to make it seem a confident gesture. "I think you'll find that our returns are accurate."

"Do you keep a record, sir?"

"Naturally." He opened the bottom drawer of his desk and took out a red ledger book. "It's all in here. Every Realbrew vehicle is listed."

Diamond held out his hand for the book. His hopes were dashed the moment he opened it. The mileage was in monthly totals. As evidence, it was no help at all. He went through the formality of asking how the figures were supplied and heard about the mileage logs kept by each driver.

"And when the logs come in, do you photocopy them?"

"No. I don't believe in paperwork for its own sake." Buckle made a pistol of his fingers and pressed them to his head in a mime of suicide. "Now tell me it's obligatory."

Diamond opened a page of the ledger fully in front of him. "The Mercedes-Benz 190E 2.6 Automatic Saloon."

"Which one? The company owns two. One is for my personal use and the other is driven by the company chauffeur."

"Two cars of the same model?"

"Bought at the same time. It all went through the books quite properly and I keep my own log religiously. You're welcome to examine it if you wish."

"Yes, please. And the other . . . ?"

"Should be with the other vehicle which—unfortunately—is not on the premises at the present time. If you'll excuse me a moment . . ." He called someone on the intercom and asked them to fetch the log from his car.

"The other vehicle, the one the chauffeur drives," Diamond said. "Is that the one being held by the police?"

Buckle's eyes snapped into sharper focus. "You're bloody well informed."

"It's public knowledge, sir. I can examine the log for that car at the police station—is that what you're telling me?"

"Not really," answered Buckle. "I gather it's gone missing. The police were onto me about it. They wanted to know if the log was on the premises here. There was no reason why it should have been. The system is that the books are kept in the cars and checked at the end of each month. The job never takes more than a day."

"Your chauffeur's in trouble, I understand," Diamond ventured.

"To borrow a phrase of yours, it's public knowledge," Buckle said smoothly.

Equally smoothly, Diamond asked, "Is she guilty?"

"I should think so. She was in pretty deep with the dead woman's husband. Mind, I'm not faulting her as an employee. She was a good driver. Reliable."

Diamond felt a gut contempt for this man. He was finding it hard to subdue. "She drove the one car, did she?"

"Just the one. She never used mine, if that's what you're asking."

"It wouldn't have mattered if she did," Diamond pointed out, "seeing that they're both company cars."

"True. But mine is exclusively for my own use."

"And did you ever have reason to drive the chauffeur's car, sir?"

"Never. I had my own. Look here, if there's any suspicion that I'm on the fiddle in some way, you'd better come out with it."

"I'm more interested in Mrs. Didrikson," Diamond candidly answered. "You said she was reliable. Was she at work on the day of the murder?"

"She took the day off, but I don't see what this has to do—"

Diamond overrode the protest. "And the next day? Was she at work the next day?"

"She was late. When she got in about half-past ten, she looked to me as if she'd been up all night. I didn't go to town on her. With a chauffeur as dependable as Dana, you know there had to be a damned good reason. I've told all this to the police."

And Diamond could imagine what John Wigfull had made of it. Stanley Buckle was going to be a formidable witness for the prosecution, apparently believing the best of his chauffeur, while disclosing facts that were open to the worst interpretation.

"Who exactly are you?"

Diamond was saved from replying by a secretary who brought in a small black book. "The log?" he said, holding out his hand. "Thank you, my dear."

All the entries were in one hand, presumably Buckle's. The book was fully up to date and appeared to have been kept as meticulously as Buckle had claimed. The monthly totals tallied with the office ledger. On the critical day of September 11, two short journeys of nine miles were entered, and the same on September 12.

Diamond thanked Buckle, said he would delay him no longer, and left. On the way out, he looked for Buckle's Mercedes in the car park. It was parked in the space reserved for the managing director. The mileage on the clock matched the latest figure in the book.

His morning's work had come to nothing. The case against Dana Didrikson looked stronger still.

7

THERE FOLLOWED A HIATUS of three months during which Peter Diamond tried to persuade himself that he could do nothing more for Dana Didrikson, that it would be better for all concerned if he let the law take its course. His thinking came down to this: He expected her to be found guilty, and his knowledge of the case suggested that the verdict would be right. He didn't expect the trial to last long. It wouldn't surprise him if she changed her plea to guilty.

She would probably serve a dozen years of the life sentence and be released on parole. She was no danger to society. Most of the murderers he'd known had been like her—a group apart from other criminals—people driven by family pressures or their own obsession to commit one crime in their lives.

And yet . . .

A vestige of unease lingered in his mind. Certain things about the case still challenged an explanation. The Jane Austen letters had not been found. No doubt the prosecution would suggest that Geraldine had destroyed them as an act of jealousy, and Dana Didrikson had killed her in a fit of outrage fired up by her infatuation with Jackman. Yet Geraldine had known that those letters were valuable. According to Jackman, she had been overdrawn three thousand pounds. Mightn't she have seen the letters as a way out of her financial mess?

Maybe it was mistaken to assume that Geraldine would make that kind of calculation. According to Jackman she had been mentally unstable, if not actually unhinged.

According to Jackman . . . So many of the assumptions in the case depended on Jackman's statements. He had interpreted the fire in the summerhouse as an attempt on his life, a manifestation of Geraldine's paranoia. It was worth remembering that Jackman's field of expertise was English literature, not psychiatry.

What other evidence had he provided of her mental illness? There were the persecution fantasies such as her belief that he was conspiring with her doctor. There was the time she had accused him of stealing the hand mirror from her vanity set.

The incident had appeared trivial when Jackman had described it, and still did. Other mirrors were in the house, and Geraldine had already taken possession of Jackman's shaving mirror, yet she had gotten into a state because hers was missing.

Hardly worth repeating. People—perfectly sane people—were forever getting into huffs with each other over things they foolishly mislaid.

Diamond plumbed his memory for more significant evidence of Geraldine's instability, and recalled that some had been provided by Dana Didrikson herself. Dana had witnessed that curious scene in front of John Brydon House when Geraldine had wrestled with the blond man called Andy to prevent him from leaving. And on another occasion, Dana had arrived home and been deluged with what she had termed a torrent of abuse from Geraldine, apparently unjustified.

One night in April, six months since he had quit the police, he was going over the incidents in his mind when the realization came to him that changed his understanding of the case. Ironically, something he had disregarded galvanized his thinking—the mirror Geraldine had lost.

The next morning he phoned Jackman and asked to meet him at John Brydon House. There was no reluctance on Jackman's part. The voice, bleak in its greeting, abruptly changed when Diamond spoke. "It's you—I thought you'd lost interest." The words gushed from him with hope on tap again. "I tried reaching you several times."

Diamond knew. He'd avoided the calls.

"This could take some time," he said when he got to the house. "I want to make a search."

Disappointment spread across Jackman's face. "They already pulled the place apart."

"I know. I'll start in the bedroom. Okay?"

"If you're looking for those letters, forget it."

"I'll start in the bedroom."

Jackman's back was stiff with dissension as he led the way upstairs. Apparently he had built himself up to expect some blazing insight that would transform the case, not just one more search of his home.

Diamond went straight to Geraldine's dressing room and found the switch for the frame of lights around the dressing table. The publicity photos on the walls gleamed. While Jackman watched him from the doorway, he opened the center drawer and began examining the contents, sifting through the jars and tubes of face creams, opening them, sniffing them, and in the case of a box that turned out to contain talcum powder, dipping his finger in and tasting it. He took the drawer right out of its housing, placed it on the floor, and explored the space. He repeated the exercise with the other drawers.

Jackman asked, "What are you hoping to find?"

"Do you remember telling me about the fuss she made when her hand mirror was missing?"

"Yes—but it turned up later in the garden, of all places. Is that what you're looking for?"

"In the garden, was it? Maybe someone else used it." He didn't enlarge on this. He replaced the drawers and turned to the wardrobe, running his hand along the shelf. He scooped out some silk scarves and a black straw hat. Then he knelt and began rummaging among the boots and shoes. "Mirrors have many uses. It's just an idea I have."

But there was nothing in Geraldine's dressing room to support the idea, so he said, "Do you mind if I make a search in yours?"

Jackman shrugged.

His room was as austere as a sauna after Geraldine's, the walls devoid of decoration, the chest of drawers functional, all the surfaces bare except for a newspaper and a couple of books of poetry. "Do you want to open the drawers yourself?" Diamond asked.

"Be my guest."

They contained nothing remarkable. Nor did the bathroom and the other rooms upstairs, for all the painstaking search. After two unprofitable hours, Diamond accepted the coffee Jackman offered. They sat in the kitchen and Jackman started angling again. "I'm still not sure what you hope to find."

"Do you cook for yourself?" Diamond asked.

"I wouldn't describe it as cooking. Without Marks and Spenser and the microwave I wouldn't survive."

This wasn't the time to embark on a debate about microwave cookery. Diamond feared that Stephanie hadn't yet mastered their new oven. Some of the meals that came up sizzling were cold by the time you got them into your mouth. There had been government warnings about food insufficiently cooked. In any other circumstances—across the bar of the Old Sedan Chair, for instance—he would have gotten into a helpful discussion now. However, his sleuthing took priority.

"Was she much of a cook?"

"Gerry? That's a laugh."

"Except for barbecue sauce, I take it?"

Jackman looked unamused.

"So what do you keep in those jars marked tarragon and oregano?"

"Tarragon and oregano. Just to impress her friends."

Diamond worked his way through the spice rack,

unscrewing the lids. The jars still had their seals. He tore each of them aside and sniffed the contents. "When the police made their searches, they didn't bother with your kitchen, then?"

"You bet they bothered. They stripped the cupboards bare."

"But they didn't look in these."

"You couldn't hide an antique letter in a jar that size."

"True." He moved along the fitted units, opening the cupboard doors.

"What do you want—sugar?"

"No, thanks." A large box of drinking straws had taken his attention. "Are you lemonade drinkers?"

"What?"

"The straws. A box of five hundred. Plenty have gone. I suppose you had them for the party."

"I didn't notice."

He replaced the box and took out a half-used packet of flour and set it on the kitchen table.

"Going to bake me a cake?" Jackman morosely jested.

Diamond was sniffing again. "Do you have a spoon —a large one? Thanks." He dipped deep into the flour, scooped up a spoonful and tipped it back, repeating the process several times. Then he returned the bag to the cupboard and took out an unopened one. It was folded at the top and fastened with a small piece of Sellotape.

This time he felt some resistance when he dug the spoon into the flour. Encouraged, he said, "I'll have that plastic bowl from the sink."

Jackman handed it to him without a word.

He tipped the contents of the flour bag into the bowl and immediately found what he had come for: three small polythene bags about the size of table-tennis balls containing a substance as white as the flour.

He picked at the wire fastening around one and opened it. "Do you mind turning on the light?"

The powder inside glistened. It was definitely not flour, but crystalline in form.

"Drugs?" whispered Jackman.

Diamond wet his finger, dipped it into the bag, and tasted the substance. Bitter. He washed out his mouth at the sink. "Cocaine—the champagne drug. Didn't you know your wife used it?"

Jackman's expression switched rapidly from disbelief to shocked acceptance. It was the reaction Diamond would have expected. "I see—the straws."

"Not only the straws," Diamond told him. "I don't know how familiar you are with cocaine use. The stuff has to be chopped into fine powder first. They use a razor blade and a mirror. Glass is an ideal surface. They form the powdered coke into a line and sniff it through a straw or a rolled bank note. Your wife didn't have many bank notes left."

"You mean she spent all her money on this?"

"It isn't cheap."

Jackman was tugging abstractedly at the side of his face. "Jesus Christ. How could I have failed to see it?"

"Too engrossed in your job. From what you told me about your marriage—your worlds hardly overlapped, I think you said—you weren't best placed to make sense of what was happening. It's taken me a hell of a time to work it out, and I'm supposed to be a detective, or was."

"Her odd behavior—was that totally due to cocaine?"

"I don't know about totally. I think it's safe to say she wasn't mad. My understanding of the drug is that after the well-being wears off, the user—I'm speaking of heavy users—can be prey to all kinds of fears and anxieties. They think people are against them. Paranoid delusions leading to violent behavior are well-known symptoms."

"I'm surprised her bloody doctor didn't get onto this. So when she tried to kill me, she must have been high with cocaine."

"She'd probably been snorting it at the party."

"Is this what they call crack?"

"No, crack is cocaine dissolved in warm water and

heated with an alkali, like baking powder. It comes in the form of flakes or crystals. Try that and you have an immediate compulsive addiction. A physical addiction. This isn't crack."

"But it is addictive?"

"Psychologically, yes. It can take some time. I would guess from the size of your wife's overdraft that she was hooked."

Jackman was silent for a moment, piecing together the logic of what had seemed incomprehensible at the time. "I'd like to find the bastard who supplied her."

"So would I," said Diamond. "And fast."

"You think it has some bearing on her death? You do, don't you?" He smacked his hand on the table. "My God, it could change everything!"

Diamond was way ahead of him. "There was an incident that took place on the drive in front of this house last summer, witnessed by Mrs. Didrikson and her son. It was a Saturday morning. I think you were out at the time. You were very busy with that exhibition. The two of them—Dana and Matthew—were in the road hoping to catch a glimpse of you. Mat had seen you on television and recognized you as the guy who rescued him from the weir. Instead, they saw a man come out of the house—clean-shaven, strongly built, with straw-colored hair. Blue shirt, white jeans, and trainers. Oh, and he had a gold chain around his neck. Know anyone like that?"

"Nobody springs to mind."

"He had a maroon-colored Volvo. His name was Andy."

"Andy? The only Andy I know is fat and sixty. What happened?"

"He walked out toward his car and your wife came running after him, wearing a dressing gown. Her feet were bare, but she was in too much of a state to bother. She didn't want him to leave. She was asking him to come back in. She called him Andy and said something like, 'Do you expect me to go on my knees and beg?'

She had quite a wrestling match with him before he shoved her away and drove off."

"Dana saw all this?"

"Yes, and reasonably enough she took it to be a lovers' tiff. She steered Mat away in some embarrassment. Now that we know about the cocaine, I'm tempted to see the incident in a different light."

"This Andy was her supplier?"

Diamond gave a nod. "That's my assumption. Probably he was holding out for a higher price. More than your wife was willing to pay at that time."

"We've got to find him."

"That isn't easy. If I were still in the police, I'd bring in the drugs squad. They're better placed to find him. We ought to report this, anyway."

Some reluctance may have escaped in Diamond's voice, because Jackman immediately said, "We're in a different ballgame here. This isn't just about our civic duty. Dana faces a life sentence, and that Inspector Wigfull's reputation is on the line. He's handed the prosecution a neat case of murder with an eternal triangle motive and evidence to back it. He doesn't want it complicated with a drugs connection."

"He couldn't stop it."

"Yes, but he can soft-pedal. I think we should follow this up ourselves. It's the first scrap of hope for the defense. Let's not chuck it to the opposition right away."

Diamond was uneasy. As a senior policeman, he would have come down hard on anyone who failed to report a drugs find, however small. Yet he'd also known as a senior policeman how murder inquiries worked. New evidence wasn't greeted as good news when the file had already been passed to the Crown Prosecution Service. Jackman's remark about soft-pedaling was persuasive. And the earlier cock-up over the car log still troubled him. By drawing attention to its disappearance they had undoubtedly handed the prosecution a trump card. Why not hold this one back to play when the time was right?

Following it up for themselves, as Jackman had suggested, would be fraught with difficulties, but thanks to a well-trained memory, Diamond had one possible lead. "Cast your mind back a few months. Do you recall going through your wife's address book with me? I'm pretty sure one of the names we didn't pin down was Andy."

"You're right! It didn't mean anything to me."

"There was no address, just a phone number. If we could get that number . . ."

"Right on!" Then Jackman's expression altered. "But the address book must be still in the hands of the police."

"The defense solicitor could ask to examine it. They can't refuse. It's a reasonable request, and he doesn't have to say what he's looking for."

"I'll call Siddons right away."

It was easy—too easy for Diamond's cynical mind, which warned him that nothing you really want comes without hassle. Siddons the solicitor went straight to Bath Central and saw John Wigfull. The address book was produced for him. Within an hour of asking for it, Jackman had Andy's phone number.

The snag came when they tried it. An Asian voice answered. The Bristol number was an Indian restaurant in the Saint Paul's district of the city. They didn't know anyone called Andy. It gradually emerged that the restaurant had opened in January, having taken over empty premises that had been boarded up for a couple of months. Before that, it had been a gents' hairdresser's.

Diamond succeeded in contacting the estate agent who had handled the transfer of the property. The man wasn't too pleased to be asked about Andy. He'd had to deal with a number of inquiries from a variety of callers. The barber's name had not been Andy. He had been Mario, and he had died in the flu epidemic just before Christmas. The estate agent gathered that Mario the barber had made a secondary income by taking messages for scores of dubious people who called into the shop from time to time.

Diamond put down the phone and told Jackman, "It's a dead end."

8

MATTHEW DIDRIKSON sat eating his second slice of chocolate fudge cake in Charlotte's Patisserie in the Colonnades. Facing him were Jackman and Diamond. They had sought out a table under an arch at the rear of the shop; even so, they looked conspicuous among the shoppers and business people refreshing themselves for the journey home. Diamond, in the crumpled check suit he habitually wore, was shoehorned into the space between the table edge and the upholstered seat that went halfway around; and Jackman, elegant in brown corduroy and a black shirt, could have been straight out of a color-magazine fashion feature. Matthew was wearing a white shirt, striped tie, and navy pullover, having peeled off his school blazer at the first opportunity. Diamond had predicted that at this hour of the day they would find the boy somewhere in the Colonnades making a nuisance of himself on the escalators or in the elevator, and he'd been right. It remained to be discovered what they would get in return for their bribe of unlimited cake.

"How's your head these days?" Diamond asked. "No more blackouts, I hope?"

Clearly sensing that he had the high ground here, Matthew was in no hurry to respond. He glanced toward some schoolgirls at a table nearby, ran his fingers through his dark hair, and finally admitted, "It's all right."

"It's some time since we spoke. It was here, wasn't it? I was in disguise, if you remember." When that got no reaction, Diamond added, "I don't think Professor Jackman knows I played Santa, unless you mentioned it."

Jackman said quickly, "It's Greg. He calls me Greg."

This earned a smirk from Matthew, a more positive response than Diamond had achieved so far, so Jackman took up the conversation. "Mat and I haven't seen much of each other for a while, come to that. His mother wanted it that way after a misunderstanding and of course I respected her decision, but we had some good days out, didn't we, Mat?"

Matthew nodded.

The setup was fast becoming ridiculous, two grown men trying to coax information from a schoolboy over afternoon tea. Diamond tried to sound less avuncular. "Have you been to see your mother in the remand center?"

A nod.

"This week?"

"Sunday."

"How's she bearing up?"

"All right."

It was difficult to tell whether the brevity of the responses demonstrated unwillingness to answer or a wish to consume the cake without interruption.

"Mat, we're trying to help her," Jackman said.

Diamond added, "And it's up to you to help us."

Matthew made no comment at all.

"I don't know if you understand how serious this is," Diamond said gravely. "Do they teach you anything about law at that school of yours? Your mother is being put on trial for murder, but she has a barrister to defend her and he must try to show that there is reasonable doubt. Follow me, Mat?"

The boy pushed aside the empty plate and wiped his lips. "Yep." He looked away from the table, over his shoulder.

"Another piece?" Jackman suggested.

"If I can have a Coke to wash it down."

"Bring me some change, then." He handed over a five-pound note.

While Matthew was at the self-service counter, Diamond said, "Talk about sweeteners. Does this come out of Mrs. Didrikson's defense fund?"

"Couldn't justify it on what we've heard so far," said Jackman.

When the boy returned and put the plate of cake on the table, Diamond reached out and moved it deftly out of range. "Now I want you to cast your mind back. Your mother told me about an incident she witnessed in front of Professor Jackman's house one day last summer. You were with her."

Matthew was silent. His eyes were on the cake.

"There was some kind of dustup between Mrs. Jackman and a man."

"Andy."

"What did you say, son?"

"Andy. The man's name was Andy."

"You've got a good memory, obviously. We'd like to find this Andy. You see, if he and Mrs. Jackman were seen grappling with each other—as I understand they were—he has to be regarded as a possible suspect. Let's test that memory of yours and see exactly how much you can tell us about him."

"What's the point?"

Diamond reined in his irritation. "Son, we explained. Reasonable doubt."

"I mean why ask me, when you can see him for yourself?"

"If we knew where to find him, we would. That's the point."

"I know where."

"What?"

"I know where you can see Andy. I've seen him heaps of times."

The entire seat creaked as Diamond braced. "Where?"

"In the baths."

"The Roman Baths, do you mean?"

"Mm."

He slid the cake back toward the boy. "Tell me more."

"I told you," said Matthew. "If you want to talk to Andy, that's where to look."

"He works there?"

"Don't know." Matthew stuffed some cake in his mouth. "Listen, all I know is that I've seen him down there quite a few times."

"What were you doing down there?"

"Nothing much." The dismissive answer appeared to be all they would get. Then the boy's bravado triggered a statement that was the longest Diamond had ever heard from him. "I go down after school. It's a spooky place. I like it. The kids in my form started this dare. You have to go right through the baths without being caught by the security men. You walk into the souvenir shop in Stall Street, and when no one is looking, you whizz down the stairs marked 'Staff Only'—which is really the exit—and you're inside. You have to watch out for the security men, of course, but if you're smart you can walk right through the whole of the baths and come out in the Pump Room. No one stops you there because it's the restaurant. I've done it zillions of times. It's a doddle."

"And that's where you see Andy?"

Matthew nodded.

"Doing what?"

"Pointing at stuff and talking mostly."

"He's a guide, then?"

"Sort of. He has these students with him."

"*Students?*" said Jackman, reddening suddenly.

"Not every time. Sometimes he's alone."

Diamond was far ahead, assessing the implications,

but the process of question and answer had to be completed. "So he may be a lecturer of some sort?"

"Don't know."

Matthew added nothing else of significance. And little was said at that stage between the two men. If Andy, the presumed supplier of Geraldine's cocaine, had connections with the university, Jackman was going to face some questions himself.

When they got up to leave, Diamond invited Matthew to visit the Roman Baths with him after school on Monday, the next opportunity. "Meet me here," he suggested, adding craftily, "and if you're early, there may be time for another slice of fudge cake. Then you can help me do some detective work. But I want one thing clear: We enter the baths the regular way, through the front. I'm too visible to creep down the backstairs."

Matthew grinned and went off to look for his friends.

Out in Stall Street, Jackman was burning to say something. "Before you ask, there's no school of archaeology at the university."

"History?"

Jackman was actually shaking his head when he clapped his hand to his forehead and said, "Wait a minute. I'm wrong. A section started up this year. Just a handful of lecturers and first-years. I can't say I know any of them. That's the truth." He paused. "I suppose you want me to make inquiries."

"If you can manage it without alerting anyone," Diamond said. "I want to surprise Andy."

"Want some support?"

"There's no need. I'll let you know what happens, naturally."

"Actually I'd quite like to be there," Jackman offered with a self-conscious clearing of the throat. "I haven't seen much of Mat in recent weeks. I like the kid."

"That isn't the point of the exercise," Diamond told him in the tone he'd once used to keep the murder squad in line. "I'll be in touch."

If the truth were told, he liked the kid, too, for all his rough edges.

Jackman phoned on Monday with news of a part-time lecturer attached to the university history section. He was called Anton Coventry, and was known as Andy. His specialism was the history of Roman architecture, and he was presently leading a study of the Roman Baths with a first-year group from the School of Architecture and Building Engineering. They met on Mondays and Thursdays at 4:30. By special arrangement they had the use of the baths those days for an extra hour after the public had left, until 6:00. Jackman's inquiries had confirmed that Coventry had blond hair and dressed in a macho style. Moreover, he was a triathlon specialist.

"A what?"

"Triathlon. It's a sport, the ultimate in endurance, a kind of triple marathon, involving running, swimming, and cycling."

"Sounds to me like the ultimate in folly. Triathlon. When you mentioned it first, I thought maybe someone had invented the ideal sport for people like me, giving you credit for trying, and the hell with achievement."

"Trying, yes. I get it," said Jackman without amusement. "Coming back to Andy, I find it hard to square a passion for fitness with pushing drugs."

"Nothing strange in that," said Diamond, the pure-born cynic. "Drugs are commonplace in sport."

"I'd like to make it clear that I've never met the guy, so far as I'm aware," Jackman stressed.

"Point taken." Diamond grinned unkindly as he put down the phone.

On Monday afternoon, Matthew must have raced out of school or skipped a lesson, because he was waiting in the Colonnades by the entrance to the patisserie. Consequently there was ample time for the cake. Diamond, under instructions from his doctor to limit calories, confined himself to a frugal black coffee, averting his eyes from the boy's plate as he issued instructions. "Get this clear, Mat. Your purpose in being there is to satisfy yourself that the man in the baths is the same one who you saw having a set-to with Mrs. Jackman in the drive of John Brydon House. If you made a mistake, or can't be sure, then you must have the guts to say so, right? But whatever happens, I want you to stay quiet while we get a look at him, and remain hidden after that."

If proof of Mat's commitment were required, it came when he put down the cake half-eaten and suggested they start. Diamond told him there was plenty of time to clear his plate.

"I can't. I'm too excited," Matthew admitted.

Diamond's self-control wavered. "Pass it across, then."

At 4:20 P.M., they left the Colonnades, crossed Stall Street and entered the baths. To reach the ticket office, it was necessary to pass through the Pump Room, the meeting-place of Georgian society that now serves as a restaurant. The teatime ritual was fully in session, every chair occupied, the waitresses in their black waistcoats, white blouses, and aprons trying zealously to keep up and the trio at the near end lustily performing the Toreador music from *Carmen*. It was a relief to penetrate to the more serene atmosphere beyond.

Not many visitors were entering the baths at this stage of the day. The woman in the ticket office warned them that the exhibition closed to the public at 5:00. Attendants would ask everyone to leave. Diamond gave a nod of understanding. As soon as they were out of earshot, Matthew, the veteran interloper, confided to Diamond that he knew hundreds of places to hide.

Diamond didn't care to admit that he'd never previously made the official tour of the baths. Two terms of Latin in his youth had killed any interest in the Romans. Once he had attended a civic dinner in the Pump Room, preceded by cocktails beside the Great Bath; looking up to admire the lighting supplied by flaming torches attached to the columns, he had tripped on the uneven paving and spilled most of his drink down the dinner jacket he'd hired for the evening.

They came first to the remains of the temple of Sulis Minerva, picked out by discreetly sited lighting, so that the weathered limestone effigies of the gods glowed red-gold on the altar. The tourists down there were lingering to gaze, if not to read the guide notes, but Matthew, striding through as if it were his home, said, "You don't want to waste time here. Andy covered this bit a month ago. He's doing the Great Bath this week."

They moved along a walkway and down several flights of stairs, taking a series of turns that confused Diamond's sense of direction until they passed a window that looked down on to an open-air bath. The surface of the water was bubbling. "That's only the sacred spring," Matthew mentioned dismissively, seeing Diamond hesitate. At a still lower level, they heard a steady rush of water and saw the arch where the overflow from the spring tipped out as a miniature waterfall.

Ahead was daylight and the Great Bath, its blue-green rectangle overhung with steam. After the spotlights in the tunneled approaches, the sense of space and light could not fail to impress. The bath itself was some seventy feet by thirty, with steps down to the water. Rows of columns on stone piers surrounded it, supporting a canopy for the flagstoned aisles where Romans once promenaded, watching the bathers. The stretch of water was open to the sky. Visitors stood in ones and twos along the aisles, staring up at the columns and the sculptured figures mounted above them. "Most of it's Victorian," Matthew informed Diamond. "The Roman stuff barely comes up to your knees." His education had profited from his trespassing in the baths.

Diamond wasn't there for the architecture. A group of young people had gathered at the far end. Their style of dress and their absorption in conversation, rather than the surroundings, confirmed them as students. The lecturer had not appeared yet.

For the moment, Diamond had no need to get

close to the students. Around the sides of the bath, under the canopy, were a series of recesses where miscellaneous bits of masonry were displayed on stone plinths. Most were too low or too narrow to be useful to someone of Diamond's size, but at the center of the south side was a larger bay that housed an assortment of broken pilasters and columns. It looked possible to get behind it without attracting attention.

He and Matthew strolled casually around the pool until they were level with the bay. After glancing around, he touched Matthew's arm and steered him behind the plinth. They didn't even need to crouch.

Visitors continued to drift by for the next ten minutes, and then two of the security staff came through, evidently to warn any lingerers that the exhibition was about to close. Mercifully, although they passed quite close to the plinth, they didn't look behind it.

By degrees the surrounds of the bath emptied except for the history class and its hidden observers. The daylight was starting to fade. High above the Great Bath, the figures of the Roman emperors appeared more dramatic against the sky.

"You okay, son?" Diamond inquired.

Matthew nodded.

A moment later, footsteps clattered on the flagstones quite close to them, steps too brisk for a sightseer, even a belated one trying to get around. And it wasn't one of the attendants.

"It's him," Matthew whispered. "Definitely."

Andy Coventry passed within a few feet of them on his way around the perimeter to his students—his head and torso visible from their vantage point, the shoulders so broad and well muscled that the black T-shirt he was wearing was a second skin. The striking feature was the bleached mass of hair swept back from the forehead over the skull in the style of some sports idol of the 1950s.

Diamond said, when it was safe to speak, "Let's watch for a bit."

There was some lively barracking from the students

when Coventry approached them. He was probably ten minutes late. He opened a sports bag and took out what presently proved to be a number of steel measuring rules and handed them round. His voice was audible only in snatches across the water, but it was clear that he was issuing instructions, setting the class some kind of project. He knelt beside one of the original Roman piers supporting a column and measured its length and height. There was some discussion about the additional masonry used to reinforce the structure that had once supported a timber roof. The students had produced clipboards and were recording the information. Coventry started assigning them in pairs to the six main piers along the north side of the bath.

In a few minutes, all of the students were busy, measuring and taking notes. Satisfied, apparently, that they were usefully occupied, Coventry picked up his bag and strolled away from the class toward one of the exits at the west end.

Diamond put a restraining hand on Matthew's shoulder. This was going to require the stealth of a professional. He left the boy, stepped back into the shadows, and crept off in the direction Andy had taken. Conscious of his size, he moved with a lightness of step more appropriate to a much slimmer man.

A suspicion had dawned in Diamond's brain even before Andy had appeared with the sports bag. The next few minutes, he sensed, would be crucial to the investigation he had started all those weeks ago and was pursuing to its climax.

The need to remain unnoticed was essential, and so was the need to see what Andy Coventry was up to. It meant venturing into a complex of warm and cold baths at the west end of the Great Bath—with a high risk of discovery now that no visitors were left. He passed through the open door. Making use of every feature of the building that offered the possibility of cover, he approached the circular cold plunge bath known as the *frigidarium* and stared around its perimeter for a sight-ing of his man. The subdued lighting was a mixed blessing.

He seemed to have lost the trail already. The walkway system lined with Plexiglas sides began again in this section. All he could see as he peered over the handrail opposite was the site of another bath, practically empty of water. Obliged to move on into a section still more in shadow, he found himself looking down on a sunken area where columns of copper-colored bricks stood in ranks like the Terracotta Army discovered in China. He knew what it was from postcards he had seen: an early form of central heating. The columns had once supported a floor, enabling hot air from a charcoal-burning flue to circulate in the cavity. Above, in their Turkish bath, Romans had once sat and sweated and been oiled, scraped and massaged. The hypocaust, as it was labeled, was one of the most notable features of the baths, mainly because of its function, and also for the strange, unforgettable spectacle of more than a hundred of these knee-high columns, filling the floor space in symmetrical formation, no less impressive for being worn and damaged, a chromatic mix of copper and ochres that time had rendered into what could easily have passed for a masterpiece of modern art.

If Diamond's thoughts had really taken on aesthetic overtones (which is doubtful), they must have been galvanized by the sight of Andy Coventry crouching down on the floor among the columns at the far end.

Diamond froze, undecided whether to go down there. Coventry hadn't looked up; he was absorbed in whatever he was doing.

The right course, Diamond decided, was to watch and wait. He backed away, out of Coventry's sight, up a flight of stairs that led to the toilets.

There was an interval of two or three minutes when nothing happened; then the scrunch of shoes on the gritty underfloor of the hypocaust, followed by the sound of Coventry hoisting himself back on to the walkway; and brisk steps as he returned toward the Great Bath.

Peter Diamond was down the steps and over the barrier before the drumming of the footsteps had ceased. With agility born of urgency, he sidestepped between the columns until he came to the place where he had seen Coventry. As he had anticipated, there was a cavity near one of the vents to the flue. He knelt, put his hand inside, and touched something most unlike a Roman relic. It was soft, smooth, and light in weight.

He lifted it out—a plastic bag containing a white, glittering substance.

In appearance it was identical to the cocaine he had found in the bag of flour in Jackman's kitchen. He felt inside the cavity again and located similar bags, stacks of them, too many to remove now.

As a hiding place for drugs, the hypocaust had advantages. Unlike much of the site, it was dry. The cavity was masked by one of the brick columns, and nobody had reason to look there, because this section of the baths had been comprehensively excavated. The public were kept well back behind the Plexiglas. Yet it was neutral ground that Andy Coventry could visit twice weekly without fear of being seen. Whether collecting or depositing, he could carry the stuff in and out of the building in his sports-bag. And who in his right mind in the Avon and Somerset Drugs Squad would suggest the Roman Baths for a bust?

Diamond stood. The immediate problem was what to do about it. He was entitled to make a citizen's arrest. But was that the wisest course of action? Ideally he wanted to question the man about the murder. Drug dealing was dangerous and despicable and Coventry would take the rap for it, but not immediately.

Then the lights went out.

This part of the building had no windows. It was pitch black. Diamond reached out to steady himself. He didn't want to blunder into those columns of bricks and lose his balance. His first thought was that the lights had been routinely switched off now that the place was officially closed.

His second thought was more alarming, prompted

by a sound somewhere ahead like the scuffing of a shoe
on limestone grit. Of course it might simply have been a
fragment of stone dislodged by some natural means. He
doubted that. Suppose Coventry had returned and spotted him at the hiding place. Suppose he had deliberately
cut the lights.

It wasn't wise to remain where he was.

There was no question of finding a way through the
hypocaust. He would have to edge along the back wall
like a spider trapped in a sink. Tentatively he slid his
hand along the surface, put out a foot, and shifted his
weight sideways. He paused, listened, heard nothing,
and repeated the move, this time finding one of the
columns in his way. Still with his palms flat to the wall,
he edged around the obstruction, intent on putting as
much distance as possible between himself and the cavity where the drugs were hidden.

By this means he negotiated three more columns.
He was feeling his way around a fourth when he heard a
scrunch from the far side. No doubt about it: Someone
had climbed down from the walkway and let himself
onto the gritty surface of the underfloor.

A voice, definitely Coventry's, called out, "I know
you're there, fatso."

Diamond made no response. Remaining still and
silent was the best way to limit the damage.

Coventry was on the move. The steps were quick
and even. Either he was willing to risk skinning his
knees on the columns of the hypocaust, or he knew the
layout perfectly.

It was a test of nerve. Diamond waited, tense and
poised to defend himself.

Coventry was heading for the place where the
drugs were hidden. He must have moved right along
one of the aisles between the columns, because he
didn't falter. Only when he reached the wall did he stop.

There was a short silence. Then Coventry spoke up
again. "All right, you bastard, let's see where you are."
With that, a cigarette lighter flamed.

He held it at arm's length and moved it in a wide

arc, casting long shadows across the floor of the hypocaust. Inevitably, the light picked out Diamond.

The triathlon was Coventry's sport, but he could
certainly have made a success of pro wrestling. He came
at Diamond as if he'd just rebounded off the ropes. The
lighter went out—too late to be of help to Diamond,
who stepped back to avert the force of the charge, and
fell. A brick column that had endured for two thousand
years was flattened under his bulk. On a reflex learned
in rugby scrums, he brought his knees and arms to his
chest and swung his body hard to the right. He felt a
searing pain in his side as he was crushed against the
debris. One of his ribs had snapped. Using the leverage
of his thighs, he succeeded in forcing the man aside and
followed it up with a jab with the elbow that made contact with yielding flesh.

The pain in his side was severe. In a hand-to-hand
fight, he wasn't going to last long. He groped in the
darkness and made contact with another of the columns. Blessedly, it took the strain. He hauled himself
on to his haunches. Then something hard hit his head.

Coventry must have picked up a brick and swung it
wildly. The full force would have brained Peter Diamond. Instead, it scraped down the side of his skull,
raking the skin just behind his right ear, and sank into
the muscle tissue of his shoulder. He staggered, held
onto the column, and lurched forward. His shoulder
went numb.

Andy Coventry meant to kill him.

He was upright and moving between the columns
with no idea which direction he was taking, except that
it had to be away from his assailant. The darkness was
absolute. Heightened by the deprivation, his other
senses gave him a vivid animal awareness. The dank,
dead smell of the stones filled his nostrils. The chill
ripped through his flesh. The crunch of his steps re-
sounded from the roof and walls. This was the blind
rush of the hunted. He didn't care if he transformed the
hypocaust into a heap of rubble, so long as he survived.

Taking huge, audible gasps, he stumbled through the black void, hands outstretched.

And stopped.

His hands were flat against a smooth surface which had to be the Plexiglas side of the walkway. Reaching up, he found it impossible to make contact with the rail, so he worked his way to the left until a stone obstruction stopped him. The wall again. Behind him, he could hear the crunch of Coventry's steps.

He reached up with his right hand to see if there was any chance of scaling the wall, and got an agonizing reminder of the injury to his rib. Using the left hand instead, he discovered a ledge about three feet above the ground. He got his knees up to the level and hauled himself higher. A second step now presented itself. Laboriously, he scrambled up, made contact with the Plexiglas again and then—mercifully—the rail of the walkway. He got his legs over and felt the flat rubber surface under his feet. Now he could discern a faint gray light. Daylight. He staggered toward it, conscious that Coventry must reach the walkway at any moment.

The Great Bath was ahead. There, common sense argued, he would be safe from further attack. Coventry could hardly carry on the fight in front of his students.

Diamond assessed his injuries as he moved. The rib was the most disabling, and there was also blood trickling down his scalp from the head wound. He could feel its warmth on the side of his neck. The blood was conspicuous. When he reached the Great Bath, he didn't want the students crowding around him asking questions. Somehow he must hold himself together and convince anyone who was watching that he was walking normally. That the blood, if they noticed it, was some sort of blemish, a strawberry mark on the skin. Then he needed only to get to one of the doors leading to an exit.

He would have to leave Matthew to find his own way out. Thank God the boy was familiar with the place. He was smart enough to escape.

But Diamond was not. Within a few yards of the

entrance to the Great Bath, he was surprised by a sudden movement to his right. He turned. Enough daylight had penetrated the place to show him Andy Coventry coming at him with a spade, a heavy-duty, long-handled spade of the sort used by builders. There was no escape this time. Wielded like a sledgehammer, it was about to cleave Peter Diamond's skull.

PART SIX

Trial

1

———————

A BLACK BAR across white. A thin black bar, dividing the field of vision like a cable across the sky.

Too uniformly white for sky. It had to be something else.

A ceiling.

A cable across the ceiling? No. Something more rigid. A black bar. Or rod. Or rail.

Maybe a rail. There was something right about a rail. A connection, but with what?

With a sound. The rustle and scrape of something metallic. Curtain rings. So why not a curtain rail?

What would a curtain rail be doing across a ceiling? Curtains were for windows. No window here.

Unless this was a bed, a hospital bed with curtains for privacy. That would explain the scrape of the rings. It ought to be easy to check, because the rail would go at least three sides around the bed.

Unfortunately it wasn't so easy when one couldn't move one's head to left or right. When one felt muzzy and tired, too tired really to care . . .

"He opened his eyes again, sir," the voice of a woman announced, a woman difficult to place.

"Didn't move his lips, I suppose?" A man's voice.
"No."

"Poor sod. Keep your ears open, just in case. I know it's bloody tedious, but it has to be done. You want to try talking to him when you're here by the hour. Anything that comes into your head. Tell him the secrets of your love life. That's what the nurses do. Anything to stir up the brain cells."

"Do you mind? My private life isn't for Mr. Diamond's ears, sir."

"Relax, Constable. Even if he heard you, which is doubtful, he wouldn't remember a thing. Well, I'm off. See you tomorrow."

"Gutso."

"Mm?"

"You see?" The voice was triumphant. "It is a response. He heard. Peter Diamond, you fat slob. What do we have to do to bring you 'round? What's your taste in music? The Hippopotamus Song, I reckon."

"He's moving his lips, sir."

"Jesus Christ, he is. Peter? Can you hear me?"

"Mm."

"Again."

"Mm."

"Terrific. Mr. Diamond, do you understand? This is Keith Halliwell. Remember me? Somerset and Avon Police. Your old sidekick, DI Halliwell."

"Halliwell?"

"He spoke! Did you hear that, Constable?"

"Yes, sir."

"Brilliant. Put a call through to Mr. Wigfull. We're in business at last."

His eyes were open, and instead of the curtain rail in front of them, there was a face, a dark face dominated by a mustache. A face he didn't particularly care for.

"Mr. Diamond?"

"John Wigfull."

"How are you feeling?"

"I can't move."

"Don't try. Your head's clamped. You're lucky to be alive."

The trite remark irked Diamond, even at this level of consciousness. "Where am I?"

"In the RUH. You've been in a coma. They said if you did come 'round, there was no obvious physical damage to the brain, but no one can stay in a coma too long. Do you follow me?"

"Perfectly," said Diamond.

"You were found in a pool of blood in the Roman Baths. The Didrikson boy alerted us."

"Good lad."

"Your skull was cracked and impacted. The only reason your head isn't in two pieces is that the spade was curved at the edge. Do you remember being struck?"

"Not really."

"It may come back to you slowly. We'll be needing a statement."

"You pulled Coventry in?"

"You remember a certain amount, then?"

Diamond summarized what he remembered, up to the moment when Andy Coventry had set off in pursuit of him.

Wigfull informed him that the drugs squad were holding Coventry on a charge of possession. "We'll do him for dealing, as well. He had two kilos of cocaine stashed away in the baths."

The brain was functioning, sluggishly, but reliably. "He was supplying Mrs. Jackman, the woman who was murdered."

Wigfull frowned. "What's your evidence for that?"

"The boy and his mother witnessed Andy coming out of the house."

"The Jackman house? When was this?"

"Months ago. Last summer. You remember. Mrs.

Didrikson told us in her statement. Geraldine Jackman was begging Coventry not to leave."

"That was Coventry?" Wigfull's tone was skeptical.

"The boy is certain of it."

"What exactly are you suggesting, Mr. Diamond—a drugs angle on the Jackman case? Is that the best the defense can think up?"

"I'm talking facts, John. Geraldine Jackman was snorting coke. Go to the house. You'll find packets of cocaine hidden in bags of flour in the kitchen."

Wigfull moved away from the bed, out of Diamond's limited range of vision. "The post mortem samples were negative for drugs. If you cast your mind back, Dr. Merlin ordered a full screening test for drugs and alcohol. Chepstow found nothing."

"This is something you should check with Merlin," Diamond advised. "It doesn't mean she hadn't used cocaine. Unlike marijuana, it doesn't hang about in the body for long. A few days at most. If she hadn't snorted the stuff in the few days prior to her death, it's unlikely that traces would have shown up in the samples."

"Even if what you're saying is true, it's a side issue," Wigfull insisted. "Nobody's suggesting Gerry Jackman was nice to know. That's no part of the prosecution case. All right, you tell me she was a junkie. I'll see that it's investigated, but the fact remains that Dana Didrikson killed her. The evidence is unassailable."

"When is the trial?"

"In just over a week."

"A *week?*"

"You've been here ten days. Take it easy. They bring the papers round. You won't miss a thing."

Later that morning, he met the surgeon who had pieced together his splintered skull. The operation, he learned, had been a five-hour job, and no one had been able to predict with confidence that he would come out of the coma, let alone come out of it with his brain unimpaired. The contraption clamped around his head

was essential to his recovery. In twenty-four hours it
would be replaced by something that permitted more
movement. As for other injuries, two of his ribs had
cracked, and there were superficial abrasions, but there
was no reason why he shouldn't be on his feet in a week.

"On my feet and out of here?" Diamond asked.

"On your feet and as far as the toilet, Mr. Diamond. As a ward sister once remarked to me, bedpans
are nobody's cup of tea."

At least he had an opportunity to think. The matter that
exercised him most was Andy Coventry's behavior. He
would dearly have liked to question the man, only it
wasn't possible, now or later. John Wigfull must have
taken a statement already, but John Wigfull was
blinkered.

The ferocity of the attack had been out of all proportion. Coventry could easily have killed him. Was a
crack over the head with a spade a reasonable response
to being caught with a couple of kilos of cocaine? People can panic, certainly. The chances were that Coventry
wasn't a big wheel in the drugs trade, not an importer or
a trafficker, just a pusher, probably with no form at all.
Those are the people who are liable to strike back when
threatened. The real professionals weigh the consequences.

However, there was a more persuasive scenario.
Andy Coventry had clearly been Geraldine Jackman's
supplier. He'd kept her in cocaine and systematically
emptied her bank account. Fine, until her funds ran out.
She had been heavily overdrawn at the bank. He must
have watched her become increasingly desperate, knowing that ultimately there would be no point in offering
the stuff to someone who couldn't pay. Maybe he'd told
her the arrangement was at an end. Then—the scenario
ran—Geraldine had got in touch again. She'd offered
something of value in exchange for drugs. Coventry had
gone to the house, and she had shown him the Jane
Austen letters she had pilfered from her husband.

Coventry must have been unimpressed. He would have foreseen the problems in turning the letters into cash. The discussion had turned ugly. Gerry, in one of her towering rages, had threatened to expose him as a pusher, and the hell with the consequences for herself, because without cocaine her life was closing down anyway. Andy Coventry, desperate, had silenced her forever.

Through the months since then, the man must have lived in dread of the truth emerging. When he became aware in the Baths that someone had been watching him stow away drugs, he had panicked. He had killed once to stop someone blowing the whistle on his dealing, so why not a second time?

Toward the end of the week, Gregory Jackman came to the hospital on a visit. Hollow-eyed and drooping at the shoulders, he looked ten years older than when Diamond had seen him last. "The drugs story has broken," he explained. "They came to the house—Chief Inspector Wigfull and some people from the drugs squad—and I showed them the bags of flour. Today it's all over the tabloids. 'Drugs Find in Prof's House. Dead Woman's Cocaine Habit.' The top brass in the university don't like it one bit. I've been told to take a year's sabbatical directly the trial is over."

"Told? Do they have the right?"

"Asked, then. They're being as decent as they can. I'll get a year's salary, but the understanding is that I'll go to America on a research fellowship, and while I'm there I'll apply for other posts."

"Welcome to the club," said Diamond.

"What?"

"It's the old heave-ho. Will you go?"

"Try and stop me."

"Can it really be as quick as you say?"

"Thanks to the wonders of fax, yes. The only thing to be settled is the day I fly out. I've been called as a witness, naturally."

"Presumably a prosecution witness."

"Yes. It's a warrant. I've talked to Dana's lawyers. I don't seem to have any choice in the matter. It's the way they want to play it, apparently."

"These days the forensic evidence is often so cut and dried that you don't call defense experts to challenge it. If the defense calls no witnesses except Dana, they'll have the right to make the final speech to the jury before the judge sums up."

Jackman said bleakly, "I just hope they've talked to Dana about this. God knows what she's going to make of me appearing for the prosecution."

"She still intends to plead not guilty, does she?"

Jackman tilted his head, surprised by the question. "Certainly. Is there any reason why she shouldn't?"

"I don't know. Wigfull was here a day or two ago, looking as smug as a winning jockey. He's sure they'll convict."

"So I gathered."

"Nothing has altered, then?"

Jackman said gloomily, "It looks as hopeless as ever. I thought perhaps what happened to you would help the defense by pointing to Andy Coventry as an alternative suspect."

"Well, doesn't it?"

He shook his head. "Her lawyers don't want to go down that road."

"Why not, for God's sake?"

"They say it doesn't address the crucial points that the prosecution will raise—the fact that Dana admits she was at the house on the morning of the murder, and the evidence that her car was used to transport the body to Chew Valley Lake. That forensic report is dynamite. She has no answer to it. And that leaves out all the circumstantial stuff about motive. A good prosecutor will eat her alive."

Privately, Diamond had to admit that the lawyers were right.

•   •   •

By Friday he felt sufficiently recovered to phone Siddons the solicitor and ask whether the defense team were fully aware of Andy Coventry's involvement in the case.

"Absolutely," Siddons assured him. "The drugs bring another dimension to it. Mrs. Jackman's outbursts obviously had their origin in her cocaine habit."

"Yes, but have you considered the possibility that Coventry killed her?" He outlined his theory.

From the tone of Siddons's responses—the polite, yet qualified murmurs that came down the phone each time Diamond paused—it was clear that the solicitor wasn't exactly turning cartwheels of joy at the other end. He thanked Diamond for his interest and said, "Unfortunately for us, your theory isn't tenable. Coventry was questioned by the police about his movements at the time of the murder, and he was three hundred miles away, in Newcastle. For the entire week. They checked it. He was lecturing to an Open University course at Hadrian's Wall. It's a cast-iron alibi. Infuriating, isn't it?"

2

_____

DEPRESSING as it was, the doctors were right. Peter Diamond was still in hospital when Dana Didrikson's trial for murder opened at Bristol Crown Court. True, he'd reached a stage of convalescence when he was no longer considered enough of an emergency to justify occupying a room of his own near the sister's office; instead, he'd been moved into a six-bedded ward near the stairs that was, in effect, a poker school. The inmates were all concussion cases restored to sufficient consciousness to tell a sequence from a flush. Their slick play was a testimony to the nursing. Diamond had never been much of a cardplayer, so after a few hands to demonstrate goodwill he had escaped to the day room and the morning papers.

There was not much call in the RUH for the quality newspapers, according to the news agent who supplied the wards. Diamond's information about the first day of the trial had to be drawn from the tabloids. Among the glamour shots of Gerry Snoo and banner headlines of the ANGRY GERRY'S LAST HOURS variety were meager accounts of the court proceedings. Diamond managed to glean that Dana had pleaded not guilty and a jury of eight men and four women had been empaneled. Prosecuting Counsel, Sir Job Mitchell, QC had opened the prosecution's case with his outline of the events leading up to the charge of murder. Reference was made to the accident at Pulteney Weir that had brought Dana Didrikson into the ambit of the Jackmans. She was portrayed as a single parent—"Desperate Dana," in one paper—struggling to bring up a son and stretched to pay his school fees. Jackman's fatherly acts of kindness to the boy in the summer months were seen as the seed of a motive—"Lone Mum's Love Plot"—nurtured by Dana's discovery that the Jackman marriage was in crisis. The lengths to which she had gone to obtain the Jane Austen letters as a gift for Jackman were stressed as significant, and so was the acrimonious visit of Mrs. Jackman to her home—"Gerry's Man-Stealer Fury." It was pointed out that Dana had admitted visiting the Jackman house on the morning of the murder when she'd heard that the letters were missing. Motive and opportunity were thus spelled out to the readers at least as vividly as they had been to the jury.

Each paper insisted that recent developments in forensic science would dominate the case. The Crown would be calling experts in DNA analysis—genetic fingerprinting—to prove that the body had been placed in the trunk of Dana's car prior to its being recovered from Chew Valley Lake. She had sworn a statement that the car had never been driven by anyone but herself. And she had been unable to explain the disappearance of the mileage log.

Thus outlined, the prosecution case appeared formidable. So, also, did the hostility of the tabloids toward Dana. Diamond had long ago ceased to believe in unbiased reporting. But he did feel embittered by two feature articles eulogizing genetic fingerprinting as the infallible method of detection. No direct reference to the Jackman case was made, but when an editor chose to publish such a piece on the day a major trial opened, the inference was clear. One paper had a center spread of forty mug shots of murderers and rapists trapped by the DNA test in the past two years.

The old antagonism stirred again. He'd thought he

had gotten it out of his system when he'd quit the police.
Yet here he was bridling at the assumption that science
had taken over completely from the detectives.

He heard a sound behind him and saw a staff nurse
and probationer approaching with a trolley.

"How is my Mr. Diamond this morning?"

"Just about coming to his senses," he answered.
He'd given up trying to speak normally to this Nightin-
gale who reduced every exchange to the level of the
children's ward.

"Ready to have his dressing changed?"

"Indeed. And if staff could arrange to make it a
little flatter to the head—a little less obtrusive, shall we
say?—Mr. Diamond would be mightily obliged."

"Why? Going to the pictures, are we? Or a football
match?"

There was a supportive giggle from the probationer.

Diamond said, "A murder trial, actually."

"What are you saying?"

"That your Mr. Diamond will shortly be leaving
you. Discharging himself."

A shocked silence was followed by, "We'll see what
Sister has to say about that."

"Fair enough. And when she's said it, Mr. Diamond
will thank Sister sincerely for her tender, loving care
and bid her good day."

By 11:30 he was sitting in the public gallery in Bristol Crown Court listening to Dr. Jack Merlin giving evidence. The pathologist was being as cautious as ever,
declining to name a cause of death. Pressed by the Prosecution to comment on asphyxiation as a likely cause, he
would say only that it was not inconsistent with the findings. The main thrust of the forensic screening that had
followed the autopsy had been towards toxicology to
determine whether drugs or alcohol had been present.
The screening tests carried out by the Home Office forensic laboratory had proved negative. Under cross-examination, Merlin admitted that there was a threshold
point for analytical suitability, and that samples from a

corpse submerged in water for more than a week might
not yield significant traces. However, he believed it was
unlikely that death had been caused by a toxic substance.

Merlin was followed in the witness box by another
forensic scientist, called Partington, who spoke somewhat long-windedly about fibers found in the bedroom
at John Brydon House. Peter Diamond's attention
moved elsewhere.

Dana Didrikson, dressed in a dark green suit, listened from the dock, her hands clasped in her lap. She
had her brown hair pinned back severely, perhaps to
discourage the suggestion that she was a husband-
stealer. She wore no makeup. Image was an important
consideration, and her solicitor would have advised her
to dress demurely. It appeared to Diamond that the
months in the remand center had marked her. She'd put
on weight—not much, but enough to give her face a
decidedly mumpish look that combined with her sagging
posture to suggest that she was already resigned to a
long prison sentence.

"The color was distinctive?" Sir Job Mitchell was
saying to his witness.

"Certainly," the scientist responded. "A shade of
dark red or maroon achieved by dyeing the garment
with some home dye. We matched it with samples taken
from a lambswool jumper found in the defendant's
home."

The judge—a world-weary Welshman—intervened.
"Sir Job, unquenchable as my interest is in the findings
of the forensic science laboratory, I should like to know
where this line of questioning is taking us."

"My lord, the Crown is seeking to establish that the
defendant was present and wearing the garment in the
bedroom where the murder took place. Taken together
with the hair samples and the skin tissues also found in
the bedroom, and subjected to DNA analysis, the evidence is fundamental to the prosecution case."

"The evidence of what?" persisted the judge. "My
understanding is that several weeks passed before the

house was searched. We cannot safely conclude that these fibers and tissues were deposited on the day Mrs. Jackman was murdered. Suppose the defendant visited the house some day after September eleventh?"

"In that case, my lord, with the greatest respect, it would be highly relevant to inquire what the defendant was doing in Professor Jackman's bedroom some day after September eleventh, or—one might conjecture— some night."

There was some subdued amusement at this and defense counsel was on her feet. "My lord, I must object."

"Sit down," said the judge. "That remark was unworthy of you, Sir Job."

"I withdraw it unreservedly, m'lord, and apologize to the court." Smoothly, Sir Job added, "We now pass on to the matter of the Mercedes car driven by the defendant. Did you examine the car, Mr. Partington?"

"I did. On October eleventh. I removed samples of skin and hair from the trunk of the vehicle and subjected them to DNA analysis."

"For the benefit of the court, would you now explain the significance of such a test? This is what is commonly known as genetic fingerprinting, is it not?"

"Yes. It is a way of producing genetic profiles of individuals which are unique in each case except for identical twins. The genetic material known as DNA can be extracted from samples of blood, skin, semen, or hair roots and separated into strands. Chemicals known as restriction enzymes are used to chop the strands into unequal pieces which are sorted on a piece of gelatin by a process known as electrophoresis. We then tag the bits with radioactive probes and expose them to X-ray film to produce a series of black bands not unlike the bar codes used in supermarket checkouts."

"Every one unique to the individual?"

"Exactly. So that comparisons can be made with certainty."

"And you produced genetic profiles of the traces of

hair and skin found in the trunk of the Mercedes car driven by the defendant?"

"Yes."

"With what result?"

"They matched the samples taken from the victim."

"Matched them absolutely?"

"In every respect."

There was a pause in the proceedings while comparative photographs of the results were passed around the jury.

"Is there anything else you can tell the court about the skin and hair found in the car?"

"We found four hairs altogether, all matching the victim's DNA profile. Three were from the pubic region, suggesting that at some stage the body in the trunk was unclothed."

"And the skin particles. How many did you find?"

"Twenty-three."

"So many. Is that indicative of anything?"

"It suggests to me that the body was dragged across the lining of the boot, causing some scaling. There may also have been some movement when the car was driven."

"Summing up, then, Dr. Partington, you are quite certain in your mind that the body of Mrs. Jackman was conveyed somewhere in the boot of the defendant's car?"

"Entirely certain."

"Thank you."

Dana's defense counsel rose to cross-examine the witness. She was Lilian Bargainer, QC, a doughty, silver-haired advocate, ample in voice and girth. Diamond had been cross-examined by her on one occasion. The defense was in capable hands.

"Dr. Partington, there is just one thing I would like to have clear. Is it possible, is it conceivable, that the skin and hair samples you took from the trunk of the car could have been introduced there?"

"What exactly do you mean?" Partington knew very well what she meant. It was a defense red herring, dangled in front of the jury in case they were influenced by stories of police corruption.

"If some person of malicious intent wished to convey the impression that the car had been used to transport the body somewhere, might he or she have misled you by planting some skin and hair samples in the trunk?"

Dr. Partington was categorical. "No. The appearance and positioning of the skin samples was entirely consistent with a body having lain there and been lifted in and out. They adhered to and mingled with the fibers of the inner lining entirely as one would expect. In my opinion, it would not be possible to reproduce this effect artificially."

"Thank you."

The court adjourned for lunch.

In the corridor outside, Diamond spotted Jackman briefly, but he was in conversation with a lawyer, possibly the solicitor, and it seemed inopportune to approach them. So it was a solitary lunch in the pub across the road, where the head bandage attracted wary looks from other customers.

He next saw Jackman in the witness box. The people in front, in the first row of the public gallery, craned for a better view. In the dock, Dana Didrikson lowered her eyes as if taking an interest in the state of her fingernails. Her expression remained placid, but she couldn't do anything about a nervous twitch in a muscle close to her jawbone.

After Jackman had taken the oath, he was steered gently by Sir Job into the account of his marriage that he had given in his statement to Diamond many weeks ago. To his credit, he adhered closely to the original, admitting the imperfections in his relationship to Geraldine, the steady increase in arguments and accusations. Some of it was going to make juicy reading in tomorrow's papers, in particular the night Geraldine had set fire to the summerhouse.

"You were convinced that your wife intended to kill you?"

"Yes."

"Yet you chose not to report the incident to the police."

"That is correct. She was mentally unstable, or so it appeared at the time. As I now know, she—"

Sir Job cut in sharply, "We're dealing with matters as you understood them at the time, professor. Would you tell the court whether you had met the defendant, Mrs. Didrikson, prior to the fire in the summerhouse."

"I saw her that evening, yes."

"Where precisely? At your house?"

"She came to the house. I met her outside, in the road."

"Why was that? Didn't you want her at the party for some reason?"

"It wasn't appropriate. She hadn't come for a social evening. She came to clear up a misunderstanding."

"So you cleared it up in the road?"

"We went to a pub."

"In her car?"

"Yes."

"At your suggestion?"

"It was a place to have a conversation."

"And a couple of drinks, I presume. It didn't cross your mind that your connection—I employ the word in a platonic sense—your connection with Mrs. Didrikson might have come to the notice of your wife?"

"She knew of it. She took the phone call."

"Ah."

Jackman had been lured into deep water and now he was floundering. "But it didn't amount to anything at that stage."

"At that stage?"

"I mean a connection in the sense you hinted at. Then, or later."

"Come, come, professor," said Sir Job, smiling indulgently. "I scrupulously avoided suggesting anything that may have happened later, but since you have raised the matter, would it be true to say that the platonic connection blossomed into a friendship?"

Jackman blushed deeply. He was making a terrible hash of this if he wanted to help Dana. "A platonic friendship."

"A friendship that lasted through the summer?"

"We met a few times, but it was for the boy's sake. I took him swimming a number of times."

"And to other places?"

"A cricket match, on one occasion, and a balloon festival."

"And at the end of these outings, you returned young Matthew to his mother?"

"Naturally."

"She must have felt some obligation to you."

"No."

"No?"

"I mean that wasn't the intention at all. I had no ulterior motive."

"But your wife thought otherwise."

At this, defense counsel rose to object that Sir Job appeared to be cross-examining his own witness. For some minutes both counsel and the judge were embroiled in an argument over the legal niceties.

Diamond listened unhappily. He'd come here to follow the trial at first hand instead of reading the garbled newspaper accounts, and it wasn't at all as he had hoped. Powerless to influence what was going on down there, he sensed that Dana's attitude of resignation was preempting the verdict. The prosecution were riding high.

The examination-in-chief was resumed. "Professor, we were discussing your late wife's reactions to your occasional meetings with the defendant. Would you tell us what she had to say on the subject?"

"She twisted everything."

Sir Job glanced toward the judge, who said wearily, "Tell the court what your wife said, professor."

"She hinted that I was having an affair with Mrs. Didrikson."

"Only hinted?"

"Well, toward the end she was more specific."

Diamond ached inwardly. This was disastrous for the defense. Far better if Jackman had come out with the worst Geraldine had said. By his reluctance to tell, he appeared to be confirming that he and Dana had been lovers.

"What did she say precisely?"

"You want the exact words?" Jackman hesitated. "She said we were shagging like rabbits. It was a complete and utter lie."

Sir Job said, "Did you say lie, or lay?" The quip was well timed. General laughter covered the embarrassment and the cheap point was scored. The defense would gain nothing by protesting.

Jackman's misery continued for another hour. Sir Job went on to secure the important admission that Geraldine had visited Dana and accused her of using Matthew as bait. He took Jackman through the events of the weekend before the murder and made much of Dana's gift of the Jane Austen letters.

"She wanted you to have them as a gift—these letters of potentially great value?"

"Yes."

"A farewell gift?"

"That was my understanding. After what had taken place between my wife and Mrs. Didrikson, it would be impossible for me to go on seeing the boy."

"And you accepted the letters?"

"Yes—but if they proved to be genuine, I always intended to return them to her after the Jane Austen exhibition was over."

"So this farewell was more of an *au revoir* than a final parting. When were you next in contact with Mrs. Didrikson?"

"On the Monday morning. I phoned."

"The day your wife was to be murdered? What did you have to say to Mrs. Didrikson that Monday morning?"

Scarcely a statement of Jackman's had passed without being given a damaging twist by Sir Job. It was cross-examination masquerading as direct examination, and so skillfully had it been done that the defense would only have damaged its own case by repeatedly objecting. By the time Sir Job had done, the jury must have been convinced that Dana was a woman in the grip of an infatuation, and that Jackman had encouraged her.

The cross-examination proper was cut to the minimum. Lilian Bargainer looked over her half glasses at Jackman and asked, "Professor, can you account for your wife's erratic behavior in the months prior to her death?"

"I believe I can. She was using drugs."

"There is evidence of this?"

"Yes. On April 25th last, the police found packets of cocaine hidden in the house. I understand that a person addicted to cocaine may exhibit symptoms of paranoia."

The judge interrupted. *"Drugs?* I heard no mention of drugs before this. Sir Job, is the prosecution aware of this? You made no reference to it in your outline of the case."

Prosecuting counsel coughed and wrapped his gown protectively around him. "We are aware of it, m'lord. A man has been charged with supplying the deceased with cocaine. The matter has no connection with the case for the Crown."

"That may be so. I am surprised we have not heard of it already."

"I intend to call a police witness at a later stage, m'lord. Undoubtedly the matter will be touched upon. I do not wish to overstate its importance."

The judge turned to Mrs. Bargainer. "I take it that you attach some significance to it. Did you wish to pursue this matter with this witness?"

She said, "I think the point is made, my lord. I shall, of course, wish to cross-examine the police witness in due course."

The rest was routine questioning, attempting to

mend some of the fences broken by the prosecution. Jackman did what he could.

When the court adjourned for the day, Diamond didn't stop to speak to anyone. There seemed no point anymore. Anyway, his head ached. He went home to take some painkillers.

3

HE WAS IN THE SAME SEAT in the public gallery next morning. By the time Dana was brought in, every place was taken. She looked small, too small to be the focus of this elaborate ritual.

The court rose for the judge.

Prosecuting counsel remained standing when everyone else sat down. "My lord, with your permission, before we commence the proceedings, I beg to advise the court of some new evidence which has come to light."

"Sir Job, you know the position regarding new evidence," said the judge. "The prosecution is not at liberty to spring surprises on the court."

"Then I must request an adjournment. I assure you that the matter is crucial to the proper administration of justice."

The judge fingered his wig, thought for a long interval, and then announced testily, "The court is adjourned for thirty minutes. Both counsel will attend in my retiring room."

Diamond filed out with the others, sensing that there would be a longer delay than the estimated half hour. Something sensational must have occurred.

The recall came after almost two hours.

"After hearing submissions from both counsel, I have decided to allow the prosecution to present its new evidence," said the judge. "We shall then adjourn until tomorrow to allow the defense to consider the implications."

With the tact of a lawyer who knew he had stepped close to the limit, Sir Job pitched his voice on a low, unassertive note. "Call Chief Inspector Wigfull."

In the public gallery, Diamond's toes curled.

Wigfull stepped up and took the oath in a voice redolent with self-congratulation. To Diamond's prejudiced eye, his mustache seemed to have been brushed upward, into an exultant curve.

"Chief Inspector, would you tell the court what you informed me this morning," said Sir Job in little more than a whisper.

"Early this morning, I conducted a further search of the defendant's house in Bath. It has not been occupied since she was taken into custody. In the course of the search, one of my officers, Detective Inspector Halliwell, removed the drawers from the dressing table in the bedroom, the defendant's bedroom, and discovered something taped to the underside of the section that housed the drawers. It was in a position where it would not have been visible by simply removing the drawers. Inspector Halliwell felt underneath and detected a transparent folder. He immediately drew it to my attention."

"Describe it, please."

"The folder contained two antique letters with the signature 'Jane.' They were dated in the year 1800. From descriptions given to us previously by Professor Jackman, I believe them to be the letters written by Jane Austen that had allegedly been stolen from his house."

Sir Job addressed the judge. "M'lord, the Crown submits these letters as Exhibit Six." He handed a folder to one of the court officials, who passed it up.

After a cursory examination, the judge asked whether the defense wished to put any questions to

Wigfull at this stage, and Mrs. Bargainer said she reserved her cross-examination. The judge gave his customary warning to the jury not to discuss the case and called the adjournment.

Diamond watched Dana Didrikson while this scene was enacted. Her composure had shattered. A look of extreme shock registered on her features. Her counsel approached her and an earnest exchange took place.

The corridor outside was abuzz with Wigfull's announcement. Every phone was occupied by the press. In the crush, Diamond managed to catch Jackman's eye. He was in animated conversation with a gray-suited, silver-haired man who had to be Siddons, the solicitor, but their words were lost in the turmoil. They both gestured to Diamond to join them. He had some difficulty. Someone—a reporter—recognized him and asked for a comment. He refused point blank and forced a passage through the jostling, shouting crowd.

"What do you make of it?" Jackman demanded, and then answered his own question with, "It's devastating. Couldn't be worse. I thought my showing yesterday was damaging enough, but this on top . . . a disaster."

"It looks bad," Diamond agreed.

"They wouldn't have framed her, would they?"

Siddons, shocked, said, "Come now!"

Diamond said, "No chance. John Wigfull isn't the sort. He plays the rules. And I can vouch for Keith Halliwell. No, they found the letters for sure."

"Why didn't they find them before? They searched the place weeks ago."

"Two possibilities," said Diamond. "Either someone overlooked them, or they weren't there at the time."

"Weren't there?"

"Feel like a drive to Bath?"

On the dual carriageway near Keynsham, Jackman unburdened himself of some guilt. "You know, I felt a bloody hypocrite when I was giving evidence yesterday. I had to make it appear as if all my dealings with Dana were altruistic—that I acted out of sympathy for young

Mat. I like the boy, it's true, and I enjoyed taking him swimming, but I looked forward to every meeting with Dana. You know. I've tried to explain."

"Say so, then," said Diamond, ever a man for frank speaking. "You love her."

"All right," Jackman muttered. "I do. I was hoping against all the odds that the jury wouldn't convict. Then I was going to ask her to come to America with me. And the boy. A clean break for all of us." He sighed. "No chance of that now."

"You believe she did it?"

"I can't believe that, feeling as I do about her, but I can't see that she'll get off now."

Diamond didn't comment.

They drove up to Lyncombe and the terraced block where Dana had lived. A uniformed constable was stationed by the front door. They could see him from the end of the street.

"Drive on. There's a way into the back garden from the street behind," Diamond said, recalling the day Dana had escaped to her car when he and Wigfull had called at the house.

He picked his trilby off the backseat and covered his bandaged head. Without obvious subterfuge, but in silence, they entered the back garden and approached the back of the house. Diamond bent to examine the door frame, and in particular the lock. It was an old-fashioned mortise that had probably been in use for forty years. By aligning his eye with the edge of the door, he spotted the shapes of finger bolts at top and bottom. No one had forced an entry that way.

He examined the kitchen windows and found no signs, but when he came to the sash window to the sitting room and traced his finger along the lower edge, he located a distinct indentation in the painted surface of the ledge.

He invited Jackman to feel it.

"The window's fastened securely inside," Jackman said. "I wouldn't say it's been forced."

"We'll find out presently." Diamond returned down

the garden path and got into the car. "Would you drive us 'round to the front?"

This gave the impression that they were just arriving. The young constable at the door recognized him as he opened the gate. "Mr. Diamond?"

"We'd like to see inside, if you don't mind."

"Sir, I'm under instructions from Mr. Wigfull—"

"You'd better come in with us then and see we don't steal the silver."

Whether or not the news of Diamond's departure from the force had percolated to this level of the uniformed branch, the voice of authority prevailed. With the constable in tow, they went straight to the back sitting room and examined the window fastening. The frame had a substantial brass fitting of the kind that rotated on a pin and slotted snugly into a catch to secure both sections of the window in the closed position.

"Nothing wrong with that," Jackman observed.

Diamond turned to the constable. "See if you can find me a screwdriver, lad."

A few minutes later he unfastened the four screws that held the main fitting in place and lifted it clear of the wood. Then he stood back. "See what you make of that."

If Diamond's tone of voice wasn't quite so self-admiring as Wigfull's had been in court, it was close to it. Undeniably the wood below the fastening had recently been splintered. You could see where the screws had been forced. Tiny splinters of clean, white wood had been jammed into the holes to give the screws something to bite into when they were replaced.

"The intruder got in this way and tidied up afterward," he said. "I spotted a chip of fresh wood on the floor between the boards. Years ago, in the days when real detectives worked out of Scotland Yard, we had a saying: 'Give your eyes a chance.'"

Ideally, the dictum merited a moment's contemplation. It got none at all from Jackman. "When was the break-in? Last night?"

"Could have been any time in the past two weeks.

The letters were hidden upstairs ready to be discovered if and when they were needed."

Diamond grinned from ear to ear. After so many months in the doghouse he was entitled to be satisfied. The discovery was detective work at its finest, worthy to secure his place in the pantheon with Fabian of the Yard and the other trilby-hatted heroes of yesteryear.

4

_____

LILIAN BARGAINER, QC, disposed of John Wigfull next morning with appropriate irony.

"Chief Inspector, the entire literary establishment salutes you today for recovering the missing letters of Miss Jane Austen. The newspapers are bracketing your name with Sherlock Holmes and Miss Marple. Pray how did you make this happy discovery? Was it, to paraphrase Miss Austen herself, the result of previous study, or the impulse of the moment? Was it sense, or sensibility, that guided you to the hiding place?"

Wigfull frowned and said, "I'm afraid I don't follow the question."

"I'm surprised it causes any difficulty to a man of your acuteness. Let me put it another way. Who tipped you off?"

He swayed back like a boxer. "I'm unable to answer that."

"Somebody did, presumably. Surely you didn't order the search of the house yesterday morning on a whim?"

"Well, no."

"So . . . ?"

Wigfull passed the tip of his tongue slowly around his lips.

After an appreciable pause, Mrs. Bargainer said, "Do you understand what I am asking this time?"

"Yes."

"Then you really must give an answer."

He said softly, "There was a phone call—"

"Speak up, Chief Inspector."

"There was a phone call to the main police station in Bath late the previous evening. The caller rang off before we could get his name."

"So you were tipped off. You didn't tell us this in your statement yesterday."

"I didn't consider that it was needed at that stage."

"I'm pleased to hear it. I really didn't have you down as a glory hunter. Now we know. An anonymous caller. Do I have it correctly now?"

"Yes."

Mrs. Bargainer drew her gown aside and rested her hands on her hips. "Let us consider another point. When you gave us this startling information yesterday, we were supposed to deduce, were we not, that the defendant, Mrs. Didrikson, had obtained the letters and hidden them in her dressing table herself?"

"I simply reported what I found," Wigfull said guardedly.

"And—you can tell us now—were you surprised to have made such a discovery? After all, you had searched the house from top to bottom on a previous occasion."

"We must have overlooked it the first time. As I explained—"

"Oh, don't sell yourself short, Chief Inspector. Have you considered the possibility that someone entered the house sometime in recent days and planted those letters there?"

Wigfull looked across to the table where the prosecution team were seated, but no help was forthcoming. "I don't think that's likely. The place has been kept locked."

"So would it surprise you to be informed that the sash window in the sitting room at the back has recently been forced, and the fitting repaired and screwed back into place?"

"Is that true?" said the hapless Wigfull.

"That is my information. You are the detective, Mr. Wigfull. I suggest you investigate. Your findings will interest us all, as will your deductions afterward. We accept that your statement yesterday was made in good faith. However, craving the court's indulgence, I venture to describe the testimony as somewhat colored by pride and prejudice. No further questions, my lord."

The judge looked faintly amused. He leaned forward, his chin propped on his right hand. "Sir Job?"

Some hurried shuffling of papers at the prosecution table underlined their confusion. "At this point, m'lord, we propose to move on to the chief inspector's evidence-in-chief."

"Then I suggest you do."

The next hour and fifty minutes was an exercise in damage control, a painstaking recapitulation of the police investigation. By switching back to the discovery of the body in Chew Valley Lake and plodding systematically through the process that had led to Dana's indictment, Sir Job masterfully contrived point by point to rehabilitate Wigfull as a credible witness.

To the Wigfull's credit, his testimony was equal to the challenge. He spoke with restored assurance, making a point of facing the jury as he gave his responses, and his language was simple and direct. He didn't hesitate again. He must have been aware that Diamond was watching from the public gallery, yet he described the first phases of the inquiry, when Diamond had been in charge, with impeccable recall—the search of the lakeside and the delay in identifying the body; the television and press appeals for information; and how Professor Jackman had eventually come forward and identified the body. Sir Job took him through the search of John Brydon House, the interviews with Jackman and the transatlantic phone conversation with the American academic, Dr. Junker (an affidavit from Junker had been filed by the prosecution). Wigfull explained how checks had been made at University College and with Air France that established an alibi for Jackman, and how the focus of the investigation had then switched to Dana.

"What happened when you went to interview her?"

"She ran out of the back of the house. I gave chase, but she got into the Mercedes and drove away. It happened that she met another car in a narrow road near the house—met it head-on. There was a slight collision."

"She was unhurt?"

"Yes, sir."

"And did she admit to running away from the police?"

"Her words were, 'I was trying to escape.'"

So it went on through the morning, this process of assembling a case that would allow no reasonable doubt. Sir Job omitted nothing. He took Wigfull through the interview of Dana and established that she had insisted she had no more to tell when in reality there had been much more to come. He plotted the stages of her disclosures, showing how she'd eventually admitted to having visited the Jackmans' house on the morning of the murder and had seen Geraldine lying dead in bed. Finally, he testified that when the reports had come back from the forensic lab confirming that the body had been placed in Dana's car trunk, he had formally charged her with murder in the presence of her solicitor.

It was 12:50 when Sir Job concluded the examination-in-chief. The court adjourned for lunch. Dana, ashen after the morning's ordeal, was led down to the cells.

Siddons, her solicitor, was waiting for Diamond at the foot of the stairs from the public gallery. "Do you have a few minutes? Mrs. Bargainer would *so* like to meet you."

"Her memory can't be too hot," Diamond commented. "She cross-examined me in this court six months ago."

They invited him to join them for a pub lunch across the road. Out of her wig and gown, Lilian Bargainer passed for one of the mainstays of the lounge bar, drinking dry sherry from a schooner and dragging at a cigarette that she held between thumb and forefinger. "God, what a production old Claws is making of it," she said. "He's working on the principle that if Wigfull talks for long enough the jury will forget the balls-up of the missing letters. Never fear—I'll remind 'em." She gripped Diamond's sleeve. "Pete, old sport, I owe you one for that. What are you drinking?"

"Orange juice," said Diamond, tapping his head bandage.

She pushed a ten-pound note at Siddons. "Be an angel. Get one for yourself. I mean a beer or something. And see what food there is." Alone at the table with Diamond, she said, "I want to tap your brain."

"Gently, if you must."

"I cross-examine Johnny Wigfull this afternoon. I intend to keep it short and devastating, but I mustn't miss anything. What are the weak points in the evidence?"

"I wouldn't trouble with the weak points if I were you," Diamond told her. "Go for the strong one."

"The body in the trunk?"

"Right. If you hadn't suggested this meeting, I was going to whisper in Siddons's ear."

"Ah—so you know something?"

"I wouldn't put it so strongly as that—particularly after brain surgery. I don't know how reliable the little gray cells are, but they've been working overtime to catch up."

He wasn't really underselling the importance of what he was about to tell her. He quietly relished this moment as much as he relished the sensation to come in court. For all her hail-fellow manner, Lilian Bargainer had a shrewd brain. She would appreciate this. She would understand its significance, a triumph of canny detection over the men in white coats.

"Get to the point, my love. Time's at a premium."

"If I'm right about this, there's a detail—an important detail—you can check with your client. She won't appreciate the significance, by the way."

"She's in no shape of mind to appreciate anything, sport, but I'm willing to try."

"Ask her to cast her mind back to that morning she took Matthew up to John Brydon House and saw the blond man walking out on Geraldine."

"The pusher—Andy Coventry?"

"Yes. In her statement, she told me he appeared familiar at the time, but she couldn't place him. I think we may be able to refresh her memory. Ask her if she could have seen him swimming."

"Swimming? You'd better explain, you cryptic old bugger."

Wigfull looked apprehensive as he entered the witness box again. With good reason. His rehabilitation had owed everything to Sir Job Mitchell. Lilian Bargainer wouldn't be wearing velvet gloves for the cross-examination. Up in the public gallery, however, Peter Diamond was in a forgiving mood. The last words he had spoken to Mrs. Bargainer were, "Wigfull's not a bad detective. He's wrong, but he's not bad. You don't have to wipe the floor with him."

She was on her feet. "Chief Inspector, I shan't detain you long. You've given the court a copious account of your investigation, but you neglected to mention that the late Mrs. Geraldine Jackman was a user of cocaine. Did you not consider this of relevance?"

"It came to our notice only recently," Wigfull stated with a smoothness suggesting he had anticipated the question.

"But it doesn't affect the present case?"

"That is correct."

"That is your judgment." She turned toward the jury and rolled her eyes upward as if in despair of the police. Then she swung back to Wigfull. "There is one other matter I should like to clarify, and that concerns the interrogation of the accused, Mrs. Didrikson. She was taken by ex-Superintendent Diamond and yourself to Bath Central Police Station for questioning on Tuesday, October tenth. Am I right? You may refer to your notes. I want to get this clear."

Wigfull produced his notebook and thumbed through it. "October tenth. Yes."

"She was detained overnight? Is that correct?"

"Yes."

"And on October eleventh her car was collected for forensic examination?"

"Yes—but with her permission."

"Granted. Your personal conduct toward Mrs. Didrikson cannot be faulted. I believe you went so far as to notify her employer, Mr. Buckle, that she would not be able to drive him in the morning."

Wigfull agreed modestly, "That's true. I did."

"A very considerate thing to have done, if I may say so," Mrs. Bargainer complimented him.

Plainly, Wigfull saw an opportunity here. "Yes, but there was another reason for doing it. I wanted to check with the employer, Mr. Buckle, whether the accused had reported for work on the day of the murder. And she hadn't." He glanced toward Sir Job and was rewarded with a nod of acknowledgment for scoring a point under cross-examination.

"So when did you speak to Mr. Buckle?" Mrs. Bargainer asked.

"Sometime between eight and nine in the evening."

"The evening of October tenth?"

"Yes."

"Thank you, Chief Inspector."

There was a moment's hiatus before the court fully grasped that Mrs. Bargainer had finished the cross-examination. The whole exchange had taken less than two minutes.

Wigfull looked as bemused as anyone.

The judge asked whether the prosecution were proposing to reexamine. They were not. Wigfull was told to step down. Sir Job and his team had been thrown again. The disarray at their table was all too apparent.

"Are you calling another witness?" the judge inquired.

"Directly, m'lord," said Sir Job, scattering papers across the floor.

The witness was Stanley Buckle, dressed for his appearance in a three-piece dove-gray suit and an Institute of Directors' tie. The usual rosebud was missing from his buttonhole, possibly in recognition of the solemn occasion. Once in the box, he reinforced the punctilious image by making a performance of putting on half glasses to read the oath. He exuded importance; it was in the tilt of his chin and the set of his shoulders.

Sir Job's junior, by comparison a man with a poor posture and an unfortunate high-pitched voice that would probably ensure that he remained a junior forever, was assigned the undemanding task of establishing how the Mercedes car came to be in the prisoner's possession.

"She was the driver for my company, Realbrew Ales," Stanley explained.

"She kept the car overnight?"

"Yes. There was an understanding that she could use it privately outside office hours provided that journeys were entered into the log."

"All journeys were entered into a log?"

"That's what I said."

"To your knowledge, Mr. Buckle, did any person other than Mrs. Didrikson ever drive that car?"

"Not a soul. It was new when we supplied her with it."

"The log—is it kept in the car?"

"That's the drill. We check it at the end of the month and enter the mileage in our ledger."

"Did you know that the log was not in the car when it was taken for forensic examination?"

"I heard about that. We made a search at Realbrew just in case, but I didn't expect to find it. Dana got it back from the office on September first. It should have been in the car, as I believe she told the police." Buckle glanced across at Dana for confirmation and she actually gave a nod. He added gratuitously, "I'd like to have it put on record that she was a respected member of my staff."

"We are obliged to you."

When Lilian Bargainer rose to cross-examine, nothing in her manner suggested that this would be anything but a formality.

"Mr. Buckle, you described yourself as the managing director of Realbrew Ales, but you have a number of other business interests, don't you?"

"I didn't think you needed to know. I'm a supplier of novelty goods to stationery shops and other outlets. I'm also on the boards of several companies in the entertainment business."

"Novelty goods?"

"Toys, Christmas crackers, metal puzzles—you name it. . . ."

"You import these items, presumably?"

"Well, yes." Buckle answered in a way that showed he was more interested in talking about other matters.

"From the Far East?"

"In the main."

The judge, too, was uneasy and signaled it by resting his hands on the bench and leaning back stiffly against his padded chair.

Lilian Bargainer made no concessions. "The toys. Would they include such items as miniature teddy bears from Taiwan?"

"Certainly."

"Last summer you asked Mrs. Didrikson to collect a consignment from Southampton Docks."

"That's right."

"She told you, I believe, that she was stopped on the way back by two policemen in plain clothes who searched the cartons containing the bears. Is that so?"

"That's what she told me."

The judge leaned forward to interrupt. "Mrs. Bargainer, I am trying to see the pertinence of these questions."

"The matter has direct relevance to the case, my lord, as I shall presently demonstrate. Mr. Buckle, you're obviously—literally, in fact —a man of the world. You must have divined the reason why the police were interested in this consignment. Toys from the Far East, collected by a company driver from the docks."

"They were clean," said Buckle, affronted. "Teddy bears—for charity. They were handed out to kids at Longleat."

"So it emerged," Mrs. Bargainer conceded. "But clearly in the view of those policemen there were grounds for suspicion that you were importing drugs."

Sir Job bounded up to interrupt. "M'lord, I can't believe my ears. This is outrageous. It's a blatant attack on the reputation of the witness. Nothing in Mr. Buckle's testimony can warrant such character assassination."

"Both counsel will approach the bench," the judge instructed them.

From the gallery, Diamond strained to overhear the earnest argument that ensued. If the judge ruled in favor of the prosecution now, Mrs. Bargainer's task would be next to impossible. In the dock, Dana nervously repinned a strand of hair. Whether she fully understood the significance of this moment was unclear, but she could not have failed to sense the tension in the court.

After almost ten minutes of wrangling, counsel returned to their positions. Sir Job was crimson, Lilian Bargainer still serene.

"My apologies, Mr. Buckle—for the delay," she resumed. "I have been asked to come quickly to the point, and I shall. Is it a fact that Anton Coventry, known as Andy, is an associate of yours?"

Buckle's hands gripped the ledge of the witness box. "I've met a man of that name, if that's what you mean."

"I mean a little more than that. Have you entertained him at your house?"

"Well, yes."

"He swam in your pool on at least one occasion?"

"Yes."

"Doubtless you've heard that he is at present in custody on several charges, including offenses relating to the supply of cocaine?"

"I read something about it in the paper." Buckle was unconvincing. It was too late now to distance himself from his odious friend.

"Did you know that Andy Coventry is alleged to have supplied cocaine to the late Mrs. Jackman?"

Buckle was silent.

"Come now. It is public knowledge, is it not?" Lilian Bargainer probed.

"Why ask me, then?" said Buckle.

"Why not admit it, then?" she rapped back. "We're getting closer to the truth, aren't we? The whole truth that you promised to tell. Mr. Buckle, I put it to you that you came under police suspicion as an importer of illegal substances. My client's trip to Southampton at your behest to collect the teddy bears was just a charade, a diversionary tactic to spike their guns, was it not? How interesting that when she returned to your house at the end of the day, you were entertaining, among others, Andy Coventry."

Sir Job rose to protest that the charges against Coventry were *sub judice* and the imputation was misleading, and Mrs. Bargainer withdrew her last comment.

"But you agree with my account of the facts?" she pressed Buckle.

"The whole thing is irrelevant," he said without conviction. "I'm here to talk about the car."

Mrs. Bargainer smiled. "Very well, let's talk about the car. The Mercedes 190E 2.6 automatic that you bought when Mrs. Didrikson joined Realbrew Ales. You bought two cars of that model for the company at that time, didn't you?"

"Yes."

"One for your personal use and the other for Mrs. Didrikson's?"

"Yes."

"Good." She beamed at Buckle; he didn't smile back. "I'm going to ask about the use you made of the cars, notably on Monday, September eleventh, and Tuesday, October tenth, last year. Am I making myself clear, Mr. Buckle? The first date was that of Mrs. Jackman's murder. We have already heard from you that Mrs. Didrikson did not report for work that day, so presumably you had to drive yourself about?"

"Yes."

"And ever since Tuesday, October tenth, you have been without a chauffeur, because that's the day Mrs. Didrikson was taken in for questioning by the police. When were you informed?"

"I can't recall."

"Chief Inspector Wigfull testified that he phoned you between eight and nine that evening, October tenth."

Buckle shrugged. "Fair enough."

"I must insist on a better answer than that. Do you recall being telephoned?"

"All right. It was sometime that evening. I didn't check my watch."

"It's important, you see, because there was a delay of some twelve hours before the Mercedes Mrs. Didrikson drove was collected for forensic examination. The car stood outside her house for twelve hours. When it was collected, we now know, the impossible was shown to have happened. The scientists proved with their genetic fingerprinting that the body of Geraldine Jackman had been in the trunk of that car. I say it was impossible because Mrs. Didrikson has told me so, and I believe her."

Buckle stared rigidly ahead like a guardsman being bawled at by a drill sergeant. Actually Lilian Bargainer had not raised her voice one decibel.

The skill of this cross-examination was profoundly satisfying to Peter Diamond. Compelled to hear his own deductions voiced by proxy, he was locked into every word the barrister uttered.

"I put it to you that the impossible can only be explained this way. When you got the call from Chief Inspector Wigfull, you decided on a plan to confuse the police and divert suspicion from yourself. For it was you, wasn't it, Mr. Buckle, who deposited the body of Geraldine Jackman in Chew Valley Lake?"

Nobody protested and Buckle made no pretence of a response. A paralyzing curiosity gripped the court as Mrs. Bargainer talked on. "On the night of September eleventh you drove there with the dead woman in the boot of your Mercedes. And when, a month later, you heard that Dana Didrikson was being held overnight, you thought of a way of confirming the police in their suspicion that she was the murderer. The spare keys for her Mercedes were held by your company. You drove up to Lyncombe where the vehicle was parked. You opened the boot and unclipped the fabric lining."

Buckle's eyes flicked toward the jury, as if in search of a doubter. The looks that met his were not encouraging.

"Are you listening, Mr. Buckle? You unclipped the lining. Then you removed the lining from the boot of your own car, the lining the body had lain on, and fitted it into the other car. Do you deny it?"

Peter Diamond so completely identified with the question that he started to say aloud, "Speak up." He clapped a hand to his mouth.

Buckle was saying, "You've got me totally wrong. I didn't kill Gerry Jackman. Before God I didn't."

"You put her in the lake."

He hesitated.

"You put her in the lake," Mrs. Bargainer insisted. This had become a contest of wills.

Buckle stared around the court. In the dock, Dana had put her fingers to her throat."

"Do you deny it?" Lilian Bargainer demanded.

He capitulated. "All right, I did. I put her in the lake." As a murmur from all sides of the court broke the tension, he added with more voice, "But I didn't kill her."

Mrs. Bargainer frowned, put her hand to her face and let the fingers slide down to the point of her chin in an attitude of incomprehension. "You're going to have to help me, Mr. Buckle. What you are claiming now is curious, if not incredible. Let's have this clear. On the night of September 11th you drove to Chew Valley Lake with the body of Mrs. Jackman and deposited it in the water, and yet you didn't kill her. You insist on that?"

"Yes."

"Why? Why behave in such an extraordinary fashion?"

He was silent.

"You must explain, Mr. Buckle, you really must if we are to believe you."

His mouth remained closed.

Mrs. Bargainer said, "Let's approach this another way. You didn't kill her. Did you know she had been murdered?"

"No," said Buckle, freed from his constraint. "That's the point."

"Good. I'm beginning to understand. You found her dead, is that right?"

"Yes."

"You didn't know she'd been murdered, is that right?"

"Yes."

"You thought she'd overdosed."

"Yes—I mean no." Buckle stared about him. He'd been snared, and he knew it.

Lilian Bargainer said without even a hint of irony, "You said yes and you meant no. Which is it? I put it to you that your associate Andy Coventry was supplying Mrs. Jackman with cocaine that he got from you. You're the importer and he was the pusher. Am I right?"

Sir Job sprang up, but the Judge gestured to him to be seated.

"You had better consider your position, Mr. Buckle," said Lilian Bargainer. "It's too late now to deny your involvement in drugs. If you do, you lay your-self open to suspicion of murder. Which is it to be?"

Buckle swayed slightly in the witness box, sighed heavily, and then the words tumbled from him. "What happened was this. Come September, Andy bunked off to Scotland on some course. He was her supplier, like you said. I got word from my contacts that she was shouting for the stuff. She was making trouble about Andy being unavailable. Big trouble. She was threatening to blow the whistle on us. So I went to see her on the Monday."

"September eleventh?"

"Yes."

"What time?"

"About lunchtime. When I got no answer at the front, I went 'round the back. The kitchen door was open. People with a habit aren't too clever about things like that. I called out and still got no answer, so I tried upstairs. She was dead on the bed. It got to me, I can tell you, finding her like that. She's overdosed, I thought. They say cocaine can kill you, just the same as heroin. I could see real trouble ahead if the doctors opened her up. So I decided to move her. That's what I did. Carried her downstairs and put her in the car. That night I dropped her in the lake." He closed his eyes and added, "I was hoping that would be the end of it."

"And the Jane Austen letters?"

"They were stuffed down the front of her night-dress, like she was hiding them. I thought it must be something she meant to trade for the coke, so I took it. I didn't even look at them till later."

"And what happened when the body was found in the lake?"

"I was really scared—but not a word was said about drugs. She'd been smothered, the papers said. I realized what I must have done—I'd moved a murdered corpse. The next thing, they arrested Dana—my driver—and it was all too close to home for my liking. I could be done as an accessory. So when the chance came, I switched the linings, just like you said. I only did it to cover myself. Dana had been stupid enough to kill her, I thought, so I wasn't causing her any more aggravation than she deserved."

"What happened to the log?"

"I burned it, obviously."

"Obviously?"

"Well, every trip was accounted for. If the police had seen it, they'd have found out that her car wasn't used to move the body, wouldn't they?"

"And presumably you falsified the log in your own car?"

He nodded. "It's a simple matter when you're behind with the entries, as I was." Then Stanley Buckle drooped like a bull pierced with bandilleras.

But Mrs. Bargainer had another ready. "Let's turn to something else that was brought to the court's attention. I put it to you that when you heard Coventry had been arrested, you broke into Mrs. Didrikson's empty house and taped the letters into her dressing table as another diversion."

Buckle hesitated.

"Why did you do that?" said Mrs. Bargainer gently, as if he had made the admission already.

He dipped his eyes. "As a kind of insurance. I was dead worried the drugs would come up at the trial, and they did—on the first day. So I needed to switch the interest back to the letters. I phoned the police and told them to look in the house. Until today, I believed Dana was guilty. I wouldn't have done it otherwise. Have I said enough?"

"More than enough for me," the judge acidly commented. "Does the prosecution propose to reexamine?"

Sir Job declined. "And in view of the testimony we have just heard, we shall not be calling any further witnesses, m'lord."

"The prosecution case is closed?"

"Yes, m'lord."

Up in the public gallery, Peter Diamond sat back in his chair, mentally spent.

Lilian Bargainer rose again. "I submit, my lord,

that the case we have heard from the prosecution is not strong enough to lay before the jury."

The judge agreed and directed the jury to acquit Dana Didrikson.

Dana covered her face and sobbed.

5

"YOU LOOK like a piece of chewed twine," Stephanie told him that evening after they'd eaten. "And no wonder. Why don't you get an early night?"

"Presently."

"If it's the news you're waiting for, I saw it all at six-thirty. She appeared at the press conference and scarcely said more than a couple of words. She didn't even smile. The papers are offering terrific money for her story, but she's told them what to do with it. You've got to admire her."

"Yes."

"That lawyer of hers was a woman, I noticed. She must have been brilliant to fathom what really happened. You can't put that down to feminine intuition."

"I don't," said Diamond.

"What a brain!"

"Lilian Bargainer?"

"Well, yes. That Inspector Wigfull was way off beam and so were you."

The injustice wounded him less than being coupled with Wigfull. "Off beam? What about?"

"The cocaine. You should have been onto that from the beginning."

"We got diverted. The forensic tests were negative.

They didn't show Geraldine Jackman was using the stuff. Yes, I know," he added sheepishly. "I'm the one who says never rely on bloody scientists."

"What went wrong with the tests?"

"She hadn't taken any of the stuff before she was killed. Not for some days. She was desperate to get some, which was how Buckle was drawn into it. The irony is that she had several packets in the house, the ones I found. They must have been left over from one of the parties she gave, and she forgot they were there. She focused totally on her supplier."

"And he killed her."

"Oh, no," said Diamond.

"I mean Buckle. He's been arrested."

"Yes, but on a drugs charge."

She frowned. "Isn't he the killer, then?"

"No."

After he declined to add any more, she said, "I suppose you know who it was, cleverclogs. You ought to be back in the police." As if instantly regretting the remark, she reached out and squeezed his hand. "But I'm glad you aren't. I see more of you."

"Hmm."

"Let's have a pub lunch tomorrow, just the two of us."

He shook his head. "Sorry, I'm already booked for lunch."

"Oh? Who with?"

"The murderer." He reached for the TV remote control.

Conceding no hint of surprise, curiosity, or concern, she said, "All right, Saturday."

He got to bed soon after. Stephanie's insouciance and his cussedness kept them both awake for a few hours more. Some time after midnight he told her everything.

6

HE SAT HUDDLED under a big black umbrella on a bench
in front of the Abbey, his raincoat buttoned to the neck
and the collar up around his ears, touching his hat brim,
indistinguishable from the plainclothes men seen in
grainy black-and-white films of forty years ago. He had
bought two portions of fish and chips from the shop at
the end of Abbey Gate Street. They waited, wrapped, in
his lap. A fine drizzle had blown in from the Bristol
Channel and settled over the city. It was so misty that
half the Abbey front was invisible. Even the pigeons had
abandoned the place, but he was content to be there.
This was what it was all about.

He was keeping a close watch on everyone who
crossed the paved churchyard. Most were shoppers or
tourists. A line of schoolchildren chattering in French
approached the West Door and went in. From Stall
Street came the opening bars of the Bruch Violin Con-
certo; the street musician played regularly, backed by a
taped orchestra. He had done well to find a dry pitch
this morning. But he would have done better to have
waited a few minutes longer, because the Abbey bells
started chiming midday.

"Do we really have to talk here?"

The voice came from behind Diamond. He turned

and saw Matthew Didrikson at his shoulder. "Come and sit down. It's dry under the umbrella, and the fish and chips won't stay warm forever."

The boy came around the bench and accepted the packet Diamond handed him. He remained standing.

"At least we can talk in private here," Diamond said. "Have you seen your mother?"

"Yesterday evening. Greg took us out for a meal. It's impossible at home with the press and all that."

"A celebration feast?"

"Not really." Matthew stared down at the pavement, frowning. "Greg's going to America."

"Yes, I heard."

"He wants my ma to go with him and bring me, too."

Diamond asked straightforwardly, "Did you tell them you killed Mrs. Jackman?"

Matthew caught his breath and shivered. He continued to look downward. Today the child in him was more obvious than the man.

"You should."

"I can't."

"Why not?"

"It's too much."

"You mean after everything she's been through?"

Matthew gave a nod.

"I believe she knows," said Diamond. "That's why the acquittal left her unmoved. In her heart of hearts she has a sense of what really happened, Mat. And she's staying silent because she's your own mother and she loves you. But she knows the truth has to come out, and she'd rather hear it from you than someone like me."

The boy was scanning Diamond's face to satisfy himself that the words were totally sincere. "Are you going to tell?" A playground phrase.

"I will if necessary."

His frankness measured up to the scrutiny, because Mat said, "I'll speak to her." He looked away, at a child crossing the yard on a BMX bike. "Will I go to prison?"

"Not prison. You're underage."

"Will there be a trial, like my mother had?"

"Probably." This wasn't the time to speculate on the problems the judicial system faced in dealing with a twelve-year-old accused of murder. Nor was it useful to explain what detention During Her Majesty's Pleasure would really amount to. "Want to sit down?"

This time Matthew accepted. He had to sit close to Diamond to get under the umbrella. There was moisture at the edges of his eyes. "I didn't mean to kill her. When I went to the house, I only meant to find those letters. I knew she must have taken them just to spoil everything."

"Why don't you tell me about it from the beginning? That Monday morning your mother had a call from Professor Jackman to say the letters were missing."

"She was really upset. I could tell how angry she was, and I was angry, too. Mrs. Jackman was a wicked woman. I hated her. She called my ma some horrible things and it was only because of her that I couldn't go swimming with Greg anymore. *He* didn't want it to stop. He'd been really kind to me. He saved my life when I fell in the weir. Greg wasn't using me as some kind of worm on a hook, like she said, just because he fancied my ma, or something. He was . . ."

"Like a father?"

"Yes." Then Matthew rapidly added, "I still love my real father."

The "real" father who preferred playing chess, who hadn't bothered to come to England for the trial. The reality was that the father had rejected his son. Matthew's blind loyalty suppressed a terrible, a deadly despair.

"What happened on that Monday morning?"

"When Ma was driving me to school, I could see she was all upset about those letters. I decided to try and get them back from Mrs. Jackman. On the first day of term, we always have to hang around the vestry for hours while they issue us with clean robes. They're too busy with the little kids to bother with us older boys.

You can go off 'round the shops and nobody gives a monkey's. I went up to Widcombe on a minibus. I knew the house, of course. I thought I might find a window open somewhere, but it was easier than that, because the back door was open. I just turned the handle and walked in. Nobody was about. I crept upstairs and found her bedroom. She was in there, still asleep. I wanted to look for the letters, but I was afraid she might wake up and catch me."

"Did she wake?"

"Not until I lifted the duvet over her face. She was lying on her back and I pulled it up to cover her eyes. I don't think I would have killed her if she'd stayed asleep. She moved, and I pressed the duvet down. She struggled, but it was no good because her arms were trapped under the quilt. The more she struggled, the harder I pressed. I was kneeling on her. I was angry and frightened at the same time. I didn't panic, exactly, only I didn't want her to wake up and find me there, so I kept on pressing and pressing down on her face until she went still. I was even more scared then, when I knew what I'd done. I pulled the quilt down again and uncovered her face. I knew she was dead. I didn't stop to look for the letters, or anything. I just ran out."

"Caught the bus back to Bath?"

"Yes."

"Later on, when you heard that the body had been found in the lake, you must have been amazed."

"Yes."

"What did you think had happened?"

"First, I thought Greg must have found her in the bedroom and moved her, to make it look as if she killed herself. Later, I believed my mother put her in the lake. They said her own car was used. I didn't know what to do. If I owned up, I could get my ma into trouble. That day you came to our house and she tried to run away, and you caught her, I didn't really have a concussion. I thought you might have to release her if I was taken to hospital."

Diamond gave a nod and said nothing.

"I'm sorry you lost your job because of me," said Matthew.

"Forget it," Diamond told him. "You probably saved my life by getting help as quickly as you did after Andy Coventry brained me in the baths. That could have been permanent. Eat up your fish and chips."

In the silence, Diamond weighed the significance of what Matthew had told him. The Crown Prosecution Service would have a real problem deciding the sensible way to deal with this. In reality, it would save everyone a headache if Jackman and Dana flew off to America and took the boy with them. There was no extradition of minors.

As if he read the thought, Matthew said, "I want to own up properly. If I go to the police, would you come with me?"

"Sure."

"First I want to tell Ma."

"Okay."

"What do you think she'll do?"

"I don't think she'll be in any hurry to go to America."

"And Greg?"

"It wouldn't surprise me if he changes his plans when he hears what you have to say."

They finished their lunch and got up to leave. Diamond rested a hand lightly on the boy's shoulder. Ahead, the mist was starting to lift, and he could make out one of those stone angels on the lowest rung of the ladder, caught in the attitude of moving upward.

ABOUT THE AUTHOR

PETER LOVESEY, Golden and Silver Dagger Award-winning author of both the Sergeant Cribb and Prince of Wales Victorian mystery series, is one of the most acclaimed British crime writers of his generation. He has just completed his second Detective Superintendent Diamond mystery, DIAMOND SOLITAIRE. Peter Lovesey lives in Wiltshire, England.

If you enjoyed THE LAST DETECTIVE, you will want to read Peter Lovesey's next Peter Diamond mystery, DIAMOND SOLITAIRE, available soon from Doubleday Perfect Crime. Look for it at your local bookseller.

Here is a special advance preview chapter from DIAMOND SOLITAIRE.

DIAMOND SOLITAIRE

by
Peter
Lovesey

1

AN ALERT SHATTERED the silence in Harrods, a piercing, continuous note. The guard on duty in the security control room, Lionel Kenton, drew himself up in his chair. His hands went to his neck and tightened the knot in his tie. On the control panel in front of him, one of the light-emitting diodes, a red one, was blinking. If the system was functioning properly, someone—or something—had triggered a sensor on the seventh floor. He pressed a control that triggered the video-surveillance for that floor. Nothing on the monitors was moving.

Kenton was the senior security guard that night. He was so senior that he had a shelf above the radiator for his exclusive use. On it were framed photos of his wife, two daughters, the Pope and Catherine Deneuve; an ebony elephant; and a cassette rack of opera tapes. Puccini kept him alert through the night, he told anyone so philistine as to question opera in the control room. *Non shall sleep.* Listening to music was more responsible than reading a paper or a paperback. His eyes were alert to anything on the panel and his ears to any sound that clashed with the music.

He silenced Pavarotti and touched the button that gave him a direct line to Knightsbridge Police Station. They must already have received the alert electronically. He identified himself and said, "Intruder alert. I'm getting a signal from the seventh floor. Furniture. Section nine. Nothing on screen."

"Message received 2247 hours."

"Someone is coming?"

"It's automatic."

Of course it was. He was betraying some nervousness. He tried another survey on the seventh floor. Nothing untoward was visible, but then he hadn't much faith in video surveillance. Every terrorist knows to keep out of range of a camera.

And he had to assume this was a terrorist.

Twenty-two night security officers were posted in various parts of the store. Kenton put out a general alert and asked for a second check that all the elevators were switched off. The security doors between sections were already in position and had been since the cleaners left. In the business of counter-terrorism nothing can be taken for granted, but really it wasn't feasible to break into Harrods. The intruder—if one was up there—must have hidden when the store closed and remained out of sight. If so, someone's job was on the line. Someone who should have checked section nine. You weren't allowed one mistake in this line of work.

His second-in-command that night, George Bullen, burst in. He'd been patrolling when the alert sounded.

"Where's it from?"

"Seventh."

"It bloody would be."

The furniture department was high risk: a brute to patrol. Wardrobes, cupboards, chests of drawers and units of every description. The nightly check for devices was a wearisome chore. It was conceivable—but in no way excusable—that the guard on duty had been so bogged down opening cupboards and peering into drawers that he'd missed someone lurking out of sight behind the damned things.

Another light flashed on the console and one of the monitors showed headlights entering the delivery bay. The police response couldn't be faulted. Kenton told Bullen to take over and went down to meet them.

Three patrol cars and two vans already. Marksmen and dog-handlers climbing out. More cars arriving, their flashing alarms giving an errie, blue luminosity to the delivery bay. Kenton felt a flutter in his bowels. The police weren't going to vote him security man of the year if this emergency had been triggered by a blip in the system.

A plain clothes officer stepped out of a car and ran across to him. "You're?"

"Kenton."

"Senior man?"

He nodded.

"You put out the call?"

He admitted it, and his stomach lurched.

"Seventh floor?"

"Furniture department."

"Points of access?"

"Two sets of stairs."

"Only two?"

"The section is sealed off by security doors."

"No elevators?"

"Swtiched off."

"Any of your lads on the stairs?"

"Yes. That's routine. They'll be guarding the stairways above and below level seven."

"Lead the way, then."

Thirty or more uniformed officers, dog-handlers and men in plain clothes, several carrying guns, came with him as he set off at a run through the ground floor to the first stairway. A squad of a dozen or so peeled off and raced up that staircase while he led the remainder to the next.

Mounting seven floors was a fitness test for Lionel Kenton. He was relieved to be told to stop after six and a half, and even more relieved to find four of his own security staff in position as he'd claimed they would be. Now he had a chance to recover normal breathing while radio contact was made with the party on the other stairs.

"What's the layout here?"

Essentially the police marksmen wanted to know how much cover they could rely on. One of Kenton's team, a burly ex-CID officer called Diamond, gave a rapid rundown of the furniture display positioned nearest to the stairs. Peter Diamond was the man responsible tonight for this section. You poor bugger, thought Kenton. You look more sick than I feel.

A team of three marksmen was sent up the final flight. Others took up positions on the stairs. The rest moved down to the landing below.

This was the worst—waiting for the unknown, while others went up to deal with it.

Someone offered Kenton some chewing-gum and he took it gratefully.

Perhaps six nerve-racking minutes went by before there was a crackle on the senior policeman's radio and a voice reported, "Negative so far."

Two dogs and their handlers were sent up to help.

Another long interval of silence.

Security Officer Diamond was just to the left of Kenton. He had his hands clasped, the fingers interlaced as if in prayer, except that the fingernails were white with pressure.

The last dregs of Kenton's confidence were draining away when someone announced over the scratchy intercom, "We've got your intruder."

"Got him under restraint?" said the man in charge.

"Come and see."

"You're sure he's the only one?"

"Positive."

The tone was reassuring. Strangely so, as if the tension had lifted altogether. Police and security staff dashed up the stairs.

The seventh floor lights were fully on. The marksmen had converged on a section where armchairs and settees were displayed. But they weren't in the attitude of gunmen. They were lounging about as if at a wine and cheese party. Two were seated on the arms of chairs. There was no sign of anyone under arrest.

Suddenly cold with his own sweat, Kenton went over with the others. "But you said you found someone?"

One of them flicked his eyes downwards, towards a sofa.

It was the kind of vast, black corduroy thing that an advertising executive would have in his outer office. At one end was a heap of scatter cushions, brilliant in colour. The face looking out from under the cushions was that of a small girl, her hair black and fringed, her eyes oriental in shape. Nothing else of her was visible.

Kenton stared in bewilderment.

"Ah, so," said the senior policeman.

2

"YOU'RE SACKING ME." Peter Diamond, the guard responsible for section nine on the night the child was found, spoke without rancour. "I know the score."

The score was heavily against him. He wasn't young. Forty-eight, according to his file. Married. Living in West Ken. No kids. An ex-policeman. He'd risen to the rank of detective superintendent and then resigned from Avon and Somerset over some dispute with the Assistant Chief Constable. A misunderstanding, someone said, someone who knew someone. Diamond had been too proud to ask for his job back. After quitting the police, he'd taken a series of part-time jobs and finally moved to London and joined the Harrods team.

"I shouldn't say this, Peter," the security director told him, "but you're bloody unlucky. Your record here has been exemplary, apart from this. You could have looked forward to a more senior post."

"Rules are rules."

"Unfortunately, yes. We'll do the best we can in the way of a reference, but, er . . . ."

". . . security jobs are out, right?" said Diamond. He was inscrutable. Fat men—and he was fat—often have faces that seem on the point of turning angry or amused. The trick is to guess which.

The director didn't mind exhibiting his own unease. He shook his head and spread his hands in an attitude of helplessness. "Believe me, Peter, I feel sick to the teeth about this."

"Spare me that."

"I mean it. I'm not confident I would have spotted the kid myself. She was practically invisible under the cushions."

"I lifted the cushions," Diamond admitted.

"Oh?"

"She wasn't on that sofa when I did my round. I definitely checked. I always do. It's an obvious place to plant a device. The kid must have been somewhere else and got under them later."

"How could you have missed her?"

"I reckon I took her for one of the cleaners' kids. They bring them in sometimes. Some of them are Vietnamese."

"She's Japanese, I think."

Diamond snapped out of his defeated mood. "You *think*? Hasn't she been claimed?"

"Not yet."

"Doesn't she know her name?"

"Hasn't spoken a word since she was found. Over at the nick, they spent the whole of today with a string of interpreters trying to coax her to say something. Not a syllable."

"She isn't mute, is she?"

"Apparently not, but she says nothing intelligible. There's almost no reaction from the child."

"Deaf?"

"No. She reacts to sound. It's a mystery."

"They'll have to go on TV with her. Someone will know her. A kid found in Harrods at night—it's just the sort of story the media pick up on."

"No doubt."

"You don't sound convinced."

"I'm convinced, Peter, all too easily convinced. But there are other considerations, not least our reputation. I don't particularly want it broadcast that a little girl penetrated our security. If the press get on to you, I'd appreciate your not making any statements."

"About security? I wouldn't."

"Thank you."

"But you can't muzzle the police. They have no interest in keeping the story confidential. It's going to break somewhere, and soon."

A sigh from the director, followed by an uncomfortable silence.

"So when do I clear my locker?" Diamond asked. "Right away?"

The priest looked into the widow's trusting eyes and rashly told her, "It's not as if it's the end of the world."

The words of comfort were spoken on a fine summer evening in the sitting-room of a country villa in Lombardy, between Milan and Cremona. Pastoral care, Father Faustini termed it. Ministering to the bereaved, the sacred obligation of a priest. True, the ministering in this instance had continued longer than was customary, actually into a second year. But Claudia Coppi, cruelly widowed at twenty-eight, was an exceptional case.

Giovanni, the husband, had been killed freakishly, struck by lightning on a football field. "Why did it have to be my husband when twenty-one other players, the referee and two linesmen were out there?" Claudia demanded of the priest each time he came on a visit. "Is that the Lord's will? My Giovanni, of all those men?"

Father Faustini always reminded Claudia that the Lord works in mysterious ways. She always gazed at him trustingly with her large, dark, expressive eyes (she had worked as a fashion model) and he always told her that it was a mistake to dwell on the past.

The priest and the young widow were seated on a padded cushion that extended around the perimeter of the sunken floor. As usual, Claudia had hospitably uncorked a Barolo, a plummy vintage from Mascarello, and there were cheese-biscuits to nibble. The sun had just about sunk out of sight, but to have switched on electric lights on such an evening would have been churlish. The scent of stocks, heavy on the cooler air, reached them through the open patio doors. The villa had a fine garden, watered by a sprinkler system. Giovanni, not short of money—he'd made it to the top as a fashion photographer—had called in a landscape architect when the place was built. For Father Faustini, the remote location of the villa meant a three-mile trip on his moped, but he never complained. He was forty and in good health. A rugged man with tight, black curls and a thick moustache.

"You're doing so much better, now," he remarked to the widow Coppi.

"It's window dressing, Father. Inside, I'm still very tense."

"Really?" He frowned, and only partly out of concern for the tension she was under. It was a good thing the room had become so shadowy that his disquietude wouldn't be obvious to her.

"My usual problem," she explained. "Stress. It shows up in the muscles. I feel it in my shoulders, right across the top."

"As before?"

"As before."

There was a silence. Father Faustini was experiencing some tension, also.

Claudia said, "Last week you really succeeded in loosening the muscles."

"Really?" he said abstractedly.

"It was miraculous."

He cleared his throat, unhappy with the choice of word.

She amended it to, "Marvellous, then. Oh, the relief! I can't tell you how much better I felt."

"Did it last?"

"For days, Father." While he was absorbing that, she added plaintively, "There's no one else I can ask."

She made it sound like a plea for charity. Father Faustini sometimes fetched shopping for elderly members of his flock. He often collected medicine for their ailments. He'd been known to chop wood and cook soup for poor souls in trouble, so what was the difference in massaging Claudia Coppi's aching shoulders? Only that it set up conflicts within himself. Was it right to deny her Christian help because of his moral and spiritual frailty?

On the last two Friday evenings he had performed this service for her. Willingly he would have chopped wood instead, but the villa's central heating was oil-fired. He would have fetched shopping with alacrity, but she had a twice-weekly delivery from the best supermarket in Cremona. She had a gardener, a cook and a cleaner. What it came down to in practice was that the only assistance Father Faustini could render to Claudia Coppi was what she was suggesting. The poor young woman couldn't massage her own shoulders. Not well enough to remove muscular tension.

There was another factor that made him hesitate. Once a week in church he heard Claudia Coppi's confession, and lately—he wasn't certain how many times this had occurred, and didn't intend to make a calculation—she had admitted to impure thoughts, or carnal desires, or some such form of words. It wasn't his custom to ask for more details in the confessional once the commission of a sin was established, so he couldn't know for sure that there was a connection with his visits to the villa.

"I found something you could rub in, if you would," she said.

He coughed nervously and crossed his legs. This was new in the routine. "Embrocation?" he queried, striving to limit his thoughts to muscular treatment, remembering the overpowering reek of a certain brand favoured by footballers. The stuff brought tears to the eyes.

"More of a moisturizer really. It's better for my skin. Really smooth. Try." She reached out and smeared some on the back of his hand.

He wiped it off immediately. "It's scented."

"There's a hint of musk," she admitted. "If you'd like to hold the pot, I'll just slip my blouse off."

"That won't be necessary," he quickly said.

"Father, it's silk. I don't want it marked."

"No, no, *signora*, cover yourself up."

"But I haven't unbuttoned yet." She laughed and added, "Is it as dark as all that?"

"I wasn't looking," he said.

"That's all right. I've got my back to you anyway."

As she was speaking he heard the blouse being slipped off her shoulders. Now he was in a real dilemma. She sounded so matter-of-fact, so nonchalant. By protesting, he was liable to inflate this into a moral crisis. It could appear as if he were letting himself be influenced by things she had said in the confessional.

"Not too much at once," she cautioned. "It goes a long way."

He suppressed his misgivings, dipped in a finger and spread some over his palm.

Claudia's back was towards him, as she had claimed. He

reached out and applied some of the moisturizer to the back of her neck.

She said, "Oh dear, the straps are going to get in your way."

"Not at all," protested Father Faustini, but the brassiere-straps were tugged aside, regardless.

On the previous visits, he'd been persuaded to massage Claudia without using a liniment, through her tee-shirt. This was a new experience. The contact with her flesh unsettled him more than he cared to admit. He traced the slope of her shoulders, feeling the warmth under his fingers. The smoothness was a revelation. When his hands cupped the round extremities of her shoulders he was compelled to pause.

She sighed and said, "Bliss."

In a moment he felt sufficiently in control to resume, spreading the moisturizer liberally across the shoulder-blades and up the spine to her neck. She had her head bowed so that her long, dark brown hair hung in front of her. He gave some attention to the deltoid muscles, gently isolating them, probing their form. In spite of what Claudia had said about tension, everything felt reasonably flexible to him, but he was the first to admit that he was no physiotherapist.

"Let me know if I'm causing any discomfort," he told her.

"Quite the reverse," she murmured. "You have the most incredible hands."

He continued to apply light pressure to the base of her neck until quite suddenly she raised her head and drew the hair back behind her shoulders.

"Enough?" he enquired. He hoped so. The movement of her hair across the backs of his hands had given him a physical sensation not to be encouraged in the priesthood.

But Claudia Coppi remained unsatisfied. She told him that there was still some tension at the tops of her arms.

"Here?"

"Yes. Oh, yes, just there. Do you mind if I lean back against you, Father? It's more comfortable." She didn't wait for his answer.

The back of her head was on his chest, her hair against his cheek. In the same movement she placed her hands over his own and gripped them firmly. Then she pushed them downwards.

He hadn't discovered until now that she had altogether uncovered her breasts. She guided his hands over them. Exquisitely beautiful, utterly prohibited breasts offered for him to experience. For a few never-to-be-forgotten seconds of sin,

Father Faustini accepted the offer. He held Claudia Coppi's forbidden fruits, passed his hands over and under and around them, thrilling to their fullness and their unmistakable state of arousal.

A monster of depravity.

With a supreme effort to banish fleshly thoughts, he blurted out the words, "Lead us not into temptation," and drew his hands away as if they were burned.

Tormented with shame, he stood up immediately and strode resolutely through the patio doors and around the side of the house without looking back. He didn't respond to Claudia Coppi's, "Shall I see you next Saturday?" He knew he had to be out of that place and away.

He thought he heard her coming after him, probably still in her topless state. As swiftly as he could manage, he wheeled his moped out to the road, started it up and zoomed away.

"Fornicating fool," he howled to himself above the engine's putt-putt. "Weak-willed, degenerate, wanton, wicked, wretched, sex-crazed fellow. Miserable sinner."

The little wheels bore him steadily along, his headlight picking out the road, but he was barely conscious of the journey. His thoughts were all on he depravity of his conduct. A man of God, a priest behaving like some beast of the field, only worse, because he was blessed with a mind that was supposed to be capable of overcoming the baser instincts.

How will I answer for this on the Day of Judgement? he asked himself.

God be merciful unto me, a sinner.

Precisely at which stage of the journey he became aware of what was ahead of him is impossible to say. Certainly he must have travelled some distance before he was ready to submit to anything except the writhings of his tormented conscience. It had to be spectacular, and it was. Father Faustini stared ahead and saw a pillar of fire.

The night sky was alight above the Plain of Lombardy, fizzing with hundreds of brilliant fiery points. Their origin was a fiery column, perhaps three thousand metres away, and towering over the land. Emphatically this was not a natural fire, for it was more green than orange, bright emerald green, with flares of violet, blue and yellow leaping outwards. Father Faustini was seized with the conviction that the Day of Judgement was at hand. Otherwise he might have suspected that something had been added to the Barolo he had swallowed, because what he was seeing was psychedelic in its extraordinary combination of colours. He'd seen large fires before, and mammoth firework displays, but nothing remotely resembling this.

What else could a wretched sinner do in the hour of reckoning, but brake, dismount, go down on his knees and pray for forgiveness? He felt simultaneously panic-stricken and rocked with remorse, that this should happen on the very night he had transgressed, after a lifetime of blameless (or virtually blameless) service in the Church. He knelt on the turf at the roadside, his hands clasped in front of his anguished face, and cried, "Forgive me, Father, for I have sinned."

He couldn't discount the possibility that his lapse with Claudia Coppi was directly responsible for what was happening. By speculating that his few seconds' fondling of a pair of pretty breasts had hastened the end of the world, he may have been presumptuous, but he felt an ominous sense of cause and effect.

He sneaked another look around his clasped hands. The state of the sky remained just as awesome. Streaks of fire were leaping up like sky-rockets, leaving trails of sparks.

As yet there were no avenging angels to be seen, nor other apocalyptic phenomena. He heard no trumpets, but nothing would surprise him now.

Instead he saw two brilliant lights, so dazzling that they made his eyes ache. And immediately there came a low droning, becoming stronger. The source wasn't supernatural. A car, its headlights on full beam, was moving at high speed towards him along the road, from the direction of the pillar of fire. Father Faustini could understand people fleeing from the wrath to come, but he knew that they were deluding themselves. There could be no escape.

And so it proved.

The engine-note grew in volume and the lights intensified in brilliance. Ordinarily, Father Faustini would have waved to let the driver know that he was dazzled. But of course he wasn't mounted on his moped. He was on his knees at the side of the road. He'd abandoned the bike when he'd first seen the pillar of fire. Abandoned it where he had stopped, in the middle of the narrow road.

The car was racing towards it.

He clapped his hands to his head.

There simply wasn't time to drag the moped out of the way. He could only hope that the driver would spot the obstruction in time and steer to the side. It might be academic at this late stage in the history of the world whether an accident—even a fatal accident—mattered to anyone, but Father Faustini had always been safety-conscious and he couldn't bear the thought of being responsible for anyone's death.

In truth, the driver of the car would share some blame, for his speed was excessive.

What happened next was swift and devastating, yet Father Faustini saw it in the curious freeze-frame way that the brain has for coping with danger at high speed. The car bore down on the moped without any let-up in speed until the last split-second, when the driver must have seen what was in front of him. The rasp of tyre-rubber on the surface of the road as the brakes were applied made a sound like a siren's blare. The car veered left to avoid the moped, and succeeded. But it hit the curb, went out of control and ricocheted to the opposite side. Father Faustini registered that it was a large, powerful saloon. The white light from the headlamps swept out of his vision and was replaced by intense red as the car skidded past with its brake lights fully on. It mounted the curb and started up a bank of turf that bordered a field. The band of rear lights lifted and spun in an arc. The whole thing was turning over. It was thrown on its back not once, but three times, tons of metal bouncing like a toy, smashing through a fence and finally sliding on the roof across the ploughed earth.

One of the rear lights was still on. It was out in a spray of sparks. Smoke was rising from the wreck.

Father Faustini's legs felt about as capale of holding him up as freshly cooked pasta, but he stumbled across to see if he could get anyone out before the entire thing caught fire.

The weight of the chassis had crushed the superstructure. The priest got on his knees beside the compressed slot that had once been the driver's window. There was a figure inside, the head skewed into an impossible angle. Too late for the last rites.

Round the other side was the passenger, another man, half on the turf. Literally. The other half, from the waist down, was still trapped inside. The halves were separated at the waist.

The priest crossed himself. A wave of nausea threatened, but it was vital to stay in control because the air reeked of raw petrol and the whole wreck was likely to turn into a fireball any second. Still troubled that someone might be alive and trapped inside, he lay on his stomach to try and get a sight of what had been the back seat. He needn't have troubled. There wasn't a centimetre of space between the torn upholstery and the impacted roof.

As he braced to get up, a sound like the rushing mighty wind of the Pentecost started somewhere to his right. The petrol had caught fire.

He sprang up and sprinted away. Behind him, there was a series of cracking sounds followed by an almighty bang that must have been the petrol tank exploding. By then, he was twenty metres away and flat to the earth.

He didn't move for a while. His nerves couldn't take any more. He actually sobbed a little. It was some time before he thought of saying a prayer. In his embattled mind, the car-crash had overtrumped the Day of Judgement.

Finally, he sat up. The wreckage was still on fire, but the worst of it was over. Filthy black smoke was taking over and the stench of burning rubber stung his throat and nostrils. He stared into the flames. The charred, mangled metal that remained barely resembled a vehicle.

Every muscle he possessed was trembling. With difficulty, he got to his feet and walked past the burning wreckage towards the moped, which still stood untouched in the centre of the road, a testimony to his stupidity and his responsibility for this tragedy.

Beyond, the night sky was still rent by the vast pillar of fire that had so distracted him. The colours were still unearthly in their brilliance and variety. Even so, Father Faustini was forced to reconsider whether it could really be Judgement Day. The shock of the car-crash had altered his perception. He couldn't explain the phenomenon. There had to be a reason for it, but he hadn't the energy left to supply one.

He got astride the moped, started up and rode off to report what had happened.

BANTAM MYSTERY COLLECTION